Hideaway

Safe Havens 4

Sandy James

Hideaway

Cover design by Dragonfly Press Design
www.dragonflypressdesign.com
Book design by Sandy James
Published by James Gang Publishing

All characters and events in this book are fictitious. Any resemblance to actual persons living or dead is strictly coincidental—and honestly, a bit creepy if you think about it.

Sandy James
sandyjames.com

Printed in the United States of America
First Printing: April 2020
ISBN: 978-1-940295-20-6

A note from Sandy:

After writing as many books as I have, it sometimes becomes difficult to think of acknowledgments and dedications. Not because I don't have TONS of people to thank, but because the sentiments start to sound repetitive (at least to me).

This book is different. So…here goes…

Acknowledgements:

I lost my husband of nearly thirty-four years to colon cancer in September of 2016, and I felt as though the rug had been pulled from under my life. If not for the myriad people who caught me when I fell, I'm not sure where I'd be right now. I wish I could list each and every one of them—family, friends, colleagues, students, authors. So many! I thank you all from the bottom of my heart.

And to Nancy Reinhardt and Cheryl Brooks—thank you for having my back. You helped me get back into the swing of writing and made sure *Hideaway* was ready to go.

Dedication:

Life threw me a hell of a curve ball in May of 2018 when I went on a date with a man who would change my life.

Brian—this book is for you.

Not only are you an amazing husband, you are my best friend. Thank you for making me laugh, for being the best "idea" person when I'm writing, and for promising to share the next adventures of life at my side.

I love you.

Chapter One

Montana Territory—September 1886

There wasn't a single part of him that didn't ache.

Drake Myers swiped the muck from his face, casting aside the sticky mess as he glared up at the hefty woman who'd just tossed him out of her brothel and onto the muddy street. Damn if everyone in the place didn't spill out onto the porch to watch his humiliation.

He'd been warned. More than once. But he simply didn't give a damn about anything anymore. He'd also underestimated Madame Marie. The woman might be as wide as she was tall, but when it came to protecting her working girls, she had every bit as much strength as a heavily muscled man.

Hands on her ample hips, she stood in the moonlight and glared right back at him as even more curious people poured from the whorehouse to gawk. Madame Marie's red satin dress strained at the seams as the peacock feathers protruding from her upswept hair bounced each time she nodded her head. "You go on and git now! Ain't got no time for scoundrels like you."

"My money's good as anyone else's," Drake grumbled, more to himself than her.

He groaned as the two women he'd hoped would entertain him for the evening hovered behind Marie. The skinny blonde frowned as she clutched her silky robe together to cover her breasts. The redhead showed no emotion at all, simply stared at him with eyes that held little intelligence and not an ounce of spark. After seeing him wallowing in the mud as though he were some hog, they were probably relieved he hadn't had a chance to be intimate with them.

Drake hadn't even had the opportunity to touch either of them. After he'd ridden just outside the town of White Pines to the well-known but seldom talked about brothel, he'd paid his money to the young hostess and grabbed the only two comely faces from among the available working girls. They'd barely closed the door to the bedroom when angry shouts had accompanied Marie's heavy footsteps up the stairs. The door had slammed open, and moments later, he'd found himself grabbed by his shirt collar and the seat of his pants, hustled down the stairs, and tossed out in the street like so much garbage.

Probably what he deserved, wallowing in mud, what with the way he'd been floundering in his own misery of late.

Marie shook her head and then started wagging her finger at him like a mother scolding a naughty child. "I done told ya and told ya. I cain't have ya occupying two of my girls at the same time. It ain't right. It just ain't natural, I tell ya."

After wiping the rest of the mud from his face, Drake dragged himself to his feet. He'd drunk enough to be a tad unsteady, but unfortunately not enough to forget this humiliation come morning. "You sell girls, and you want me to think you're outraged that I wanna bed two women at the same time?"

One of the girls handed Marie his hat.

With a snort of disgust, Marie tossed it at him. "Git out and stay out."

Drake caught it before it ended up in the mud, too. After slapping the weathered hat against his thigh, he put it on his head. Then he threw the vastly amused people from the brothel one last scowl before weaving his way to his horse, Rusty. Snatching the chestnut gelding's reins from the hitching post, he held them tightly as he hauled himself into the saddle. His eyes caught the blonde's—the prettier of his two potential companions. "You wanna earn some coin you don't have to share with Marie, you know where to find me." He dug his heels into Rusty's sides, hoping to hell the horse's hooves would throw some clumps of dirt Marie's way.

When he reached the town, it was peaceful as ever. Quiet. All but abandoned by this time of night. The only place with signs of life was the Four Aces, the local saloon that catered to the rail workers and cowboys who often passed through White Pines. The other businesses had shut their doors tight for the night hours ago.

It wasn't until he reached the boarding house that he allowed his anger to finally ebb. The whole situation had been ludicrous. Two women at the same time? Even *he* wasn't truly that disgusting. The plan had been nothing more than another attempt to forget his wretched life.

The boarding house's manager was sitting on the big porch, rocking in his chair, and smoothing a cloth over the barrel of the shotgun in his lap. No doubt he'd want to discuss past-due rent. Again. Drake rode right past him to the barn, where he cared for Rusty's needs, Afterwards, he gave the gelding a gentle stroke on the muzzle and an extra handful of grain for being his only real friend.

When he reached the front door, he tipped his hat to Earl Hammonds, who hadn't budged an inch. "Evenin', Mr. Hammonds."

Earl didn't even look up, simply kept rubbing the dirty cloth on the barrel of his gun. "You be owin' me money, Mr. Myers. That sum be past due."

Drake took off his hat and raked his fingers through his unruly hair before wincing as he realized there was still mud in it. "I know, Mr. Hammonds. It's just..." He shrugged. "I don't have it. Not yet." Mind scrambling for some logical explanation why he couldn't seem to cough up the money to keep renting his room, he finally let out a resigned sigh. What little money he'd had was now in the hands of the brothel, and they weren't likely to give it back. He only had three things of value, two of which he'd never peddle. Rusty and his gun. "I'll sell my saddle tomorrow and pay you."

Earl let out a snort as he rocked in his squeaky chair.

"I mean what I say," Drake insisted. Instead of waiting to hear more of the owner's derision, he put his hat back on and opened the front screen door. "You'll get your money tomorrow."

"You be bathin' a'fore you sleep in that bed."

"I have every intention of doing exactly that." Without a backward glance, he pulled the door shut behind him.

The rain barrel that served as the boarding house's bathtub held water cold enough to set Drake's teeth chattering. He fingers went numb long before he'd finished washing away the dirt. He slipped into clean long johns before heading upstairs.

The room he'd called home for the last few months was smaller than Rusty's stall, but it had a bed and a table, which were really all he needed.

Sitting on the bed, he jerked on clean socks, flexed his toes, and gave his head a disgusted shake when his big toes popped through holes. Since he had no talent with a needle, he hadn't darned the damn things.

God, but he led a sorry existence.

His gaze fell on the wooden model of a house that rested on the table. Not *a* house; *his* house. At least the one he'd dreamed of owning when his cattle driving days eventually ended and he'd earned his fortune. A fortune he'd never earn now, thanks to a previous ill-fated trip to a whorehouse in Denver. The woman he'd hired that night had drugged him, stolen the payroll entrusted to him, and left him with a reputation as an undependable dimwit. Even though he'd hunted the woman down and returned the money, all those noble tasks did was solidify a popular notion that he'd stolen it himself and fabricated the story about Sara Fuller—now Sara Young.

Funny how she'd come here to start a new life and found a good one. A husband. A home.

All Drake had found here was misery.

He'd tried to forgive her. He had. And for a while, he'd convinced himself he'd moved on. White Pines seemed as good a place to settle as any—until it appeared as though everyone in town thought poorly of him. While the fault probably lay right at his own feet since his behavior had been pretty disgraceful, it was easier to blame Sara Young. Much easier.

The small house taunted him, reminding him of how his earlier models had earned him nothing but criticism. *"A waste of yer time,"* his uncle had always grumbled, often accompanying his censure by tossing whatever Drake had been working on into the fire and then giving him a cuff upside the head.

Is that what his work represented? A waste of his time? He had no job. No prospects for employment. Very little money. Yet still he carved and built and created.

With a mournful howl, he swept his arm across the table, sending his house model crashing against the wall and falling to the floor. The V of the roof tumbled off the structure as two of the walls separated and dropped away. He'd reduced it to kindling.

Uncle Herbert would've been proud.

There'd be no more time given to creations no one but him would ever see. His life was in the shitter, and he'd sunk as low as he could possibly go.

The time had come to pull himself up from the mire. He'd have to try harder to find employment, even if it meant mucking out stalls or digging ditches. A man had to eat, and Earl Hammonds wasn't going to wait much longer for his rent.

Blowing out the candle, Drake flopped onto the bed, vowing to stop feeling so damned sorry for himself and start to make a new life. Before sleep claimed him, he had one important epiphany.

There's really nowhere to go now but up.

* * *

"I'm sorry, Kayla."

Kayla Backer tried to hide her gloomy reaction to Drew's announcement. He was clearly in mourning for his older brother and didn't deserve the added

weight of her disappointment. She folded her arms under her breasts and waited
for the reasons he'd refused her request.

Drew Pearson frowned. "I know you had your heart set on starting
construction on your new home, but..." He shook his head and cast his gaze to
the wooden floor.

Her heart ached for him. "No, Drew," she said, laying a hand on his arm.
"Please express no regrets. I apologize for making you feel as though you owe
me anything. You should go to your mother. She needs you now."

With a hard swallow, he nodded. "I cannot imagine her grief. My brother
was everything to her." Head bowed, he ran his hand over his blond hair. He
wore it much longer than was the fashion, often tying it behind his neck with a
leather cord. But the man was an actor. White Pines folks loved his
eccentricity. They *expected* it. The fancy suits. The air of whimsy. They even
ignored the fact that he was a man in his early thirties who lived with another
man.

His lover—although people would never acknowledge the men's
relationship as anything more than a fast friendship—stood next to the couch,
keeping close watch over Drew and Kayla as they spoke. Gideon Young was
every bit as dark as Drew was light, his black hair and brown eyes so very
different than Drew's hair the color of sunshine and eyes the hue of the summer
sky.

Now she was being far too fanciful. She loved Drew as though he were
her brother, but despite having lived in their home as the men's housekeeper for
close to nine months, she was still wary of Gideon. Not that he deserved her
misgivings. He'd been nothing but kind. His aloof manner sometimes reminded
her far too much of her former fiancé.

And those wounds still ran too deep to dwell upon.

"I can easily bide my time until late autumn," Kayla said, hoping to raise
Drew's spirits. "Once you return from seeing your family, then we shall begin
work." A nod to the drawings piled on the side table. "Perhaps in the time you
and Gideon are away, I can find someone who can turn my dreams into reality.
Heaven knows I have no idea how to transform my thoughts into a home."

At least Drew looked up, although his smile seemed forced. "I fear my
skills at building are somewhat limited." He tossed a glance to Gideon.

Gideon heaved a sigh. "Told you already, Kayla. I'm gonna build it when
I can, but I'm going to Missoula with you first, Drew. Snows come in October,
so I'm not gonna start this year. Next spring. Maybe. We gotta get your ma
settled first."

Settled. Gideon's way of letting Drew know that his mother wasn't
returning to White Pines with them as Drew hoped. Kayla had tried to make
herself scarce whenever the men had quarreled about the fate of the widow,
which was often since the news of the death of Drew's brother had reached
them. While Drew claimed his mother would be happy moving away from
Missoula and coming to live with the men, Gideon wanted Drew's sister to care
for her, insisting they needed their privacy.

"I am quite sure she shall settle fine in one of our bedrooms," Drew
asserted.

Gideon started shaking his head before Drew even finished his sentence.

"We wouldn't have any privacy, what with her putterin' around."

The contradiction couldn't go unmentioned. Kayla's penchant for speaking her mind always got the better of her. "If you do not wish to have a woman 'putterin' around,' then why did you welcome *me* into your home?" She waited a beat. "Oh yes. Now I remember. You were trying to remedy what you believed was your brother's error in summoning me as his potential bride." She'd crossed her arms again and now drummed her fingers against one forearm. "I have explained to you many, many times that I hold him no ill will. Nor do I hold any ill will for Sara."

Eyes narrowed, Gideon responded to her gibe. "Caleb should've married *you*, Kayla."

Although he was always kind to his sister-in-law, Sara, Gideon often let Kayla know he preferred her education and refinement to Sara's shady past. "Sara cannot help what she was. Surely, you've come to terms with her former life. She had no choice. Life is... difficult for women who have no protectors."

His gaze hardened. "Don't see you selling yourself to men."

"Had you and Drew not taken me in," Kayla countered, "my future might have been every bit as bleak as Sara's past. As I have said on many occasions, Gideon, I have forgiven her and Caleb. You should as well. She is your brother's wife now, and he cares greatly for her. They have a son. Leave the past where it belongs. In the past."

Gideon simply stomped to the door. He snatched his jacket from the wooden pegs where it hung next to hers and Drew's and left them, slamming the door behind him.

The man's temper would cool quickly, as it always did where Drew was concerned. All Gideon required were a few sweet words from Drew, and he would no doubt be moving Drew's mother to White Pines in short order.

Stepping up to the window, Drew glanced through it, a pensive sulk on his handsome face. "I fear he shall never truly accept Sara. A sorrow, that. She is such a wonderful woman, and she makes Caleb happy."

Kayla took a place at his side. "He will never be unkind to her."

"You're right on that point, my dear."

The western view from the window was beautiful, more so since it included the five acres that Gideon had gifted her for her service to them as well as a guilt offering. "I should never have agreed to accept the land," she whispered.

Drew's brows drew together. "Why the devil not?"

"Gideon had no need to rectify whatever injustice he believes his brother dealt me. I came to White Pines to be a bride. Should I have truly wished that end, I have had more than enough opportunities for matrimony from many of the men in and near town."

His frown eased. "That you have, but nonetheless you accepted the land. It pleased Gideon for you to have it." He lifted her hand and brushed a kiss on her knuckles. "You have been a gift, dear Kayla. You take very good care of us, and his conscience will bother him if he doesn't make recompense for Caleb luring you here under false pretenses."

Kayla shrugged off the thought, knowing she could never tell them the whole truth—that she came to White Pines for something other than marrying a man she'd never met. Her life had changed for the better when Sara married Caleb, for Kayla hadn't been forced to hand her life over to a man. She could be her own woman, not some mail-order bride marrying a stranger. A home of her own would only aid her in that end.

"The whole affair was nothing more than a comedy of errors," she insisted. "Caleb wanted a bride, and when Sara arrived, he was convinced she was the one he'd sent for. I bear neither him nor Sara any malice." A glance back to the lush acres that Gideon would soon deed to her. "Yet I find I crave what Gideon has offered."

"You wish a home of your own." Drew gave her a quick embrace. "You took the land, Kayla. Let us build you a home on it. Perhaps when it is ready, you might wish to accept one of the many proposals of marriage and make a family there."

Chapter Two

Drake ran a brush over Rusty's rump as he kept a close watch over the three men who were coming down the livery's aisle. The first was Earl. Dressed in his typically patched and worn clothing, his skinny frame all but disappeared if the man turned sideways. The other two gentlemen, Drake didn't know, although he'd seen them before.

White Pines was such a small town. Unlike other railroad stops, it never grew by leaps and bounds. Instead, the same families had lived there for generations—would probably still be there long after the territory became a state. Perhaps that was why Drake was sticking around. Because that sort of home appealed to him.

That, and he was as poor as a preacher without a flock.

One of the other men was close to his own age and walked as though he'd spent a lot of time in the saddle. Dressed like it, too. The other was a dandy—far too fancy a man to ever hang around a barn. An extravagant suit, right down to one of those stuffy neck ties, which was white as snow. No, this man hadn't mucked out a stall in his whole life. Hell, he'd probably never even stepped in manure without pitching a hissy fit.

So why was Earl leading them Drake's way? And why in the devil was he carrying the pieces of the model Drake had broken the night before?

Rusty sidestepped into him, the horse nervous at having strangers approach. Drake nudged back with his shoulder and continued his chores. "What can I do for you gentlemen?" he asked when they stopped to stare at him.

Earl was the one to answer him. "They be wantin' to know about this." He dropped the pieces of the model onto one of the tack trunks.

"Why?" No one had ever been remotely interested in the things he'd built. Even more perplexing was that this one was broken, probably beyond repair.

Instead of giving a reply, the younger man nodded at Rusty. "Fine-lookin' animal." He stroked the horse's muzzle, and damn if the normally skittish Rusty didn't allow the attention.

Drake's hackles rose. "He's not for sale."

"Didn't ask," the man said with an easy smile.

"Then why are you here?"

"Came to speak to Earl." The man stuck out his gloved hand, quickly snatched it back to remove his weathered glove, and then offered his hand to Drake again. "We ain't met. I'm Ty Bishop." He inclined his head at the dandy. "This is Drew Pearson."

Drake recognized their names. Both had been entangled in the drama surrounding his coming to White Pines. "Drake Myers."

The dandy stroked his chin with this finger and thumb. "Ah, the illustrious Mr. Myers. Our paths should have crossed months ago, yet I find this is our first face-to-face meeting. I believe you followed our Sara to this fair town."

So that *was* where Drake had heard Drew's name. From Sara.

The thief who'd destroyed his life.

Damn, but he wanted to find forgiveness for her. The circumstances of his existence now wouldn't allow him that luxury. Had she not snatched the payroll he'd been holding, he would still be working his way up the hierarchy of the cattle company.

Instead, he was stuck in the middle of Montana without two bits to rub together.

And it was all *her* fault.

He saw no reason to respond to Drew's statement, so he finished brushing Rusty, tossed the worn brush at the tack trunk, and led his horse back into the stall.

"They be wantin' a builder," Earl said as Drake closed and latched the stall door.

Taking a piece of wire he'd prepared, he twisted it around the gate and the post.

"Got an escape artist?" Ty asked with a note of humor in his tone.

Drake nodded, pleased that there was a man here who spoke the same language. "Not a gate in the world he can't open."

A grin filled Ty's face. "Got me a mare like that. No matter what I do, still find her grazing on the front lawn most every damn day."

Had he not felt as if the weight of the world resting on his shoulder, Drake might have smiled in return. "They can be pretty clever animals when they wanna be."

"Are you capable of building that home in real life?" Drew asked, nodding at the model.

What an odd question. "I s'pose so," Drake replied. "Built a barn or two in my day. Only helped on one house, though."

"Why'd you build *this*?" Ty asked, running his fingers over the line of the wrecked model's roof.

Drake shrugged, not about to open his thoughts to these men. He knew nothing about them beyond their connection to Sara, and that certainly wasn't a point in their favor.

Ty's gaze shifted to Drew. "Looks familiar."

"I agree," Drew replied before turning back to Drake. "Would you please answer Ty's question? Are you capable of building this home?" He fished in his pocket and pulled out a folded piece of parchment.

"Why would you wanna know?" Were these men thinking he was a carpenter? What other reason could they be asking such strange questions?

"We're searching for a builder," Drew replied. "Thus far, our search has been fruitless."

"No one in this whole town can build a house?" Drake couldn't stop the incredulous tone of his voice.

"Oh, there may be many who *can*," Drew said. "Unfortunately, we have discovered most *won't*." Unfolding the paper, Drew held it out to Drake. "This is exactly what we want."

Drake looked at the picture, startled at the nearly perfect rendering of the model he'd made. "Who drew this?"

"The woman who will live in the house."

"How did she...?" None of this made any sense. Drake swept his free hand at the broken model. "How did you even find this?"

Ty was the one to reply. "We were askin' Earl about a man who did some work on his roof, hopin' he might be a builder. Saw this resting on top of the firewood pile. Was mighty impressed, especially since it looked so much like the one Kayla—er, Miss Backer drew."

Kayla Backer. An uncommon name, and one Drake could have sworn he'd heard before. "Why's she drawing a house?"

"It's the house she wishes to live in," Drew replied.

"Why can't her husband build it?"

"She's single," Ty replied. "Wants the house for herself."

A single woman? In Montana?

Hell's fire, the woman must be as ugly as a donkey.

But even that shouldn't have discouraged the lonely men of White Pines. Some were desperate for feminine companionship. He was aware of the town gossip that Drew and Gideon had no intention of taking brides, so he wondered if they kept her around to help her out since no one else wanted her.

Drew pulled Drake back into the conversation. "A shame to waste such a creation as kindling." His gaze found Drake's. "If you are capable of building this home—a true-to-life-size version of this home for Miss Backer—we would like to discuss employing you to do exactly that."

Earl jumped in where he wasn't welcome. "He be owin' me money. His first pay comes to me." Emphasizing his point, he thumped his chest with his thumb.

"Ah, yes. *Important* things first," Drew drawled with just the right amount of scolding to make Drake consider grinning. "We will be happy to settle Mr. Myers debt should he accept our offer."

"How far is it to where you want this built?" Drake asked. If they offered him a fair salary, he would consider building the damn place. "It's a bit too late in the year to start, but come spring—"

"Miss Backer wishes you to begin promptly," Drew said. "The house will be built on some acres we've given her as her own... homestead, you might say."

"Winter will set in and—"

Once again, Drew cut him off. "Should you complete the frame and the roof promptly, the remainder could easily be built in the less hospitable months."

Drake shook his head. "I won't make my horse trudge through the types of snow we get out here to get to the site."

At least that statement gave Drew pause.

However, Earl, looking a bit giddy, had something to say. "He could live at yer place. Then he ain't gonna be needin' one of my rooms no more."

Seemed Earl was as anxious to get rid of Drake as Drake was to leave Earl's company.

Ty paused as though deep in thought. "Could close himself off the loft in the barn. Might make a cozy place to stay while he works." He focused a hard stare at Earl. "He won't be troublin' you then."

"You or your damnable bedbugs," Drake added, happy to see Earl sputter at the insult. "If I could live in the barn, and if Rusty won't have to trek through blizzards, then I'll build Kayla Backer her house."

* * *

Kayla put her hands on her hips and glared at Drew. Her thoughts were tumbling and turning, and her anger couldn't seem to find the right words to let him know exactly how ridiculous it was to even consider having Drake Myers build her home.

"You seem angry, my dear," Drew said as he laid his gloves on the table.

The words finally came. "Sara is my friend, Drew. You simply cannot believe I would wish to spend time with a man who...who...wronged her so."

"Wronged her?" Ty said as he strode into the house, obviously hearing what they'd been saying. He held the door as his wife, Cassie, followed him in.

Drew helped Cassie remove her coat, but he kept up the topic. "You know I love Sara like a sister, but it would seem to me that *she* wronged *Drake*."

After Cassie gave Kayla a kiss on the cheek, she whirled to Drew, her pretty brown braid flying with the motion. "Sara merely did what she had to do to survive. You should not be criticizing her so. I also believe she returned whatever money she borrowed from Mr. Myers."

"Borrowed?" Ty snorted, drawing a stern frown from his wife.

"Then say the same to Kayla," Drew said in his defense. "She is the one who began this conversation by claiming that Drake Myers in some way hurt our Sara."

Her face heating, Kayla tried to clarify, hoping they wouldn't press her too hard. "I was not referring to the money she might have taken in a time of desperation."

As though he enjoyed seeing her so flustered, Drew grinned and pressed on as though he knew what she would say. "Then what exactly did you mean, Kayla, dear?"

"He... visited her. At that...that... And then they..." She threw up her hands and tried to toss out a different bone for Drew to chew upon. "I shall cease my objections. Drake Myers will be acceptable, should you believe he can do a good job on my home."

"Heard something about visitin'. Who visited what?" Gideon asked after he came in through the same door Drew, Ty, and Cassie had used.

With a mischievous smile, Drew replied, "I believe our Kayla is a bit concerned that Drake Myers has been to visit women who work in brothels."

Kayla felt as if her cheeks were on fire. "Must we speak of this?"

Ty burst out laughing. "When you say 'women,' you don't know how right you are. Heard he tried to take two to bed at Madame Marie's place and got tossed out on his drunken ass."

A gasp ripped from Cassie as she placed her hand over her husband's mouth. "Ty! You mustn't speak of such things with ladies present."

Even though he nodded, his brown eyes were full of the sharp humor Kayla normally enjoyed. In her months in White Pines, she'd grown close to Cassie and Ty Bishop. They'd embraced her as though she were a sister, and when Sara and Caleb Young joined them, everyone had a marvelous evening of stories, charades, or cards. Sometimes, the five of them simply shared a meal and comfortable conversation.

Should Drake come to the farm to build her home, Kayla had no doubt that she would only be able to see her friends by going to them for a visit. Sara would never come while he was around, nor would Kayla wish to put her friend through that kind of odd reunion.

After the men stopped chuckling, Cassie finally removed her hand from her husband's mouth, but not before Ty grabbed it back and quickly kissed her palm.

Dropping her gaze to the floor, Kayla swallowed the heartache such an intimate and loving gesture caused. Both Ty and Caleb were openly affectionate with their wives, and Cassie and Sara returned that affection wholeheartedly. Although she genuinely loved her friends, Kayla admitted—if only to herself—she longed for a husband she could make a home with. A man she could love.

A future that could never be since the right man had been taken away from her.

"What's this?" A crooked finger under her chin, Drew raised her head so he could look in her eyes. "Are you sad, Kayla dear? What brought a frown to your pretty mouth?"

Shaking her head to move his hand away, she said, "Just a fleeting thought, no more."

"Then it's settled," he announced. "Mr. Myers shall come to begin work tomorrow. That way Gideon and I will have a few days to get him settled in the barn loft and be sure he has all the supplies he needs before we leave for Missoula."

"There are some things we have yet to consider," Kayla pointed out. "I will remind you that my living out here with Mr. Myers and no chaperone will make us fodder for gossip."

"Hell, Kayla," Ty said. "He's already every gossip's favorite subject."

Cassie let out a little laugh. "Ty's right. But then again, you and I have never cared what the busybodies of White Pines think of us. For that matter, neither does Sara. I often consider that the basis of our wonderful friendship." She offered Kayla a comforting smile. "Let the man come. Let him build you a home. I shall be sure Sara understands that we mean her no offense by hiring him."

Kayla tried one more tack. "I've yet to hear what makes you so convinced he is capable of the task."

With a hand on her shoulder, Drew said, "I've seen what he can do. Trust me, Kayla. He can do this for you. If you'll let him."

Although she still wasn't convinced it was a wise idea, Kayla nodded. She desperately wanted a home of her own, and if that meant dealing with a man she could never respect—a man who frequented brothels and, if the talk around town was to be believed, often drank far more than he should—she would do so.

And once her house was done, she would never have to see Drake Myers again.

Chapter Three

The ride to Gideon Young's farm was a treat for Drake's eyes. He'd spent most of his time in the territory in and around White Pines, so he'd had little opportunity to take in the beauty of Montana. Mountains to his left; meadows to his right. No doubt they'd be full of buttercups and chicories come spring. Fresh air filled his lungs, and the sounds of birds cheered his spirit. His horse moved in an easy, smooth lope, and Drake rode far enough behind the wagon Gideon drove to avoid the rocks and tufts of mud that were often tossed his way by wheels and hooves. The whole package made for an enjoyable afternoon.

Until he thought about the task that lay ahead.

Although he loved to work with his hands, he was still worried that he couldn't give Drew and Gideon exactly what they wanted. They'd explained quite a bit of the situation after they'd offered him this job, including a welcome explanation that Ty and Caleb Young would be there from time to time to help him with the framing—a task requiring at least two or three men. Once Gideon returned, he'd work side-by-side with Drake.

He'd accepted their proposal, grateful to be away from the confinement of the boarding house and the rebuking eyes of many of the townsfolk. Yet he worried at his fate being held in the slender hands of a woman who was clearly unpleasant. A bossy bundle of goods, if he'd understood all the men had told him about her demands.

He'd seen her a few times when she'd come to town. Kayla Backer was far too prim and proper to suit him. Her starched blouse was always buttoned to the throat, gloves covered her hands, and she seemed inclined to keep her nose in the air with everyone she met. She spoke to few people, keeping her own company rather than spending time in conversation.

He might not have been properly introduced to her, but he'd listened to whispers. No man had been able to convince her to marry. The many eager males inclined to woo her were quickly turned away. The fact she lived with two single men, even if there were rumors about those men and their relationship as well, made him speculate at what made her so undesirable.

A shrew, no doubt. The woman obviously had Drew and Gideon dancing to her tune. Why, they were even spending a large amount of money to build her a home of her own, something unheard of. What woman in Montana would chose to isolate herself so deliberately?

"What have I gotten myself into, Rusty?"

Drew turned to look back at him? "Are you speaking to me?" he called, loud enough to be heard over the clatter of the wagon.

Drake shook his head, which made Drew frown and face the road again.

They rounded one last bend, and the farm came into view. The house was grand, far nicer than any he'd seen in Montana. That only made him think Kayla wasn't entirely in her right mind. Who wouldn't be happy living in such an extravagant home? Hell, even the barn was elaborate. Sleeping there wouldn't be a hardship, judging from the small chimney that rose from the loft area. Beat the hell out of the boarding house.

"Welcome." Drew climbed down from the wagon and swept his hand at the barn. "Gideon spent most of yesterday enclosing a nice space for you in the loft. He also added a pot belly stove to help keep you warm, but please remember to use caution with it since you will be living in a barn." He pointed at the double doors near the peak of the roof. "Should the snows rise too high, you can exit there and make your way to the house." His finger shifted to a small door on the second floor of the house."

"Added those after a really nasty blizzard," Gideon said as he hefted Drake's bag from the wagon's bed. "Snow was too deep to get to the animals. Had to crawl out a window."

Then the weight of the situation settled on him. "You get snowed in often enough to need those doors?"

Gideon's chuckle was the first Drake had heard from the man who seemed to keep tight control over his emotions. "If you're hopin' that was a one-time blizzard, 'fraid you're in for a disappointment. Used it three times last winter."

His stomach plummeted to his boots. Not only would he be out here alone with an unpleasant woman, he'd likely spend quite a bit of the winter unable to escape for his normal nights at the Four Aces. Or at Madame Marie's. Surely the woman had forgiven him by now. He'd have coin in his pocket, and women like Marie could always smell profit.

Just as Drew and Gideon led Drake to the front porch, the door to the house opened and Kayla Backer stepped outside as she finished buttoning her coat.

Having never seen her up close, his first thought was that she was much prettier than he'd expected. Her hair was bound in one, thick braid that was the color of wheat. It was long enough to brush against the middle of her back. When she fixed her big, brown eyes on him, every thought drifted right out of his head.

"Welcome, Mr. Myers." Her voice was husky. Sensual. It hit him like a jolt to the groin. "I hope we can help make your stay here pleasant."

"He's not a guest," Gideon grumbled, clearly not happy to see Kayla being so accommodating.

"Not exactly a *guest*," Kayla replied with a smile as sweet as honey. "I dare say he shall be on our farm for quite some time as he builds my house. I simply hope his time here is enjoyable."

The woman wasn't at all what Drake had expected. With only a few nice words, his prediction of her being a shrew were tossed aside. Instead of a problematic female, he found a woman beautiful enough to make his head spin, who also seemed to have a kind, gentle nature.

So what exactly was so wrong with her that no man had married her?

She offered her hand.

Drake quickly tugged off his glove and gave her hand a shake. "Thank you kindly, Miss...er...Baker."

"Backer," she corrected. "You may call me Kayla. Since we'll be sharing meals together, you need not be so formal." Her gaze went to Drew. "Were you able to arrange for the lumber?"

Drew nodded. "Deliveries will come regularly, so long as the weather holds."

"And Ty and Caleb have agreed to help?"

"From time to time."

"Wonderful. Then perhaps Mr. Myers would like to see the spot where my home shall be built?" she asked, pulling a blue knit cap from her pocket before tugging it on her head.

"Please call me Drake."

That charming smile of hers was going to be the death of him. "As you wish." Kayla skirted around him and beckoned the men to follow with a flip of her hand. "The day holds enough warmth, I believe we can walk."

"Is it far?" Drake asked, hurrying so he could walk by her side.

She shook her head while the other men nodded. She showed them a frown. "Although they believe it's a bit too distant from their home and that I am foolish for wanting a bit of privacy. They merely worry for my safety."

"As they should. A woman shouldn't live out here all alone."

Both Drew and Gideon nodded again, which only made Kayla sigh. "I can assure you that I am quite capable of taking care of myself."

Figuring that starting an argument wasn't a good way to begin his new job, Drake kept the rest of his thoughts to himself.

She was wrong, of course. The woman had undoubtedly never learned of the evils in the world or of the horrible things that could happen to a lady living alone, especially in the wilderness. While the town was close—only a couple hours' ride away—and Gideon and Drew would be within walking distance of her home, she wouldn't be immune to men who would want to rob her. Or worse.

But the topic was pushed aside. For now. Drake would have to work up the courage to explain things to her before he put the first board in place. Maybe that way she'd be smart enough to change her mind about exactly where she wanted her house.

* * *

Kayla still harbored worries about the man who now walked beside her.

Once Gideon and Drew left for Missoula, she'd be all alone with a person none of them knew well. What she'd heard, while it could only be called gossip, didn't paint a pretty picture of Drake Myers. He'd been called a drunkard and a debaucher. She could tolerate neither type of man.

She was quite proud of herself that she'd successfully hidden her distaste when he'd arrived. Slapping a smile on her face, she used her best manners to try and make Drake feel welcome. Had there been any other options, Kayla would've been happy to send the man away. But her desire to be in her own home was stronger than her disgust at a man who clearly wasted his time on alcohol and loose women.

Her mood improved vastly when they reached the spot for her new house. The view of the mountains from the top of the hill was breathtaking, and she would never tire of seeing the snowcapped peaks. Drew had promised her a large window, an extravagance she wouldn't protest. The rest of her house would be frugal, just enough for her with nothing ornate. A simple home, but she considered it a sin not to be able to see the beauty of those mountains.

While Drew and Gideon helped Drake pace off some of the dimensions of the foundation, Kayla found herself studying the man who would spend quite a bit of time alone with her. She'd learned much—none of it good—of his character, but she'd only seen him in passing. Now, especially while he was otherwise occupied, she could take his measure.

He was an attractive man, something she hadn't truly noticed before. His brown hair was longer than she preferred, but it was clean. Perhaps he'd welcome her taking a pair of scissors to it. Until she got to know him better, though, she would feel far too forward offering her services.

His clothes were worn and in need of mending. Since she was handy with a needle, she could inquire whether he'd like her help with that instead. It was a much less personal task than a haircut, and asking him might be a nice way to break the ice.

As Kayla watched him, Drake suddenly turned and locked his gaze on her, almost as if he'd known she was gawking. Her face heated, but she didn't flinch. She'd learned a long time ago that holding a firm stare instead of glancing away made her seem stronger.

Even if I'm not all that strong.

That voice in her head was immediately dismissed as nothing more than the ghost of Chantal Carrington and her constant criticism. From the moment her former fiancé Gregory had introduced Kayla to his mother, the woman found nothing but fault in anything Kayla did. She was too thin. Too opinionated. Too beneath a man like Gregory Carrington.

Gregory might have wanted Kayla to be his bride, but it became perfectly clear that Chantal would never have allowed that to happen. If only he'd known about his mother's plots and plans, things could have turned out differently. If only he'd heeded Kayla's warnings. If only...

No. No more. It was high time those memories were buried deep enough they would cease to haunt her and cause her such pain. Gregory was her past.

This home was her future.

"Miss Backer, um, Kayla?"

Drake's voice brought her back from her unpleasant reveries. "Yes?"

"You truly only want one bedroom?"

She nodded.

"But what if you decide to marry? To have babies?"

"I shall *never* marry." Despite her efforts to conceal it, anger tinted her tone and she had to force herself to relax.

His confusion was plain on his face. "Why on earth not?"

"That, sir, is none of your concern."

He cocked his head, considering her for long enough that she grew uncomfortable. "Anyone ever tell you you're an odd duck?"

Dare he bait her? "Probably the exact number of people that have called you the same."

Drew burst out in laughter, and even the normally glum Gideon grinned.

"I should have warned you, Drake," Drew said. "Our Kayla has a tongue as sharp as any properly stropped razor."

"I noticed that," Drake said. At least his mouth had bowed into a smile, and the twinkle in his chocolate eyes made her wonder at his motives.

"Can you build my home or not?" Kayla snapped. An apology at her rude question immediately tickled her tongue, but she bit it back. Drew was correct. She *did* have a sharp tongue—often sharper than most men could handle. But she refused to swallow her words anymore, even if that meant Drake wouldn't agree to help them.

"I *can*," he drawled. "Now I just gotta figure out if I really *want* to."

"What's this?" Drew's brows knit. "I believed we had reached an agreement. Did we not come to terms yesterday?"

"We did," Drake admitted.

"Then have you changed your mind?"

Swiping his hat from his head, Drake kept his hard stare directed at her.

Kayla knew her face had to be a bright red, but she continued to hold his gaze. "Have you changed your mind because you've made my acquaintance and found me lacking?"

He let out a sigh. "We're likely to be spending a good amount of time together, and I have to admit, I'd like it if you weren't so...so..."

Having been on the receiving end of so much censure in her lifetime, Kayla tossed him a few possible words. "So tart? So rude? So insolent?"

"So damned pretty."

His words took the wind right out of her sails. That, and the way his dark eyes seemed to draw her in made something inside her stomach flutter.

A bad sign.

"What I meant to say is that we'll be out here. Alone. And what with you being such a comely woman..." Then he shrugged.

Gideon stepped up to Drake, his hands clenched into fists. "Are you sayin' you'd take advantage of her while we're away?"

"No, sir. I'd never take an unwilling woman."

"Then what are you saying?" Drew asked as he set a restraining hand on Gideon's arm.

"I'm saying that two people—a man and a woman—all alone out here..." Drake shrugged. "Nature's bound to take its course."

Kayla let out a little snort. "I assure you that nature will do nothing more for us than heap snow upon our shoulders."

He appeared as angry as a cat with ruffled fur. "Other women seem to like me just fine."

Her anger soared at his obvious belief that he was irresistible—that she was the kind of woman who would wish to be associated with him. "I assure you, *Mister Myers*, that I am nothing like the ladies you pay to like you 'just fine.' We shall have a working relationship and nothing more."

"You don't have to get your petticoats in a twist. You might be a right nice-looking woman, but it's clear we're far too different." He offered his hand to Drew. "I'll build your house."

"*My* house," Kayla couldn't help but point out.

Drake acted as though she hadn't spoken. "And I promise to keep my distance from Miss Baker."

"Backer," she said through gritted teeth, fairly sure he'd mispronounced her name on purpose.

After the men shook hands, Gideon led Drake back to the barn to show him the loft that would be his home. Drew remained behind, throwing an arm across Kayla's shoulders.

"I know he's not what you expected..."

God love Drew. He always knew how to defuse her anger. "He's exactly what I *expected.* He's just not what I *wanted.*"

His lips brushed her cheek. "Gideon and I will only be away as long as absolutely necessary. I'm sure once I speak to my mother, I can convince her to come stay with us."

Thankfully, Gideon was nowhere near to hear that boast or there would've been yet another quarrel. "You can be quite persuasive when you wish to be."

"We'll leave in three days, once we're sure Drake has settled in and has everything he needs. But I promise to return as quickly as humanly possible."

Kayla leaned her head against him. "I shall miss you."

"And I you. Don't be afraid to turn to Drake should you need anything in our absence."

"I have Ty and Caleb should I need assistance," she reassured. "I can promise you that I shall never need Drake Myers for anything other than to build my house and stay out of my way."

Chapter Four

"We shall return before you even have time to notice our absence." Drew kissed the top of Kayla's head and held her a little tighter.

She tried to restrain her tears, sniffing hard as she rested her forehead against his chest. The last thing Drew and Gideon needed before they left was a weak, weeping woman hanging all over them. She'd been alone before. She could be alone again and not fall apart.

That was a lie, and she well knew it. Her childhood and her long journey to flee New York might have forced her to be alone, but she hadn't enjoyed being by herself. Until she came to live with Drew and Gideon, she hadn't grasped exactly how lonely her life had become. The months she'd been in their company had created a bond, one she hadn't realized the strength of until she was now faced with losing them, even if only temporarily.

"Look there." Drew eased away from her. "Cassie and Sara have arrived to keep you company."

A wagon approached, leaving long lines on the muddy road in its wake. Kayla had known Ty and Caleb were coming to help Drake with the house, but she hadn't known their wives would come along.

"There, all is better," Drew said with a smile. "'For if they fall, the one will lift up his fellow.'"

One of the things she loved most was how Drew challenged her mind. His library of books remained at her disposal, and one of his favorite games was to quote the Bible—sometimes Shakespeare as well—and expect her to cite the source. He and Cassie often played the same game. His keen intellect kept Kayla on her toes, and she'd yet to best him while he constantly left her baffled. Kayla had to think a moment for the origin of his words, not wanting to send him away with the hubris of victory. "Um... Ecclesiastes?"

He tweaked her nose. "Correct. Chapter four, verse ten. See? You have already cheered to our friends' arrival. I'm quite sure they will keep you from being too lonely while we're away, and do not forget that Drake will be here to come to your aid—day or *night*." His eyes sparkled with mischief.

"You may not matchmake, you rascal," she said with a playful swat at his chest. "Especially not with a man of such ill repute. I have no intention of allowing him anything more than friendship—if even that."

Drew merely winked, the grin never leaving his face.

Kayla let out a censorious scoff. "You could not ever believe that I would consider that man for anything but a hired hand. His... *habits* leave much to be desired."

Even as she claimed disinterest, she found her gaze wandering to where Drake was sorting through a large delivery of lumber that had arrived only the day before. How Gideon was able to obtain it so swiftly, she would never understand. But she was beyond grateful. Although the weather might quickly turn against them, the men could use the warmth that remained to get a good start on the house.

Cassie and Sara both leaned over the side of the wagon and waved as Ty drove the team closer. Kayla returned the gestures, even finding a smile for her friends.

"I don't see the children," she commented to Drew.

"No doubt they are at the Twin Springs visiting Grace."

Kayla nodded, a little pleased to have some of Cassie and Sara's precious time without their children underfoot. Grace Morgan lived on the Twin Springs ranch with her husband Adam, Ty Bishop's adopted father. Kayla had quickly learned that Grace considered herself to be a surrogate mother to Cassie and Sara, and in turn, that made her grandmother to Cassie's daughter, Diana, and Sara's son, Isaac. While Kayla sometimes enjoyed the noise and frivolity of their children, she wished everyone to keep their focus on getting a frame and roof on her house before the snows flew.

As Ty secured the wagon, Caleb climbed down from the seat and lifted Sara out of the wagon bed. She gave him a quick kiss and then waited as he helped Cassie to her feet. Then he and Ty tended to the horses.

The women were bright with smiles, both beautiful in their own way. Cassie Bishop was a little bit of a thing, but she had the face of an angel. Her eyes were a deep brown, her hair tawny with a tint of sunshine. Although small, she commanded attention, and should she fix her focus on any man, she held him captive. Kayla had seen the jealous looks her husband Ty aimed at any man who chose to gape at her. Then again, a woman that comely was hard to ignore.

Sara was taller with a lithe figure, her black-brown hair shorter than Cassie's. Her eyes were the clearest blue, the color of cornflowers, and full of hard-earned wisdom for one barely in her twenties.

Kayla felt plain next to her two friends. As they both embraced Drew, she realized exactly how much he meant to them, perhaps even as much as he meant to her.

A knot suddenly formed in the pit of her stomach. Although Drew had asked Drake if he had objections to seeing Sara—something he claimed would not disturb him—Kayla couldn't help but worry whether there would be angry words exchanged. She watched Drake, who was still sorting supplies, and felt a pinch of guilt that she was forcing him to face a woman who had wronged him.

A hand settled on her arm. "Kayla?" Cassie asked.

With a forced smile, Kayla hugged first Cassie and then Sara. "Where are the children? With Grace?"

Sara nodded. Her gaze went to Drake. "He was told I was coming today?"

"Gideon spoke with him," Kayla replied, even as she nodded. "He believes Drake bears you no grudge."

"There!" Cassie said, taking Sara's hand and giving it a squeeze. "I told you there was nothing to worry about. Why, I'm sure he's forgotten all about—"

Sara let out a rather loud snort. "Forgotten? Sweet Jesus, Cassie. I *stole* from the man. How could he forget that?"

Since Kayla was of like mind, she stayed silent as Cassie endeavored to convince Sara that it was high time to bury the past. At least Sara seemed to be listening, and it wasn't long before she was nodding along with Cassie's wisdom.

"The money was returned," Cassie pointed out.

"That doesn't excuse my actions," Sara insisted.

"I would suggest," Kayla finally said, "that we first focus on preparing some food for the men."

"Then we can gather more stones for your foundation," Cassie said.

"And hearth," Kayla added. "I was thinking how homey it would be to have one made of the same stone as the home's foundation."

Drew beckoned to Kayla, so she hurried to him. Gideon was holding the reins to both of the ready horses, which meant the time to part had arrived.

She swallowed hard to try to banish the tears that stung her eyes. "May God watch over you both and bring you safely home."

Gideon surprised her by handing the reins to Drew and giving her a quick, breath-stealing hug. Then he mounted his horse while Drew embraced her. He gave her nose another tweak before gaining his saddle. With a tip of their hats, they left on their journey.

"Godspeed," she whispered.

Cassie wrapped a reassuring arm around her waist and guided her toward the porch. "Time for us to get to work."

* * *

Drake let his fake smile drop the moment the women went into the house.

He couldn't deny he'd need all of their help. The men would handle the lumber needed to begin the frame while the women helped hunt and carry the stones for the foundation. One man couldn't build an entire house by himself. It simply wasn't possible. But the assistance being offered to Drake made him wish it were.

Just seeing Sara Young made his blood boil, especially when she looked so damned happy. From the day she'd robbed him, her life had been going steadily uphill. His, on the other hand, was near the bottom of a deep, dark well—landing him here instead of as the boss of some cattle company.

Ty and Caleb came striding toward the building site, forcing a sigh from Drake's lips. He'd have to make nice with them, which would be a hell of a lot easier than it would be should he find himself face-to-face with Sara. Then he'd have to bite his tongue until he drew blood.

Even *that* might not stop him from saying his piece.

"Fine morning for some work," Caleb said. There was a hint of nervousness in his voice that was a bit of surprise. His gaze wandered the deliveries that had arrived only the day before. "Where'd all this come from?"

Drake took off his hat and wiped the sweat from his brow with the back of his sleeve. "Drew and Gideon called in a few favors from some craftsmen. Got a lot of things readymade that would've taken me a good long time to work on."

"I'd say." Ty walked around a stack of wooden spindles meant to be used on the large porch Kayla wanted. "These are nice pieces of work."

"They are," Drake replied. "Better than I could ever make."

"Me, either," Caleb said. "So where would you like us to start?"

Drake finished cutting one last board before nodding at the pile of lumber for the frame. "Been cuttin' these so we can start the outside walls. Figured if we could get the stones in place for the foundation and get a good beginnin' on raising a roof, I'd be able to finish on my own."

Glancing at the sky, Ty frowned. "Think we can get a roof up before the snows come hard and heavy?"

After setting his handsaw aside, Drake sighed. "No. Not really. But I promised the men I'd give it my best, and that's exactly what I plan to do."

"Fair enough." Caleb picked up one of the uncut boards. "You're the boss, tell us what you want us to do."

The boss. That was exactly what he should have been had it not been for Sara Young. Of course, he'd known her as "Princess" first—nothing more than a working girl from Denver. One of many he'd paid to take his ease.

Ty and Caleb exchanged looks, probably because Drake hadn't immediately set them to work. Then Caleb swept his hat from his head and threaded his fingers through his dark hair. "Look, Drake... We should clear the air."

"No need for that."

"I think there *is* a need." Caleb cleared his throat loudly. "I know what Sara... was. What she did to you. She feels mighty bad, but she was in a tough spot. If you got to know her, you might understand she ain't a thief. Not deep down inside."

Drake tossed aside another piece of wood, harder than necessary. "It's over and done."

"She needs you to understand."

Drake hefted one of the large stones for the foundation. "I understand fine. We don't need to discuss it. Ever."

Ty shook his head but picked up one the stones to follow Drake. After a few moments, so did Caleb.

They barely spoke as they worked. Only enough words were exchanged to coordinate as they set the boulders on the four corners of what would be Kayla's home and then formed the lines for the rest of the foundation. Despite the crisp air, Drake shed his coat, loving the feel of his muscles burning and sweat trickling down his spine. Hard work was reprieve. Hard work was forgetting.

The sounds of the bell made his head snap up. Kayla always rang an enormous bell hanging on the large porch to announce a meal. He could hardly believe that much of the day had passed since they'd begun work.

"We best be going," he said. "Doubt the women will be patient if they're ready to feed us."

"What about Sara?" Caleb asked.

"Water under the bridge," Drake replied, trying to keep the anger from his voice.

He hiked briskly toward the house, hoping if he simply continued to ignore Caleb's prodding the man would give in and stop gnawing that particular bone. Caleb and Ty followed, and Drake caught their wary exchange of glances.

God, he needed a drink. Damn good thing he'd thought to bring a bottle of rot gut with him. Once this day was over, he would drink away the memories, the anger, and the regret.

Chapter Five

Kayla waited on the porch long after the wagon had disappeared from her sight. The twilight air was crisp, and her breath rose in cloudy puffs around her face. The day had been productive, ending too soon for her taste. But daylight hours waned rapidly this time of year and would continue to shrink until the next year arrived.

Her guests had graciously stayed for an evening meal, although Drake had eaten with the speed of a starving dog before making his excuses to head to his home in the barn. She'd seen neither hide nor hair of him since, although she kept casting glances to the door from the moment he'd left, hoping he'd return.

After the ladies had cleaned away the mess made by the meal, they'd all had a nice conversation about whether women should ever be allowed to vote should Montana become a state. Remembering the rather lively discussion brought a smile to her lips.

Wrapping the thick shawl a little tighter around her shoulders, Kayla looked out toward the beginnings of her home. The foundation had risen well as the day progressed, the rocks now forming a large rectangle that would one day support a house. She felt selfish seeing it, knowing that she was asking far too much of Drew, Gideon, and Drake to keep working on the building with the weather ready to turn harsh.

A home. All she'd ever wanted, and her heart seemed to be set on this house being the pinnacle of finding a home. She would own it. She would put her stamp on it. She would lovingly place each piece of furniture, each knickknack, each rug.

Would it truly be the elusive *home* she'd sought when her tasks were done?

A sharp noise caught her ear, and her gaze shifted once again to the large double doors on the upper loft of the barn. One had been flung open, and Drake—holding tight to a half-empty bottle—leaned his shoulder against the frame.

Kayla almost shouted for him to take care because of the height of his perch. Any forward movement might send him plunging to the ground, so she bit the inside of her cheek. If the man had been drinking yet again, he wouldn't have the wit or skill to save himself should she holler at him.

With a shake of her head, she turned to go inside before she became an icicle.

"Thank God!" Drake's loud proclamation made her whirl back around.

"What did you say?"

"They're gone. Good riddance," he called back to her, saluting with his bottle before taking a drink.

Shaking from cold and anger, she wanted to dismiss him. Yet she needed him to understand exactly how much the help from the Bishops and Youngs meant to her. "How dare you! They have done nothing but offer kindness and assistance!"

He responded by taking another long pull from the bottle.

"You will not speak poorly of them!" Heavens, she felt the fool, shouting with the man across the way from porch to barn.

"Fuck 'em."

Kayla let out an enraged gasp. "How dare you use such language!"

Drake's reply was a grin that she found too attractive in such a shameful man.

"Have you ever considered that you drink to excess?"

All he did was shrug hard enough she feared he would tumble over the side.

With a shake of her head, she turned to go back inside. Standing on the porch and screeching like a harpy was no way to have a conversation.

"Wait!"

She whirled to his shout only to find that he'd left his perch and was no doubt on his way down from the loft. If he'd consumed what was missing from his bottle, he was likely to break his neck when he fell off the ladder.

A few moments later, one of the barn doors slid open and Drake came marching across the yard, his bottle still in his hand. "Wait right there," he said, wagging his finger at her. "I got somethin' to say to you."

Folding her arms under her breasts, Kayla braced herself. She hadn't intended to have a confrontation with the man who'd been hired to help her, but she simply couldn't abide by his reprehensible habits.

His drinking. His cursing. His whoring.

He was a grown man and it was high time he took responsibility for himself. If she was the only one brave enough to tell him that, so be it.

"Look here, woman…" Drake stumbled up the four steps to the porch. He caught himself on the railing.

"My name is Kayla."

The man rolled his eyes, listed to one side, and then had to cling to a post to regain his balance.

Perhaps he was too deep into his cups to have this discussion. She nodded at the bottle he still held tightly. "Did you drink *all* of that?"

He lifted the bottle and squinted as if judging exactly how much was missing. "S'pose I did. Why's it matter to you?"

His words weren't as slurred as she'd expected. Perhaps the man had a high tolerance for drinking, something she'd knew happened after a soul had used spirits for a long time. Years.

Like her father.

She stared at Drake. The man was handsome, well spoken, and had a true talent for building. And yet he was wasting his life on alcohol and women who sold their bodies. How could he not see the danger he was putting himself in?

She suddenly felt sad for him, a deep sorrow that was ridiculous after only knowing him a few days.

"What?" he demanded. "Whatcha starin' at?"

Kayla refused to answer. He wouldn't want her pity. With a shake of her head, she turned to go inside.

A strong hand circled her upper arm, stopping her with a tight squeeze. "I asked you a question."

Since he refused to let her make a tactful exit, she faced him and straightened her spine. He deserved the truth, and perhaps the truth might set him free. "Fine. You want to know what I see when I look at you?"

He nodded, his unruly hair falling over his eyes. He brushed it away with the back of his hand.

"I see a tragedy. A horrible tragedy."

"What's that s'posed to mean?" he said, following the words with a feral growl.

"In all of your days of debauchery, have you ever tried walking away from alcohol? It dulls the senses," she insisted, "and it rots the mind."

"In all of *your* days, have you ever drunk a drop?"

"Certainly not!"

"Then quit talkin' about somethin' you know nothin' about." His words ran together in a sing-song manner. He lifted the bottle and shoved it toward her. "Here. Take a drink. Live a little."

She pushed his hand away. "I will not."

"Afraid?"

"Certainly not."

"Then here." He thrust the bottle at her again. "Show me how brave you are, Kayla. Show me you're not afraid to try some whiskey."

She shook her head.

He let out a snort. "Knew it. You're nothin' but a sanctamin...er...sanctaprim...er..." Hoisting the bottle to his lips, he downed several swallows and then grimaced as though the liquid burned as it traveled down his throat.

"I believe the word you are searching for is sanctimonious, is it not?"

"Yeah," he drawled. "That's what you are. You don't know what I've been through. You don't know what I've suffered."

"Are you speaking of Sara taking your money?"

"Damn right, I am."

Kayla narrowed her eyes, her anger rising so fast and hot that the cold no longer plagued her. "Tell me, sir, how have you *suffered* because some poor creature tried to escape life as a virtual slave, a life of degradation, by taking money that was not even yours?"

In a heartbeat, Drake's face flushed crimson and he sputtered as if so many words were trying to crowd their way out of his mouth that he couldn't figure out which ones would arrive first. "I'm suffering, all right. I'm here, ain't I? Stuck *here*." Lifting his arms, he spun in a circle and then nearly dropped his bottle as he gripped a post to keep from falling until he could get his feet back under himself. "Middle of nowhere. Fuckin' Montana. Ain't even a damn state."

"I've asked you not to curse in front of me. Now, I must insist. I shall not abide by foul language."

A sly smile crossed his lips. "I'll speak any damn way I want to. Damn. Shit. Fuck." Each word was slow. Deliberate. Cruel.

She'd reached her fill of his self-pity, an emotion she'd never allowed herself to indulge in regardless of her circumstances. Anger ruled her tongue. "How *dare* you? You believe you are suffering because you live in this beautiful territory, among some of the nicest people in all of the United States?" She stomped her foot, instantly sorry because the cold made her toes sting. "You know nothing of suffering, of having your life destroyed simply because someone believes you are not nearly good enough for—"

She clenched her hands into fists. Dear Lord, she'd almost blurted out her sordid tale. Her anger made her speak without thought, and she couldn't allow that to happen again. Ever.

Temper back in check, she let her gaze wander over the man. He'd clearly started drinking the moment the evening meal had ended. His clothes were disheveled and badly in need of mending. Sawdust clung to his sleeves and the legs of his pants. For pity's sake, he'd barely washed his hands. As far as she could tell, he'd tossed his hat aside, grabbed the bottle of devil's brew, and started indulging.

"Quite starin' at me," he snapped.

"You have no idea how pathetic you appear, do you?" she asked.

"What?"

An idea blossomed. "Come with me, Mr. Myers. I've a need to show you something important."

Kayla opened the door, pleased to see Drake following without her having to prod him too much. Walking was rapidly becoming more difficult for him, so she tried to keep a few steps ahead to be sure he wouldn't trip forward and tackle her to the ground.

"Where're we goin'?" he asked.

"I need you to take a good, long look at something. Perhaps it will open your eyes."

"Whatcha mean, woman? My eyes are already open."

"Literally, not figuratively. And my name is not 'woman.'"

"You ain't makin' sense," he insisted.

She moved right through the living area to head to the bedroom wing. Passing by her room, she cast a quick glance to see that the tabby cat she'd taken a shine to was waiting on her bed, curled up in a ball and sound asleep. Only when she entered the largest bedroom—the one Drew and Gideon shared—did she stop.

"Well, well, well." Drake tossed her a wicked smile. "You wantin' me in your bed, Kayla?"

"No, Mr. Myers. Not only do I *not* want you in my bed, this is not even my room. It belongs to Drew." *And Gideon.*

"I ain't sleepin' with no man."

"No one has asked that of you."

He lifted a hand to rub his furrowed forehead. "You're makin' my head ache with tryin' to understand what you want. You invited me in. We're in a bedroom. You're a woman—"

"So I noticed."

"—and I'm a man. What else is there for a man and woman to do in a bedroom?"

A deep breath helped her keep from blistering his ears. She grabbed his wrist and dragged him to the tall looking glass—the one Gideon had bought for Drew as a birthday present. "As I told you, I need to show you something." She stopped when she'd pulled him right in front of his own reflection. "Look."

Drake's eyes shifted to the mirror. "At what?" He nodded at his image. "That's me. So what? I've seen a lookin' glass before."

"No, Mr. Myers. I would like you to truly *look* at yourself—at what you've become."

"What are you sayin'?"

She jerked the bottle from his hand and then pointed at the mirror. "You need to see what others see. Your eyes are red and dull. Your hair is far too long and dirty. Your face is dirty. You haven't shaved in days. And your clothing looks as though you slept in it."

"I *did* sleep in it."

"Clearly. But what breaks my heart—what I pity most—is that you were probably a very handsome man."

"What'cha mean *were?*" He fixed his eyes on the mirror. "I'm handsome."

Kayla shook her head. "The reflection I see in this mirror bears little resemblance to the man who came to White Pines last year. Drew told me you were kind—that you'd helped Sara when her child arrived early. He told me you had wit and humor. So tell me, Mr. Myers... Do you see a handsome man in that looking glass now? Do you see a man with wit and humor? Or do you see what we all now see, a pathetic drunkard who is throwing his life away like so much rubbish?"

As Drake stared at himself, she shook her head and left the room, hoping the next few moments would be illuminating for him. That, and she wasn't sure she wanted to consider her own reflection too awfully long.

God only knew what she'd find if she looked too deeply inside herself.

She left the bottle on the wash table on her way out.

* * *

Drake let out a scoffing laugh as Kayla left.

Look in the mirror?

What the hell was she trying to prove?

Even though he'd always assumed people with looking glasses suffered from pure, naked vanity, he decided to oblige her.

With a snort, he shook his head and let his gaze fall on his reflection.

His heart took a leap before it began slamming in his chest the moment he realized that the wretched waste of man he was seeing was himself. He blinked and blinked, thinking what he saw was an illusion, a vision drawn in his mind from Kayla's scolding and criticism.

The man in the mirror didn't change.

His hair was long and tangled, hanging to his shoulders in strings. Dirt was smeared on his face—at least what he could see of his face since it was covered with a week's growth of whiskers. There were dark circles framing his bloodshot eyes, and his nose was red and dripping as though he had a nasty cold.

Despite his disgust, he kept gaping. First at his ragged clothes—a tattered shirt, a coat that was dirty and ripped, and pants that were filthy and too large for him.

When had all this happened?

Drake had arrived in Montana a healthy man, a good-looking one in his opinion. Now, he was a man who'd aged a decade in less than a year. As he raised a hand to comb his fingers through his hair, he stopped and held that hand in front of his face. No matter how hard he tried, he couldn't stop the damn thing from trembling.

Angry at Kayla for forcing him into this uncomfortable enlightenment, he snatched the bottle from the table. He lifted it to his lips, chugging the last of the whiskey he'd brought out to the farm. Fire burned down his throat and into his stomach, where it churned what remained of his evening meal. He wanted—*needed*—the forgetfulness the strong drink gave him.

His image blurred as he swayed, willing himself to stay on his feet. He shook his head at the disgusting, broken man staring back at him from the mirror. It was some magic trick. It had to be. That was the only explanation.

Yes, that was what had happened. The woman was playing him as though he were some rube at a carnival.

He thumped the looking glass with his knuckles, checking the thickness, hoping to discover exactly how Kayla had pulled off such a ruse. Yet the thickness wasn't abnormal. He stumbled behind the freestanding mirror, searching for a handle or a button that might restore the image to a true reflection.

God, his head hurt, pounding hard and making his heartbeat echo in his ears. With a grunt, he moved back to stare at the reflection of the man he'd become—a man who was wasting away.

Drake's stomach lurched, and he dove for the empty chamber pot resting near the bed. Wave after wave assaulted him as the food and drink emptied from his sore belly. After several moments, he was reduced to dry heaves as his nose ran and his eyes watered.

Suddenly, a cold, wet cloth was laid on the back of his neck. "Are you finished?"

He swiped the sleeve of his coat across his mouth before he nodded. A glass of water was thrust in front of face.

"Take a sip and spit it out," Kayla said in a gentle voice.

He obeyed, although after he took the glass from her, his hands shook hard enough that it was difficult to get the water to his mouth. After swishing the cold drink around his sour mouth, he spit it into the chamber pot.

"Now, take a few small sips."

Again, he obeyed. Although he'd brought up some of the whiskey, all he'd drank before supper was rapidly taking away the world. Kayla's voice seemed to come from a distance, and what he could see grew fuzzy and dark.

As he stretched out on the cold floor, a pillow was suddenly under his head and a blanket draped over his body.

"Sleep," she said.

Drake let go of his thoughts and allowed the fog of the whiskey claim him.

Chapter Six

Drake was fairly sure death might be better than what he was suffering now that he'd awakened. Light spilled through the window, drilling like hot pokers into his eyes. There were birds singing just outside, and each trill and whistle was akin to a hammer being struck against his skull.

He opened his burning eyes enough to try to figure out where he was since his memory was a dark void. The room wasn't at all familiar, and his view from where he lay on the floor made the furniture seem out of proportion. A bed with a brass headboard took up a good portion of the room. A dark chest of drawers stood on one wall, and a table with a pitcher and bowl was within his reach. It wasn't until he saw the expensive looking glass that memories of the night before began to blossom in his mind.

With a groan, he tried to push himself up on an elbow. There wasn't a single part of him that didn't ache—from the roots of his hair to his toenails. His tongue was covered with a foul-tasting film. A clean chamber pot rested next to him. He remembered getting sick, but his mind was blank after that.

Drake dragged off the quilt that had covered his body, figuring Kayla had taken pity on him and arranged it over him after he'd passed out. She'd also been kind enough to shove a pillow under his head. He'd have to swallow his pride enough to thank her.

He forced himself to sit up, setting the room to spinning. A few deep breaths kept him from upchucking again.

"Coffee?"

Although she'd only spoken one word, Kayla's voice bored into his skull. He let out a groan and put his hands against his ears.

"I feared you might suffer this morning," she continued. "You did drink a great deal last night. In fact, you became quite ill. I'm sorry I wasn't able to help you into a bed, but you were simply too heavy for me to lift after you'd passed out on the floor."

Squeezing his dry, irritated eyes tightly shut, he wondered if there was anything he could do to convince her to bring him some whiskey. The only cure for what ailed him was hair of the dog, but all of the brew he'd brought with him was now gone. He'd finished it last night.

"I brought you coffee," she said.

Drake opened his eyes to mere slits. "Coffee ain't what I need."

She set a delicate cup and saucer on the table next to the water pitcher. "Coffee is what I have." She turned to face him, her skirts swishing loudly around her ankles. The smirk on her face made him believe she knew exactly what he'd like to drink. "Or I could brew some tea, should you prefer it."

"Breakfast," he mumbled. Having some food in his tender belly might help him get past this misery.

With another shake of her head, she folded her arms under her breasts and frowned. "Breakfast has come and gone." As though to punctuate her words, a far-too-loud clock down the hall chimed twice. "As has the noon meal."

"Need some food." The simple act of talking made his head throb harder.

"We need to speak on an important matter first," she insisted. "Then I shall prepare you a light fare."

If his head hadn't felt as though it would shatter into a thousand pieces, he would have given it a shake. "Eat first."

She shook her stubborn head.

Although Drake wasn't sure he could even carry on a coherent conversation, he acquiesced with a curt nod. Would the pain never cease?

"I have come to a decision regarding your assistance with building my home."

He would've quirked an eyebrow had he not known it would cost him dearly. Instead, he flipped his hand in agitation, wondering how quickly he could hop on his horse, get to town, and find some whiskey.

Kayla drummed her fingers against her forearm and let out an exasperated sigh. "Should you wish to remain at this farm and employed in the building my home, you will no longer consume spirits."

"Spirits?"

"Alcohol, Mr. Myers."

Her words took a long time penetrating his foggy thoughts. She couldn't be serious. Not consume spirits? No alcohol?

The woman was daft.

"Why?" was all he could choke out.

"I have no need of explaining myself, but I simply refuse to tolerate the behavior I saw last evening. It is quite evident that you cannot exercise any type of moderation; therefore, I have no choice but to bring an end to this reprehensible habit."

Drake would chew off his own tongue before he admitted that he couldn't understand half of what Kayla had said. Her speech was far too refined for him—*she* was far too refined for him. But the gist was unmistakable. "I can't have my whiskey?"

"No, you may not have your whiskey."

He wanted to shout at her, to scoff at her and ask how she could dare stand there judging him. She was nothing but a prim and proper virgin who knew absolutely nothing about life. Hell, she'd never even sipped whiskey, probably thought it was for other people. Common people.

Then it dawned on him. What was really eating at him was her belief that he was beneath her—not fit to kiss her dainty feet.

Anger making his temples throb in rhythm with his rapidly hammering heart, he got to his feet. "Lady, you can kiss my hairy ass."

Standing her ground, she drew her lips into a thin, angry line.

"I mean it. Kiss. My. Ass. You can find someone else to build your stupid house. Ain't a man in the world who'd share it with an ice queen like you anyhow. Likely freeze my pecker off if I put it in you."

She didn't even blink at his crude tirade. "I can understand that you might be angry, but if you—"

"Angry don't even scratch the surface." He got to his feet, holding tight to the bed's footboard until the room stopped shifting beneath him. "I'm gettin' my things and leavin'."

Damn if she didn't shake her head yet again.

"I mean it, lady. I'm not stayin' here."

"I'm afraid that you have no choice," she calmly announced.

Confusion reigned. She was shoving him out the door, then she was telling him he couldn't leave? He chose to focus on one important thing. If he wanted to quit this job, there wasn't a damn thing she could do about it.

Drake snorted. "You think a little bit of a thing like you could stop me?"

Why did her eyes seem to sparkle with humor? "I have no doubt you possess superior strength. What I know that you clearly do not is that we had a great amount of snow fall overnight. I doubt you will be able to go anywhere for at least a few days."

"What?" Even nature was conspiring against him now. He made his way to the window, squinting hard against the light and finding more snow than he thought should've been able to accumulate in the short amount of time he'd been dead to the world. "Damn." His gaze shifted to Kayla. "Did you take care of—?"

"The animals have all been tended to."

Shame washed through him. While his main job was to build the house, he'd promised Drew and Gideon that he'd also tend the livestock while they were away. Instead, he'd slept through the morning feeding and milking. Had Kayla not done his chores, the poor milk cow would've been in pain from a swollen udder.

"Thank you," he mumbled.

"I didn't take care of the animals for you."

He dragged his fingers through his dirty, messy hair. "All the same, thanks."

She moved to stand by the mirror. "Have you peered at your reflection this morning, Mr. Myers?"

The woman knew good and well he hated it when she called him that, especially when she emphasized his name with what he heard as snootiness. "No," he snapped, unable to keep his voice down despite his aching head.

Her eyes widened at his near shout. "You should. Just as last evening, I believe what you shall see staring back at you is a man I am quite sure you never wanted to be. You might also try to remember exactly how long it has been since you've passed a day—an entire day—without needing the swill that is slowly destroying you." On that, she left him alone, shutting the door quietly behind her.

Even though he wanted nothing more than to march right out of that room—out of that house—and forget all about the looking glass, he found himself stepping closer again. The cursed thing had been difficult for him to gaze into last night, the reflection one that made him wince. But his appearance had been altered by the amount of whiskey he consumed. Surely by this morning, even though his head and body were suffering, he would look more like himself. That was the tale he told himself before he stepped in front of the mirror.

A stranger still stared back. Eyes more red than white. The lines on his gray face were deep, marking him a man much older than his thirty years. His hair would've made a great nest for the barn mice judging from the tangles. He'd grown thin, no doubt from his erratic pattern of taking meals—or from drinking them. The food Kayla had made the night before had been tasty, but he'd been in such a hurry to drown his anger that he'd wolfed it down too fast to enjoy. The whole meal had ended up in a chamber pot anyway.

As he raised his hand to try to straighten his collar, he realized how badly it was still shaking. Holding it at eye level, Drake concentrated hard on keeping his outstretched hand steady. He'd always taken pride in his shooting skill because of that stable, sturdy hand. Now, it trembled enough that anyone who saw it would think he suffered from the ague.

His shocking appearance paired with the misery of the pain he suffered made him wonder if some of the people in White Pines had refused to hire him because of his pathetic appearance. He looked, quite simply, like a drunkard.

Denial raced through him. "I can stop whenever I want," he said to himself with a firm nod. *I can. I can take or leave whiskey.*

So why did his stomach knot at the thought that he might be snowed in at this godforsaken farm for a few days?

Because there wasn't a drop of the brew anywhere near.

A shudder raced through Drake when he thought hard about all Kayla had said, especially when she challenged him to remember a day when he hadn't had a shot of whiskey. There was no memory of a time when the drink hadn't been a part of his life, at least not in the last handful of years. Even on the trail, he'd indulged with the other cowboys, probably more often than not. In fact, one of the other bosses had pulled him aside and cautioned him not to get so friendly with the men, saying they wouldn't respect him. He especially advised Drake to temper his drinking.

Clarity rang like a bell. All this time he'd heaped responsibility on Sara Young's slender shoulders, blaming her theft of the payroll on him losing his job even though the money was returned. In reality, the decision to dismiss him had been because of his drinking. The payroll had merely been a good reason to finally act.

"What you shall see staring back at you is a man I am quite sure you never wanted to be."

Kayla's words haunted him, and he looked at his reflection again, knowing she was entirely right. That face wasn't his—not the true Drake Myers.

Where had he gone?

He'd drowned in bottles of cheap whiskey.

Truth was, he needed this job. Desperately. He had no place else to go, and while he wanted to stomp right out of there to escape Kayla's knowing stare, he simply couldn't.

Which meant one thing.

No whiskey.

"It'll all come out in the wash," he whispered to himself. He would do this. He *could* do this. She wanted him to walk away from whiskey; he'd do exactly that.

I'll show her!

Heading to the door, he jerked it open, not surprised to find her waiting nearby. "Fine." He growled. "I'm not gonna drink anymore. Not 'til the house is finished." He inclined his head at the window. "Won't be working on it today, though."

The corners of her mouth twitched as though a smile threatened. "I can understand why that might be difficult with so much snow." She made a delicate gesture toward the kitchen. "I could make you something to eat now."

Drake nodded and murmured his appreciation, following her into the kitchen. He sat at the table and sipped at the cup of coffee she'd offered earlier that was now set in front of him while she whipped him up a meal.

She hummed softly to herself, appearing quite pleased with the day's turn of events. No wonder since she'd gotten exactly what she wanted. After a short time, she put a plate full of eggs, pork, and potatoes in front of him.

His stomach churned cruelly at the scent, but he swallowed hard before forcing himself to eat. He'd bluster his way through this hangover, although he wished he had a drop or two of drink left in the barn to help take the edge off his headache.

Would he always want just one more drink?

Well, when this ordeal was over, he could have all the wanted.

That reminder buoyed him.

As Kayla went about cleaning the kitchen, Drake finished his meal. He finally took the empty plate to the sink. "Thank you kindly."

"You're quite welcome," she said, taking the dish from his trembling hand.

"I'm gonna head to the barn. I need myself some more sleep."

Her brows knit as she let her gaze sweep him from head to toe. "I was thinking it might be a good idea for you to stay in the house, at least for a few days."

He thought for a moment he'd misheard her. His head was still pounding every bit as hard as it had when she'd awakened him, and he found that his thoughts were as hard to grasp as tendrils of smoke. He'd broken out in a cold sweat, and his legs were now shaking as much as his hands. "Why?"

"I dare say you might suffer from the loss of your drink. I have seen the like before, and you are showing quite a few of the symptoms."

"What in the hell does that mean?" A moment later, his stomach rebelled, and Drake had no choice but to dive for a bucket sitting next to the sink. The meal he'd eaten came up, making his throat and nose burn and his eyes water.

When he was reduced to dry heaves, he felt a cool, damp cloth draped over the back of his neck again.

"It is as I feared. You will suffer for a while, Mr. Myers."

Suffer was the correct word, but he could only wonder at why this hangover was so much worse than any he'd had before.

As though her train of thought followed his, she said, "My father went through this malady when he was forced to abandon his habit. I know ways to ease your misery, and it would be best for both of us if you remained in the house. I do not relish the notion of trudging through the snow and climbing a ladder to tend you, which I dare say shall be often in the next few days."

As weak as a newborn foal, he pushed the bucket aside and sat back on the floor. He grabbed the damp cloth from his neck and dragged it over his heated face. While he wanted to tell her that he'd be grateful for anything she could do to bring whatever this illness was to a swift end, all he could do was nod at her suggestion.

"Let's get you in bed." Kayla grabbed his elbow and tried to help him get to his feet.

Once he was up, he leaned heavily against her as he made his way back to the room he'd used the night before. She released him long enough to turn back the bed's quilt, and he flopped on his back, wondering if death would bring him faster relief.

"I fear you are going to have some miserable days ahead," she said, pulling the quilt over him and laying her cool hand on his forehead. "I'll do everything I can to make you more comfortable."

As she turned to leave, he grasped her hand. Through his hazy thoughts, one thing was crystal clear. She was the only person who could help him now. "Thank you."

With a weak smile and nod, she left him to his wretchedness.

Chapter Seven

Drake smelled a hell of a lot better, but he wasn't entirely sure the ordeal of the bath had been worth it. At least now that he was stretched out on the clean linens and dressed in freshly washed and mended long johns, he could relax.

Relax? Not hardly. He still suffered from shivers for no reason. Thankfully, his legs had stopped their strange and rather painful involuntary dance, and his hands no longer shook uncontrollably. His stomach had settled enough to allow him to eat the light offerings Kayla gave him each meal time. Toasted bread. Broth. Tea.

A big, hot bowl of stew would taste mighty good 'bout now...

A glance out the window told him the snow hadn't abated. Although it was late in the evening, he could still see the thick, white flakes dancing in the wind. For all he knew, the snow was waist-deep. He'd been stuck inside, battling his body's reaction to being without whiskey.

The days had dragged by—days full of sickness of his body and his mind. The worst part was knowing Kayla had seen him at his weakest. The woman had to be disgusted with him.

Hell, he was disgusted with himself.

How had he ever allowed himself to sink into such depravity?

The hinges of the bedroom door squeaked as Kayla nudged it with her hip to force it open a little wider. In her arms were his clothes—all of them—now clean and no doubt mended. She set the pile on the end of the bed just as an exaggerated yawn forced her shoulders back a moment before one of her slender hands covered her open mouth.

"Beg pardon," she murmured as she went about putting his clothes inside the bedroom's bureau as though it belonged to him.

Then Drake noticed the shadows under her doe brown eyes. The woman was clearly exhausted, no doubt from the constant care she'd given him through his misery. He recalled the cool rags against his feverish face, the gentle words she used to calm him, and the mugs of broth laced with herbs to help him weather the storm. He owed her more thanks than he could ever offer.

In all honesty, Drake owed Kayla his very life. Had he kept up his steady drinking, he wouldn't have been long for this world. Only his sober mind could grasp the danger he'd constantly placed himself in by swilling that rot-gut day and night.

She yawned again, swaying on her feet. "Pardon. I cannot seem to stop yawning."

Drake patted the soft mattress. "Come. Sit. I–I need to talk to you."

"We can talk quite adequately from here."

"Please, Kayla. You're dead on your feet, but I gotta tell you something." He patted the spot again. "Please."

With a weary sigh he tried not to take offense to, she moved to the open side of the bed, sat down, and leaned back against the headboard. He wasn't at all surprised when she closed her eyes. She probably hadn't sat down all day.

He felt like a cad. Not only was Kayla taking care of his sorry ass, she was also feeding and caring for the livestock, chopping the firewood, and cooking.

Doing his chores as well as her own.

"I–I want to tell you how much I appreciate all you done for me," Drake said. The guilt was so overwhelming that he couldn't even look her in the eye, so he stared at the wall in front of him. "I know it wasn't easy taking care of me. I acted like a wounded bear, but you never quit on me."

Her silence gave him confidence to continue. "You were right, you know. I was a–a...mess. A drunkard. I don't know if I can even find the words to tell you how grateful I am." He took a quick glance around the bedroom. "You put me up here in the house. Took all my clothes and sewed up the holes and tears." His gaze came to rest on the pile of clean clothes. "And you washed 'em up nice for me. I just wanted to tell you how much it all meant to me."

She still didn't reply.

Drake found the courage to glance at her face.

Damn if Kayla hadn't fallen asleep. Her chin had dropped to her chest, and her breaths came deep and even.

The woman hadn't heard a single word of what he'd said.

"Serves me right," he whispered.

Afraid she'd end up with a nasty crick in the neck if she slept that way, he thought about carrying her into her own bedroom. Problem was he wasn't entirely sure his returning strength had reached a level to allow him to do so. He wasn't about to drop his savior on her ass simply because he was trying to make her more comfortable. No, he'd be a gentleman and give up his bed for her. It was the least he could do.

Drake had no sooner made up his mind to leave when Kayla mumbled something in her sleep and leaned over to drop her head against his shoulder. Knowing that position was likely to leave them both cramped and sore, he eased his arm around her shoulders and guided her to lie down so that her head rested on his lap.

Letting out a resigned sigh, he relaxed against the feather pillow propped behind his back. If she needed him to be her pillow so that she could rest, he'd be glad to accommodate her. She deserved no less than any kindness and comfort he could offer.

Admitting that he was wrong hadn't been easy, especially when he'd also had to admit Kayla had been right all along. When she was awake enough to listen, he'd simply have to open himself up again and spit out the words he somehow knew she needed to hear.

Why had she done all she had to help him, especially when he'd been nothing but a pain in the ass from the moment he'd arrived at the farm? Shameful as it was to admit, Drake had treated her with such disdain, never once offering her a kind word or action. Despite his cruelty, she'd nursed him through what had been the worst time of his life. And she'd done so even knowing he'd brought his wretchedness on himself.

As gently as he could, he smoothed the hair away from her face. Then he stared at her as she slept, amazed at how unguarded she now was—how the lines of worry faded while she rested.

She was young—awfully green for someone who was wanting to have a house all to herself. Instead of worrying about a homestead, she should be doing what other young women did. Flirting and sparking with young men.

Talking with her friends about ribbons and dresses. Going to church picnics with her family.

Instead, she lived far away from town, caring for two men who could never care for her as anything approaching a wife. And she'd seemed to have given up on being with a man. No one in town had claimed her.

Or had she refused to be claimed?

Perhaps she hadn't stumbled across the right man yet.

Exactly what kind of woman was this Kayla Backer?

With a smile, he traced the lines of her dainty ear with his fingertip and figured it might be a good idea to find out.

* * *

Kayla was sure Drake had taken a turn for the better.

Despite the late hour, he was still sleeping, which wasn't unusual. For the better part of a week, he'd been asleep more than awake. The difference this morning was that his slumber was peaceful.

As his body adjusted to the loss of the alcohol, he'd suffered badly. When he slept, he tossed and turned as what she assumed were nightmares made him call out in fear. There were hours spent at his bedside, smoothing her hand across his furrowed brow, stroking his hair, and whispering softly to try and chase the demons away.

Whenever he'd been awake, Drake was angry. Since Kayla understood the irritation wasn't about her, that she was simply the lightning rod for all his misery, she took his insults and profanity with grace. Not that she enjoyed his tirades. But she'd endured worse with her father, and Drake had never once become physical. In that, he was much better than her father. The only thing that had prevented her from major injury was her father being trapped in his bed or his chair, his legs useless. He still found ways to strike out at her, often with words, which could seem every bit as hurtful.

With a shake of her head, she set the physic she'd prepared for Drake aside. She'd used a special mixture of herbs that her aunt had taught helped balance a person's body. A pinch of calendula to ease his raw throat. Some elderberries, dried and ground to powder, to ease his fever. Ginger to soothe his stomach. Garlic—something her aunt swore by, despite the pungent smell that tended to offend—because it seemed to help many different problems.

Thankfully, her herb and flower gardens had done well this summer, not only yielding healing supplies but giving beauty to what had been a stark piece of land close to the house. She'd planted everything from the seeds she'd carefully gathered from her aunt's garden. Licorice. Milk thistle. Nettle. And so many more. Each new item she'd harvested had been dried and preserved to rebuild the supply.

She could have been content in Chicago with her uncle and aunt, but she'd had to flee their home. Chantal Carrington had made sure that Chicago would never be safe, which was why Kayla had been forced to run to St. Louis and now found herself in the obscurity of the Montana Territory with no chance of seeing any of her family again.

A tear spilled from Kayla's eye. She swiped it away with the back of her hand. Her aunt had been such a gentle, kind soul, and her uncle had treated her like one of his own. She might've been happy with them.

"Kayla..."

Grateful to have something to pull her from her sad memories, she forced a smile. "You look as though you are feeling much better this morning."

Pushing up on his elbows, Drake found the first smile she'd seen from him in a week. Locks of his hair hung over his forehead, long enough to almost hide his eyes. She'd insisted he bathe and wash his hair the day before, and he'd taken it upon himself to shave since his hands were steadier. Now, with that crooked smile, he was so appealing that he stole her breath.

"I brought your morning tonic." She stumbled over the words, unsure as to why she was suddenly so nervous, especially after she'd awakened with her head in the man's lap. Her hand was trembling as she handed him the mug.

His smile turned to a grimace. "I can't abide the way that tastes."

"So you have told me. Over and over. Yet look at how much my potions have helped you heal."

"Heal? Is that what you call sleeping off my drinkin'?"

"That is *exactly* what I call it. You had an illness, Mr. Myers, and—"

"Damn it, Kayla..." Drake took a deep breath and let it out slowly. "You've nursed me near to a week. Why in the hell can't you call me Drake?"

He had her there. For the entire time she'd cared for him, she'd kept as much emotional distance as she could. Last night, she'd simply been too weary to keep her eyes open and had fallen asleep in his room. When she'd awakened, she'd been so embarrassed that she was sure she'd blushed to the roots of her hair.

One thing that helped her maintain some aloofness was not using his familiar name. With a small smile, she admitted to herself she enjoyed how much it irritated him. "Fine. I will endeavor to call you Drake from this moment on—*if* you drink your tonic without a fuss."

"You got yourself a deal." Taking the offered physic, he gulped it down quickly. As he shuddered, he handed it back to her. "Tastes like sh...er...terrible. Tastes terrible."

"I would imagine it does. When you rise and come to the table to eat, I shall have fresh water for you to chase away the flavor."

"Oh, goodie. *More* water."

"Water cleanses the inside as well as the outside, Mist...um...Drake."

"Drunk enough of it to fill a lake."

"And that water has improved your health, has it not?"

Drake chuckled. "Gotta admit that it has." He tossed the quilt aside and stood. He wore nothing but his gray long johns, and the back flap had loosened so that only one button held it in place.

Kayla caught a good look at his tight backside before she glanced away. "I shall leave you to dress."

He laughed and was buttoning the loose flap when she turned to go.

A hand snaked around her upper arm. "Wait. Please," he pleaded.

Since he was no longer showing her the better part of his derriere, she acquiesced, arching an eyebrow in curiosity.

"I... I..." He dragged his foot across the wooden floor. "I just wanna thank you. If you hadn't helped me... Well, I've never had anyone take care of me like that before when I was sick." He gave his head a shake. "Wasn't really *sick*, either. I was drunk, and I'm ashamed of myself."

A bit surprised at his epiphany, she didn't try to pull away, even as his hand moved down her arm to grasp her hand. If she was honest with herself, she'd have to admit how much she liked feeling her hand encased in his.

"You were right. I *was* a pig."

"I do not believe that I ever called you a pig," Kayla protested.

"No, but I was one. You just said it nicer." He cleared his throat roughly. "You made me look at myself. Made me see what I was doin'." Slowly, he raised her hand until he was able to brush a kiss over her knuckles. "Thank you."

"You're quite welcome. I'm happy to have helped."

"I'm not gonna get drunk like that again."

"I believe it might be prudent," she advised, "not to drink at all." Drake took a long time thinking over her words, so she squeezed his hand. "Would you wish to find yourself right back in this situation?"

He shook his head, but the fierce frown didn't leave.

"I am of the opinion that even one drink could be enough to cause you to abandon all you've achieved here."

"Why?"

"Why what? Why would it toss you back into that storm?"

He shook his head again. "Why do you know that?"

Aware that she was opening up a part of herself, she didn't hesitate to reply. "Because of my father."

Drake's frown eased, and a softness came into his eyes. His thumb began to rub gentle circles on her palm. "Your father was a drunk?"

"He was—until he had no choice but to abandon his ways."

"No choice?"

"One night after drinking far too much, he stepped in front of a fast-moving carriage. His back was injured and he lost the ability to walk. I refused to allow him to drink as he recovered, and since I managed the household from that point on, I would not bring alcohol into our home."

Oh, how that had angered her father! But there had been times—far too many times—the man had sworn he'd changed his ways only to be tempted back into a life ruled by spirits.

"Where is he?" Drake asked.

"Pardon?"

"Why isn't he here with you?"

She sighed. "He died more than a year ago."

Drake watched the sadness steal away every bit of spark from Kayla's face, and he wished he hadn't pushed for answers. Yet he was glad to learn a little about her, even if what she shared came in such small bits and pieces.

"I'm sorry," he said, taking a step closer until he stood before her. Then he cupped her soft face in his hands and kissed her forehead.

He owed her so much. Until this morning—the first truly clearheaded morning he'd had in almost as long as he could remember—he hadn't realized exactly how low he'd sunk. Nor could he continue to blame Sara's theft for his debauchery. Even before the day she'd stolen the payroll from him, Drake had been lost to drinking and whoring.

When he sat in bed, contemplating his life, his first thought had been shame. His Uncle Herbert, the man who'd raised Drake as though he were his son, would have been disgusted with what he'd become. That thought made Drake vow never to allow himself to be the kind of man he couldn't stand to see staring back from that looking glass Kayla had forced him to use. No, he would change. He'd be the kind of man his uncle would've been proud to claim.

The first thing on his "to do" list was to thank Kayla for helping enlighten him. Instead, he'd picked at a barely healed wound, and his questions had turned her sunny mood sour.

Wrapping his arms around her, he pulled her into a hug, a bit surprised she didn't try to move away. "I'm sorry I brought it up."

"There's no need," she replied, although she didn't relax in his arms. Instead, her hands rested against his chest as if she couldn't decide whether to push herself out of his embrace or continue to allow it. "You couldn't have known."

"That doesn't mean I'm not sorry that I brought back bad memories." He pressed his lips to her forehead again. Her pleasant, somewhat flowery scent and the feel of her body so close to his made it difficult to think. All he wanted was to give her a proper kiss.

Proper kiss?

Hell, he wanted to bed her. End of story.

"I should get you something to eat," she said.

Drake crooked his finger under her chin and lifted until her eyes met his. "I need to thank you."

"You already have."

"Not properly." Before she could have a chance to figure out his intent, he kissed her.

For a long moment, he waited for her to break the connection and flee his embrace. Instead, she sighed against his mouth and leaned against him as she threaded her arms around his neck. A low growl rumbled from him when Kayla's fingers tangled through his hair, tugging gently as she moaned.

God, he wanted to pick her up and carry her to the bed. Then he'd peel off that prim dress and make love to her.

If the woman could read his mind, she'd be running for the door. Despite her passionate response to his kiss, she wasn't the kind of woman a man tumbled for fun. No, she was the kind of woman a man married, and that wasn't ever going to happen in his life.

Feeling a little guilty for taking advantage of her after all she'd done for him, he eased back, refusing to deepen the kiss. But he smugly noticed how her mouth followed his. A moment later, her cheeks flushed a vivid red. What he didn't know was whether she was embarrassed or angry.

"I am so sorry," she said, stumbling back a few steps.

Considering he was the one who should be apologizing, Drake couldn't help but gape at her. "Sorry? *You're* sorry?"

"I am," she replied with a nod. "I should not have been so…so…brazen. It shall not happen again."

    She left before he could set her straight.

Chapter Eight

As Drake dressed, he wondered what could have been going through Kayla's mind to make her apologize, as though she'd offended him with the kiss. Remorseful words had been ready to tumble from his mouth, but she'd beaten him to the punch. He'd never been so surprised in his whole life, and not only from her apology, even though he'd never expected it.

The way she'd kissed him had shattered all the notions he'd held about Miss Kayla Backer. Drake had judged her as a cold woman. Why else would she remain unmarried in a place where she had her choice of men—men who desperately wanted wives? With the inordinate gossip that flew through the town, he'd heard the stories of the many proposals of marriage she'd spurned. The men in the town insinuated all sorts of wild things about her. Everything from her being frigid to her preferring the company of other women.

Then she'd kissed him and proven every story to be nothing but cruel blather.

There was nothing cold about Kayla. The woman many in White Pines called the Ice Queen was definitely hiding some heat inside her.

That knowledge left Drake torn on what to do next. He owed her so much for helping him recover from his bout of severe self-pity and depravity. Yet he still tasted her on his lips, still felt her soft curves pressed against his body. He might curse himself as nothing but a randy goat, but he desperately wanted to explore the passion her kiss had offered.

Now what?

For now, he'd wait and watch. Should Kayla give him so much as the crook of her finger in invitation, he'd give in to his desire. But should her passion never reveal itself again, Drake would leave her be.

It was the only honorable thing to do, and God knew he hadn't been acting honorably for quite some time.

"As good a time as any to start," he muttered to himself as he headed out of his room.

Kayla was setting two plates full of food on the table. "Are you hungry?"

Her question was so calmly asked, he couldn't help but think he'd misread her reaction to their kiss. Then he saw how she tightly gripped her hands together after she put the plates down.

The desire to put her at ease nearly overwhelmed him. "Yes, ma'am. I surely am." Drake glanced at the plate as he pulled out her chair for her. "Smells tasty."

"I hope you enjoy it." She scooted her chair a little closer and picked up the piece of linen she'd set on the table.

Since he had no idea what that linen was for, his first inclination was to stuff it in the collar of his shirt to protect it from spills. He watched her and was surprised to see her drape the linen napkin over her lap. The woman had impeccable manners, so he shook the cloth out and laid it on his knees. He was rewarded with a shy smile.

They ate in silence, but that quiet didn't seem to bother her. Just like him, she seemed comfortable with it. By the time the meal was over, he was exhausted. No doubt his body was still recovering, but he felt worse than useless.

Kayla carried her plate to the sink. When she came to pick up his, she knit her brow. "Are you ill? You've gone as pale as milk."

He'd wanted to get back to his chores today, but he'd need a nap before he could manage something as taxing as dealing with the livestock. "I'm not sick. Just tired. Again."

As though she didn't believe him, she pressed the back of her hand against his forehead.

"I'm fine. Truly," he insisted. "Only plumb tuckered out."

"You should go sleep for a spell," she said, picking up his dirty plate. "After I clear away the breakfast clutter, I shall tend to the animals."

"You could leave it 'til after my nap." Even as he made the promise, Drake knew some of the chores simply couldn't wait.

"I shall milk the cow and be sure to feed all of our stock. Then we can share this afternoon's chores."

"That sounds nice." Drake couldn't stop a yawn from slipping out. "Thanks for pickin' up my slack while I've been...out of sorts."

"I'm accustomed to hard work," Kayla said. "I find it soothing. Please go and rest. I'll wake you should you not rise by the noon meal."

* * *

Drake came awake with a start at a loud sound.

Was that breaking glass?

Heaven only knew how long he'd slept. As his mind cleared of the fog of slumber, he caught whispered voices from the bedroom down the hall—voices he didn't recognize. He strained to listen as he grabbed his pants from where he'd set them aside before his nap and tugged them on.

"I done told ya and told ya, Smitty. She ain't got no one here with her."

"Ya told me. Just ain't gonna believe any woman could be *that* stupid."

The intruders' feet crunched against broken glass, spurring Drake to hurry and slip on his boots. The men were inside the house, and he had no doubt their intentions were malicious.

Where in the hell was Kayla? Was she still outside?

He had to protect her.

The noise of an object crashing to the wood floor filled the air, sounding as loud as thunder. The men who'd been foolish enough to come after her weren't concerned with being heard, which meant they didn't realize Drake was on the farm, let alone in the house.

"Damn it, Grimes! Why don't ya go ahead and shout that we're here? Damn clumsy fool."

"Ain't got no worries, Smitty. She be in the barn, tendin' the stock. We can grab her up when she comes back in."

How kind of them to reveal their plan.

Drake eased open the bureau drawer where she'd put his gun and holster. He slid the gun loose, checked that it was loaded, and let out his held breath at seeing bullets in the chambers. Moving as silently as possible, he eased toward the door as he strained to hear their movements.

"Just you be rememberin', Grimes," one of the ragged voices said. "I get first poke at her."

"Yeah, yeah. Don't matter none to me. You'll just be stretchin' her out for me."

Blood lust raced through Drake, and it took every bit of his self-control not to rush out and break both of their necks. Instead, he paused as they made their noisy way down the hallway, waiting until the first was within striking distance. While he might want them dead after hearing their big plans for Kayla, he knew the best thing to do was beat them down and then let Marshal Riley sort the bastards out.

He slid his gun into his holster.

"Just thought of somethin', Smitty. Where we gonna find a parson to marry the three of us?"

"Marry? Three people cain't marry, you fool." A loud snort followed the question. "No one said nothin' about marryin' the bitch anyway. Shoulda taken our money when we offered it to her. Now, she's gonna give it to us for nothin'."

With a deep breath, Drake used the element of surprise to step into the hallway. He was able to grab the closest intruder and punch him in the face. Anger fueled the hit, and the man's nose broke. Before the guy could recoup, Drake hit him again, sending a couple of rotten teeth clattering to the floor. The man fell to his knees before his eyes rolled back in his head and he collapsed to his right side.

The other man rushed Drake, wrapping his arms around Drake's waist and slamming his back against the wall.

Breath coming out in a loud whoosh, Drake kept boxing the guy in his ear until he turned loose of his waist. Then Drake shoved the horrible smelling man far enough away that he could take a swing at him. His fist connected soundly with the would-be kidnapper's jaw.

Blood began to pour from the man's mouth. "I ongue," he mumbled as though his tongue were swollen. "Oo ade ee ite i ongue."

"Bit your tongue, did you? Well, then," Drake said, cocking his elbow. "Let's see if I can make you do that again." This undercut punch sent blood flying before the man collapsed next to his partner.

Drake looked past the bodies and down the hallway to see Kayla standing there, a shotgun in her hands—a shotgun that was now aimed at him.

"Easy there," he said, splaying his hands to calm her.

"It would appear that you handled the mischief makers without my assistance," she said, her strained voice betraying the fear her beautiful face wasn't revealing.

Wondering what to say to ease her worries, he nodded at the men. "Afraid I made a bit of a mess."

She kept switching her gaze from him to the two unconscious men on the floor. "You were able to subdue both men?"

Shooting her a smile, he nodded. "They didn't put up much of a fight. How did you know to grab the shotgun?"

"When I was returning from the barn, I spied their horses tied to the tree by the goat pen. Once I had a good look at them breaking the window and crawling through, I had to guess they were up to no good." One of them groaned, and she frowned in response. "Were you able to ascertain exactly why they chose to force their way into our house?"

"If I heard their plans right, they were going to abduct you, Miss Backer."

She quirked an eyebrow, but he wasn't sure if it was over his announcement or the polite address he'd used.

It had just slipped out as a way to show her the respect she clearly deserved. Had he not been there, she would have been able to protect herself quite well.

Both of the intruders began to stir, and Drake grabbed the collars of their thick coats, dragged them to their feet, and gave the men a hard shake. "I guess I can bind these varmints in the barn 'til morning. Then I can ride into town and fetch Marshal Riley." He frowned as he looked at both their broken faces. "I don't recognize either of them. Do you?"

"I fear that I do," Kayla said, still pointing the shotgun. "To your right is Eugene Smith, whom his friends call Smitty. The other *gentleman* is Joseph Grimes."

The fact that she hadn't put down the gun was making Drake nervous. Women and firearms didn't mix well, and he sure didn't want to end up with a hole in his belly if the damn thing went off accidentally. She might be holding the shotgun, but he had no idea if she knew how to use it. "Why don't you put that gun down now?"

"Because I do not trust either of these men, and until they are gone from this farm, I will defend myself."

Since she was being her usual stubborn self, he tried to expedite matters so he could get them secured in the barn and relieve her of her weapon. "How do you know them?"

"They accosted me on the street the last time I ventured into White Pines, so I made it a point to learn their names. I believed it important to know with whom one is dealing."

Drake's imagination ran wild as he pictured the way those scoundrels might have tried to talk to Kayla. "What happened?"

"I believe they had formed the opinion that I was a woman of…ill repute." She let out a small scoff. "They wished to engage my services."

Had there been enough light for him to see her face better, he had no doubt he'd be seeing a bright blush on her cheeks. The notion that those two men were too stupid to know a woman like Kayla was about as far from a prostitute as a woman could get made him long to punch them again just to pay them back for the insult they'd given her.

"Turn me loose, you varmint," Smitty demanded.

Still holding tight to Smitty's collar, Drake gave him another rough shake. "The only place you're goin' is the barn. You and your pal here can just cool your heels 'til I can get Marshal Riley out here."

Kayla shook her head. "I refuse to abide their presence on this farm a moment longer. They should be on their way."

"On their way?" Drake couldn't stop the loud, incredulous words from spilling from his lips. "Have you gone daft? They need to be in jail."

She gave her head another shake. "I simply do not care whether they are punished or not, although I imagine Gideon might wish that they bear the cost of the broken pane of glass."

"Then what d'ya want to do with them?"

"They can walk back to town," she announced.

"Walk?" Smitty whined. "Why we gotta walk? Got a pair of horses out there."

"I fear you are wrong in that judgment," Kayla said, a saucy smile forming on her face.

Grimes kept trying to get to his feet, which pleased Drake since it gave him an excuse to shove the smelly man right back down to his knees.

"What you sayin'?" Smitty demanded.

"Your horses are already well on their way back to White Pines," she said. "I set them loose as soon as I deduced you men had ill intentions. I also gave each a good, hard slap on their rumps to be sure they would make a hasty exit. You two gentlemen shall have to walk back to the town to fetch your animals. My guess is that they will find their way back to the livery where you stable them."

Grinning at her clever way of handling the two idiots, Drake dragged them toward the front door. "It's still mighty cold out there, boys. Hope you don't lose a toe or two to frostbite getting back to town."

"You ain't really tossin' us out in the snow, is you?" Grimes asked as he stumbled to keep up with Drake's fast pace.

"Damn right, I am," Drake said. He wasn't surprised that Kayla had hurried ahead to open the door for him.

"We'll freeze to death!" Smitty complained.

"Shoulda thought of that before you came out here tryin' to hurt the lady," Drake said.

As soon as he got close enough, he dropped Grimes on the floor. Then he gripped Smitty's collar tighter, took hold of the back of the man's pants, and heaved him out onto the porch. Grimes followed close behind.

Although the two men continued protesting, Drake kicked each in the ass to get them off the porch, and he watched as they trudged away in the snow, following the tracks left behind by their fleeing animals. The door closed softly behind him, but he maintained his vigil in the freezing cold until he could no longer see them.

"Good riddance." He opened the door and headed back inside, hoping his hands and feet would warm quickly. Those men were in for some miserable hours.

Kayla was nowhere to be seen.

"Miss Backer?" he called.

Her sweet voice sounded from down the hall. "I am in my room."

He found her trying to stuff a blanket into the broken window. "You're gonna cut yourself if you're not careful."

Glancing over her shoulder, she let out a rueful chuckle. "I have already done so."

"What?" Marching across the room he jerked her hands away, letting the blanket tumble to the floor. "Where?" Then he saw the smeared blood on her palm. Smoothing it away with his fingers, he found small gashes across two of her fingers. "Damn it."

As she tried to tug her hand away, she said, "Please do not curse in front of me. I have asked you before, Mr. Myers."

"And I've asked you to call me Drake."

"I can care for my injury later, but the snow is still coming through the window, and I have no wish to build a snowman in my bedroom. Please allow me to finish my task."

"I'll go fetch a wood panel to put over it 'til I can get a new window pane."

Why did his stomach flip each time Kayla smiled at him? He'd seen pretty women before. An innocent smile shouldn't affect him so profoundly.

"That would be very kind of you," she said.

He gave her a brusque nod.

"Now, I shall tend these cuts." When she tried to pull her hand back again, Drake refused to let go. "Please release me, Mr…er… *Drake*."

Drake shook his head. "Come with me. I'll help get you bandaged up."

Chapter Nine

Kayla would never have expected such tender care from a man as rugged as Drake Myers. His calloused hands were surprisingly gentle as he helped clean the cuts the glass had made on her index and middle fingers.

Although the bleeding had been fierce when she'd caught her hand against the jagged edge of the broken window pane, the wounds had finally ceased to bleed. He had still insisted on washing the cuts and wrapping clean linen strips around each finger.

She held up her hand, considering the finished bandages. "I look a bit ridiculous with cloth rings on two of my fingers."

With a chuckle, Drake took her hand again and brushed his lips against the back of it.

Warmth spread across Kayla's cheeks, a heat that moved down her neck and chest. The nearness of him flooded her senses.

He smelled good. A surprise since when she'd first met him, he'd often carried the scent of the livestock he tended as well as the odor of unwashed clothes. And, of course, the odor of whiskey that had floated around him like a cloud. As he'd gone through his withdrawal from alcohol, she'd made sure all of his clothing was given a thorough washing. He'd obviously given himself just as thorough a cleansing.

Now, his scent reminded her of the outdoors. Clean and crisp. With a touch of something she could only think of as his own unique, masculine allure.

And alluring he was, especially when he still held tightly to her hand. Before he'd pulled himself from the mire, she'd found him attractive— unkempt though he'd been. With him being clean and sober, she found him nearly irresistible.

Thoughts of the kiss they'd shared couldn't be pushed aside. While she'd been kissed before, back when she was engaged to Gregory Carrington, she'd never experienced anything more than a chaste press of his lips to hers. Kayla hadn't known that a kiss could be so…splendid. Her body had flushed with heat and a need that she'd hadn't recognized. One that Gregory had never inspired. One that made her want to get closer to Drake, to have him wrap himself around her.

With a frown, she worried the temptation to have him teach her more about what a man and woman could share might be too hard to resist.

He cocked his head. "Why are you frownin'?"

She tried to tug her hand back.

He wouldn't let it go. "Was it something I said?"

"I am quite well, thank you. I have chores to do." Pulling a little harder, Kayla had to gape at him when he still refused to turn her loose. "Unhand me, sir."

With a shake of his head, Drake smiled. Then he leaned down to press his lips to hers.

Although she knew that she shouldn't allow him to take such liberties again, she closed her eyes and surrendered with a sigh.

His lips were warm and soft against hers, and as he wrapped an arm around her waist and tugged her closer, she felt her heartbeat speed in anticipation, loving the surge of desire that raced through her as his lips caressed hers.

When he quickly dropped his hold on her and stepped back, her eyes flew open. The anger that she saw on his face was confusing. The kiss had been so enjoyable. Why did he look mad enough to spit nails? "Drake? Is something amiss?"

Raking his fingers through his hair, he stared at the floorboards. "I'm sorry, Miss Backer."

The man wasn't making any sense. She'd been quite willing to participate in their kiss, and she wasn't at all ready for him to stop. The change of his mood had been swift, and his apology was puzzling. "Why would you be sorry?"

"I shouldn't have… You're just too… That was so damned…" He took another step back. "Forgive me." Turning on his heel, he grabbed his coat and the cap she'd knitted for him from the wooden peg and headed outside.

She almost followed him to the porch to call after him, wanting him to stop and explain what he'd been thinking. Not once had she protested him kissing her, and his words had done nothing to clear her confusion. Surely, he knew that she'd never allow anything beyond that simple show of affection, and yet it seemed as if the kiss had been so unsatisfactory that he felt the need to flee her presence. It was as if his use of her formal name built some barrier between them.

Still staring at the closed door, she pondered one other important thing. Why did she wish he would at least *try* to do more than kiss her?

* * *

Drake gave Rusty a few affectionate pats. "Sorry you've been cooped up in here. We'll go for a nice long ride soon." He closed and latched the gate to his horse's stall and looked around the inside of the barn.

Kayla had done a wonderful job with the animals, and she'd even chopped a bit of firewood. He'd finished the few chores that remained, and then he'd promptly run out of things to do. His body was tense, but he wasn't sure if the tightness was from residual anger at the two idiots who'd tried to grab Kayla or if he was merely in need of a woman.

No, not *a* woman.

Kayla Backer.

Normally one to prefer big-breasted, wide-hipped ladies, he had to admit that her slender form had felt perfect pressed against him. That was why he'd ended the kiss. Touching her, having her lips against his, made his head swim and his mind fill with impossible thoughts.

Perhaps accepting this job had been a mistake. Perhaps he'd have been better off trying to find work in White Pines.

But there hadn't been anything for him there. Not when he'd been a no-account drunk. Coming here had probably saved him in more ways than he could count.

Drake stepped out of the barn and glanced to where the beginning of Kayla's house was barely visible among the snow drifts. After all she'd done for him, how she'd taken such good care for him, he owed her more than he could ever repay.

He figured building her the perfect house would be a good start.

* * *

Kayla had a pleasant surprise three days later.

For this first time since he'd become temperate, Drake had awakened without prompting and began his chores without prodding, actually performing some of his duties before she'd risen. When she'd dressed and gone into the kitchen, she'd seen him through the window, feeding the chickens. His gaze had caught hers, and he'd given her a tentative smile—another first. A little embarrassed, she waved before feeling silly and setting herself to the task of making breakfast.

She was just putting their plates on the table when he came inside. After brushing the fresh snow off his shoulders, he made a point of wiping his feet on the braided rug she'd made to keep mud off her clean floors. He even shot her a smile to show her he'd remembered her instructions. Then he tossed aside his hat, scarf, and gloves—the ones she had knitted for him.

"Breakfast smells mighty good," he said as he pulled his chair out. A frown crossed his face before he hurried to the chair she was going to use. He eased it away from the table as though waiting for her to sit.

A bit confused, Kayla mumbled her thanks. Up until today, Drake's manners had been practically nonexistent. She'd let each slight pass because she'd realized exactly how much he'd been suffering.

Today was definitely one of turning a corner in his conduct, and she couldn't be more pleased.

Meals—at least the ones Drake took at the table rather than on a tray in his room—had always passed in silence. Another change in his conduct, for now he kept up steady chatter.

"You shoulda seen Rose this mornin'. Why, she's as big as the barn she lives in," he said.

Funny, but his stream of comments about the farm and all its animal occupants was comforting, reminding her of the men she tended. She missed Drew and Gideon, but for the first time since they'd left, she accepted Drake's companionship. Enjoyed it.

"Think I'll go see what I can get done on your house," he said, scooting his chair away from the table and then helping with hers.

His announcement took her by surprise. Between his recovery and the amount of snow that had fallen recently, Kayla had assumed her home would see little or no progress until spring. "But what about last night's snow?"

"Ain't all that much," he replied. "There's plenty I can do now that I'm not drink...er...now that I'm feeling better."

"Is there anything I can do that would assist you?"

He rubbed his fingertips against the stubble that covered his chin.

At least he was thinking it over. She was so desperate to get out of the house and so happy that she finally had someone to talk to rather than care for, she added another argument. "Surely two of us would see much more progress than if you labored alone."

"I s'pose there is. Tell you what, let me help you with cleanin' up this mess, then we'll get to work."

For a moment, Kayla was struck speechless. Drew might assist her in what Gideon usually called "woman's work," but Drake helping with dishes?

Perhaps now that he wasn't pickling his brain, he might develop a pleasant and endearing personality. "I'd be quite pleased to have your help."

* * *

Drake finished pounding in a nail and then glanced up. Kayla was doing her damnedest to pick up a rather large stone. Since the foundation was almost complete, he had no idea why she felt the need to move such a heavy rock.

He was about to call out to her when she let out a rather unladylike grunt, tried to lift the stone, and slipped in the fresh snow. Her backside hit the ground, and then she did a backward somersault down the slight incline. Sprawled in the snow, legs and arms akimbo, she looked a bit dazed.

Tossing aside his hammer, he ran to help her. Damn if he didn't stumble over her rock. Although he tried hard to regain his footing, he ended up sliding face-first down the small hill, not stopping until he slid right between her open legs, his face pressed into her bunched-up skirts.

It took a moment for his thoughts to clear, and when Drake glanced up, he found Kayla sputtering in indignation, her face red as fire.

Laughter bubbled up inside him at the absurdity of the whole situation until he couldn't contain it. God, how long had it been since he'd had something to laugh about?

Since she was struggling to jerk her skirts from under him, he rolled to his side, his laughter coming so hard and deep that his sides began to ache.

"How dare you laugh at me!" Scrambling to her feet, she'd tried to repair her appearance. Her hands brushed hard at her skirts, trying to settle them back into place.

All Drake could do was wrap his arms around his middle and keep laughing.

"Stop laughing at me!" When Kayla stomped her booted foot, she hit a piece of ice. Her arms flailed in circles as she tried to keep from falling to the ground again. Just when it appeared she'd succeeded, her feet went out from under her and she landed on her backside right next to him.

She slapped his arm before rubbing her hip. "Stop laughing at me!"

Only the hurt in her voice helped Drake regain a little of his self-control. "I'm not laughing at you."

"You most certainly are." Rolling so she was on her hands and knees, she prepared to stand.

He hurried to his feet so he could grab her under the elbow and assist her. "Not *at* you. I was laughin' because... Well, because it was funny, what with both of us finding ourselves on our ass— On our backsides."

Fussing with her clothes, she wouldn't allow his eyes to catch hers. "I fail to see any humor in wallowing around on the ground like a piglet."

Snow still stuck to most of their clothing, so he tried to help her brush herself clean. He was smoothing the snow off her shoulders when she looked up at him with those big eyes of hers. Her cheeks were bright with color, her eyes sparkling as though she now saw the humor.

Drake had to kiss her.

It only took an instant for him to realize that he was playing with fire. The mere touch of his lips to hers was enough to tell him that he was in trouble. As he mentally warned himself to stop, he pulled her into his arms.

Kayla always responded with heat when he kissed her, melting into him and looping her arms around his neck. Despite the cold, his body's response was swift. When he was trying to justify carrying her into the house and making love to her, he forced himself to grab her arms and set her away from him.

As she glared up at him, her brows gathered and her eyes boring through him, Drake had to fight the nearly irresistible desire to kiss her again.

"Why?" she demanded.

He cocked his head. "Why what?"

"Why do you keep…?" She closed her eyes and let out a sigh. "Oh bother. Never mind."

"Why do I keep kissing you?"

"Why do you keep pushing me away?" Her words were mere whispers.

Realizing exactly how little he knew about nice women, Drake replied honestly. "Because I shouldn't be kissing a lady like you."

The confusion was still plain on her face. "Why on earth not?"

"Because you're too good for the likes of me."

Kayla blinked, at an absolute loss at what to say to such a ludicrous comment.

Too good for him? According to Gregory's mother, Kayla was nothing more than white trash. To have Drake believe she was too far above his touch rendered her speechless.

He turned and walked back up the small hill as she watched him walk away, unable to call him back and demand that he get his foolish notions out of his mind and do so immediately.

Didn't he know how his kisses affected her? How much she enjoyed his touch? No man had ever inspired the feelings that Drake Myers created so effortlessly. Not once had she considered getting closer to any man since she'd been torn from Gregory's life and sent on the odyssey that had brought her to Montana as a potential mail-order bride.

Kayla had been so relieved to find that Caleb Young had already married by the time she'd arrived. Back then, she fancied herself still in love with Gregory. Even considering another man's offer for marriage—and Lord knew there'd been plenty—had been untenable. She'd settled in nicely taking care of "confirmed bachelors" Drew and Gideon and had figured she wasn't meant to have a family of her own.

Then Drake had come into her life.

Now, she was reassessing her future, and more and more she saw Drake Myers as a part of it.

"I am a fool," she muttered to herself before returning to the rock she'd been trying to move. "An utter fool."

Chapter Ten

"Such a beautiful day," Kayla said, stretching her arms high before settling her hands back in her lap. It was joyous to be able to take a wagon ride to town for supplies and not be hemmed in looking at the same four walls as she had for six straight weeks.

When hard winter finally settled over the farm, she knew things would get worse. Fear nudged her, telling her that she might go mad from boredom. The only thing that might relieve her tedium was the library Drew had amassed. With her voracious reading habit, there were few stories she'd yet to read, but she had no aversion to rereading good books.

And then there was Drake. While she had been reticent of his living so close, his company would be a blessing in the coming months. Yet she fretted over what might happen between them in such close quarters when heavy snow kept them isolated from the rest of the world. He still occupied a bedroom in the house, and she didn't have the heart to tell him that he should probably return to his loft in the barn. While she might have handled herself well with the ruffians who'd come to take her, she was comforted that Drake was close should a similar event occur.

She also abhorred the idea of the poor man being out with the animals and shivering in the cold as he tried to sleep. The stove in his loft surely didn't put off much heat, and it was, of course, a fire hazard. She had good reasons for wanting him to continue his stay in the house.

Who exactly are you trying to fool, Kayla?

She wanted him there. Plain and simple.

"Beautiful?" Drake let out a snort, forcing two white puffs from his nostrils. "Beautiful if you wanna freeze your a— If you wanna freeze your backside off."

"My *ass* is quite toasty," she said, patting the fur hide that covered their legs. "Thank you very much."

His laughter always made her smile. "It would appear that I'm teaching you some new words."

"Oh, I assure you, they are not *new* to me. There have been many men who have spoken them in my presence, even if they were forced to apologize for those transgressions. However, I have surrendered any attempt to teach *you* not to curse when I am around since it is clearly a nasty habit. Therefore, to break you of that pastime, I will use those shameful words as well to show you how repugnant they are."

He turned to grin at her. "No, you won't."

"I most certainly will. When the moment is right, of course." She punctuated that promise with a curt nod.

Drake laughed again and gave the reins a shake to get the horses moving a little faster. "We'll just have to see about that. Can't see a dainty thing like you letting a few damns or shits slip out. Not in your nature."

"Why, I can *damn* well curse with the best of them."

He said nothing, but he wanted to let out a laugh at how strange it sounded to hear her curse. A few moments passed before he glanced at the paper she'd pulled from her coat pocket and now held in her mittened hands. "Think you've got enough on that list?" he asked. "We're likely to be snowed in for at least a couple of months."

Pursing her lips, she considered what she'd written. "Perhaps I shall increase a few of these quantities." Then she looked over to him. "You truly believe we shall be unable to leave the farm for two whole damn months?"

He nodded. "Maybe even longer. Better give that list another check, Miss Backer. Don't forget the pane of glass with all that food. Although it's better to have too much in the larder than go hungry. I'd hate to have to eat a horse or two."

She grinned at him. "I would dare say that Rusty feels the same damn way."

When had Kayla grown comfortable teasing him?

Drake wasn't sure, but he liked this side of her personality. Then he scowled when he remembered her cursing. It just wasn't right, having a lady like Kayla saying bad words.

"A bad memory?" she asked.

"Pardon?"

"You were frowning so fiercely for a moment. I thought that perhaps an unpleasant memory had taken your thoughts."

"I was frownin' because you keep sayin' 'damn.' I don't like it."

She had the nerve to grin at him. "Neither do I."

"Then don't say it."

"What I meant was that I dislike hearing *you* saying 'damn.' So long as you choose to curse, then I will follow suit. Damn right, I will."

"Stop that!"

Still smiling sweetly, she began to hum a happy little tune, probably because she was so pleased with herself at getting him riled up.

"You're an exasperating woman, Kayla Backer."

She heaved an exaggerated sigh. "So I have been told. By quite a few people."

The clear skies made for a cold ride, and she snuggled tight against his side. Not that he minded in the least. The more time he spent with her, the more he realized exactly how wrong he'd been to assume that no man wanted her. Truth was that she was the kind of woman who deserved better than the unmarried men living around the town, and he was glad she'd never accepted any of their offers to marry.

A spark ignited in his thoughts, and try as he might, he couldn't stop it from burning.

What if I married her?

A ridiculous notion, and yet Drake couldn't make himself push it aside. Not that he was the marrying kind, but now that he saw the world through clear eyes, he knew that life as a cowboy wasn't something a man could enjoy for long. It was dangerous work, and if even a body survived without a major injury, he simply couldn't herd cattle as he aged. Time took too high a toll on a man.

If he wasn't going to be a cowboy, then what exactly *was* he going to do with his life?

That was a question Drake had no answer for. Yet.

He tried to divert his attention from stressing over his future. "Where are you from, Miss Backer?"

"Would you kindly answer a question for me?" she asked, sounding a bit exasperated.

A glance to his right revealed a stern frown on her face. "Fire away," he said, not at all sure of her change in mood.

"Since you insist upon me using your given name, why have you fallen back to calling me Miss Backer?"

Drake grinned. "After seeing how well you handled those varmints, I'm just bein' respectful, ma'am."

At least she smiled in return. "While I genuinely appreciate that respect, I have given you leave to call me Kayla."

He shrugged.

She sighed.

A change of topic was in order. "Tell me where you're from," he suggested again.

"Are you speaking of what city I grew up in or from which country my ancestors came?"

"Ancestors?" He chuckled. "No, ma'am. The city."

"New York City."

Drake waited for her to say more, but several moments passed without Kayla elaborating. Glancing over, he was surprised to see a fierce frown on her lips. "What's wrong?"

"I should not have revealed that."

"Why?"

With a shake of her head, she glanced away.

Would the woman ever make sense to him? "Why's it matter that you told me you're from New York City?"

When she returned her gaze to him, he saw a fleeting moment of fright in her eyes. Then she straightened her spine. "The past is often best left in the past. May we please change the topic now?"

Still puzzled over her naming New York City—so very far away—as her home, Drake kept up his questions. There was so much he didn't know about her, and before the winter was out, he intended to find out every detail she appeared to be protecting. "I thought Caleb said you were from St. Louis. I remember him saying he thought Sara was sent by a preacher in St. Louis to marry him. But now you're sayin' you're from New York?"

"I do believe we are in for more snow soon," she said, pulling the wolf pelt a little higher on her lap.

"You had to have come from Missourah at some point if that preacher sent you as a mail-order bride," Drake insisted.

"We must remember to check the wire around the chicken coop again," Kayla said with a too-sweet tone in her voice. "That pesky fox is sure to find a way in if we do not protect the hens."

He released a frustrated sigh. "In other words, you're not gonna tell me."

"How astute of you."

Perhaps if he opened up about himself, she'd be encouraged to do the same. "I'm from Texas originally. Youngest of ten kids, so I knew I'd have to make my own way in life pretty early."

"Ten children? Oh my."

"Mama and Pa probably still live there. Haven't seen 'em in years. Not since I was ten and left with my uncle to learn to work the steers. Spent more time with him than I did my parents. Ended up calling Denver home. At least until Princess…er…Sara led me here."

"I am familiar with the story of her theft of your company's payroll," Kayla said. "Surely you have forgiven her by now."

Drake frowned. "Hard to pardon a woman who steals from you and sends you chasin' her all the way to Montana to get the money back."

Placing her hand gently on his arm, Kayla said, "You must understand why Sara stole from you. The woman was in an impossible situation, the kind that can make a person desperate. Sometimes the only way a woman can protect herself is to run as far away from danger as she is able—even all the way to a territory thousands of miles from her home."

It wasn't exactly what she said but how she said it that made the hair on the back of Drake's neck stand on end.

Kayla was afraid of someone. *Very* afraid.

"There!" She pointed to the distance. "I see White Pines."

Sure enough, the town was drawing near. Not close enough she should be so excited, but he took her enthusiasm for what it probably was—an excuse to end what was clearly an uncomfortable conversation.

"Yes, ma'am." Drake gave the horses' rumps a mild slap of the reins. "We'll be there directly."

Leaning closer to him, she let out a sigh that escaped her lips in a tendril of white. "I am ready to be warm."

He chuckled. "I'm afraid that you're in the Montana Territory. That might not happen until May."

* * *

"Miss Kayla."

Kayla glanced away from the stack of canned goods she'd been considering to find Matthew Riley, the marshal of White Pines. His heavy coat was trimmed in beaver fur, an addition that his wife had surely provided. Victoria Riley was talented with a needle, as Kayla had learned whenever they'd attended quilting bees for newly married couples.

He tugged on the brim of his hat. "Good day, Miss Kayla."

"And a fine day it is, Marshal Riley." She inclined her head in greeting. "So nice to see you. Where is your wonderful wife?"

"Victoria's at home, ma'am. She huddles pretty close to the fire lately."

"Her time is drawing near, is it not?"

He nodded. "Pretty soon, Grace will have to stay in town in case the baby decides to come during a blizzard."

"I'm sure Victoria will be grateful for your sister's company."

Matthew shifted his weight between his feet, and Kayla realized that this hadn't been a chance meeting. He had something to say to her.

"Is there anything I can help you with, Marshal? Your wife, perhaps?"

Doffing his hat, he raked his fingers through his wavy brown hair. "I had a telegraph message about you. In fact, I might've had *two*."

A chill ran the length of her spine. "I beg your pardon?"

"First one was definitely for you. It came about a week ago from that pastor who sent you out here to marry Caleb."

"Reverend Hayes? Why on earth would he send a telegraph?"

"Got it written down back in my office, but the gist of it was that he was concerned about you. Wanted to know where you were stayin' and whether you'd gone ahead with the weddin'."

"That makes no sense, Marshal. I sent him a long letter explaining exactly what happened with Caleb and that I was planning on settling here with Drew and Gideon. There is no reason he should be asking such questions."

"Maybe he didn't get the letter?"

Kayla frowned. Although that was the best explanation, she couldn't help but wonder why the good reverend was sending the message now. She'd been in White Pines for many months. If he hadn't received her letter, he would have reached out to her well before now.

"You said there were *two* messages," she reminded him. "If the first was from Reverend Hayes, from whom did the second come?"

"That one came from a Pinkerton detective. Said he was looking for you— at least I *think* he was lookin' for you, 'cause I don't know any other lady who settled in White Pines last year. Could be the telegraph receiver took the message wrong. The detective asked for Carolyn Burton, not Kayla Backer. Could he mean you?"

Her heart began to pound at hearing her true name, the one she'd left behind in Chicago. And that name was being used by a Pinkerton, a man who'd obviously been hired to track her down like a common thief.

Which can only mean…

Gregory's mother was searching for her.

Again.

Kayla had fled New York City to escape Chantal Carrington's wrath. But that hadn't been enough. Kayla had barely made a home with her aunt and uncle in Chicago when Chantal's minions were hot on her trail, sending her running to St. Louis with a new identity. Had the good reverend not helped her flee, she would have lost her life to the vengeful heiress.

It was now clear that Chantal wouldn't stop until Kayla was dead. And all because her son had fallen in love with a woman Chantal believed was far below the Carringtons' elite station in life.

"Miss Kayla? You all right?"

She squared her shoulders and tried to muster up some bravado. "I am perfectly fine, thank you."

"Went kinda pale there for a moment."

It was vital that Matthew send a message back to the Pinkerton detective that discouraged any more inquiries into where she was. "I assure you, I am quite hale, Marshal. But I do have to disappoint you. I am afraid I do not know anyone named Carolyn Burton. You shall have to tell that poor detective that he is searching in the wrong place."

"I was hoping that message was meant for you, but that was only wishful thinkin'."

"It definitely was *not* for me." She had to calm the panic she heard rising in her own voice so that man wouldn't grow suspicious.

"I'm sure it's nothing," Matthew said.

"What's nothing?" Drake said, startling her and causing her to jump.

Whirling, she put her hand to her chest, wondering if she'd ever calm her racing heart. "You nearly scared the life out of me."

With a grin, he patted her shoulder. "Sorry 'bout that." He inclined his head at Matthew. "What's nothing, Matthew?"

The marshal kept shifting his gaze between the two of them as though unsure of whether to continue the discussion in front of Drake.

This wasn't a subject she wanted to share with him. Ever. "Were you able to find the supplies you needed?" she asked.

A frown filled Drake's face. "Don't change the subject."

Kayla tried to quit the topic and turned to Matthew. "Thank you for your assistance. We have quite a bit to do before going back to the farm, and I believe the gray skies are warning of more snow."

Drake narrowed his eyes, and she was pretty sure she heard a low growl coming from him.

After putting his hat back on, Matthew tugged on the brim once more. "I'll pass your best wishes on to my wife, Miss Kayla." He looked to Drake. "Good to see you, Drake." Then he walked away.

Hands on his hips, Drake stared at Kayla. "What was *that* all about?"

She tried to dismiss the question with a wave of her hand. "I still have a few things to get before I shall be ready to leave."

"In other words, you ain't tellin' me."

Drake wanted to grab her and shake her. For her to pretend that nothing was wrong was absurd. Her face was ghostly white, and her hands were trembling. Whatever Matthew had told Kayla had upset her a great deal.

Another frustrated growl slipped out before he squelched it. Trust was something earned, and in the time she'd known him, Drake had been nothing but a drunkard. Hopefully, time would mend that rift and she would feel better about sharing her life with him. "Let's get the rest of what we need and head back. It started snowin', and we need to be on our way."

"I'm ready." She followed him to the front of the store.

He waited while she haggled with the storekeeper over the price of some of the items, and he grew antsy, wanting to get back on the road. Finally, she counted out the money for the things she'd purchased, and Drake sent her to the wagon while he made two trips from the store to the wagon to carry out the supplies she'd bought.

Instead of crawling up into the seat to wait for him, Kayla stood at the rear of the wagon. "What is in this crate?" she asked.

"Beats me," Drake replied, placing the rest of the supplies in the wagon bed. "Came addressed to you."

"Where on earth did you find it?"

"Will Spencer from the Four Aces ran me down when I was loading the wagon. Said it arrived for you 'bout a week ago. Drew sent it. Probably knew that shipping it to the farm wasn't wise in this weather and that if he sent it to

Will, he would find a way to get it to you."

At least now she was smiling, something he much preferred to the fear he'd seen earlier. "May we open it?"

Drake shook his head. "Let's get on the road before the snow piles too high."

"But—"

Setting a hand on her shoulder, he smiled at her eagerness. "We'll open it soon as we get home. Promise."

Chapter Eleven

Drake had never seen Kayla so excited. As he struggled to open the wooden crate Drew had shipped to her via Will Spencer, Drake smiled at the enthusiastic way she clasped her hands and kept rocking on her feet.

He'd barely gotten the crate out of the wagon—a struggle because of the size of the damn thing—before she begged him to bring it inside and get it open. Had he not stressed that the horses needed attending, they'd probably still be hitched to the wagon and waiting in the cold. Normally, she insisted on the animals coming first. After the two of them made sure the horses were tucked away in their stalls, he picked up the pry bar and headed to the house with Kayla practically skipping by his side.

Once he'd lugged the crate inside, she'd cast her coat aside and tugged on his until he'd gotten it off and grabbed the pry bar.

"Hurry, Drake. I want to see what's inside."

With a chuckle, he pushed hard on pry bar until the nails finally gave up the fight and the side of the crate began to open. Soon, he was able to remove the lid and set it away, figuring he might be able to use the wood as kindling later.

As though unable to control herself, she resorted to the first unladylike action he'd ever seen from her. She bumped him hard with her hip to push him out of her way.

He laughed at her and gave in as she responded by digging through the curly wood shavings, sending them tumbling over the side of the small crate. Then she let out a joyous squeal as she clapped her hands. "Books!"

Peeking over her shoulder, Drake saw her tug a book out of the shavings and hold it to her chest. "That big crate and only one book?" he teased.

When she turned to face him, her radiant smile sent heat running through him. He suddenly wanted that smile to be because of him, not some silly books.

Don't be a fool. She deserves better than the likes of you.

She opened the cover reverently, as though it would shatter if she touched it too roughly. "*Around the World in Eighty Days*," she said, reading the title. "Oh my. How exciting that sounds, even if the notion of traveling that quickly is ridiculous!" Turning the pages, she was obviously reading because her lips were moving silently.

Drake fished through the shavings to find another book and then read the title on the spine. "*Twenty Thousand Leagues Under the Sea*? Drew must like adventures."

Kayla stopped reading. "Heavens, no. He prefers more serious stories. Shakespeare, especially."

Setting the book aside, he grabbed another from the crate. "This one's called *The Mysterious Island*." He put it aside and searched for more.

"I shall no longer suffer from boredom this winter," she announced as she took each of the books he plucked from the shavings and began to stack them on the sofa. "So many! Drew has been far too generous."

Although he realized it was ridiculous, Drake couldn't push aside the jealousy that she clearly had a great amount of affection for Drew. The man was in love with Gideon and could never feel more for Kayla than a brotherly affection. There was no need for jealousy.

What right did Drake have to feel any jealousy at all? He was nothing to her. Only a man building her house.

He understood, now, why she remained unmarried. Kayla was far above the touch of most of the men in White Pines. She was educated, refined. Her impeccable manners and speech made her clearly destined to be the wife of a man with money and connections.

He was suddenly overwhelmed with the need to know more about this woman. Why was she in Montana? When she should be attending teas and social events, she was feeding livestock and keeping the home of two bachelors.

"Mr. Myers!"

Her excited shout pulled him out of his thoughts. "What?"

Hands on her slim hips, she glared at him. "Did you not hear a word I said?"

He rubbed the back of his neck. "Sorry, I guess I didn't."

"I was asking if you'd like me to share these wonderful books with you."

Accustomed to her generosity, he nodded. A shame he found none of the joy in the books that she had.

"As soon as I finish each, I shall pass them along to you." Kayla punctuated the promise with a decisive nod.

"Um… I was thinkin'…" Drake lowered his gaze, embarrassed at what he had to admit. "Maybe you could read 'em to me?"

She cocked her head. "Do you not enjoy reading in privacy? Perhaps there isn't sufficient light in your loft?"

Since it was the first time she'd mentioned him returning his loft, he frowned. He was content to sleep in a warm, soft bed and had hoped Kayla wouldn't insist on his moving back to the barn.

"I can see from your crestfallen expression that either there isn't enough light for you to read, or…" Reaching out, she placed her slender fingers on his hand. "Is that scowl an indication that you do not wish to sleep in the barn again?"

His head shot up at her touch and her keen perception. "I don't wanna be too forward."

"So you'd like for me to extend an invitation?" Her face lit with a smile. "I would be happy if you would stay on in the house. After our intrusion, I would feel safer knowing you are near."

Drake turned his hand so he could grasp hers. "That's right kind of you."

"Now, you may read whenever you wish."

"About that… I'd like it better if you read to me." He didn't want to admit his problem, but the way her brows gathered told him she'd figure it out eventually. He swallowed his pride. "Readin' can be…difficult for me."

"Were you taught to read?" She let out a sigh. "Of course, you can read. You told me the title of a book."

"Yes, ma'am. But the letters, they don't seem to want to make it easy."

"What do you mean?"

At least she asked as though she truly cared, so he tried to explain what no one else could ever seem to understand. "They're slippery suckers. Wanna turn around on me and look backward. Or the letters jump around in different spots."

"I've heard of such problems, but I fear I have no remedy." She squeezed his hand and smiled. "Which means I will be quite happy to read to you so that you may share these wonderful stories with me."

Drake didn't smile in return. Instead, his gaze locked on hers, and the tenderness he saw there was something new, something that made his breath catch. He let his eyes drop to her mouth, and all he could think about was kissing her.

Unable to stop himself, he leaned closer, waiting for her to put an end to his foolish notion.

Kayla's eyes widened when she realized that Drake intended to kiss her again.

It was an impertinence. She should put her hand against his chest—the same one she now allowed him to cradle in his—and push him away. He was taking liberties, and she should protect her virtue and her reputation.

Her reputation? *What* reputation? Her name had been blackened before she'd journeyed to White Pines, and since her appearance, the townsfolk had all looked down on her. A mail-order bride was suspect, let alone one who refused to marry once she arrived.

And when the same women lived alone on a farm with two unmarried men?

Her name was "Harlot" already. Why shouldn't she find some simple pleasures in life—like a kiss from a handsome man?

Then she saw his eyelids drop to half mast, his blue eyes revealing a hunger that made something inside her ignite. She could no more resist him than she could stop the sun from rising every morning.

Instead of putting his lips against hers, Drake eased back and stared down at her. When his brows knit tightly, she feared he'd been disappointed. Her fault, clearly, since she knew next to nothing about men and women and things like kissing.

"I–I have little experience, I fear," she said, her voice quavering with her nervousness. "In kissing, I mean."

Suddenly, his arms were around her, and after a growl rumbled from his chest, his lips were no longer merely touching hers.

They were crushing them.

Kayla's mind was tossed into chaos, her thoughts lost in the melee of sensations that now engulfed her. She was helpless against Drake's onslaught, unable to keep her arms from rising to put around his neck. The feelings were too strong to fight, and having her body pressed so intimately against his was inviting in a way she'd never known.

Just when she was beginning to think this was the closest to heaven she could ever find on earth, he did something even better. He slid his tongue between her lips, capturing her surprised gasp with his mouth.

She'd been kissed—or at least she *thought* she'd been kissed. Now, she wasn't so sure. Gregory had put his lips to hers. Chaste kisses that were in line with what society expected of a couple who had announced their betrothal.

But those were pecks, nothing more.

Drake was *kissing* her. Thoroughly. And Kayla wanted to drown in the feelings rioting through her.

Her blood had turned to liquid fire, racing through her veins and making her feel alive for the first time in her life. Never had she thought that her body could respond in such a way. Tentatively, her tongue returned the caress of his. The way his arms tightened around her, holding her even closer told her that he liked her boldness.

She thought she was getting the way of it, her tongue every bit as wild as his, when Drake suddenly pulled back, all but shoving her away. The horrified expression on his face made her stomach plummet to her feet.

"Wh–what did I do wrong?" Kayla asked, her hand rising to touch her lips. They felt hot and swollen and she wanted to demand he kiss her again and do so immediately.

He didn't reply, only stood there looking a bit confused before his face became unreadable.

The kiss had been the most intoxicating thing she'd ever experienced, and she couldn't understand why he didn't want it to continue.

"That was wrong," Drake said, backing a step away. "Very wrong."

Embarrassment flooded her, making her face heat.

What was the matter with her? She'd thrown herself at him. No wonder he'd wanted to put some distance between them. Her behavior had been no better than that of the women he'd paid for their services. No doubt he believed she was a wanton who didn't even require a coin in her palm the way a working girl did.

Mortified to the soles of her feet, all she could think of to do was apologize. "I'm sorry," she mumbled.

"You're sorry? *You?*"

"I am." The manners her father had instilled in her didn't cover the way she'd just behaved. Were her father still alive, he'd probably toss her out of his home and wash his hands of her. "I am very sorry, Mr. Myers. It shall never happen again."

Gathering up her skirts, she hurried down the hall to her room and slammed the door behind her. Then she threw herself on her bed and began to mentally berate herself.

* * *

Drake could hear Kayla angrily whispering to herself, but he couldn't catch her words. He couldn't make his feet move, as though he was anchored to the spot. So filled with confusion, he simply couldn't comprehend what had just happened between them.

A kiss. They'd shared a kiss.

But it was so much more.

Accustomed to women who were paid for their affection, Drake hadn't known that a woman could ignite such feelings inside him—especially a good woman.

Or was she truly good? Although his experience with anything other than whores was limited, he couldn't help but wonder where she'd learned to kiss the way she'd kissed him.

All sorts of theories began to fly through his mind. Perhaps she wasn't what she appeared to be. The only information Drake possessed had come from his dealings with Sara and Caleb, and he couldn't say that he'd paid much attention to what they'd told him. He'd been too busy being angry at Sara to give two figs that Kayla had been intended to be Caleb's mail-order bride.

What had driven her to such a drastic action? What could've made her leave wherever she called home—New York City?—to come out in the middle of untamed land and marry a man she didn't even know?

Had she been a woman of ill repute who had fled to start a new life? She sure as hell wouldn't be the first. Had she run away the same way Sara had run from a life of selling herself in Denver?

It hurt to think of Kayla in the same light that he thought of the prostitutes he'd known. Even Sara, no matter how furious he'd been with her, didn't seem to fit their ilk. They were hard women, used and discarded. They painted their faces, colored their hair, and acted exactly like what they were.

Whores.

Kayla was no whore.

Maybe it was only one man—one man who had ruined her reputation and sent her packing. Lord knew there had been plenty of good women who'd suffered the same fate. What better way to escape a tragic relationship than to run west and start a new life? Plenty of people did, although they were usually criminals or were trying to leave the poverty of cities behind. Had she come here to marry Caleb and start her life over again?

Gossip about her had plagued the town since she'd exited the stage that had borne her to White Pines. Despite the fact that she'd been living with Drew and Gideon almost from the moment she'd arrived, speculation about her past and her reasons for first agreeing to marry Caleb and then becoming housekeeper to his brother still raged like wildfire. Why hadn't she married despite the numerous proposals that had come her way since she'd arrived? Why was she content to hide away with Drew and Gideon?

Drake raked his fingers through his hair and then shook his head. He should go to her and apologize. Regardless the reason she'd had the skill to kiss him with such passion, he had no right to flaunt propriety that way.

Her dialogue had ended, and before he could head down the hall and knock on her door to give her his regrets, that door opened. What he saw shocked him.

Had Kayla been a woman wronged, one who'd been kissed by a man whose advances she didn't want, she would have appeared with red-rimmed eyes after weeping over being so shamed. Instead, she faced him with a hesitant smile that flabbergasted him.

"I should prepare our supper," she said in such a calm tone that she appeared bored. "And you, Mr. Myers, have animals to attend to, do you not?"

Then she walked right past him as though their kiss had never happened.

Chapter Twelve

Drake set the last of the dishes he'd dried on the shelf. He glanced to Kayla, still unable to find the right words. There'd been almost no talking throughout the rest of the day, which was now winding down. The sun had already set by the time she put their supper on the table. In Montana, winter days were almost too short for him to take care of all the livestock let alone work on her house. The foundation was complete, thanks to the periodic help from Ty and Caleb. But there was little Drake could do while that foundation was buried in snowdrifts.

They'd been lucky so far this winter, with snow not cutting him and Kayla off from the rest of the world. Judging from the thick, gray clouds that ominously loomed in the distance all day, that luck wasn't going to hold much longer.

Soon, the Montana winter would be snowy, bitter cold, and difficult to survive. Drake would do whatever was necessary to keep Kayla safe and warm until spring. Thanks to a successful hunting trip he'd made a few days ago and their trip to the general store, the larder was full, and they were prepared should a blizzard strand them on the farm.

Hanging the towel on the wooden rod he'd installed for her, she brushed her hands down her skirts. "Thank you for your help with the supper dishes."

Drake gave her a brisk nod. He still felt so awkward around her, and he wished he knew what she was thinking and feeling so he'd know what to say. No doubt she regretted their kiss. Regret was the furthest thing from his mind. No, he wanted her. Now. Desperately.

This was going to be a long, trying winter.

Kayla wasn't a woman a man tumbled and then forgot. Not only was he unfamiliar with her kind, he also didn't know how to discuss his intentions.

But what exactly *were* his intentions?

His lust was still running high, making it difficult to think straight. But he finally came to a decision. She deserved better than what he had to offer. As though Drake had *anything* to offer... He was flat broke and living on the farm only to complete a task—to build her house. Then he'd be right back to living hand to mouth.

That was no kind of life for Kayla. He silently vowed to be a person he'd never been before.

A gentleman—although he was clueless as to how to be something he was not.

The beautiful smile she tossed his way as she lit the lamp in the sitting area knotted his gut. Had she any clue about the things he'd thought about doing to that slender body, she would be pushing him out the door and barring it against him.

"Would you still enjoy having me read to you?" Her gaze caught his, and her smile slowly faded. "What's wrong, Mr. Myers?"

"Drake, dammit. I thought we were past this! I've told you a hundred times to call me Drake!"

Now, her dark eyes shot fire. "You needn't snap at me."

He sighed, a long, drawn-out affair that gave him time to calm himself.

His anger and his desire seemed to get tangled up in each other. If he didn't get a strong grip on both, he'd never make it through the winter without tossing her on a bed and having his way with her. "I'm sorry. I just... Please, for the love of God, call me Drake."

Kayla cocked her head. "Why does it bother you so that I use your formal name?"

Because that kiss was anything *but formal.* "We're friends. Friends don't use formal names."

Her expression was unreadable. "Is that what we are? Friends?"

"Well, yeah. At least I think so. Don't you?"

She didn't reply, only stared at him for a few moments looking a bit bewildered. Then she let out a small sigh and dismissed him by picking up a book from the stack she'd left on the sofa. "Shall we begin with *Around the World in Eighty Days*? It is the one which intrigues me the most." Tucking her skirts beneath her, she sat in the chair closest to the light.

Drake flopped on the sofa next to the books and hoped he wouldn't yawn much. He was dog tired from his chores and the trip to town. Add the darkness, and he was ready to find his bed, regardless of how chilly it might be. While there was a large hearth in the bedroom Gideon and Drew shared and in the room Kayla used, the smaller bedchamber only had a small fireplace. He'd opted for that room out of respect for his hosts.

Perhaps the cold would make him rethink that decision.

Kayla held the book reverently. "The title promises a wonderful journey for us."

"A journey?"

"Oh, yes. Every book takes readers on a delightful journey." Gently opening the cover and turning the first few pages, she smiled. "Shall we begin?"

He couldn't help but smile in return. "I'd like that."

So she did. "'Chapter One: In Which Phileas Fogg and Passepartout Accept Each Other, the One as Master, the Other as Man Around the World in 80 Days.'"

* * *

As Drake walked Kayla down the hall to her bedroom, he thought about their kiss. Despite his wish to banish the interlude from his thoughts, it refused to budge. He stepped into the room and went to the hearth. Kneeling, he tossed a couple of fat logs on the fire and used the iron to stoke the flames. "You've got plenty of wood for tonight."

"Thank you kindly for fixing my window pane."

He nodded.

"Would you like me to heat a bed-warmer for you?" she asked, her arms folded around her waist.

With a shake of his head, he got to his feet and dusted his hands against his thighs.

"Good night, then."

The light from the fire painted her features in a soft glow. Her eyes sparkled, and he wanted to go to her, to kiss her again and see if she'd have him. He'd lay her down on that quilt and—

"Good night, Drake."

"Good night." Angry the words had come out so harsh that her eyes widened, he simply turned on his heel and left. A moment later, the door closed softly behind him.

His room was next in the hall, and he pushed it open and strode inside, shutting the door a little too forcefully. Instead of lighting the lamp, he let his eyes adjust to the small fire and the pale moonlight filtering through the window. When he noticed a folded quilt that Kayla had obviously left on the bed for him, he smiled.

In her own way, she cared for him.

After tossing aside his boots, shirt, and pants, he added the quilt to the other blankets covering his bed and then crawled between the sheets. Chilly though it was, he couldn't turn off thoughts of Kayla and their incredible kiss. The feel of her curves pressed against his body. The way her tongue had glided over his. The taste of her.

Before too long, his cock was hard and throbbing, and he knew that despite his weariness, if he didn't take matters into his own hands, there'd be no sleep for him that night.

* * *

Kayla folded her petticoat and set it with the rest of her clothing. She hadn't realized how paper-thin the wall between her room and Drake's was until she heard him moving about. Knowing he could hear her as well was disconcerting. Did he know she was undressing? She'd clearly caught him throwing his boots aside, and she found herself straining to listen to more of what he was doing.

A shameful thing, to find herself so infatuated with a man, let alone a man like Drake Myers. She'd resorted to using his full name again to try to distance herself from him, but that tactic hadn't worked. Instead, she'd angered him, and in doing so he'd revealed that he considered her a friend.

Hang that!

She had no desire to be merely his friend. After that eye-opening kiss, Kayla had made a decision, one that would surely shock anyone who knew her.

I want Drake to be my lover.

Simply thinking about it was enough to warm her inside. How scandalous to think of lying with a man without the benefit of matrimony. Before coming to Montana, she would never have allowed herself to even consider such a notion.

Being in this place had been…liberating. She'd discovered so much about herself. Instead of being resigned to being nothing but another society wife, she'd learned to value herself because others valued her. Drew and Gideon depended on her now, and they were giving her the best gift of all.

A home of her own.

But where did Drake fit in that new independent life she'd made here?

He was sure to move on after he finished his task. A man like him didn't stay in one place too awfully long. There was no tying down a cowboy, a lifestyle which Drake had been enjoying before following Sara to White Pines to retrieve the stolen payroll. Once her home was complete, she'd be watching him ride a horse into the sunset, never to be seen again.

Ah, but he was here *now*. Why not take advantage? He was clearly a man who knew the ways of making love, judging from the stories she'd heard in town. While she normally didn't put too much stock in gossip, she'd listened intently to the stories women whispered about him. Had she not known how seldom he left the farm, she might've believed he'd taken nearly every woman in White Pines as a lover.

Of course, the tales were exaggerated, but there had to be at least a kernel of truth involved.

Kayla meant to find out for herself exactly how much prowess he possessed.

What had she been saving herself for anyway? Marriage?

That prospect had evaporated, thanks to her former fiancé's mother and her machinations. At least as far as New York City was concerned. While she could easily make a marriage here in Montana, the potential grooms were downright reprehensible.

Except for Drake…

But Drake was not a man who would marry—probably ever. He was a man a woman could take as a lover, who could show her passion, something she was never likely to know again once he exited her life.

Then she heard something coming through the thin wall between them. A few squeaks of his metal bed frame followed by a gasp. When she distinctly heard an exaggerated groan, Kayla began to worry. Was he getting sick? Was he having a horrible nightmare, the likes of which she was so familiar? When the groan was quickly followed by a low moan, she flew into a panic. She tossed the covers aside and jumped out of bed, hurrying out of her room to find out what was wrong with Drake.

Pushing the door open, she stopped short when she saw he was in bed, the only part of him visible was his head resting on the pillow. "Are you all right?" she asked, taking a few steps toward the bed.

"Wait!"

Stopping in her tracks, Kayla frowned at him. "I heard you through the wall. The sounds you were making… I feared you might be ill."

"I'm fine, damn it all."

"Do you need a chamber pot? Is your stomach sour?"

"I said I'm *fine*," he snapped.

She ventured a few more steps.

He began fumbling under the covers and glaring at her. "Get out, Kayla!"

"You needn't shout at me. I was merely—"

"Get out, woman!"

Eyes wide, she was ready to bellow at him the same way he'd shouted at her when it dawned on her exactly why he might have been making the sounds that she'd heard. Her mouth formed a surprised O before she promptly whirled around and fled the room, slamming the door behind her.

Standing in front the fire to warm herself from the chill that she'd received, Kayla couldn't help but smile. While she should've been embarrassed at catching him in such an intimate act, she simply wasn't. In fact, she found the idea of him giving himself pleasure more than a little arousing. She even held out hope that his actions were because of her—because he desired her. Another scandalous thought, but she wanted Drake to have been thinking only of her.

Because if he had been thinking of her, then seducing him would be that much easier.

Chapter Thirteen

"Sweet heavens." Kayla stared out the barn door, amazed at the incredible amount of snow that could fall in the span of a few hours. What had started as thick, fat flakes covering the grass now piled above her ankles.

Drake brushed the snow that had stacked up on his shoulders when he'd gone to the pump to grab the bucket he'd left there. Although he'd barely stepped out into the weather, he'd come back coated in the white flakes. "It'll get worse," he predicted.

She glanced to the open door again, both thrilled at the beautiful picture and worried about what the rapid accumulation meant. "Will the animals be safe?"

"Yes, ma'am. They're all cozy and warm. Even brought in the chickens." He took her hand and led her to the ladder to his loft. "Wanna see the precaution I made?"

Unsure as what the loft had to do with preparation for the snow, she knit her brows.

"Up the ladder," he urged. "I need to show you something. Don't worry. I'll be right behind you. I won't let you fall."

Putting her hand on a rung, she glanced over her shoulder and gave him an easy smile. "I trust you."

As she began to climb the ladder, Drake could only stare at her, speechless.

Of all the things she could possibly say, those words were the last he would've expected.

Their relationship had started off so rocky, he'd never thought to be her friend let alone earn her trust. That was a prize she seldom offered. Only Drew and Gideon were in her confidence, and Drake doubted even they were privy to her whole story. As far as he knew, she'd never opened up to anyone.

Yet she'd just declared that she trusted him.

He might not have believed her if he hadn't seen with his own eyes that she was quickly ascending without glancing back to check if he followed.

Could she be telling the truth?

Drake hurried behind her, staying close. It wasn't until she was at the top of the ladder and kneeling on the loft floor that he let out a sigh, relieved that she was safe. After he followed her into the loft, he took her hand and led her to the double doors that used to be opened for bringing hay into the barn. Now, the bales were stored in empty stalls.

The loft itself still bore the scent of the hay that had been stowed there for years before Drake had enclosed it to be his temporary home. Before the hard freeze had set in, the place always made him sneeze.

He was pleased she didn't pull away, and it seemed so natural to encase her small hand in his, even if their thick gloves prevented their skin from touching. "See the rope?"

"Rope?"

Drake inclined his head at the cord that was knotted to the inside of one of the double doors.

"Oh, *that* rope. What is it for?"

"You can grab it and slide down instead of taking the ladder. Much quicker that way. Are you ready?"

Her eyes widened and her mouth dropped open. "But I…I… You can't expect me to…"

He squeezed her hand. "I'm teasin', Kayla. I strung it to the attic door of the house today."

The smile she gave him made his groin tighten. "You called me Kayla."

"I did."

"Thank you."

Drake smiled in return, a bit drunk on the affection in her voice.

"For what purpose did you hang the rope?" she asked, returning him to the conversation.

After letting go of her hand, he flipped the latch and opened one of the doors. The view was spectacular. White as far as the eye could see, the mound of her home's foundation barely discernable in the distance under a blanket of white. "So when the snow gets deep and the wind makes it impossible to see where you're goin', you can hold the rope and still get home."

The incredulous look on her face didn't ease. "But it's too high. The attic is… And this door is…"

"First winter this side of the Mississippi?"

She nodded.

"Then you're in for a shock. Snow piles up mighty quick."

"Surely not up to the second level of our home?"

"*Our* home?" Drake winked.

Kayla blushed. "*The* house, then."

"I'll have another rope on the lower level. It'll string from the barn door to the kitchen door."

Staring out the doors, she said, "Why would we need a rope? It's barely a good stone's throw to the house."

Drake could only chuckle at her naiveté. "As I said, you're in for a shock."

"But I can see the house quite plainly."

"Once the winds pick up, you won't be able to see past the nose on your face." He had to playfully tweak her pert nose. "I guaran-damn-tee it."

"Oh my."

"Don't you worry none. It'll be me going out in the worst of it. Just wanted you to know the ropes are there if you need 'em." Since his morning chores were done, he found himself wanting to hear her melodious voice again. "I don't s'pose you'd read me some more of the book?"

Kayla's radiant smile made him smile in return. "Are you enjoying the adventures of Phileas Fogg?"

"Yes, ma'am, I am." Not a lie. Drake found he liked the story, but it was spending time with her that he relished more.

"Then let's have a quick lunch, and we can read a chapter or two before afternoon chores."

* * *

Kayla stared out the window, trying to tamp down her rising anxiety.

The snow still fell heavy and deep, but the winds had risen significantly. Soft whistles filled the kitchen, probably from small cracks around the windows and between the boards. Every now and then, a gust would come so forcefully the panes would rattle. A mound of snow had all but buried the hen house, and the porch would soon be enveloped.

The wind blew so briskly, the snow appeared to move sideways instead of falling from the dark clouds. She'd never seen the like, even in cold, snowy St. Louis.

Glancing over her shoulder, she found Drake thrusting his arms into his coat sleeves.

"You're going to the barn?" She went to the wooden pegs and grabbed his fur hat. After he buttoned up his coat, she held the hat out to him. While he tugged it on his head, she fetched the scarf she'd knitted for him.

"Yes, ma'am. Need to feed and water the livestock. Gonna milk the cow again in case I can't get out there in the mornin'." He took the scarf she offered and draped it over his neck.

"I shall go and help you." Kayla reached for her coat.

Drake stopped her with a hand on her arm. "You need to stay inside." The tone of his voice suggested she not argue.

She argued nonetheless. "If we work together, we can get done quickly."

With a shake of his head, he jerked on his gloves.

"I insist," she said, taking her coat off the peg.

He stopped her by grabbing her wrist and gently pulling her arm down. "The storm's too strong for me to let you go out there."

"But you're going."

"I have to. The animals depend on me. I'm gonna make sure they're good and cared for just in case we're snowed in for a spell. Once the snow eases, well, then you can go out with me." He tossed her a teasing smile. "We can build snowman."

For once, Kayla refused to be charmed by him. "Drake…" She reached for her coat again and plucked it from the peg.

This time he was more insistent, taking her coat from her and hanging it right back up. "I got enough to fret about goin' out in this storm. I can't be worryin' about you. Too many bad things can happen in a blizzard like this." He shot her a fierce frown. "Promise me you'll stay in the house."

Folding her arms under her breasts, she leveled a hard stare at him. "I am going."

"Kayla, please. Don't do something foolish. Promise me you won't follow me. Promise me right now."

She couldn't help but respond to the fear in his voice. Easing her stance, she sighed. "I'll stay in the house."

"Promise?"

"I promise."

He nodded. "As soon as I'm out that door, you shut it tight. Hear me?"

"Yes, Drake."

With another stern nod, he wrapped the scarf around his face and pulled on his gloves. Then he took a deep breath and jerked the door open.

Snow immediately spilled onto the floor as more swirled in on the wind.

Kayla hurried to the door. As soon as Drake waded out into the storm, she put her shoulder against the door to force it closed. Then she hurried to find some old towels and the broom to get rid of the large amount of snow that had filled the house.

The whole time she worked on righting the mess, she worried about the danger Drake was facing on the short trip to the barn.

* * *

A second hour had passed, and still Kayla fretted that Drake hadn't returned.

While she knew there were a lot of things to be done to help the livestock, she couldn't help but worry that he should have returned by now.

Crouching next to the fire, she set two more logs on it to keep the home heated. Drake would surely have need of its warmth. The temperature had dropped considerably, and the wind howled around the house. Thankfully, the sturdy structure could withstand the onslaught.

I should have things ready for him.

To give herself something to do, she fetched a couple of quilts and some of his clean clothing. No doubt he'd need to strip out of his wet garments, then she could help him dress, wrap him in a blanket, and set him in front of the fire. She'd also make a pot of strong, hot coffee to warm him insides.

Then she ran out of things to do.

As she waited for Drake, she paced in front of the hearth and rubbed her hands together to appease both her worry and the chill in her fingers. She couldn't settle enough to do anything more, even read. Besides, she was sharing the story with Drake, and he'd be disappointed if he missed any of the tale.

The door rattled, and Kayla hurried to see if he'd returned only to be saddened that the wind had been the cause. Instead of cleaning up the snow that had blown inside when she'd opened the door a crack, she looked to where her coat hung.

She'd promised him that she'd wait inside. Yet each of her thoughts forced her closer to breaking that pledge.

What if he'd fallen and couldn't get back to the house? What if something had happened in the barn, causing him to become trapped? What if—

She banished the worries with a shake of her head as she made up her mind. She wouldn't wait a moment longer.

After donning her coat, she bundled herself snugly in a hat and scarf. Content that she'd be well protected from the cold, she pulled on her mittens and faced the door. With a bracing breath, she opened it and waded out into the blizzard.

* * *

One last look around, and Drake felt assured the animals would be fine until he could return.

The cold was jarring, and he'd had to stop several times to shake life back into his hands and stomp it back into his feet. While he'd milked the cow, he'd enjoyed warming his hands against her teats, but that was the only luxury of the afternoon. Now, the milk was nearly frozen. Not that it mattered. He'd have his hands full getting himself home. There was no way he could tote the milk or the few eggs the hens had laid back to the house. Thankfully, neither was needed, and there would be more to come in the long days ahead.

A few of the chickens clucked at him from their temporary home in one of the horse stalls. He envied their thick feathers and the protection nature gave them.

"You all stay safe," he said to the animals. "I'll be back as soon as I can." He couldn't help but shake his head at his words. It was Kayla's fault that he talked to the animals now. Rusty, sure. Horses were smart. But she always insisted all the critters understood her, so she'd made a habit of it. He'd adopted the same practice, silly though it was.

As if animals knew what people were saying. He scoffed at the notion.

Knowing he could put it off no longer, Drake made sure he was protected against the intense cold by wrapping the scarf around his face until was nearly covered. Then he forced open the barn door just enough to slip through.

The wind hit him like a punch, sending him stumbling to the side as he held tightly to the rope. No matter how many times he'd been caught in a blizzard, he'd never grow accustomed to the mind-numbing cold. Bracing himself, he began to follow the line back to the house he couldn't even see through the intense snowfall.

Thank the Lord, Kayla was safe and warm. Drake would need her help to get out of his sodden clothing. Perhaps he could get her sit next to him by the fire, and he pictured the two of them snuggling under a quilt. As he warmed himself, he would listen to her sweet voice read him more of a book that had captured his imagination.

Then he'd probably kiss her again.

Hand over hand, plodding his way through the hip-deep snow, Drake endured the ordeal, comforting himself with the knowledge that a warm home and a beautiful woman waited for him. The winds were brutal, and he had to fight his way slowly along the rope, sometimes turning his back to take the brunt of the gales for a moment or two before he could continue.

Funny, the thought that she was waiting for him was far too tempting for a no-account cowboy like him. What business did he have daydreaming about Kayla being his and his alone?

The house slowly appeared, a good thing, because he was chilled to his very bones. He couldn't feel his feet or fingers and knew he was in for a world of hurt when they were again warm.

Then he saw something just ahead of him, a dark form lying still as death nearly buried in a snowdrift.

No, it couldn't be. She'd promised him she'd stay in the house.

His mind raced as he stumbled toward what he'd now recognized as Kayla.

Please don't let her be dead.

Chapter Fourteen

Kneeling beside Kayla, Drake tried to roll her to face him. She was nearly hidden in the snow, and the wind whipped so loudly around them that he couldn't hear anything but the roar.

She had to be fine—she just had to be.

Since they were close to the porch, he let go of the rope and wrapped his arms around her waist. Tugging her along, he stumbled toward the house, sending them both sprawling back into a drift when he tripped on the bottom step that was buried deep in the snow. Righting himself, he hauled her up to the porch, setting her down against the wall while he opened the door. Then he had to fight past the snow that followed them inside. He was finally able to lay her on the floor.

Strength rapidly waning, Drake shouldered the door closed and then quickly cast aside his sodden gloves, scarf and hat. His stiff fingers didn't want to cooperate, but he was finally able to get his coat off. All he could think of was getting Kayla warm. She was curled up on her side where he'd left her, unmoving.

After shedding his boots and wet socks, he knelt beside her. Damn if his jaw wasn't seized in cold spasms that made his teeth rattle. He couldn't help but let out a relieved sigh when she groaned as he turned her to her back.

She was alive.

A glance around the sitting room gave him hope. She'd clearly prepared well for his return with blankets and towels waiting on the table. Drake sent up a thankful prayer for her foresight. He half carried, half dragged her to the sofa. Then he tossed a couple more logs on the fire, careful not to get his numb hands too close to the flames.

As he undressed her, she began to rouse. Her teeth chattered hard enough he feared one might crack, but he refused to stop when she weakly tried to push his hands away. Where survival was concerned, modesty had no place. It wasn't until he had her stripped down to her shift that he was satisfied. Grabbing one of the towels, he rubbed her braid, wondering if he should loosen her long hair to allow it to dry. Figuring the braid was probably easier to manage, he left it in place and spread one of the blankets on the rug in front of the fire. Picking her up, he carried her to the quilt and placed her on the center.

"Where are my clothes?" Her voice was slurred and sleepy. She sat like a discarded rag doll, boneless, as she glanced down at herself.

Drake untied the ribbons around her thighs and peeled down her thick stockings. "I can't believe you went out in that blizzard in damned skirts."

"What?"

"You shoulda worn pants, woman," he snapped.

"A lady does *not* wear pants."

With a shake of his head, he pointed to the blanket. "Lay down, Kayla."

"Why did you take my clothes?"

"They were wet," he replied as he went to work on his own clothing. Had his long johns not been damp, he would have spared her the embarrassment of his nudity. But he shed those as well, wrapping one of the towels around his hips. Thankfully, her shift had been dry so he hadn't needed to remove it, too.

After rubbing his hair dry, he picked up the second blanket and sat down next to her on the floor. "Lay down," he said again. "We need to help each other get warm."

Kayla slumped over, and he helped her stretch out in front of the fire.

Drake spread the blanket over them before he fit his front to her back, trying to keep the cloth around his hips. With his clumsy fingers, the task proved impossible, so he gave up that fight and wrapped his arms around her, trying to will heat back into both of their bodies.

"We should have eaten something," she said, her voice still unsteady.

"Not until I warm us up." He let out a snort. "I'm plum exhausted. Couldn't make us supper if I wanted to."

"I shall prepare a meal later—" An exaggerated yawn interrupted the last word.

He kissed the top of her head where it was tucked next to his chest. "You do that, Kayla. But for now, just sleep."

Holding off his fatigue as long as he could, Drake finally surrendered when Kayla's breathing became slow and rhythmic. His last thought before sleep claimed him was that holding her felt too right to ignore.

* * *

The dull ache in her head woke her, the same type she tended to get when her monthly was due or she'd overexerted herself. She kept her eyes half-closed to try to figure out exactly why a fire was shining directly on her face.

Things came back in a rush when she felt the hard planes of Drake's body pressed tightly to her back. One particularly firm part of him was nestled against her backside, and knowing that his body had responded to her in such a fashion sent heat straight to her core.

Then she remembered that her father had often teasingly offered a theory that some men were able to respond to nothing more than a stiff breeze. Although Kayla might not be the cause of Drake's arousal, she was quite content to be held in his strong arms and take advantage of the situation. Headache or not.

The reason she was in his embrace now seemed foolish. She'd broken her promise to him and ventured out into weather more intense than she'd ever experienced before. When the first gust of wind had caught her, she'd been slammed into one of the porch posts so hard that she'd eventually blacked out. She only recalled a little of tumbling off the porch into a snowdrift before Drake had dragged her back inside.

Trying to move slowly as not to awaken him, she felt for the sore spot on the side of her head where she'd hit the post. A small knot had formed, and simply touching it made her wince.

The warm body behind her stirred. "Kayla?"

"I did not mean to wake you."

She could hear him let out a yawn. "God, I'm tired." The hand he'd rested on her hip moved to her stomach and gave her a gentle stroke. "Are you well?"

"My head aches. I remember hitting it against—" Before she could finish her words, she found herself flipped to her back with Drake looming over her.

"Where'd you hit your head?"

"My right temple struck a porch post."

His hand was suddenly in her hair, and when his finger rubbed the sore spot, she sucked in a breath.

He frowned down at her. "You've got a knot there. Why didn't you tell me?"

"I fear I don't remember much after that. Please stop touching it."

"It pains you?"

"A little," she admitted, not wanting to complain.

"I can scoop up some snow for you to hold against it." Although Drake offered, he didn't move a muscle. Instead, his eyes kept gazing into hers, a penetrating stare that sent her blood racing and banished any thought of her headache.

The firelight painted his skin bronze, and she found that she was attracted to the patch of brown hair on his chest. She lifted her hand to lightly touch the crisp hair before splaying her fingers through it. Touching him was intoxicating. All she wanted was more and more.

He jerked as though she'd burned him. "Don't..."

Kayla refused to heed him. Instead, she placed her palm against his chest as she stretched her other arm up to grab his neck, intending to pull him down to kiss her.

Drake resisted—for a moment. Then he settled his mouth on hers.

After a quick, no-nonsense kiss, he eased back and stared down at her, a confused expression on his face.

She tried to tug him closer again, wanting the same type of kiss he'd given her before, the one that had made her toes curl.

He remained rigid, not giving into her insistent pulling. "Kayla...no."

"Why?"

"Are you kiddin' me?"

"I assure you, I am *not* teasing. I want you to kiss me."

"You don't know what you're askin'."

"I'm asking for a kiss," she said sternly, a little insulted that he didn't seem to want her.

Although his breath quickened, he shook his head.

"Kiss me, Drake."

"If I kiss you, I'll want more." With another shake of his head, he started to move away.

Kayla held tight, trying to keep him right where he was. "Perhaps I'd like some of that...*more*."

His eyes widened.

"I find that I enjoy your kisses. I should like to see where they might lead us."

Drake's heart was pounding, and his mouth had gone dry.

The woman couldn't possibly know what he wanted of her. He had no doubt she was a virgin, a sheltered one at that, despite her bravely venturing to the West on her own.

Problem was that he was naked and she was nearly the same, and even though the kiss he'd given her had been chaste, he wanted her desperately. All that kept him from smoothing his hands over her soft skin was a thin shift that he could rip from her body with little effort.

But he'd made himself a promise. She deserved the kind of life he could never give her.

She clung like a vine when he tried to roll away again. "Kayla…"

With surprising strength, she pulled him closer and brushed her lips against his. Once. Twice. Then she took his lower lip between her teeth and he was lost.

Sweeping his tongue into her mouth, Drake pressed his body against hers, pinning her to the floor as her hands went to his back to caress and explore until her palms covered his backside.

Nudging her legs apart with his knee, he settled between her thighs as he ravaged her sweet mouth. Her tongue was every bit as wild as his, and it didn't take long until his control slipped away.

He shifted to her ear, running his tongue around the ridges before he brushed kisses against her slender neck. Soft, little bites were soothed with long licks, and the way she purred in pleasure and squeezed her thighs against his hips had his cock hard and aching.

Kayla's fingers skimmed up his back, her nails leaving trails of gooseflesh in their wake. She seemed to want to touch him everywhere, and her innocent exploration of his body only added to his desire.

She let out a soft mewl of displeasure when he stopped kissing her. But when he laved a hardened nipple through the thin fabric of her shift, she dug her fingers into his hair and tugged hard. He merely chuckled and shifted to her other nipple, drawing the linen-covered nub deep into his mouth.

Her legs wrapped around his hips as she rubbed her core against his erection. All he needed to do was shift his hips, and he could plunge deep inside her warmth.

A gust of wind came whipping down the chimney, sending a flurry of sparks from the fire to hover over them like shooting stars. The sting of the ashes against his shoulders sobered him so quickly that his head spun.

"No," Drake said in a strangled whisper. Dear Lord, he'd been ready to take her right there on the middle of the sitting room floor. What kind of animal was he?

"Drake?" Her voice quavered with uncertainty.

He flopped to his back, breathing hard, still wanting her but knowing he would never forgive himself if he took advantage of her in such a degrading way. It wasn't until Kayla tried to crawl on top of him and kiss him again that he was able to force himself to move. He scrambled to his feet and scooped up the blanket that had covered them. He wrapped it around his waist, trying to shield himself.

She stared up at him with wounded eyes. "I don't understand."

"I–I can't do this."

"Drake…"

"I won't!" He tripped on the blanket as he tried to hurry away. Righting himself, he headed to his room, slamming the door in his wake.

Kayla shivered, as much from Drake's rejection as the cold. Fighting back the threatening tears, she put a few more logs on the fire to bring some heat back into the house. No doubt the fires in their rooms had gone out, but she didn't want to worry about that now. Her mind raced as she tried to figure out why he'd left her.

Left me?

Ran away is more like it.

He fled with the speed of a startled rabbit, and no matter how much she searched her thoughts, she could find no reason.

There had been passion in his kiss, in his touch. She'd tried to return that passion, following his lead and not letting any blood-cooling modesty keep her from responding with all the affection she felt for him.

And affection was the correct word. This went beyond physical to her. Kayla wasn't trying to fool herself into believing Drake could feel more for her than lust, but she couldn't remain every bit as emotionally aloof. She was growing to care for him. A great deal. That caring made her need to make love to him blossom.

Yet he'd spurned her.

But why?

Brushing away a stray tear, she got to her feet. Her head swam for a moment, and she worried that the knock she'd taken might be more serious than she'd first thought. The dizziness quickly passed, so she brushed aside her concerns and decided to confront Drake. It was clear she'd done something wrong, something that had repulsed him and made him leave her. She dearly wanted to find out what about her or what she might have done that had been so foul that he'd passed up what she'd freely offered.

Because the house was so cold, she stopped in her own room to don some clothes. Her breath came in white puffs as she tugged on her garments, and her brow was furrowed in concern. Could it be that there was something wrong with her? Had her body repulsed him? She'd never considered herself beautiful, but she didn't believe she was ugly, either.

She cupped her hand in front of her lips, huffed out a breath, and sniffed. Was the smell of her breath revolting?

The sounds of Drake moving around his room got her moving again. She hurried to his door and pounded on it with her fist, unable to control her rising anger. "Drake, I need to speak to you."

There was no reply.

She hit her fist against the door harder. "You must come out here and speak to me! This instant!"

His footsteps echoed against the floorboards and the door swung open. What right did he have to glare at her?

She narrowed her eyes. "Tell me why you left me." She hated the way her voice trembled, and she hoped he'd chalk it up to the bitter cold instead of the hurt he'd dealt her.

Instead of replying, Drake pushed past her and went to her room. Then he crouched by the hearth and went about starting a new fire as though everything was routine again.

Kayla sat on the edge of the bed watching him. The fact that he wouldn't give her an explanation only made her mind reel with increasingly frightening theories.

I'm too thin.

My breasts are too small.

He thinks I'm ugly.

As the fire caught, he fed it with a couple more logs and then rose to his feet. "We should eat."

She shook her head. "Not until you give me an explanation."

Drake raked his fingers through his hair, and she bit back an acerbic comment about it needing to be cut. "Can't we just forget that happened?" he asked.

She gave her head another shake. "If I offended you… If I did something…wrong…"

"That's what you think?" He let out grim laugh. "You think you did something *wrong*?"

"I must have! Why else would you run away from what I…wished to do with you?"

"Because you deserve better!" On that shout, he marched out of her room.

Kayla hurried to follow. "What exactly does *that* mean?"

"You're a virgin."

"I beg your pardon?"

He glared at her. "I'm not sleeping with a virgin."

"I see." She tried to keep her chin from quivering, but she was so close to tears. "You wish me to be more…experienced. Like your…other women."

"I'm not talkin' about this anymore." He stomped away and didn't stop until he was in the sitting room. After a look at the fire, he picked up a block of wood and tossed it on the pile.

She snatched up her discarded clothing. "Yes, we *are* talking about this."

"Kayla… Let it go."

With a shake of her head, she grabbed the towels that were scattered over the sofa. "I thought you wanted me. But then you jumped up and ran away."

Drake tossed the blanket aside and put his hands on his hips. "Don't you get it?"

"No. I do not get it."

"You're a…a… *lady*."

The word sounded like a curse. "You're a gentleman."

"Hell no, I'm not. I never was and never will be. You deserve better than the likes of me!"

Drake nodded, happy to have finally spit out the words. Kayla needed to know that he wasn't going to take advantage of her in that way. She'd given him such tender care, helped him through what might've been the worst time in his life as he'd dried out from his alcohol haze, and he wouldn't repay her by stealing her innocence.

Instead of looking relieved, she scowled at him, her eyes filled with unleashed anger. "You have no idea what kind of woman I am!"

"You're a good woman, Kayla."

She shook her head, forcing the tears that had spilled over her lashes to stream down her cheeks.

"You *are* a good woman."

"A good woman doesn't get her father murdered!"

Hideaway

Chapter Fifteen

Drake stared at her, not quite sure he'd heard her shouted words correctly.

She shook her head and fled down the hallway, and he pondered her words as he dressed and returned to the sitting room. When she'd finished dressing, she joined him. Then she plopped down hard on the sofa and put her hands to her face.

Reacting to the pain written all over her, he sat next to her and draped an arm around her shoulders. Instead of pulling away as he'd expected, she leaned into him and took a couple of bracing breaths, clearly fighting the need to weep.

"I can't rightly believe you had a man murdered," he said, putting as much conviction in his voice as he could. The gentle woman he knew couldn't possibly have caused someone harm—especially her father. Drake remembered well Kayla telling the story of the man's abuse of alcohol, yet the love and concern he'd heard in her voice made it plain that she loved him.

"It was *my* fault," she insisted, thumping her chest with her fist. "Had I not wanted to marry Gregory…"

Frustrated that she wouldn't finish the thought, Drake squeezed her closer to him. "Tell me, Kayla. I need to know."

She leaned back and looked up at him with eyes full of sadness. "I should never have told you anything." The shrug she gave him was anything but nonchalant considering the way she still trembled. "Why does it even matter now?"

"We're here all alone," Drake replied. "I'm responsible for our safety. If someone murdered your father… Well, who's to say they won't come for you?"

Her eyes widened. "She could never find me here."

"Tell me, Kayla. Please."

She popped to her feet and began to pace as she wrung her hands. "She has no idea where I am. I came here to escape. After what happened to Papa… I had no choice. I couldn't stay in New York."

The maddeningly slow pace of her telling the story was stretching his patience beyond endurance. Who was the "she" that kept coming up?

Drake patted the sofa. "Sit down, darlin'."

She stopped to stare at him. "His death *was* my fault."

"I need you to tell me how you came to Montana, then I need you to tell me about your pa and what happened to him. I know you never wanna talk about yourself, but it's time."

After a deep, shuddering breath, she sat next to him again, staring at the hands she folded in her lap. Then she nodded.

Drake started with what was bothering him most. "Who is Gregory?"

"I was betrothed to him. There were documents being drawn up ahead of what would've been a Christmas wedding." She let out a scoff. "I would've been a bride a few weeks from now."

He kept his gratitude that she hadn't married the man to himself. Since getting information out of her was akin to coaxing a skittish deer to eat grain from his hand, he pressed on. "Why didn't you stay and marry him?"

"His mother strongly disapproved."

Again, Drake waited for her to expand. When she didn't, he decided to push some more. "How did you meet him?"

* * *

The last thing Kayla wanted to do was relive the year of horror that ended in her fleeing west. But she knew that shielding Drake from her past wasn't wise. Her shame at what had happened made it difficult to explain. Closing her eyes, she tried to summon the past. "I met Gregory at a *soirée*. My father and I had been accepted in society because of the fortune he'd earned. He was an inventor, you see. The patents he held brought in a great deal of money."

"What did he invent?"

"All sorts of trinkets. The most lucrative was a tool specially designed to help fix pocket watches. Papa was very good with his hands."

"You never mention your mother," Drake said.

"My mother died when I was a baby. I have no memories of her." Although it might seem odd to feel sad for a person Kayla had never known, the grief of the loss still haunted her.

"What's a swahrey?"

"A *soirée*. It's a…gathering. A party, so to speak, where young society men meet young society women. Papa hoped to make a good match for me. Gregory introduced himself, and we seemed…compatible. We went on a few outings together. A picnic in the park. A costume ball. He proposed a few months after I met him, and at Papa's urging, I accepted."

"Your father liked the man?"

"He liked Gregory's family name and their fortune." Knowing exactly what Drake would ask next, Kayla beat him to the punch. "Gregory is a Carrington. His great-grandfather founded the Mid-Atlantic Bank."

Drake let out a low whistle that told her he recognized the name. Most people did, even those who were far away from New York. The Carringtons had dealings all over the world, and their reach was immeasurable.

"So why didn't you marry him?"

"His mother quickly let it be known that she did not approve of me."

"Why the hell not?"

Kayla couldn't help but enjoy the anger she heard in his voice. "In all honesty, I believe she wished Gregory to remain unmarried. She exerted quite a bit of control over his life."

Drake snorted. "A mama's boy."

"I suppose. Although I did not see him as such as first. Her need to protect Gregory was strong because of his name and his fortune. She saw me and my new social status as beneath him—beneath *them*. Once she realized that he intended to marry me, Papa and I began to have problems."

"Let me guess… Bank call a loan?"

"Exactly. And payments from buyers were often late. Then invitations were no longer being extended to either Papa or me. Friends confided that Chantal Carrington had been assuring everyone that the marriage wasn't going to happen and that she would give anyone who extended us courtesy the cut direct."

"What's *that* mean?" Drake asked.

"She held the power to banish them from social functions. When I asked Gregory, he insisted he loved me and still wanted to marry me. He told me that nothing his mother could do would stop him."

"Did you love him, Kayla?"

Turning her back to stare at the fire, Kayla let out a rueful little laugh. She'd asked herself the same question when it became clear that Chantal was doing everything she could to not only prevent the wedding but to exile Kayla and her father from acceptance in New York society. Gregory had been such a sweet suitor, and Kayla had agreed to marry him.

But did I love him?

Do *I love him?*

She mentally swept the question aside, not wanting to plumb the depth of her feelings. "He was kind and gentle, and I hoped to one day have a family. Twenty-four is well past marrying age, and I knew Gregory would be a good father and care for our children."

"Not enough reason to marry, not if you didn't love him."

All she did was shrug.

"Kayla…"

"Let me finish the story. Please."

He gave her a curt nod.

Attention back on the dancing flames, Kayla swallowed hard. "I had confidence in Gregory…until the carriage accident. Papa was convinced the wheel that came off had been tampered with. I couldn't go anywhere without different men following me. Papa guessed they were hired by Chantal to give her information on what I was doing and who I was with. Then all of our servants suddenly left. They didn't even give notice, simply gathered their things and walked out. Papa was convinced Chantal was behind all of our misfortunes. He decided to confront her."

Strong hands settled on her shoulders, and Kayla allowed herself the comfort of leaning back against Drake. His arms went around her waist, and he rested his chin on the top of her head. She drew strength from his presence.

"She came for tea at his invitation. When she arrived, she refused to dismiss her man-servant. He was a hulking man with black eyes. Otto Schneider. His size alone frightened me. I dare say he was the largest man I have ever seen."

"You met him there? At the tea?"

"No, I had met Otto before. Whenever I was with Chantal, Otto was at her side. They were…close. Gregory had even confided in me that they might be…you know…intimate. The idea pleased him because his mother had been lonely for too long."

"The rich lady had herself a lover."

Kayla shrugged again. Until things had gone so sour in their lives, she had been more focused on Gregory than on his mother and the odd man who hovered around her.

"So what happened when they got there?" Drake coaxed.

"Papa wanted me to remain out of sight. I didn't understand why, but I obeyed." She let out a little sigh. "Not exactly *obeyed.* I spirited myself into the attic where I could listen to what was happening through an opening I discovered while exploring the house as a child. I realized I could watch the sitting room without anyone seeing me. I'm not sure he knew of my trick, but I always felt it was my responsibility to look out for him, especially since he became confined to his wheelchair."

He rubbed his chin against her hair. "You're a sneak is what you are, Kayla Backer."

Hearing that name on his lips made her frown. There was more to the tale, but she would reveal the whole of her deception in due time. "Papa told Chantal that he knew she was the one responsible for our hardships. When she merely laughed at him, he assured her that he would do whatever it took for Gregory to marry me. Her response was that she would do the exact same thing to keep us from marrying and that she'd destroyed the betrothal papers." A shiver raced through her as she remembered the rising anger in their voices, the hostility that had led to cold-blooded murder.

Drake held her a little tighter. "Tell me the rest. It'll be good to get the poison out of your mind."

"Chantal got up and left, saying she hoped never to have to deal with him or me ever again and that she would protect her son at all costs. But her man didn't leave with her. He simply stood there and glared at my father. Once they were alone, Otto told Papa that Chantal wanted us both dead."

"Dear God…"

The panic was filling Kayla as though the memory were alive again. "Papa pulled out a gun. I didn't even know he owned one, but he pointed it at Otto and said he would kill him and Chantal to protect me. Everything happened so quickly. I wanted to run to Papa, but my feet seemed frozen."

Drake kissed her ear. "It's nothin' to be ashamed of."

"I *am* ashamed. If I could have gotten to them quickly, perhaps…"

"Perhaps, you woulda been shot, too."

"When I finally was able to move, I ran as fast as I could. But then…there was a shot. By the time I made it down the stairs and to the drawing room, Otto had left. Papa was on the floor next to his chair, not moving. I was so afraid." She bit back a sob and then tried to take a steadying breath.

"Was he…"

With a shake of her head, she pressed on. "He was shot here…" She pointed to her stomach. "I tried to help him, but there was so much blood. When I reached for him, he grabbed my hand and told me to stop. That he was done for." Tears flowed freely down her cheeks. "He told me to run, that I would be next if I didn't protect myself. I didn't want to leave him. So I stayed until… Until…"

* * *

Drake could only hug her and try to soothe her hurt. The past was over, and while he hated forcing her to dredge up the horrible memories, he needed to know what they might be up against. He remembered the last time they'd seen Marshal Riley when the man had said there'd been a telegraph for a

Carolyn, and Kayla had reacted icily, as though someone had walked over her grave.

Clearly, there was something else she hadn't told him yet. "Is that the whole story, Kayla?"

She shook her head. "Papa made me swear to God that I'd leave him there and run away. He told me where he'd hidden some cash, and then he…was gone. I didn't want to go…" She rubbed tears away with the heels of her hands. "I honored his wishes, grabbed the money, and hurried to the train station."

"Where did you go?"

"Chicago. He had a brother living there. I have never met the man, but I had nowhere else to go. I was only there a few months when it became clear that I had been followed. My uncle made arrangements to get me to St. Louis and to Reverend Hayes. He'd heard about the reverend's desire to help find brides for God-fearing men in the West. To keep me safe, my uncle gave me a new name—his mother's—so Chantal could no longer track me. He figured once I was in Montana with a husband and a name no one recognized, I would at last be safe."

"What's your real name?"

"Burton. Carolyn Mae Burton. Papa—Jamison Burton—called me Cara." She frowned. "Kayla was close, and I worried I wouldn't respond to any name too different from my own. So I became Kayla Backer."

"Cara. Cara Burton." It would take a while for Drake to be able to process all that she'd revealed to him, but one thing was clear.

She really *did* trust him.

There was more they needed to talk about, but she had to be weary of reliving her ordeal. He turned her in his arms and held her close, wanting nothing more than to comfort her. If he was right, she hadn't even had time to properly mourn her father. She'd had to flee her home, then her family had to send her away for her own protection.

Kayla wrapped her arms around his waist and rubbed her cheek against his chest.

"Let me make you somethin' to eat, *Cara*," he said. Although he would be content to hold her in his arms all night, his stomach was rumbling. Hers had to be every bit as empty. He wasn't even sure what time it was, because he had no idea how long they'd slept. It was dark outside, but this time of the year, it seemed to be dark all the damn time.

"It's a bit…odd hearing you use my true name. We should be careful not to say it around anyone. Please call me Kayla."

"You got a point. So are you hungry?"

"It's approaching midnight," she said, easing back. "A tad late for supper."

"Early breakfast, then." He smiled at her as he took her hand and led her to the kitchen.

* * *

Once his stomach was full, Drake knew sleep would follow soon. Kayla, no doubt, was every bit as weary. Since he didn't relish the idea of sleeping in what seemed to be the constant chilliness of his bedroom, he decided to sleep in front of the larger hearth in the sitting room.

Kayla stopped at the entrance to the hallway. "I believe I shall go to bed now. Are you ready to sleep as well?"

He grabbed the folded blanket and shook it out. "Think I'll sleep right out here tonight. It's mighty cold, and I wanna be close to the fire. You go on." After he spread the blanket on the floorboards, he was surprised to see her still standing there. "If you're worried about your fire, I checked it. Added some wood, so you'll be warm for a good, long while."

"It's not that…" She folded her arms around her waist. "I was…wondering…" She gave her head a quick shake and took a few steps into the hall. "Sleep well, Drake."

As though he'd let her leave without telling him what she wanted. "Wonderin' what, darlin'?"

Stopping, she turned back to face him. "I should like it if you shared my bed tonight."

Eyes wide, he stared at her. "Beg pardon?"

"Not in an *intimate* way," she said in a rush. "I would just…enjoy your company. And we could share our heat." When he didn't reply, she must have become nervous because she stammered out, "I promise t–to behave honorably."

It was the strangest offer he'd ever received, and a smile broke out on his face. "Are you sure?"

She nodded vigorously.

Drake picked up the blanket and folded it. "I s'pose if you promise to keep your hands to yourself…" He glanced up to catch her grin and shook a scolding finger at her. "Nothin' but sleep, mind you." He winked at her before he set the blanket back on the sofa.

Then he followed her to her room. It was awash in firelight, and the setting was so romantic that it was perfect for a seduction. When he glanced at her, he noticed she was frowning. "Change your mind?"

"No. No, please stay." Setting aside her shawl, she kicked off her shoes and went to the bed. She pulled back the covers and sat on the side of the mattress, but she made no move to lie down.

After toeing off his boots, Drake went to the opposite side of the bed. "Are you sure you didn't change your mind?"

Kayla wasn't sure how to respond. It wouldn't be very ladylike to tell him that if they crawled into the bed together that she would have a difficult time keeping her hands to herself.

The kindness he'd shown her as she spilled her story had only increased her feelings for him. While Gregory had always been polite and attentive, Drake had not only saved her life, he'd taught her about passion.

Making love to him might be a mistake, but she was more than willing to put propriety aside and live for once in her life.

But not now. Not when he was as skittish as a newborn colt. For now, she'd be content to let him hold her in his strong arms and comfort her through the nightmares that always haunted her sleep.

"Of course, I haven't changed my mind, and you may stop asking." Kayla slid between the covers, almost laughing at the absurdity of wearing her clothes. Not only would she be too warm, she'd probably have no need of the blanket, especially if she had Drake's body to cuddle against.

That thought in mind, she quickly got back on her feet and pulled her petticoats out from under her skirt.

"What are you doin'?" His question ended on a squeak when her petticoats hit the floor.

"I wish to be comfortable. I cannot do so in so many layers of clothing." To show her sincerity, she unbuttoned her shirt and took it off. Her skirt was gone soon after. Dressed only in her shift and stockings, she got back into the bed. "It isn't as though you haven't seen me in my shift." She let her gaze sweep his body. "Would you not be more comfortable if you removed your shirt and pants? Most men sleep in their long johns, do they not?"

Kayla couldn't stop a smile as she watched the emotions play across his face. Normally, Drake was difficult to read, having a true skill at hiding his emotions. Now, that guard had dropped, and she stifled a laugh as he kept shifting his gaze from her to the bed to the door.

"If we do this," he said, "I will behave myself."

His desire to be a gentleman warmed her heart, but she was determined to have him. She had never enjoyed the delicious things that Drake made her feel, and she had every intention to taking the man as her lover.

His reluctance was very clear as he slowly removed his shirt and pants. He crossed his arms over his chest. "I'm makin' you a promise right now, Kayla."

"And what is that?"

"I won't take advantage of you. Ever." On that vow, he got between the sheets, covered his body with the quilt, and stacked his hands behind his head. "Good night then," he said as he stared at the ceiling.

Refusing to be ignored, Kayla snuggled up next to his side. Placing a hand on his chest, she kissed his stubbly cheek before putting her head on his shoulder. "Good night, Drake."

With her face tucked under his chin, she felt safe smiling, knowing he wouldn't see her grin as her mocking him. He'd been so serious when he'd sworn to be a gentleman. The silly man didn't realize that it wasn't taking advantage when she wanted to make love with him. His promise might not be too awfully difficult to get him to break, judging from the way his long johns had tented in front.

Oh yes, she would get him to break that vow. The only question that remained was how long he could hold tightly to his honor.

Chapter Sixteen

Drake stomped his boots against the porch steps, not wanting to track snow into the house. After two weeks of near-blizzard conditions, nature had sent a reprieve in the form of a warm spell. The snow was still piled high, but the sun was bright and he'd had a chance to clear a walkway between the barn and the house and a narrow one to the foundation of the new home. If temperatures kept improving, those pathways could soon become muddy messes.

Promising himself he'd place some straw next time he went to the barn, he opened the door and went inside the house.

Kayla was hard at work at the stove, and whatever she was cooking smelled wonderful. She glanced over her shoulder. "Are the animals bedded down for the night?"

"They're fine," he snapped, pulling off his boots. He tried to rein in his temper. He wasn't mad at her; he was just frustrated.

For two weeks, she'd slept at his side, and Drake had done his damnedest to fulfill his pledge to keep his hands off her. But every night was an increasing challenge, a fight that became more and more difficult. This morning, he'd woken himself up trying to crawl on top of her. Thankfully, she'd been drugged by sleep and had merely burrowed deeper under the covers when he'd thrown himself out of bed. Had he not put some distance between them quickly, he might have found himself buried deep inside her before he'd awakened enough to stop himself.

Anger had been his companion all day, and he couldn't seem to shake it. Now that he was inside the house with Kayla, he couldn't help but be reminded that he was no better than some randy goat.

"You needn't be short with me," she scolded. "I shall have our supper ready in a few minutes, if you'd kindly wash up."

"Stop naggin' me." He let out a sigh. Even the simple things she said grated on his nerves. "Sorry," he spit out before he went to wash his hands.

Why she smiled in response was a mystery. As his mood fell, hers seemed to rise. She began to hum a cheery tune, then she began to sing.

The song was quite scandalous. Yet the story of a woman trying to entice a man into her bed kept spilling from her lips.

Brows knit, he gaped at her. Had she been any other woman, he might've believed she was intent on seducing him. Each time she molded her body to his at night, he had to remind himself over and over that she was innocent and clearly had no idea what she was doing to him. Whenever she'd stroke his chest, he'd flatten her hand with his own and hold it still. The times when she nuzzled his neck, he would mentally count to ten. Or twenty. Often beyond.

Kayla obviously didn't know her appeal or she wouldn't tempt him so. At night, as she removed her shirt and skirts, she always stood at the foot of the bed. All that did was allow the light from the hearth to silhouette her body through the thin material of her shift. Every curve, every hollow was visible to him, and it took all his self-control not to toss her on the bed and make love to her right then and there.

Only his vow kept him in check.

But each day was a battle, and each day he came closer to losing the fight.

After they sat down to eat, Kayla said a quick prayer before Drake dove into the food. For someone who had probably depended on servants to tend to her needs, she'd become a good cook. "Who taught you to make all this?" he asked, nodding at the spread on the table.

"Grace Morgan. I had been told she was an outstanding cook, so I went with Cassie to learn a few things from her when I realized that Drew and Gideon would have to depend on me to provide meals."

God, he loved hearing her talk. Such formal speech, and the beauty of her voice made the words sound like a song.

"I reckon I gotta get me some of Grace's cookin', then." When she frowned, he wasn't sure what was wrong. "Kayla?"

"I…I thought I was doing quite well at the task. Perhaps you believe I need more lessons?" she timidly asked.

So the woman was fishing for compliments. "Your cookin' is great, Kayla. I was only sayin' that if Grace taught you, well then, she must be a *real* good cook."

She rewarded him with a smile.

Dinner passed pleasantly, and after they finished putting away the clean dishes, Kayla pulled the big pot from a bottom shelf and put it on the stove.

"Whatcha doin'?" Drake asked.

"I haven't enjoyed a proper bath in far too long. I intend to have one now. I have a half-full tub waiting in our room, warming next to the fire, but I need to add some very hot water to make it comfortable."

"You'll need more than one pan."

"I shall work at this all night if I must, but I'm having a bath, Drake. If you help me, then I will hurry so that you may enjoy the warm water as well."

* * *

Although she knew she should get out of the hot water so Drake could have his turn, Kayla wanted to stay in the relaxing bath.

After filling the tub with steaming water, a task that required much longer than she deemed practical, she made herself a promise. She was going to find a way to convince Drew to allow Drake to install a true bathroom in her home, one with a heated water storage container. She was weary of the tedious chore of filling the brass tub just to get herself clean.

There was a knock on the door. "Kayla? You done yet?"

She smiled at the thought that Drake wanted to bathe every bit as much as she had. Standing, she grabbed a towel and wrapped it around herself before stepping out of the tub. "Give me one more minute, please."

As she quickly dried herself, she glanced at the bar of soap she'd used, wondering how he'd react if she suggested he use it as well. As it was, the water smelled of the rose petals laced through the soap. No doubt he'd feel the scent wasn't manly, but she wasn't about to empty the tub and start again.

After she slipped on her shift, she went to the door and opened it, loving how he sucked in a breath as his eyes scanned her from head to toe. So far he'd been putting up a good fight, trying to cling to his pledge not to touch her.

Now, she was going to do everything in her power to get him to break that oath. The problem was that she'd never tried to seduce a man before and wasn't sure that anything she had been doing would be successful.

"Don't you have a robe or somethin'?" Drake asked, putting his hand to his brow as though he were blocking bright sunlight.

"I fear that I haven't had time to make one yet. So many of your clothes needed mending, and there are chores… You should take your bath, Drake. The water is cooling."

He started to unbutton his shirt, and she nibbled on her bottom lip, wondering exactly how long he'd allow her to stay. It was such a pleasure watching him undress, and the thought of seeing his muscular body again, the one that had captured her thoughts since the night he'd rescued her from the blizzard.

"You're not leavin'?"

"Yes, of course. If you leave your clothes by the tub, I shall wash them before we dump the water. Please call out when you're finished." Kayla wrapped a quilt around her shoulders and closed the door softly as she left.

As Drake bathed, she decided to work on her damp hair. She spread another blanket in front of the hearth and went about removing the tangles. Task accomplished, she held the tresses up to dry, glad to have a roaring fire to assist her.

A laugh slipped out as she wondered how he'd react if she went to him and offered to wash his back.

Heavens, she was brazen, sitting there plotting intimacy with a man who would be riding away as soon as spring came and he finished her house. But she couldn't deny how he made her feel, and she suspected she was falling in love with him.

And if that didn't make her a fool, she didn't know what would. Cowboys never fell in love, and she was tying her heart to a hopeless case.

Yet there was no fighting the way she thought of him all the time, or how he made her so content by holding her close through the cold nights. The way her blood ran hot at the mere thought of kissing him again told her that protecting her heart was a lost cause.

Her common sense preached that there was the possibility of a child being created should she follow through with her plans. Her heart answered back that a baby would allow her to always keep a part of Drake at her side. There was no doubt Gideon and Drew would take a hand in raising the child. Her reputation had been lost long ago, so what did it matter that she bore a child out of wedlock?

But Drake was resisting.

Could it be that he didn't desire her? That thought made her frown. Perhaps she'd overestimated his attraction to her. After all, he was accustomed to women who painted their faces and dyed their hair. An innocent with nothing more enticing than a cotton shift might not appeal to a worldly man like him.

What else could account for why he refused to touch her?

"Kayla…"

Glancing over her shoulder, she smiled at Drake. The tender way he watched her made her nearly giddy. She held up the comb. "Come sit by the fire with me. I shall comb your hair."

Drake's mouth went dry at the vision before him. What could be more tempting than Kayla, dressed in a provocative shift, sitting in front of a fire? She was calling to him like a siren, and he couldn't have stopped himself from going to her if he wanted to.

Sitting cross-legged with his back to her, he closed his eyes and enjoyed the way she carefully tended to him, rubbing the towel he'd brought with him over his head before she combed his hair.

"You should consider allowing me to trim this," she said, tugging lightly on a bit of his hair. "It is much longer than the fashion."

"You wanna cut my hair?"

"Only if you wish me to. As long as it is, your hair gives you an air of...danger." Her voice held a note of laughter.

He chuckled. "Danger, huh?" He growled for effect. "Do I scare you, Kayla?"

Suddenly, she was on her knees, wrapping her arms around his neck. "You scare me more than you could possibly know."

"Then why're you huggin' me if I make you afraid?"

"Because what I fear is losing myself in the magic of how you make me feel."

Drake drew in a hissing breath when she rubbed her breasts against his back. There was no way she could understand what she was doing to him. His body was tied up in knots of lust. When he tensed and tried to move, she gripped him tighter.

"Please. Don't go. I...I need to talk to you."

He grabbed her wrists and eased her arms back. Then he scooted back and turned to face her, needing a little distance between them. "What do you wanna talk about?"

She let out a sigh. "Am I ugly?"

"What?"

Despite the fact that she winced at his shout, she let her gaze catch his. "Do you think that I am ugly?"

"Why in the hell would you think something that asinine?"

Her gaze dropped. "Please don't call me names."

He gently lifted her chin so he could see her face. "I didn't say *you* were asinine, I said what you were thinkin' was asinine." Seeing her sitting there so dejected, he couldn't believe what he was hearing. "What in the devil is wrong with you tonight?"

Kayla seemed to ponder for a few long moments, the whole time staring at his face and appearing close to tears. "No matter how hard I try, I cannot entice you to make love to me."

Had she said she was a visitor from the moon, he wouldn't have been more surprised than he was at that moment. His heart started hammering loud enough to echo in his ears, which had surely disrupted his hearing. There were a million things he wanted to say, but the words kept crowding together and blocking him from uttering a single one.

"Now, I have humiliated myself." Scrambling to her feet, she tried to step away, but Drake grabbed the hem of her shift. The lace ripped, forcing him to let go as to not pull the damn thing from her body. She rushed out of the room, her flight followed by the slamming of a door.

Drake dragged his fingers through his damp hair. He'd never been so confused, and he had no clue what he should do next. He was just beginning to think he might understand Kayla, and suddenly a part of her he didn't recognize had been staring right at him.

"I cannot entice you to make love to me."

At least he no longer thought he was reading more into their situation than was truly there. Until she'd confessed her actions, he'd thought that his besotted mind was making him see her actions as sexual, when in reality she was too innocent to know how tempting she was. He got an erection almost every time he saw her. He was beginning to believe the woman was going to cripple him with lust.

A smile slowly bloomed as he processed what she'd confessed. She wanted him. She wanted him in her bed, in her body. And damn if that wasn't exactly where he wanted to be.

Getting to his feet, he checked the fire and then picked up the quilt, folded it, and set it on the sofa. He needed to move slowly, to think over what he would say to her when he joined her in the bedroom—the one they'd been sharing since that cold night when they'd both nearly frozen to death.

The easiest thing to do—and by far the most appealing—was to go right ahead and make love to her. But he was having a difficult time getting his conscience to agree with his cock. Should he take her innocence, he would change everything between them. They had months ahead of them to share. A lot of that time would find them stranded and alone because of the snow. What if she discovered that she didn't enjoy making love? How miserable would it be for the two of them to be forced to endure each other's company then? What if she suddenly ordered him to leave?

He'd promised Drew and Gideon that he'd keep Kayla safe through the long winter. They were sure to take offense if he deflowered her in the process. And there was a house for him to build.

Her house.

No, he couldn't—*wouldn't*—give in to the temptation being laid in his path. No matter how much he wanted her.

That thought firmly in his thoughts, Drake went to explain his decision to Kayla.

Chapter Seventeen

Instead of barging into the bedroom, Drake knocked softly on the door.
"Can I come in?"

"Suit yourself."

The clipped response didn't fit Kayla's polite personality, which told him
exactly how upset she was. Opening the door, he stepped into the room to find
her standing at the window, wrapped in a quilt and staring out into the night.

He wanted to go to her, put his arms around her, and offer her comfort.
But he reminded himself that he was the cause of her distress, and she might
think he was mocking her by taking her into his embrace. He just couldn't
figure out how to fix this rift.

"I am sorry to have embarrassed you," she said, her voice trembling. "I
shall not do so again."

"Kayla…"

"I have humiliated myself."

"You have not."

She bowed her head. "It would be wise for you to sleep in a different
room. Perhaps you should use the room Drew and Gideon share so that you
may stay warmer at night."

That idea seemed a blasphemy. Not sleep at her side, holding her close
through the night? Until she suggested it, Drake hadn't realized how important
being near her, knowing that after a hard day of work he could look forward to
spending evenings with her, had become. She'd always cuddled against him,
and they'd talk, sharing not only the day's events but ideas about her house.

The only thing they never spoke of was the future.

He went to her, but when he tried to put his arms around her, she stepped
to the side and brushed past him.

"I want to talk about this," he insisted.

She went to the foot of the bed and stared at him with haunted eyes. "What
is there to talk about? You don't want me."

He couldn't stop a scoffing laugh from escaping. "Not want you? Oh,
Kayla. I want you somethin' fierce."

Her eyes widened. "Then why?"

"Why what? Why not make love to you?" Drake shook his head. "I'm not
the man for you."

Even as he said it, he wanted to shout that no other man would touch her
so long as he lived. His emotions were tumbling in ways that he'd never
known, making him feel dizzy. And vulnerable. She deserved so much better
than him, but the mere idea that she might one day belong to another man made
him fighting mad.

Kayla slowly lowered the quilt, baring her shoulders. The firelight painted
her smooth skin golden. "I am not asking you for anything, Drake. No
commitment. No promises."

Women were such strange creatures. This one was particularly perplexing.
She shouldn't be dangling herself in front of him like a sweet treat without
expecting marriage in return.

Yet there she stood, tempting him beyond his endurance. Only his tattered honor kept him glued to the spot.

Her arms lowered, dropping the quilt to her waist. Her breasts pressed against the thin material of her shift, nipples hard and straining. "I want to matter to someone." A tear spilled over her lashes, tracing a wet path down her cheek.

Drake was lost.

He strode to her, brushed the blanket from her hands, and then took her into his arms. "You matter to *me*." He took her into his embrace then captured her lips in a searing kiss. There was need there. His need to show her what she meant to him, even if he couldn't find the words to tell her exactly how much.

Her need to belong to him, even if only for the here and now.

Kayla broke free of any tethers on her mind and her body. Drake might not have told her that he loved her—would probably never say those words to her—but he had told her what she needed to hear.

"You matter to me."

When his tongue thrust past her lips, she returned the caress, swallowing his growl when she gripped his tongue with her teeth.

There would be no stopping this time.

Finding some strength, she stepped back, out of his arms. As she gave him a shy smile, she crossed her arms and slid the thin straps of her shift from her shoulders. When she lowered her arms, the garment fell to her waist.

Drake sucked in a long breath. "Dear God, you're beautiful."

Her face heated in response, but he reached her heart. Before she could summon a reply, he was out of his long johns, casting them aside.

His body was perfect to her, so different than her own. Well-defined muscles formed broad shoulders and strong arms. The patch of hair on his chest thinned to a line that ran the length of his torso until it thickened at his groin. His cock rose hard and long from that nest of crisp hair.

Words froze in her throat, and Kayla could only stare at him as her core tightened.

He swept back the covers from the bed and came to stand before her. After he pushed the shift over her hips to let it fall to the floor, he swept her into his arms and carried her to the bed.

Setting her on the linens, he stretched out next to her and kissed her again. This kiss was different. New. Full of a hunger she hadn't felt in him before, a ferocity that she'd somehow unleashed.

Kayla reveled in it, giving herself over to anything he wanted from her.

Drake shifted to her neck, nuzzling and licking, causing shivers in his wake. He worked his way down to her chest as she tunneled her fingers through his hair. He kissed the valley between her breasts, breathing in deeply. "You smell…wonderful," he murmured against her skin. "Like roses." His mouth covered her nipple, and he suckled gently.

Everything inside her was on fire, and she arched into him, trying to hold him where he was. He shifted to her other breast as he smoothed his hand down her stomach and then eased it between her thighs.

She tensed, but only for a moment as he nudged her legs open. His fingers combed through the hair before separating her folds. Whatever he touched there sent a thrill racing through her. She drew in a quick breath and lifted her hips off the bed.

"Easy, darlin'," he whispered. "I won't hurt you."

"I trust you," she whispered back.

He must have been pleased to hear her say that, because he rose to kiss her, his lips almost brutal in their intensity. His fingers were doing magic to her, making a knot of need form in her core.

Arms around his neck, Kayla felt as though she were reaching for something that was just out of her grasp. Everything inside her was tense, alert. When he slipped one of his fingers inside her, she gripped his shoulders, digging her nails into his skin. "Drake…"

"Let go, Kayla. Just let go."

The huskiness in his voice only added to the thrill of what was happening to her. He might not ever belong to her, but from that moment on, she belonged to him.

Drake couldn't wait any longer. His thin thread of self-control snapped when she raised her head to lightly bite his shoulder. She was wet and hot and so damned tight, and although he loved touching her and feeling the response he had pulled from her, he needed to be inside her.

Every one of her reactions was so raw, so pure. Accustomed to the way a whore would put on a show of pleasure, hoping for a few more coins, he appreciated Kayla's innocent enjoyment of what they shared. She was so lovely, her eyes sparkling in the firelight, her lips wet from his kisses.

How could she have ever believed that he didn't want her? Seemed that he'd wanted her from the moment he laid eyes on her. It had just taken him some time to sort things out after banishing the alcohol from his mind.

He pushed her thighs farther apart and settled himself against her, his cock nudging at her. But he hesitated, needing to know that she wasn't going to condemn him later for taking the most important gift she could ever offer.

Staring into her eyes, he loved the passion he saw reflected there. "Kayla, are you sure?"

"I need you, Drake. Now."

In one hard, thrust, he buried himself inside her.

Kayla let out a startled cry, and Drake worried he'd hurt her. Easing back, he thought to stop as to spare her any more pain even as he wondered how he could ever leave her.

She retaliated by wrapping her legs around his hips and holding him right where he was. "Don't leave me."

"I won't leave you," he declared. "Ever." And in that moment, he realized that he would never let her go.

Passion banished any rational thought, and all he could do was push into her, again and again, and hope he could hold off his release until she could find her own pleasure. But she felt so damned good that he was quickly losing the battle.

"Drake!" As his name fell from her lips in surprised wonder, her body tightened around him as she arched up and clutched at his shoulders.

His own release washed over him, making him shudder as he spilled himself inside her with her name on his lips.

Never had he felt the kind of contentment that filled him—in mind, body, and soul. Although he didn't want to separate from her, he was pretty sure his weight was crushing her. Rolling to his side, he pulled her up against him, pleased when she snuggled close, draping her leg across his thigh.

It felt right to hold her, just as it had felt right to make love to her.

There were promises he wanted to make, but he held his tongue. Right now, he had nothing to offer her. But in that moment when he'd realized how much she meant to him, he had promised himself that he would do whatever it took to become a man who deserved her.

On that vow, Drake kissed Kayla's forehead and let sleep claim him.

Chapter Eighteen

Kayla stirred, surprised to see bright sunlight, rare though it was, spilling through the window.

She was peaceful after the night she'd spent with Drake. Stretching like a lazy cat, she winced when she realized how sore she was from the intimacy they'd shared. Trading a bit of tenderness for the harmony that had settled on her heart and mind seemed a bargain.

"Kayla! Food's ready!" Drake shouted.

Drake cooked a meal for me?

Quickly donning her robe, she headed to the kitchen to find him setting a dish on the table. She let her eyes catch his and then quirked a brow. "Only one plate?" she asked. "Wouldn't you like to have something to eat?"

"I ate before chores," he replied with a note of humor in his voice.

Guilt swept through her at the thought of the tasks she needed to complete, tasks which she'd clearly slept through. It would surely be sundown before she caught up. "I should go check the hens."

"Done." Drake pulled the chair out for her.

"And the cow?"

"Milked. Sit and eat, Kayla. You must be hungry."

Still feeling guilty, she took a seat and glanced at the food. "Flapjacks?"

He shrugged. "Only thing I can cook good."

"I adore flapjacks," she said quickly, not wanting to appear ungrateful. "They look delicious."

Kayla cut a piece and took a bite. She was pleasantly surprised at how tasty the dish was. As she ate, she began to feel awkward when Drake simply sat across the table and watched her.

It didn't take long for her appetite to flee in wake of the awkward silence. What did a woman say to the man she'd been intimate with the night before? Should she be telling him that he pleased her? Should she be coy or pretend the things that had passed between them hadn't changed their relationship?

She wasn't embarrassed. Not over sharing her body with him. Every part of what they'd enjoyed had felt right to her. No, the discomfort she was feeling had more to do with wondering where they would go from here.

As he stared at her, she finally set her fork aside and pushed the plate away. She folded her hands and set them on the table. Better to talk about her worries than to let them eat away at her. "We should discuss a few things."

Drake leaned back in the chair and crossed his arms over his chest. A deep frown settled on his face. "I'm real sorry about last night, Kayla."

An apology was the last thing in the world she'd wanted to hear. "Sorry? You're *sorry?*"

His shoulders sagged. "It…it won't happen again. I swear it."

"It won't?" She sounded absurd, parroting the words back to him, but his attitude took her entirely by surprise. After going to all the trouble to make breakfast, she'd figured that he'd been pleased with last night. Heaven knew she was already looking forward to being with him again, but it seemed as though Drake wanted to assure her that another interlude would never happen.

Perhaps she'd been a disappointment to him. The experience had been so overwhelming, the feelings he inspired in her so new, so fresh, that all she'd been able to do was let him take the lead. Since he was accustomed to women with ample experience, perhaps her passivity had been dissatisfying to him.

She frowned, not sure what to do or say. After having the manners of a lady pounded into her from the first moment she could remember, she found it difficult to think of a way to tell him that she'd enjoyed herself. Immensely. And that she hoped to do so again and again for as long as he was with her.

"I mean what I say," Drake vowed with a decisive nod. "I won't be touchin' you again."

"But what if I *want* you to touch me again?" Kayla blurted out. Her cheeks heated, but she refused to break eye contact, even though his eyes were now wide with surprise.

At a loss of what else to say, she did the only thing she could think of to let him know that his attentions were something she craved. She stood and went to stand next to him. Then she sat on his lap, put her arms around his neck, and kissed him.

* * *

Drake was dumbfounded. Kayla's lips were so soft, so insistent, that he was captured by her kiss before he could even think to push her away. His noble intentions vanished. Quickly caught up in desire, he tickled the seam of her lips with his tongue. Once she parted them, he took advantage by rubbing his tongue across hers.

He let out a growl at the way her hips caressed his erection. The memories of the night they'd spent, the ones he'd tried to frantically to push aside, flooded his mind in the same way her nearness was flooding his senses. All of the promises he'd just made were gone in the wake of the passion she inspired.

Cradling her against him, he stood, lifted her higher in his arms, and strode down the hall toward the room they'd shared. When he saw that the bed linens were still rumpled, he couldn't help but remember how he'd felt when he'd been holding her, loving her. Now, he was nearly desperate to be inside her again.

After he set Kayla on her feet, Drake undressed with a speed he hadn't known he possessed. The way her eyes freely moved over his body with such obvious appreciation made him want to preen like a bird. He untied her robe and pushed it off her shoulders. Then he swept her shift over her head and cast it to the floor. He let his gaze drink her in. Just as he was ready to pick her up and lay her on the bed, he could only suck in a breath as she reached out to wrap her fingers around his hard cock.

Looking up into his eyes, she smiled. "My boldness pleases you?"

He answered her by nuzzling her neck, licking and nibbling until she was gripping him tightly.

Gently brushing her hand away, Drake lifted Kayla into his arms and set her on the bed. Staring down at her slender form, he was nearly breathless at the beauty before him. In the dim firelight the night before, he hadn't been able to see much of her body. That, and he'd been far too swept away by the passion they'd shared to do more than react. In the sunlight, he now drank in her ivory skin, her rose-colored nipples, and the thatch of dark hair between her thighs.

A flush spread over her face, and her hands rose to cover her breasts. "I am unaccustomed to being seen like…this. The truth is that you are the first man to see me undressed."

There was something inside him, something primitive and much stronger than he could deny, that loved knowing that he was the only man to gaze at her naked. He also had no doubt that she'd been a virgin, and that also pleased him. Gently grasping her wrists, he moved her hands away. "You're the prettiest woman I've ever seen."

He sounded like an idiot. A woman like Kayla wasn't merely pretty; she was something so precious, so unique, that he couldn't find adequate words to describe her.

And she deserved far better than a dime-a-dozen knockabout like him.

Opening her arms wide, she gave him a welcoming smile that was as strong as a punch to the gut. "Come to me, Drake."

As if he could ever deny her.

Blanketing her body with his own, he wanted to touch her everywhere, to kiss every inch of that pale, soft skin.

Her hands began to explore him, moving over his shoulders, down his sides. Each hesitant touch enflamed him. Rising above her, he settled between her legs, letting his cock rest against her core. Then he framed her face in his hands and kissed her, not holding back any of the strong emotions she inspired.

Kayla felt beautiful when she was in his arms. The way Drake's eyes darkened as he'd stared at her had set something inside her loose. In her whole life, she'd never been as free as she was when she was sharing herself with him. Every inch of her skin was alive, and the heat and tension building inside her was delicious.

Spreading her thighs a little wider, she lifted her hips, not wanting to wait a moment longer to feel him thrust inside her again. When he didn't immediately enter her, she tugged on his earlobe with her teeth. "*Please, Drake…*"

Then he did exactly as she desired, entering her swiftly and pulling a small gasp from her due to her lingering soreness.

Drake stopped moving and held himself up to look into her eyes. "Did I hurt you?"

"Just a little. It's merely some tenderness from last night. Please don't stop."

"I shouldn't do this."

When he tried to move away, she wrapped her legs around his hips. "Yes, you should."

"Kayla… I promised I wouldn't touch you again."

"A silly promise to make when you are doing exactly what I wish."

His brows knit. "You want me?"

"Oh, yes, my love, I want you." She cupped his neck and pulled him into a passionate kiss as she squeezed him tightly inside her.

Those actions seemed to make him lose his self-control. His kiss became ferocious, and she allowed herself to be caught up in the intensity. Pulling his hips back, he began to thrust into her, again and again. Harder and harder.

Kayla didn't fight the way Drake made her feel, and when the knot inside her snapped, she cried out and dug her nails into his shoulders. A few heartbeats later, he pushed into her one more time and let out a growl of surrender.

Long moments passed as sanity slowly returned, and the moment that it did, she remembered begging the man to make love to her. A laugh bubbled up as she marveled at her own boldness.

He eased out of her body and rolled to his side. Propping himself on his elbow, he shot her a frown. "Are you laughin' at me?"

Still feeling a bit awkward at being naked in front of a man, she pulled the covers over them. "Rest assured, my laughter was at myself, not you."

With his fingertip, he traced his way down her neck to her shoulder. "What's funny?"

"Me," she replied.

"Explain."

She glanced over at Drake, a bit astonished at how utterly handsome he was with his ruffled hair and a few days' growth of whiskers on his face. Her fingertips rubbed against the stubbly beard. "It would seem that in the throes of passion, I have very little modesty."

"That's funny?"

"To me, it is exceedingly humorous. I have always been such a…a…lady. Yet here I am, practically begging you to…you know."

He looked inordinately pleased with what she'd said. "You did beg, didn't ya?"

"My, you are a smug fellow."

"Smug?" He kissed her cheek. "A beautiful woman like you begs me to make love to her? Damn right, I'm gonna be smug."

* * *

It only took her a few minutes to realize that she hadn't needed to bundle up as usual. The bright sunshine was doing a wonderful job in making the winter less foreboding. After her afternoon chores were complete, she stayed in the barn to keep Drake company while he finished his work.

The pile of cut boards was slowly dwindling, but leaning against the far wall were more and more assembled structures. She couldn't figure out exactly what he was doing with the wood that was meant for her home.

She stepped up to one of the sets of nailed boards and asked, "What have you made here?"

He glanced up from the bucket he was scrubbing, gave what she was pointing to a quick look, and went right back to work. "Walls."

"Walls? These are walls? Where do you plan to use them?"

He nodded. "In your house, darlin'."

Since she knew absolutely nothing about building a home, she looked the structures over well. "I had no idea one could build a home inside another structure."

Drake set the bucket aside and grabbed the next one. "Yes, ma'am. This barn has plenty of space. With the kind of weather we've got out here, you can't count on doing everything outside. I know how much you want it done, and I don't plan to waste a day working on things. So I'm buildin' your walls."

His comments gave her pause. Now that they were lovers, would any of her plans for a future here with Drew and Gideon change?

No. She would ask for no commitment from Drake. Even though she could admit her own growing affection for the man, she doubted someone like him could nurture softer emotions such as love. Once he was done with his task, he would be gone. She refused to set herself up for heartache by nurturing any daydreams that he would decide to stay.

Besides, she was approaching this love affair as a modern, sophisticated woman. She wouldn't act like a simpering girl, trying to hold on to some man with physical intimacy. Drake wasn't the marrying type. He wasn't going to stay.

Why did that thought hurt so awfully much?

"How'd you like to go to town tomorrow?" he asked as he put another clean bucket aside.

"Do you think we could? I have so many things I would like to buy. I was hoping to make you a nice Christmas meal, and—" How foolish to almost let it slip that she wanted to purchase a gift for him.

"And...what?"

She dismissed the thought with a wave of her gloved hand. "How can we take a wagon in the snow?"

"Not a wagon, Kayla. A sleigh."

"A sleigh?"

With a nod, he pointed to the carriage house. "Gideon's got a nice sleigh. We can hook it up to Rusty and be on our way as soon as chores are done tomorrow."

"Papa and I used to take sleigh rides," Kayla said, a bit wistful at the memories. "On Christmas Day we would always share such a feast! If we can get some supplies, I shall cook you a wonderful dinner so we can celebrate the same way."

"I could do a spot of huntin'," Drake offered as he came to stand beside her. He took her hands in his, an action that made her heart skip a quick beat. "Been quite a few geese movin' through lately. Might be able to have roast goose for our Christmas dinner."

She rose on tiptoes to kiss his cheek. "Oh, Drake. That would be heavenly."

Chapter Nineteen

Kayla let Drake lift her from the sleigh, grateful to be in town and to finally have a chance to get warm again. The ride in to town had been brisk, but the sun had been high in the sky. The freedom of being away from the farm was most welcome.

"Go on inside," he said. "I'll tend to Rusty and meet you in the store."

She nodded as he took the horse's bridle and led him toward the livery. After the cold trip, the poor animal had earned some rest, water, and hay.

She walked into the general store, quickly shutting the door behind her to keep the wind from whipping inside. As she unwrapped the scarf that covered her face, she smiled at the quaint scene. The marshal was playing chess with Adam Morgan. They sat on opposite sides of a large cracker barrel, so absorbed in their game that neither looked up when she went to the stove to warm her hands.

"Good day, gentlemen." She removed her gloves and shoved them in her pockets. Then she rubbed her hands together, grateful for the heat radiating from the fire inside the stove.

The marshal moved one of his black pawns before he finally glanced up and smiled at her. "Good morning, Miss Kayla. From the way you're huggin' that stove, I'd guess you're feelin' a bit chilly."

She let out a chuckle. "The ride in was rather frosty. But the sun was warm, and in winter, I shall enjoy any sunshine I can get." Her gaze shifted to Adam. "Where is your lovely wife this morning, Mr. Morgan?"

Adam rubbed his chin as he considered the chessboard, but he did smile. "Grace is with Victoria, helping with the new baby."

Kayla clapped her hands in delight. "Oh, Marshal. How wonderful! Did you and Victoria have a boy or a girl?"

"A girl," Matthew replied. "Fat and pink and healthy. Named her Clara after Victoria's mama."

"Clara is a beautiful name. Is Victoria well?" A silly question, she realized. Victoria had always made it quite clear that she and her husband were deeply in love. If Victoria was having any problems after giving birth, he would no doubt be at her side.

"Quite well, thank you. So what brings you to town?"

"Since it was warm, I wished to get out of the house. Those four walls were beginning to be a bit stifling."

Both men laughed in response, most likely because they understood the problem well.

"It might also be prudent to restock our supplies," she added, "and I seek a Christmas gift for Drake…er Mr. Myers." She doubted either Matthew or Adam would let her slip go by without at least taking mental note of the familiar use of his name.

But did they hear the affection behind that name?

Hang it, anyway. No doubt the gossips in the town were having quite a bit of fun in speculating the connection between her and Drake. They could all call her "harlot" for all she cared. Matthew, Adam, and their wives were friends, and Kayla would never be able to hide everything from them. She wouldn't waste concern over what they did and did not know.

"If you'll excuse me," she said. "I need to complete my errands. You gentlemen enjoy your game."

Matthew stood and moved close to her side. "Before you go, I wanted you to know…there have been more telegraph messages that might be for you."

Ice ran through her veins, banishing any warmth the fire had provided. She swallowed hard and fought the strong urge to bolt. "From Reverend Hayes again?" Not that she'd believed that charade for one moment.

"Not this time. Comin' from a man claimin' to be a Pinkerton detective. Says he's in St. Louis, looking for Carolyn Burton. He seemed convinced that she'd come here, to White Pines. Are you sure there's no chance someone you know is searching for you? Family? Friends?"

She shook her head, hoping her fear didn't show.

"Carolyn Burton and Kayla Backer." He shrugged. "Figured it might just be a mistake in the name."

"I am *not* Carolyn Burton," she insisted, her tone angry. Lying was so against her nature, but she had come so far and risked so much to escape. Now that she felt at home here, she was terrified of Chantal Carrington taking everything away. Again. Kayla didn't want Gregory in her life any longer, and she wouldn't ever return to New York City. The only reason for Chantal to pursue her was for vengeance—a Carrington trademark.

The marshal didn't seem to take offense to her snapping at him. "Figured as much, judging from how adamant you were last time we talked. I went right head and told them they were barkin' up the wrong tree. If they try again, I'll give 'em the same message. They'll eventually get the hint."

"Thank you," she said, her voice barely above a whisper.

Matthew gave her a concerned frown as he put a gentle hand on her arm. "Miss Kayla, if there's something wrong, if that detective means you harm…. Well, I wanna help you."

On those words, Adam rose to come to her other side. "We protect our own," he said in a firm, strong voice. "You're among family here." His hand settled on her other arm.

"Drew asked us to keep an eye out for you while he and Gideon were away," the marshal added. "But we'd do the same even if they were here."

Humbled at their support, something she had no idea she'd earned, she nodded.

"My Gracie had a bit of trouble following her here," Adam said rather matter-of-factly. "Matthew and I can help you—if you trust us."

"Can you maybe guess what this detective might want?" Matthew coaxed.

The bell above the door rang, and Kayla glanced up, grateful for the interruption. While the marshal might've said he would support her, he also clearly believed that she knew something about all the messages he'd received. He was too much of a gentleman to come right out and call her a liar right to her face, but the implication was there. Evidently Adam was of similar mind.

When she saw Drake, she couldn't help but smile. While knowing that Matthew and Adam were on her side was comforting, she wanted—*needed*—Drake. It took all her self-control not to run to him and demand he hold her until her fear disappeared.

Wouldn't the town gossips love that *little scene?*

One look at Kayla's face, and Drake frowned. Something was wrong, a notion that was confirmed by the way Matthew Riley and Adam Morgan seemed to be offering her comfort. As he jerked off his thick, leather gloves, he hurried to where the three stood by the pot-bellied stove.

When her gaze caught his, he knit his brows. "What's wrong?"

"I shall explain later." Her voice dropped to a mere whisper. "It's about what we...discussed, about Carolyn Burton."

Drake had to bite his tongue to keep her secret, a tough thing to do since Matthew Riley and Adam Morgan were good men who were clearly concerned about Kayla. Someone was damned anxious to find her, and he was pretty sure he knew who.

Her past might be catching up with her, and he wasn't sure what to do to protect her. Instinct made him want to bundle her up and get her back to the farm, to hide her away and hope the Carringtons and all their money couldn't reach all the way to Montana.

But he wasn't that naïve. Their power and fortune could find Kayla anywhere. If he was going to help her, he needed her to tell him more about what happened—to tell him everything. And he needed allies.

Judging from the uneasiness he saw very clearly coming from Matthew and Adam, they might be a good place to start.

Kayla hurried to his side, and her eyes were entreating him to take her into his arms. While that was exactly what he wanted to do, he resisted temptation. That last thing in the world she needed was more gossip. He wasn't about to add to the trouble dogging at her heels by making her the target of every busybody in town. But the need to comfort her was nearly overwhelming.

"How you doin', Drake?" Matthew asked as he and Adam took seats on opposite sides of the cracker barrel. From the looks of it, they had been in the middle of a chess game.

"Doin' fine, Marshal. Any news from town since last time we visited?" Not very subtle, but Drake was nearly frantic with wanting to know what had made Kayla so worried.

Before he replied, Matthew glanced around the shop as though being sure there weren't any prying ears around to hear. "Been a few of those telegraphs from a Pinkerton detective. Says he's from St. Louis and lookin' for a Carolyn Burton. Wonderin' if maybe they're confusing her with our Miss Kayla. We might wanna be keepin' an eye out around Gideon's place."

"Might be a good thing there's been so much snow," Adam added. "Discourages anyone from following those messages with a personal visit."

"Who d'ja think I should be lookin' for?" Drake asked.

After moving a pawn, Matthew turned to stare at him. "According to the telegraphs, a Pinkerton might be turnin' up around the farm, lookin' for a Kayla and thinking that our Kayla is who they're after. Got yourself a shotgun?"

Drake nodded. "Got a revolver, too."

With a bit of a grin, the marshal returned to his game. "A shame there's not a way for you to call us if you need us," he remarked.

"Maybe someday we shall all have telegraph lines to our homes," Kayla said.

"For now," Drake said, "we'll keep our guard up."

* * *

The snow began again not long after they got home, and Kayla let out a sigh, knowing it might be quite some time before they were able to head back into town. Just being in White Pines had cured some of the restlessness that had settled on her at being confined to the farm. Now that she knew Chantal Carrington wasn't going to give up in her search, Kayla saw that isolation as a comfort. If she couldn't leave the farm, then it would be difficult for anyone to travel here.

While Drake was busy tending to the horse and sleigh, she tried to find a good place to hide the small present she'd purchased for him. He hadn't made acquiring the gift easy, because he'd been her shadow for the majority of the time they'd been in town. Only when he'd gone to fetch the horse had she been able to quickly complete her purchase. Thankfully, she'd been able to spirit the gift into the other packages without him seeing.

Since he rarely went into Drew and Gideon's room, she put the present in one of the drawers of Drew's bureau and then headed back to her room to remove the multiple layers of clothes. Once dressed more appropriately, she went to the kitchen to put the supplies away and prepare a nice, hot meal.

* * *

Drake poured an extra scoop of grain into Rusty's feed bucket—a proper reward for the animal deigning to pull a sleigh all the way to White Pines and back. As usual, the horse had been well-behaved.

After giving Rusty a few affectionate strokes, Drake closed the barn doors to spare the animals the wind that had begun to gust. If his instincts were correct—and they usually were—more snow was on the way. Probably not another blizzard, but surely enough to keep him and Kayla isolated on the farm.

Good.

In fact, what he wanted most was to keep her here and hide her from the world. Especially from the Carringtons.

He frowned as he thought about all she'd told him about her past. She'd been betrothed to a man who made Drake look like a pauper. Hell, Gregory Carrington made every other man on the continent seem poor in comparison. But Drake couldn't help but worry that Kayla would think that he had little to offer her for a comfortable future.

Future?

What right did he have to even *think* about making what was happening between them something more permanent? Yet he did think about it. Often. Now that they were lovers, he couldn't help but wonder if she might grow to feel the same. Kayla wasn't a woman who would give herself to a man without genuine emotions being involved.

That gave Drake pause. Did she care for him?

Yes, he was sure she did.

Could she learn to love him?

Love?

What in the hell was wrong with him?

Grumbling to himself at the foolishness his thoughts had been traveling, he stomped his way back to the house. The wonderful aroma of whatever Kayla was cooking greeted him the moment he opened the door. As he began to unwind the scarf wrapped around his face, he smiled when she came hurrying over to help him out of his coat.

"You must be freezing." She took the coat and hung it on a peg. "I have a hot meal ready."

"Thank you, Kayla." Drake shed his gloves and tossed them aside. "I'm starvin'." Before she could grab them and spread them by the fire as she usually did, he caught her hand and pulled her close. Then he gave her a no-nonsense kiss on the forehead, knowing that if he started kissing her in earnest, he wouldn't be satisfied until he could take her to bed. "Don't let those telegraphs worry you."

She frowned. "We both know that Chantal Carrington is the one sending the Pinkertons looking for me."

"Why do you think she'd do that? I mean, you left, which is what she wanted, right?"

After thinking it over, she finally said, "Chantal is known for destroying anyone she deems a threat, especially to Gregory. Perhaps she fears that so long as I'm alive, Gregory may try to find me and marry me, silly though that theory sounds."

"Not so silly." What man would voluntarily give up someone as beautiful and smart as Kayla? "Not so silly at all." His stomach let out a loud rumble, which gave him a good reason to change the subject before she could ask him to explain himself.

A smile bloomed as she inclined her head toward the table. "Seeing as you are clearly ravenous, shall we eat?"

"Yes, ma'am!"

* * *

Kayla grabbed the book and took a seat on the sofa. As he usually did once supper was ended, Drake sat next to her and waited for her to read to him.

Tonight, he was yawning. Not a surprise after such a long day. Before she opened the book, she patted her lap. "Perhaps you might wish to lay your head down and rest your eyes as I read our next chapter?"

The look he gave her told her that was exactly what he wanted to do.

So why did he hesitate?

"The story will be more enjoyable if you make yourself comfortable."

"You don't mind?"

"I would not have invited you to do so if I minded," she replied.

Turning, he stretched his legs out and placed his head against her thighs. Then he let out a contented sigh.

She couldn't help but smile in response. Before she opened the book, she combed her fingers through his hair. "As I mentioned before, you should let me cut your hair, Drake. It is far too long to be fashionable."

He snorted. "I don't give a fig about fashion. I like my hair just fine."

"I do too," she said, stopping herself before she blurted out the reason. He probably knew she nurtured a growing affection for him. He didn't need her to tell him exactly how attractive she found him and how she liked the rugged length of his hair.

After finding the proper place in the story, she held the book in her right hand as she rested the other on his stomach.

With another sigh, Drake lifted her left hand and cradled it in his as she began to read.

She didn't finish three full pages before he fell asleep.

Knowing he wouldn't want her to keep reading and miss part of the story, Kayla closed the book and set it aside. Then she stared down at Drake.

The man had turned her world upside down, but she didn't regret meeting him for one moment. When she'd been forced to flee New York City and then St. Louis, she'd resigned herself to a future that was out of her control. She'd traveled here, ready to make a man she didn't even know her husband. But that man, Caleb Young, had taken another woman to wife, someone he'd mistakenly believed was Kayla.

With no other prospects and alone in an unknown town full of strangers, Kayla had panicked. Thankfully, two Prince Charmings stepped forward to offer her a home, and she'd come to work for Caleb's brother Gideon and his lover Drew Pearson. Although she enjoyed living with the two men and keeping their house, she still felt as though she had no control over her life.

All she'd ever wanted was a home of her own. When she confessed that to Drew, he and Gideon had decided to build her one. That was how the handsome man sleeping so peacefully on her lap had become a part of her world.

What Kayla hadn't confessed to Drew—to anyone but Gregory, actually— was that she wanted a family. A husband. Children. While there were plenty of prospective spouses in and around White Pines, she'd wanted nothing to do with the rough-and-tumble sort of men that were drawn to Montana.

Until she met Drake.

It was hard to admit to herself that she'd developed feelings for a man who had no intention of ever settling down. Yet she could no longer deny that she was falling for him, and God help her, she had no idea how she was going to cope when he finished building her home and went back to herding cattle.

I shall be fine. I shall have a home of my own.

Those words of affirmation seemed a bit hollow now.

Kayla stroked his cheek, loving how he'd allowed his whiskers to grow for several days. They no longer rubbed roughly against her skin, instead feeling soft to the touch. In that moment, she decided that come what may, she'd use whatever time they had together to grab hold of all the good memories she could. They would make love, they would celebrate each day, and when the time came for him to go, she would hold firm to her resolve to set him free.

There was only one complication left to consider. Should she wind up with child, she wouldn't use that baby to hold onto him. Instead, she would love the child and be grateful to always have a part of Drake with her.

Hideaway

She laid her head back against the sofa and let sleep claim her, that vow clearly in her mind.

Chapter Twenty

Drake woke while it was still dark. The fire had burned low, so he slipped out of bed to crouch by the hearth and add a couple of logs from the stockpile to be sure Kayla stayed warm. A glance back assured him she was still sleeping, and he figured he'd let her keep dreaming for a bit since it was Christmas Day.

Rising, he went to stand by the bed. The soft firelight always made her skin appear golden, and the worry lines that often framed her eyes were gone. The news that she was still being tracked had disturbed her greatly, and he was at a loss on what to do to make that threat disappear. All he could do was shelter her and try to keep the rest of the world at bay.

Her eyes fluttered open. Then a slow smile filled her face. "Happy Christmas."

Leaning in, he brushed a kiss on her lips. "Happy Christmas, darlin'."

"What time is it?" she asked.

He shrugged. "A bit before dawn, I think."

As he started to move away, Kayla twined her arms around his neck and pulled him closer. "Come back to bed?"

Drake grinned. "If I do that, we're not gonna sleep."

"That would be my fondest desire." She tugged him harder.

Sprawling over Kayla, he kissed her, a long deep exchange of tongues that quickly made him hard. When he eased back, he was pleased to see passion reflected in her eyes. What he shared with her was so different than anything else he'd ever known, and it suddenly dawned on him that he would never enjoy this kind of closeness again with another woman.

Because he was falling for her.

Before he could react to that startling thought, she eased herself from under him and got to her feet. She whipped her sleeping gown over her head and set it aside.

His mouth went dry. Scrambling out of his long johns, he pulled the covers back and knelt on the mattress.

Kayla came to him then, kneeling in front of him as she looped her arms around his neck and pressed her breasts against his chest.

In recognizing how he felt about her, Drake found freedom. He might not be able to tell her—might never be able to let her know of his love—but he could *show* her. Although she deserved a good man, one who could give her all that she'd lost in fleeing the Carringtons, he had her now. He could hold her in his arms and make love to her, and he intended to enjoy every moment of their time together before he lost her.

There was something in Drake's touch that made Kayla wonder what had changed. He seemed desperate, his kiss so full of need that she couldn't help but respond in kind.

How much time did they have left together?

Probably not enough to satisfy her. She refused to waste a moment of it.

He was raining kisses down her throat as he covered her breasts with his rough palms. Easing to his side, he followed his hands with his mouth, drawing a sensitive nipple between his lips.

Kayla raked her fingers through his hair, trying not to pull too hard as she writhed beneath him. The suction he used seemed to reach all the way to her toes, and she could feel the familiar knot of pleasure building inside her.

A little mewl of disappointment slipped out when he moved away from her. That soft sound was replaced with a startled squeak when he separated her thighs and kissed her core. Moving to put himself between her legs, he lavished her with attention, his tongue drilling inside her and then stroking her sensitive nub until she thought she would go mad.

"Now, Drake. Please."

He refused her plea, instead increasing his attention until everything inside her burst, sending ecstasy racing through her. But he gave her no quarter, forcing her body to tighten again before he rose above her and thrust himself inside her. Feeling him buried so deeply, she shattered again, this time calling his name as the waves of pleasure washed over her. He joined her in release a few moments later, pushing into her one last time as he let out a satisfied gasp that made her smile.

Coming back to earth was slow, and Kayla loved the relaxed feeling that always came when he loved her—a peace of body and of mind that made her wish the rest of the world would simply pass them by. Here, in his arms, she'd found happiness.

And her past might snatch it away.

That thought rapidly cooled her blood, and when he rolled away from her, she jerked the covers up, trying to stop her shivers.

As always, Drake was aware of her changing moods. "What's wrong?"

She shook her head, not wanting to ruin the moment. "I should start preparing that goose as soon as chores are done. It was such a large bird, and Grace taught me that the larger the animal, the longer it should roast." Kayla pictured the goose Drake had shot—one clean bullet through the head—and worried about how long it would take to prepare. "Perhaps the hens and cow can wait until I can get the goose over the fire."

"I'll do your chores today," he offered. "You can consider the morning to cook our Christmas meal my gift to you. Although…" He jumped out of bed and knelt next to the bed. Then he lifted the mattress and reached under it, pulling out a package wrapped in brown paper and tied with twine. "I did get you this." He laid the package on her lap after she sat up to lean against the headboard.

"I did not expect a gift." She'd planned to present his at dinner, but now she wondered if she should hurry to retrieve it.

"Didn't say you did," he insisted. "Got this 'cause I know you needed it."

Pulling the string on the package, she untied it and then opened the brown paper to find thick, pink cloth. Wool, no doubt.

"You can use it to make yourself some long johns. Some for a woman. You know, to keep your legs warm."

"How romantic," she teased before giving him a quick kiss. "This was very thoughtful. I shall enjoy not having the wind whip up my skirts when I work outside." She brushed another kiss on his lips.

"I wish…" Drake let out a weighty sigh.

Kayla cupped his face in her hand. "What do you wish, love?"

"I wish I could buy you somethin' pretty. Earrings. A broach." He put his hand over hers. "I'd buy you diamonds." He looked away. "If I could."

She turned his face back so she could see his eyes. "Diamonds do not buy happiness. The beautiful fabric you gave me is much more useful and will surely give me more comfort than some silly, shiny stones."

All he did was nod, and she knew she hadn't soothed him. With a sigh of her own, she glanced to the window. "We should rise, even though the sun has yet to show its face." On her feet, she shivered before glancing back at him. "Happy Christmas, Drake."

"Happy Christmas, Kayla."

* * *

Drake pushed back from the table, stuffed and growing sleepy. "That was a mighty fine Christmas meal, Kayla." For someone who'd come from a privileged background, she'd become quite well-versed in farm life. Whether she was cooking or tending the livestock, she seemed comfortable and never once complained about everything she needed to do.

Kayla favored him with a beguiling smile. "Why, thank you kindly, Drake. I fear I should give the credit to Grace Morgan, though. She taught me how to cook everything." A yawn slipped out. "Pardon me," she ground out before another yawn overtook her. "How rude of me."

He let out a chuckle. "You mean yawnin'? Shit— Um…shoot. No need to apologize."

"Seems impolite to yawn so openly. I am simply too tired to stop myself."

"Of course, you're tired. I am too. Days are short, and we both work hard. After stuffin' myself with that great meal, I wanna loosen my belt, put my feet up, and sleep for a spell." After glancing to the kitchen, he frowned. "How about we put the food up, then save cleaning the dishes for later? We can take a short nap to get our energy back, then we'll tackle the kitchen."

"While that sounds tempting"—she cast a glance at the mess—"I really cannot leave everything so untidy."

On his feet, Drake picked up the platter with the remaining slices of goose. "Sure you can. We'll sit by the fire and nap on the sofa."

Kayla followed, still frowning.

As though to change her expression, he gave her a kiss. "It's Christmas. What harm can it to do save the work for just a bit?"

"I'm not sure… The kitchen is so disorderly."

"Who's gonna see it?"

She finally smiled and nodded. "Fine. We shall do things your way."

* * *

Drake was dragged out of sleep by a noise. What noise, he wasn't sure. But something wasn't right. A moment later, footsteps echoed from the porch.

On his feet in a heartbeat, he couldn't spare the time to worry about the fact that he'd all but knocked Kayla off his shoulder in his haste to get to the shotgun he kept close to the door.

Someone was here. No doubt some varmints from town thinking to catch them unawares. As the doorknob turned, Drake signaled to Kayla.

She obeyed his direction, quickly scrambling to move. She crouched near the sofa and waited, her anxious eyes flitting between the door and Drake.

The door slowly creaked, and he used the advantage of surprise to snatch it open. "Hold it right there!"

The man stepped back, eyes wide as he showed his hands to reveal that he held no weapon. Then he grinned. "That's quite a welcome home."

"Jesus have mercy." Drake lowered the weapon, shaken at what could've happened if he hadn't recognized the person who stood in the doorway. "What in the hell are you doing, Gideon?"

Chapter Twenty-One

Kayla let out a surprised gasp. "Gideon! You're home!" Then she looked past him, expecting to see Drew close on his heels. She was confused when all Gideon did was close the door behind him. "Where is Drew?"

Gideon shook his head. While he was typically a man of few words, the tightness of his expression told her he didn't want to talk about what had him returning to Montana on his own.

Was the hesitation because of his usual aloofness, or was he wanting to speak to her without Drake overhearing? Either way, she would follow his example and respect his desire to leave the question hanging.

He glanced to the kitchen and frowned. "Appears that a storm went roaring through here."

Kayla's cheeks heated. She went first to give Gideon a hug—one that seemed awkward for the first time since he and Drew had taken her in—and then hurried toward the kitchen. "I shall put things to right," she called over her shoulder. "After our Christmas meal, we were both so sleepy, and…" She whirled back around. "Heavens, I forgot to wish you a Happy Christmas, Gideon."

He simple grunted and inclined his head in acknowledgment.

"We took a nap," Drake said with a shrug.

"I shall not let this happen again," she assured Gideon.

Drake rubbed the back of his neck, feeling more than a little nervous that Gideon's stare had shifted from the messy kitchen to him. That gaze seemed accusatory—or was that simply his own guilty conscience?

"Didn't see smoke coming from the loft's chimney." Gideon folded his arms over his chest. "Gotta be damn cold sleepin' out there without a fire."

A pan clattered to the floor. "Pardon," Kayla said, clearly flustered.

Gideon scowled in her direction before glaring at Drake again.

The tight-lipped frown directed at him made him fidget. He couldn't have felt more uncomfortable if Gideon had accused him of raping her.

"You and me need to have a talk. *Now*." Gideon inclined his head at the door.

Drake grabbed his coat from where it hung by the door. "I was just headin' out to do evening chores."

"Think I'll join you."

Drake made his way to the barn, looking back at his "shadow" and hoping he would survive this ordeal. He shoved the barn door open with his shoulder. The last thing in the world he wanted was to have Gideon following him, especially since the man was probably going to start in on questions about Kayla.

He tried to dissuade Gideon by turning the topic. "Is Drew stayin' with his family a bit longer? Gotta say I was surprised to see you here without him. Was his mother—"

The word was cut off when Gideon fisted his hands in Drake's coat and pinned him against a stall. "You bastard. I oughta beat the life outta you!"

Although Drake felt the guilty heat on his cheeks, he refused to kiss and tell. "Don't know what you're talkin' about."

"The hell you don't. I checked the loft before I came in the house. You ain't been stayin' out here. Not for a long time."

"I've been sleepin' in the house," Drake said, before a loud huff spilled out when Gideon shoved him harder against the stall.

"In her bed, you son of a bitch. I told Drew this would happen. I knew you couldn't leave her alone. You fuckin' bastard. I oughta—"

"Gideon!" Kayla's soft voice came from behind Gideon's hulking, angry frame. "Release him. Now."

"I'm gonna whup him 'til he admits the truth," Gideon insisted. It was the first time Drake could remember when the man didn't immediately jump to Kayla's command.

Not that Drake could blame him. At that moment, he felt as though he deserved a good beating. He'd taken her innocence and given her no promises for the future.

He *was* a bastard.

"I told you to release him." There was steel in her voice, which was probably why Gideon obeyed.

"Has he been in your bed?" Gideon asked, blunt as always.

"He has," she replied. Her voice was clear and confident, but her face was crimson. "Not that anything that happens between Mr. Myers and myself is anyone's business but our own."

Gideon shook his head before shooting a threatening glare at Drake. "You sneakin' son of a bitch. I'll—"

Kayla stopped him by holding up her hand. "I would appreciate it greatly if you would stop cursing. And I believe I told you to release him."

His eyes widened. "He was s'posed to be watchin' out for you, not takin' advantage of you. He was s'posed to keep you safe."

"He did exactly that," she said. "There was a break-in, you see, and—"

"*What?*" Gideon finally let Drake go. His explosion startled the plow horse that had stuck its head over the gate, probably to check on all the commotion. "What in the hell happened?"

Drake was the one to reply. "Couple of lowlifes from town figured she was up here all alone. Broke a window and snuck in the house, plannin' to haul her off."

"Mr. Myers handled that altercation well." Kayla gave him a hesitant smile. "He was even kind enough to replace the broken window pane."

Gideon's frown showed he was less than impressed. "So you thank him by sleepin' with him?"

As Kayla let out an indignant gasp, Drake reacted to the crude question by punching Gideon in the nose. As Gideon put his hands to his face, Drake tried to shake the sting out of his gloved hand.

"Don't you dare talk about her like that!" Damn, but he wondered if he'd broken a bone in his hand.

Kayla hurried to Gideon. "Are you all right?"

He swept her aside with his arm and stood to his full height. Blood trickled from one nostril.

"Drake," she said calmly, "could you please allow Gideon and me a moment of privacy?"

Although he was hesitant to leave them alone, Drake finally nodded. Perhaps she would be able to explain the situation in a way that would keep Gideon from tossing him out on his ear. God knew Gideon couldn't condemn him any more than Drake already condemned himself.

With a nod, he left them and headed out of the barn.

Pulling a handkerchief she'd embroidered from her pocket, she stood on tiptoes to wipe the blood from Gideon's nose. Thankfully, he allowed her to care for him instead of flinching away as she'd expected.

He mumbled his thanks, took the handkerchief, and held it against his nose as she stepped back.

"Gideon…" Kayla took a steadying breath, preparing for the conversation she'd dreaded but had always known would come as soon as Gideon and Drew returned. While she knew both of them would eventually guess what had happened, she'd hoped to discuss things with Drew's romantic nature there to help curb Gideon's inevitable anger.

Gideon started the interrogation. "How could you let that bast—"

She shot him a fierce frown.

"—that *varmint* seduce you? I thought you were smarter than that."

She winced. That hurt, probably more than he would ever know. While it would have been easier to place the blame on Drake, she refused to let the rift between them stand. "You are quite mistaken."

He arched one dark eyebrow.

"Mr. Myers…" Since it seemed silly to try to be formal considering the circumstances, she continued. "Drake did not seduce me."

Gideon snorted before wiping away a few more drops of blood.

"Truth be told, *I* seduced *him*."

At least he looked properly stunned by her announcement.

"Now that you're home, I'm sure our affair is over. I won't carry on so with you and Drew back at home." She released a sigh. "I'm sure he would've grown tired of me soon anyway." She immediately wished the words back. They sounded far too much as though she were feeling sorry for herself. That wouldn't come until later, when she watched Drake ride away from her and never return.

"Why Kayla? Why him?"

Gideon's question only made her shake her head. How could she possibly give him an answer when she didn't truly understand herself?

"There's been so many men from town who'd marry you," Gideon said. "You turned 'em all down. Then you…"—he cleared his throat—"with him. He ain't gonna marry you."

"I know that," she snapped. "I'm well aware that Drake is not the marrying kind."

"And yet you…" He shook his head.

"Please, Gideon. This conversation is difficult enough. There is no need to remind me of my foolishness." She caught his eyes, trying to will him to understand that the hopelessness of her situation wasn't something she wanted to focus upon. "Please let this go."

His gaze searched her, then his features softened. "You love him."

Tears stung her eyes as she nodded.

"A foolish thing to do." Gideon shook his head and let his hand fall away from his face.

"My heart is far less wise than my head."

"That's true for most of us."

"I do not wish for Drake to know of my feelings," she insisted.

"Why not? He might marry you if you told him."

She only shook her head. The last thing in the world she wanted Drake to feel for her was obligation. If he decided to stay—which was as likely as the moon falling out of the sky—she wouldn't let him do so because he felt guilty about anything that had passed between them.

"He won't stay. You know that as well as I do. Once that blasted house of yours is done… He'll move on."

With a heaved sigh, Kayla nodded. Gideon was only giving her the hard truth she'd already faced. But hearing it said aloud was painful.

"What if… There might be a…" He took her gloved hand in his as his eyes shifted to the floor. "What if he leaves you with child?"

"I am sure that should such an event happen, I will handle things quite well on my own."

Gideon's brows knit when his eyes caught hers again. "If that happens, he should stay."

"I will not use a child to tie a man to me, especially one who has no desire to be tied down."

"You mean you wouldn't tell him?"

"Absolutely not. A child would be a burden to Drake. No, should I…conceive, I can manage to raise a child alone. I have no doubt of it."

"Kayla…"

"On this, I must insist. I hope you will honor my wishes."

Several emotions played across his face before the intensity of his expression eased. Then he pulled her into one of his bear hugs. "You ain't gonna be alone. You got me."

"And Drew, no doubt," Kayla said as she eased out of his arms.

His resulting frown the moment she mentioned Drew worried her.

"Why did you come back alone? Did Drew desire more time with his family?"

"His family. Bunch of dandies." Gideon shook his head. "Treated me like a leper."

She could see in her mind's eye how people close to Drew might view him arriving to attend his mother with another man in tow. "I dare say that most people, especially family Drew has not seen in years, have little understanding of what you and Drew share. I take it they were…unkind."

"They were horses' asses, that's what they were. Couldn't take it no more, so I came home."

"I see. And then, when you were already angered, you discovered that Drake and I had become close. That had to be a surprise."

A scoff slipped from his lips. "An understatement, if I ever heard one."

"You must be weary, Gideon. Shall we return to the house? I will warm up some of the Christmas goose, and you can get some rest."

He kissed her forehead. "Thank you kindly, Kayla."

"I'm happy you are home safe and sound. I am quite sure that Drew will be following close behind. The two of you belong together."

* * *

Drake paced the length of the sitting room yet again, waiting for Gideon and Kayla to return from their conversation. From Gideon's strong reaction, there was only one thing that was clear.

Gideon wouldn't allow him to continue sleeping at Kayla's side.

That thought made something inside Drake lurch. It hadn't occurred to him until that moment exactly how much he looked forward to being with her each night, to being able to hold her close.

He loved the way she always snuggled up against him, how she seemed to fit perfectly in the curve of his arm. Knowing that he might never enjoy that intimacy with her again soured his already nasty mood.

Funny, but it dawned on him that he was more concerned with losing her companionship than the fact they would probably not be able to make love to her any longer. Not that he wouldn't miss that. He would. Tremendously. It was only that he'd grown to need her with him all the time, not just when he wanted to touch her.

A glance to the kitchen showed that Kayla had hurried to intervene between him and Gideon and hadn't had a chance to finish cleaning up. Since he had no idea how long they'd be out in the barn talking things out, Drake figured he might as well get the pans washed and put away. At least he'd found something to do to keep his mind occupied.

As he scrubbed the last pot, the door opened and Kayla came inside with Gideon close behind. Drake rinsed the pot and dried it as they hung up their coats. He was conflicted over hearing about what had been decided in their conversation. Would he be banished to the barn or would he have to head back to town? Depended on Gideon's anger, he supposed.

She favored him with a smile that did little to ease his worries. "Thank you so much for completing my chores. You will be pleased to know that Gideon and I also made sure your evening tasks with the animals were done."

"Thank you both." Setting the dish cloth aside, Drake slowly went to her, keeping an eye on Gideon in case the man wanted to inflict a little more retaliation for what had happened while he'd been away.

With a smile still on her beautiful face, she took Drake's hand and tugged him closer. "Gideon and I have had a nice discussion about the situation in which we all find ourselves. He will keep our secret, but..."

"But what?"

"You're sleepin' in the barn now," Gideon said. His narrowed eyes still spoke of anger, but at least Drake could still work on the house.

Kayla's house. The one where she wanted to live a solitary life.

Without me.

Obviously, there would be no more privacy, and that made Drake concerned. If he couldn't even whisper to Kayla without Gideon overhearing and commenting, there would be no way they could make love. Heaven knew she could be vocal when she found her pleasure, and any such noises coming from the barn would bring Gideon running, probably thinking he was defending her.

She squeezed his hand in return. "Will you allow me to me make you some supper, Gideon? We had a nice Christmas goose."

"Thanks, but no," he replied. "I'm tuckered out. Gonna enjoy sleeping in a warm bed tonight. It was a long, cold ride."

"I built a fire for you," Drake said, rubbing the back of his neck. His relationship with Gideon and Drew had always been friendly. Seeing the accusation in Gideon's eyes hurt, making him feel like he'd taken advantage of Kayla.

Which you might have, his thoughts accused. The two of them had been stuck with each other's company, and they were, after all, a man and a woman with the needs and desires of any healthy adult.

But she wanted me.

An inexperienced woman like Kayla probably had no true idea of what she'd gotten herself into by taking a lover. Drake should've known better.

"Good night," Gideon said. "Thanks for the fire," he said with a nod to Drake. Then he headed down the hall. A few moments later, the door was loudly closed, leaving Drake alone with Kayla.

Kayla gave Drake's hand a squeeze. "I worry about you. The barn is so cold. Perhaps you should stay in the house tonight. You could sleep on the sofa, by the fire."

He was shaking his head before she even finished. "I'll be fine. We're in a warm spell. I'll get a fire goin'. I'll be plenty warm."

After a long sigh, she nodded. "It isn't right, you know."

"What ain't right?"

"Us having to be apart." Her eyes rose to capture his. "Your place is at my side."

Her last words hit Drake with the power of a blow to the chest, probably because the more time he spent with her, the more he wished he could tell everyone that she belonged to him.

Even though his heart was ready to claim her, his head always overruled that notion. Only if and when he could give her everything she deserved would he let her know how much he loved her.

Chapter Twenty-Two

Drake was pleased to finish the last interior wall of Kayla's house the next afternoon. After leaning it against the other assembled pieces, he knew the break in the weather wasn't going to last. He would have to take advantage of every temperate day to make some real progress on putting her house together.

He'd gotten much more than he'd expected done since Gideon and Drew had left, and he hoped they appreciated how seriously he was taking this job. Their approval wasn't his main motivation, though. This house meant the world to Kayla, which made it mean the world to him as well.

"You get that under a roof," Gideon said as he strode toward Drake, "you can probably get it done by spring."

"That's my plan," Drake replied. "Sent word to Caleb and Ty to come help me get the walls up and the roof on. They're s'posed to come out here tomorrow. Care to join us? Four pairs of hands, we can really make some progress."

Gideon nodded.

Although Drake hadn't spent much time with Gideon before he and Drew had left on their trip, he'd learned enough about Gideon to know that he was a man of few words. In fact, the fight they'd had over Kayla probably saw more words exchanged than Gideon had uttered in all the rest of the time Drake had been around him. So as he went about cleaning up the discarded pieces of wood, hoping to turn them into shims to use while putting the house together, he wasn't surprised when Gideon began to help without speaking.

Working in silence, they were able to not only get the construction mess put to right, but they also knocked out the afternoon chores in record speed. It wasn't until Drake was closing the barn door behind them that Gideon finally broke the stillness. "I'm gonna order some plumbing. You know, for Kayla."

"Plumbing?"

"At Drew's family home, they had everything indoors."

"Everything?" Drake cocked his head. "You mean..."

"No outhouse or chamber pots for them. Nope. They had a terlet."

"But what happens to the shit? I mean, somebody has to empty that thing, right?"

Gideon shook his head.

"Then where's it go?"

"Goes down some pipe. Just yank a chain, and it's gone."

Plucking his hat from his head, Drake chuckled. "Ain't that somethin'?"

"Had a tub with hot water. Kept it in a big tank. Only had to light the fire and then let the water spill into the tub."

"No foolin'?"

Gideon shook his head.

After raking his fingers through his hair, Drake flopped his hat back on his head. As hard as that was to imagine, he loved the idea of Kayla being able to enjoy a warm bath without the laborious chore of boiling water on the stove and carrying it to the wooden tub. "I think she'd like that."

"Heard Adam Morgan has a setup like it."

"Well, then, I'll ask where he bought the supplies, and we'll get Kayla all fixed up."

"Thanks," Gideon said. "We get that roof up, it'll give us time to work on the walls, windows, and such while we wait for the pipes to arrive."

Drake glanced to the home site. "Was thinkin' about other things we could add. Modern things."

"Like what?"

Drake shifted his gaze to Gideon, reluctant to ask for anything too fancy. While Drake wanted Kayla to have the very best, he had to remember that Gideon and Drew were footing the bill for everything to do with the house. But since Gideon had been willing to bear the cost of a heated tub, perhaps what Drake wanted for her wasn't too far-fetched. "I s'pose it depends on how fancy you wanna get. I heard that slate makes better roofing than wood shake."

Gideon pulled his lips into a tight line, revealing nothing of what he thought of the suggestion.

"Thought coal stoves might be warmer than hearths, too."

"Might be warmer, but gettin' the coal… Wood's mighty handy and we got plenty of it."

"Then wood it is," Drake said, pleased that Gideon seemed to be taking his suggestions seriously, even if he'd vetoed one of them.

"Let's go with the slate," Gideon said. "I think I can get that here soon, especially if the weather holds." He squinted against the sun that was beginning to set in the clear sky.

"We've been lucky this winter," Drake commented. "Only snowed in for a short spell, though the winds have been wicked. Kayla wasn't at all used to snow like we get in the Rockies. She's happier when it's as warm as it is now."

"Ain't likely to last. Come January…" Gideon let the thought hang.

Drake nodded, knowing that it went without saying that Montana could be a bitterly cold and snowy place to live in January and February. Even into March and April. "I wanna get the walls up so I can work inside on the house when the snow flies again."

With a clap on Drake's shoulder, Gideon said, "And now you got another pair of helpin' hands. We'll have the house done in no time."

Why did that statement cause Drake's stomach to knot in dread?

Because when that house is done, it'll be time for me to move on.

The more time he spent with Kayla, the more he feared that leaving her behind would be the worst mistake he could ever make. But how could he stay, knowing that she was a woman worthy of a man far above his station in life? She should be married to a man with wealth and power, not a knockabout cowboy, even if he was good with his hands.

He rubbed the back of his neck. "Yeah, we'll definitely have it done by spring."

Gideon cocked an eyebrow.

Aware at how forlorn he'd sounded, Drake just shook his head in reply.

"You still plannin' on headin' outta town when it's built?" Gideon asked.

How was he supposed to answer that question? Of course, he'd always planned to find a new long drive. Now that he was sober, he was sure to catch on with some ranch. There would be no reason for him to hang around White Pines.

But Drake had developed feelings for Kayla, and now he wasn't so sure that the town wouldn't play a new role in his life.

What could he possibly do to make himself worthy of her?

That would require a bit of thought…

"You're good at this, you know." Gideon inclined his head toward the building site. "Damn good."

"Thanks."

"Ever thought about leaving cows behind and doin' this for a living? Lots of people would be willin' to pay a pretty penny for a good house. More people settlin' around here every day." On that intriguing statement, Gideon walked away, a smile on his face.

Drake simply stood there, wondering for the first time if he might have some hope for a new kind of future.

* * *

The next day, Kayla straightened to her full height and groaned. Putting her hand to the small of her back, she rubbed the ache that had developed from all the bending she'd done that day. But a little pain was worth the progress that had been made on her house.

Caleb and Ty had shown up at dawn, followed not long after by the marshal and Jake Curtis, his brother-in-law. The four of them worked with Drake and Gideon, and they'd taken the pieces Drake had made and raised all four outside walls of her house so quickly that she might have missed the construction if she'd blinked. After that, she'd been given the task of pounding nails into floorboards while the men raised a roof over her head.

Now she understood why Drake had spent so much time in the barn. He'd created walls that were easy for the men to put together like an enormous puzzle. Should the men labor as well as they had today, the house would be enclosed in no time. Then Drake could go to work on the interior without having to bow to the weather.

Caleb's voice came from behind her. "Getting a bit stiff?"

Kayla smiled at his teasing. "I dare say I shall feel all this activity whenever I try to move tomorrow."

"Yeah, I'm gonna be sore myself. But we did good, didn't we?"

"You all did wonderfully. I can never thank you enough for your kindness."

"After what you went through 'cause of me…" He doffed his hat and swiped his forehead with the back of his coat sleeve. "I feel like I owe you."

"Oh, Caleb. You cannot still feel guilty. You made an honest mistake, that's all."

"I married the wrong woman." Then he let out a laugh. "Well, I s'pose I married the *right* woman. But you were left alone."

"Look around here." She nodded to where the men were taking a break, talking amongst themselves. "Does it appear as though I'm alone?"

A sigh slipped from him. "But—"

Kayla put a gentle hand on his arm. "Do you know what my father used to tell me whenever something unfortunate happened?"

"Unfortunate? You call comin' all the way to Montana to marry a man to find out he's fool enough to already get married to another woman *unfortunate*?"

"Do you know what he said, Caleb?"

He shook his head.

Smiling, she said, "Everything happens for a reason."

At least she got a grin from him. "What do you think that reason was, Kayla?"

"Why, isn't it quite obvious?" After savoring his confused expression, she said, "A Kayla and a Caleb should never dare to marry. Those names are far too similar. We would be confused all of the time."

Throwing his head back, Caleb laughed.

Kayla let her gaze drift to Drake, and she was surprised to see him staring at her and frowning.

When Caleb ended his bout of laughter, he put his hat back on his head. Then he glanced to where she'd been looking. "So that's the way of it…" He folded his arms over his chest.

How was she supposed to respond to that statement? Trying to hide her feelings for Drake had clearly been an utter failure, at least where Caleb was concerned. From the tone of his voice, she couldn't tell if he was happy for her or condemning her. Her face heated in response.

He frowned. "Don't go leapin' from the fryin' pan into the fire."

"What exactly do you mean?"

"Drake. He's a bit of a…rascal."

She quirked an eyebrow. "Are you saying that I shall be burned, Caleb?"

"His reputation ain't good."

The need to defend Drake was irresistible. "He's changed, you know. In the time he's been working out here, he's changed."

When Caleb continued scowling, it struck her exactly how much he looked like his brother Gideon. "How's he changed?" he asked.

She tempered her response to preserve a little of Drake's privacy. "He has given up spirits, and he spends a great deal of time assuring that the farm runs smoothly. There have been hours and hours of him working on building my new home."

"I see."

Her gaze caught Caleb's. "He is not the same man he was months ago. He's changed."

After he thought things over for a few moments, he nodded. "For your sake, I hope he has."

* * *

Drake had a difficult time concentrating on what Matthew was saying as he watched Kayla talking to Caleb. When she put her hand on Caleb's arm, Drake struggled mightily to keep from marching over there and punching Caleb right in the face.

"Are you listening to a word I'm sayin'?" Annoyance was plain in Matthew's voice.

"Sorry," Drake mumbled. Yet he still couldn't seem to take his eyes off Kayla.

"If she's hidin' something," Matthew said, "I need you to tell me."

The plea in Matthew's words got through to Drake, drawing his full attention. "More trouble in town?"

"Not yet. But the last telegraph message was a lot more insistent," the marshal replied. "The Pinkertons are offering a hefty reward to find this Carolyn Burton." He snorted his derision. "As if those bastards would ever pay up. But if news gets around town…"

Drake took a threatening step toward Matthew. "You told people there's a reward?"

"Of course not. How stupid do you think I am?"

Drake relaxed his stance, although Matthew's knowing, smug expression was inviting a smack upside the head.

"What I'm sayin'," Matthew continued, "is that whoever wants to find her is dead serious. Word ever gets out about the reward, you might have trouble. People won't care that our Kayla ain't the Carolyn they're lookin' for."

God forbid anyone ever finds out she is *Carolyn.*

Gideon fisted his hands against his hips. "A Pinkerton might just show up in White Pines."

"Damn it." Drake's temper kept rising, and panic was starting to set in.

All talk ceased as Kayla and Caleb joined them.

"Gentlemen." She bowed her head before favoring them with an enchanting smile. "I would like to thank you for the hard work you've done for me." As her eyes moved from man to man, her smile faded. "Something's wrong. Is there a problem with the construction?"

Drake took her hand, not caring that the others would see the affection in the gesture. "The Pinkertons are offering a reward to find Carolyn Burton."

The way the blood drained from her face made him worry that she might swoon.

"I'll protect you," Drake whispered.

"It's past time, Kayla," Gideon insisted.

"Time?" She knit her brows.

"To tell us everything. You need more than me and Drew now if you're gonna stay safe."

She winced.

Gideon narrowed his eyes. "What are you hidin' that you ain't even told us?"

"He's right," Drake said with a nod. "Tell them."

Matthew took his hat off and hit it against his thigh. "My patience is done. What in the hell is goin' on here?" His eyes drilled into Kayla. "You're her, ain't ya? The woman they're lookin' for is you." That accusing stare shifted to Drake. "You damn well shoulda told me. How can I help if I don't know what in the hell is goin' on?"

"I… I…" She appeared as frightened as a doe that had scented danger. Then, squeezing Drake's hand, she squared her shoulders. "I am the woman they seek. Carolyn Burton."

Matthew slapped his hat back on his head and stomped around in the muddy yard. "Goddammit! I knew it! I just knew it!" Once his tantrum petered out, the marshal came back to put himself in front of her. Using an imposing glare, he put his hands on his hips. "Start talkin'. *Now*."

"Don't yell at her," Drake ordered. "She's innocent in all this."

"She ain't innocent of lyin' to me."

"I simply wasn't sure whom I could trust," Kayla said.

"You can trust *me*," the marshal said with a decisive nod. "Start with who's hiring the Pinkertons."

The hand holding Drake's was tightly clenched, and it was clear she didn't want to open up.

He leaned closer and whispered, "It's time, darlin'."

She gave him a curt nod and then fixed her attention on Matthew. "I believe the person offering the reward is Chantal Carrington."

Matthew knit his brows. "That name sounds familiar."

"Her late husband was quite wealthy. His family owns Mid-Atlantic Bank."

Gideon let out a low whistle.

"Why do you think it's her?" the marshal asked.

"I was engaged to her son. She…objected. Immensely."

Matthew shook his head. "Doesn't explain why she's after you like a hound on a fox."

"It's a long story."

"Then start tellin' it."

Kayla took a steadying breath, and her courage might have fled had Drake not stepped close enough to her that their arms brushed. Drawing strength from him, she launched into the story. The more she explained what had happened, the more she realized that things with Chantal Carrington were probably going to come to a head soon. The woman seemed desperate to be sure that Kayla was forever removed from her son's life. Didn't she realize that Kayla wanted nothing to do with the man or his money? She considered sending a telegraph to tell her so, but it was clear Chantal would never give up.

Was Gregory forcing Chantal's hand, demanding the resources to find Kayla? Kayla wondered what he thought when she'd suddenly disappeared. Did he think she'd changed her mind? Chantal, no doubt, used Kayla's hasty leave-taking to her strategic advantage.

Perhaps Gregory hadn't given up on Kayla after all… That would explain Chantal's pursuit.

Papa's murder. That had to be why Chantal would hunt her down. Kayla had witnessed her father's murder. Clearly, Chantal had figured that out. Kayla could implicate her and her man-servant and send them to the gallows.

Didn't she realize that Kayla didn't have the courage nor the connections to accuse a Carrington? She'd resigned herself to the fact that her father's murderer would never see justice.

Drake squeezed Kayla close against his side as she finished explaining things to the men. It dawned on her that should she ever see Gregory again, the man would pale in comparison to the handsome cowboy she now loved.

"I assumed that my coming to Montana and changing my name would end her vendetta," Kayla explained. "It would appear that I was dead wrong."

Gideon moved closer, putting his rather intimidating height right in front of her. "You shoulda told us everything, Kayla."

"I'm sorry, Gideon. I will pack my things and leave so that you, Drake, and Drew are no longer in danger. Perhaps California—"

A roar came from Drake. "The hell you will! You're here and you're stayin' here."

All the men nodded vigorously.

Tears stung her eyes as she glanced from Drake to Gideon and then to Matthew. Even Jake Curtis, who barely knew her, had the same resolute expression.

They were going to protect her.

"Thank you." Her voice caught, making the words whispered squeaks. "Thank you all."

Every head suddenly turned to the sound of a horse trotting up the muddy slope.

When Kayla recognized the face, she let out a joyous cry. "Drew! You're home!"

Chapter Twenty-Three

Kayla broke away from Drake, hiked up her skirts, and ran to Drew. She was so focused on him that she was a bit startled to suddenly realize there was a woman riding behind him.

Clearly uncomfortable hugging the back of the saddle, the woman wiggled around until Drew turned his head to say, "Brigit, it seems as though you are ready for our journey to end."

Her reply was muffled by a brown knit scarf that was wrapped around her head and face.

"Perhaps I can convince you to dismount?" he asked with laughter in his voice.

The humor warmed Kayla's heart, and having him back felt wonderful. "I'm so happy you're home!" She reached up to help the woman dismount. Once on her feet, she was a good head taller than Kayla. "Did Drew say your name is Brigit?"

The woman mumbled something against the layers of scarf covering her face as she tried to unwrap herself from the burden.

Kayla pitched in to help, wondering if Brigit was as unaccustomed to the Montana cold as she had been when winter arrived.

When the knit scarf was nothing but a bundle in her arms, the woman smiled. "Yes, ma'am. I'm Brigit. Brigit Ryan."

Her accent was thick with Irish brogue, something Kayla had loved to hear from the shopkeepers in the New York markets. The accent had always sounded enchanting to her, and she loved it when Brigit started speaking to Drew.

"Master Andrew," she said, "I be needin' a place to freshen up." She nodded toward the group of men. "Ye'll be needin' to talk to Master Gideon to let him know ye brung me along."

Drew nodded. "He won't object. We had already discussed having you in our employ before Gideon left Missoula."

Kayla shifted her gaze from Drew to Brigit and then back again. Her stomach had fallen to her feet, because she was fairly sure she knew exactly what job Drew had offered to Brigit.

Mine.

"Employ?" she asked, not at all surprised the word ended on a squeak.

Clearly picking up on the tension, Brigit frowned. "I will leave ye two to speak in private." On that, she headed toward the house fast enough to confirm Kayla's suspicion that Brigit wasn't happy with the cold.

Kayla walked at Drew's side as he led his horse Rusty to the barn. "I assume that you have brought Brigit to keep your home. Has my work been unsatisfactory?" She'd been so focused on getting her own house that she hadn't truly considered that living in a separate residence might affect her relationship with Drew and Gideon.

Drew nodded and kept walking. "You shouldn't be at all surprised by this…change. After all"—he glanced over his shoulder toward her house—"you will have plenty to tend to caring for your own home. You would be hard-pressed remaining as our housekeeper as well."

"I would be quite fine handling both homes," she insisted. As they got closer to the barn, Kayla hurried ahead to open the door so Drew could lead his horse inside. Then she closed the door behind them.

He looped the reins over the door of an empty stall and began to uncinch the saddle. "What about meals? You intend to cook for two homes?"

She dismissed that question with a wave of her hand. "Of course not."

As he hefted the saddle off the horse's back, Drew chuckled. "So then you planned to cook for us *and* dine with us three times a day?"

"I... Well, I..." She let out a sigh. "I hadn't considered all the implications of having my own home."

He opened the stall door and led his horse inside. Then he removed the bridle. "I shall return soon to brush you." He stepped outside the stall, plucked a flake from a bale of hay, and dropped it into the stall. "For now, enjoy your hay." After a pat on the horse's thick neck, he slipped into the aisle and then closed the door firmly behind him. He wiped his hands on his jacket and wrinkled his nose. "I am in dire need of a warm bath."

"I shall be happy to heat the water," Kayla offered. "I imagine you are weary from traveling."

Grabbing her hand, Drew threaded it to his arm. "That I am. But for now, I wish to see the progress on your home."

"I dare say Brigit would appreciate a warm bath as well. Perhaps Gideon, too." Her gaze went to Drake, who was talking to Gideon. After the hard day of work he'd put in, there was no doubt he would appreciate getting cleaned up. "Perhaps we should install a larger tub so everyone can bathe in unison as I have heard they do in Japan."

"I don't think we need to resort to communal bathing. I am quite sure Brigit will help you prepare the baths, Kayla."

"She is surely tired."

Drew let out a laugh. "Even if she were, she would never allow you to have to go through the effort required for preparing four baths."

"Five."

"Why five?"

Kayla shot him a smile. "After all that work, I will be so sweaty that I shall need a bath more than any of you do."

She'd missed the sound of his laugh and the way he liked to tweak her nose. "Please don't fret, my dear. I am quite sure that once Brigit settles in, the two of you will find a way to share the necessary women's chores both here and in your new home."

* * *

Drake shook hands with Ty and then with Caleb. "Thank you both." He shifted his gaze to Kayla's house. "We made some really good progress today."

"You won't be needin' us now," Caleb said. "You can work out here whenever you want, and to hell with the snow."

Glancing back to the house, Drake realized Caleb was right. The house now sported a roof and enough exterior walls to protect him from most of the elements. Windows would come later, but for now, tarps would serve.

Ty nodded at the rapidly setting sun. "Cassie's gonna be worried if I ain't home soon."

"Sara will be the same," Caleb said. "We need to be goin'." He grinned at something over Drake's shoulder. "Looks like your woman is comin' to check up on you."

"*My* woman?" Turning, Drake saw Kayla hurrying toward them. Puffs of white clouds rose from her face as she breathed, and she bore one of the intense frowns she always got when something was bothering her. He thought about telling Caleb and Ty that Kayla wasn't his woman, but the denial never came. Probably because he wished so much that she really were his woman.

The word "mine" slammed into his brain every time he saw her, and more and more, he tried to think of some plan that would find the two of them together. Just like Ty and Cassie or like Caleb and Sara.

"Drake," she said as she marched closer. "I would really like to speak to you." Her gaze fell on the other men. "In private."

"We're were just leavin'," Ty said with a smirk on his lips. "C'mon, Caleb. Time to head for home."

She offered both men a smile, but not a genuine smile. "Thank you so very much for helping with my home."

Both men nodded and touched the brims of their hats as they passed her.

Waiting only a few moments for them to retreat, Drake frowned. "What's wrong, Kayla?"

"Everything." With no warning, she burst into tears. "Gideon and Drew don't need me anymore." She started wringing her hands. "They've replaced me."

He wrapped an arm around her shoulders, feeling entirely inadequate. Not only was he unaccustomed to women, he was at a loss on what to do with one who was crying. "Tell me what happened."

She turned to rest her forehead against his chest. "I told you. They have replaced me."

"Nonsense."

Her chin rose, then she nodded. "They have! Drew has brought a young woman named Brigit to be their new housekeeper."

While that announcement came as a bit of a surprise, he didn't understand why she was upset. "You are gonna have your own house. You won't have time to keep theirs."

She shoved herself away and shot him a piercing glare. "You agree with them?"

"What?"

"You just said you agreed with them, that you are fine with them replacing me!"

"I didn't say anything of the sort."

Although Kayla knew she wasn't making any sense, she couldn't stop the angry tears. Why couldn't Drake see that all she wanted him to do was take her into his arms, hug her, and tell her that everything would be all right?

Except it wouldn't. Brigit was here now, ready to take over—ready to be a good friend to Drew and a caretaker to Gideon.

They don't need me anymore.

No one needs me.

Whirling away from Drake, she looked at her home, the one she'd wanted so desperately that now only represented loss. What had she been thinking?

The truth settled on her like an impossible weight.

I'm alone. I've always been alone, and I'll always be alone.

With a shake of her head, she covered her face with her hands, feeling like hiding from the world. The house had been a wish, a dream, to have something just for herself. Something that was hers and hers alone. Because she'd been preparing for when Drew and Gideon would inevitably decide that they no longer needed her. And in getting that place to land, she'd brought about exactly what she'd feared.

She had a *house.*

But she didn't have a *home.*

Drake gently pulled her hands away from her face. "What's wrong?"

The concern on his face was enough to force another sob to bubble out, and she threw herself against him. In her whole life, she'd never needed anyone else. Ever.

She'd been the one who handled the household money when it had been so scarce. She'd been the strength when her father had been lost in drink. She'd dealt with the lawyers and the bankers when her father had struck it rich. No, Kayla had never needed anyone.

But she needed Drake now. She needed his arms around her. She needed his comfort.

She needed, if just for that one moment, to be his.

Once the self-pity passed, Kayla pulled away and swiped her hand across the few tears that had wet her cheeks, cheeks which were now aching with cold. "I'm sorry to have burdened you."

He brushed his lips against her forehead. "No burden, darlin'."

His nearness was suddenly too much, and she hated her own weakness. "I need to tend to my chores."

When she turned on her heel, Drake grabbed her arm. "Wait. I'll help you."

She considered refusing him, but then she realized he'd have his way. She gave him a curt nod. As she walked toward the barn, he fell in step beside her.

"Can you tell me what upset you now?" he asked.

"I fear it is… hard to explain."

"Try," he coaxed.

Introspection had never been her strong suit, but she probed her own thoughts and tried her best to explain her tumbling emotions. "My whole life, I have felt…alone. I've felt as though I had no true ally."

"What about your father?"

"Papa tried. But…it seemed as though he needed his spirits more than he needed me." Once the words were out of her mouth, Kayla wished desperately to take them back. What kind of impression was she giving Drake of her father? Papa had done his best. He simply wasn't equipped to handle a young, headstrong daughter without a wife at his side. So he'd drowned his frustration and loneliness in drink, and Kayla had been the one to deal with the ramifications.

"No brothers or sisters?"

She shook her head.

"Friends?"

"None that I can recall." Her father had been so busy with his tinkering and drinking that they seldom left their home—whatever place they called home. Before he'd earned his fortune, they'd often moved from hovel to hovel as her father tried to dodge overdue bill collectors. After his patents, the money came rolling in, but then Papa had been trying to escape people who seemed to always have their hands out in want or need.

At the door to the barn, Drake snaked his hand around her arm again and dragged her to a halt. "Can you answer me one question?"

She gave him a crooked smile in response to the irony. "It would seem as if I have been answering *many* questions. There can be no harm in one more."

He inclined his head toward the house he was building for her. "Why?"

One word, but she understood exactly what he wanted to know since it was the same thing she had been worried about from the moment Drew had introduced Brigit and she realized she'd been replaced. "I wanted a home. A real *home*. One that no one could ever take away from me. I suppose I'd never considered that in getting my own house, I might be losing the only home I've ever truly known."

"You mean Drew and Gideon, right? You feel at home with them."

"I do."

"And you think they've kicked you out now that they brought Brigit here."

To hear her fears stated so boldly made tears brim her eyes. She was being ridiculous. Absolutely ridiculous.

With a shake of her head, she busied her hands by grabbing a brush and going into the stall with Champion, Drew's horse. Always gentle, the gelding simply gave its body a quick shake and then leaned the weight off one of its hind hooves to relax. Starting at his neck, she brushed the dust from Champion's thick winter coat.

Drake started grabbing flakes of hay and tossing them into the horses' stalls. "They're not replacing you, Kayla."

She let out a deep sigh and leaned her shoulder against Champion. "I am aware of that. I truly am. It's just…"

Stopping at Champion's stall door, Drake shook his head. "They're not replacing you."

All she did was sigh again.

"You're afraid, but you shouldn't be. Drew and Gideon love you."

"I would like to believe that."

"They do." Brigit's voice was loud and firm as it echoed through the barn. "And I'm nae here to replace ye."

Cheeks heating with embarrassment, Kayla put the brush aside and went to where Brigit now stood next to Drake. "I am sorry if I offended you, Brigit."

Brigit waved that thought away with a flick of her wrist. "The truth of the matter is that I begged them to bring me."

"Why?"

"Why don't we set about making some food and I'll tell ye the sordid tale."

Chapter Twenty-Four

Kayla was both pleased and a bit intimidated with how well Brigit knew her way around a kitchen. While Brigit had been very vocal about not being here as a replacement, she was clearly a better cook. Her movements reminded Kayla of a beautifully choreographed dance.

"Will ye hand me the eggs, dearie?" Brigit pointed at the bowl of brown eggs sitting on the side table.

"Dearie?" Kayla chuckled. "My aunt used to call me that. I dare say I'm a few years older than you. I should be the one calling you 'dearie'."

"'Tis a habit I adopted from me mother. Take it as a compliment." Brigit cracked the egg with one hand and tossed the shells in the big bowl of scraps that would go to the pigs.

"Stinky and Pinky won't eat the shells," Kayla pointed out.

"Beg pardon?" There was laughter in Brigit's question.

"The pigs. The male is Stinky; the female Pinky. They will root through the scraps and push aside the shells. They are a bit…particular."

"Well, then…" Brigit plucked them from the bowl and put them with the refuse. "I shan't offend Stinky and Pinky on me first day here."

Kayla hadn't pressed Brigit to talk any more about why she'd come to White Pines. But after hearing there was a "sordid tale" involved, she couldn't help but be curious. "Why would you wish to leave Missoula?"

"Been bustin' at yer seams to ask me that, have ye now?" Brigit winked.

The teasing eased much of Kayla's worry. It seemed as though Brigit enjoyed humor as much as Kayla did. No wonder Drew and Gideon wanted her around their home. She would be a wonderfully entertaining addition to the household. "I have," Kayla replied. "You did pique my curiosity."

With a sigh, Brigit picked up a wooden spoon and began to stir the mixture she'd put in the ceramic bowl. "I suppose I did. The truth of the matter is that I couldnae stay working for Mrs. Pearson, and Master Drew tossed me a bone by bringin' me here. I couldn't stay or I'd be in a bad hurt."

Having heard many stories of how badly domestic help was often treated, Kayla couldn't believe a woman who had raised a man as caring and kind as Drew would ever be cruel to her servants. "How long did you work for her?"

"Near ta five years. Was only seventeen when me brothers brought me to the territory. They had jobs waitin' here, and I didnae like New York. I'm a quick study and knew I could find work."

Kayla nodded in understanding. "I also used to live in New York. Now that I've spent a great deal of time in Montana, I have come to realize that I prefer the mountains to cities."

"Oh, aye. The air doesnae choke me here, and there is so much…room. I was pleased nae to have to leave."

"What did Mrs. Pearson do to you?" Kayla asked, unable to rein in her interest. "Please pardon my inquisitiveness."

"'Tis fine to ask. I would be curious as well. 'Twas not Mrs. Pearson who offended me. 'Twas her son, her third son. Master Ashton."

"Drew's brother?"

"Aye. He seemed to think he had certain…liberties with me 'cause I was his mam's maid."

Men could be such pigs. Kayla hurt for what Brigit might've endured. "Did he... um..."

Brigit shook her head. "But 'twas heading that direction, if ye get my drift. I didnae wish to toss my skirts up for the man, but he saw it as his due." She stirred a bit more vigorously. "I gave him *his* due."

"Meaning?"

"I gave him my knee to his... privates."

The image made Kayla smile despite the horrible topic. "Of that, you should be proud."

"Aye, but Mrs. Pearson didnae believe me when I tried to tell her. She never saw no wrong in her boys. So when Master Drew and Master Gideon arrived after Master Aaron's death, I begged them to find me new employ, somewhere out of the Pearson reach."

The Person reach. This, Kayla understood, because she'd been running from the Carrington reach for what now seemed like forever. "It would seem that White Pines is a safe haven for us both."

Brigit cocked an eyebrow. "Were ye running, dearie?"

"I was."

"And...?"

"And I shall share my own sordid tale. I promise." Kayla glanced around at the food they were preparing. "But for now, we shall feed these hungry men. For the good Lord knows they would never be able to feed themselves."

"Aye to that!"

* * *

Kayla eased the door open, hoping there wouldn't be a telltale squeak to alert anyone that she was slipping out of the house. Wouldn't have mattered anyway. She couldn't have stopped herself even if she'd tried. It wasn't as though she'd put up even a perfunctory mental battle. She wanted Drake— needed Drake, and she would go to him. Consequences be damned.

The wind caught the door, almost ripping it from her hand. Thankfully, she was able to hold tight, but it took strength to pull it closed. Snow whipped around her ankles, forming white tornados that would have seemed pretty were she not so cold. She pulled her scarf a little tighter around her mouth and ventured toward the barn.

Drake met her halfway, catching her in his arms to halt her journey. "Oh no, you don't. Saw you slippin' out. Back to the house with you!"

"I was coming to see you."

"That makes me happy, but it's too damned cold out here for you."

"Then it is too cold for you as well." Pushing back, she took his hand. "Come inside with me."

He shook his head. "Can't do that. We ain't alone now."

"I simply do not care what everyone thinks," Kayla admitted. "I wish to be with you tonight." *I wish to be with you every night.*

"Since I can't understand a damn thing you're saying under that scarf, let's get you back in the house."

Planting her feet, she pushed her scarf down below her mouth. "I said that I wish to be with you. I am sure the barn is sufficiently warm for the both of us."

When he shook his head again, she stamped her foot, immediately contrite for the action since it stung her toes. "I shall stand here all night if I have—"

Drake swept her into his arms and started marching toward the barn. "Stubborn woman," he muttered several times on the way there.

Since she'd been called worse, she simply laughed.

When he reached the door, he set her on her feet, jerked it open, and all but pushed her inside. He had to lean his shoulder against the door to shut it again, still muttering to himself about what he clearly saw as her greatest character flaw.

Kayla sighed in resignation. She might be stubborn, but at least she'd gotten her way.

"C'mon," he said, taking her hand and leading toward a ladder. "Got the stove goin', but we're gonna have to share our heat."

"My thoughts exactly."

She loved how his eyes brightened and a smile bowed his mouth. "Oh yeah?"

"Yeah," she drawled. Despite the heat that suddenly flushed her cold cheeks, she nodded. "And perhaps we can best share that heat with fewer...obstacles."

"Such as?"

"Why, clothing of course!"

"Kayla... All I got's a straw mattress and a stove that ain't the warmest thing in—"

She stopped him by rising on tiptoes and brushing a kiss over his lips. "I am with you. I shall be quite warm."

Drake followed her up the ladder, arms on either side of her legs as though to protect her from falling. His tender care was always something that touched her heart. Her rough-and-tumble cowboy had a softer side, something she was sure few people had ever seen.

The loft was much tidier than she remembered. Of course, the only times she'd seen it was when he'd been lost in the bottle. Back then, he'd taken little care with any of his things. Even less care of himself. Now, the loft was organized and quite homey.

His clothes hung from hooks along the far wall, and the window had been covered with thick tarps. Although it seemed to breathe in and out with the wind, it held fast to protect them from the elements. The small stove was vented through the ceiling, and Drake had pulled his mattress close enough for warmth but far enough to resist catching fire. A pile of chopped wood rested within arm's length so that he could grab a log, open the stove door, and toss it in without rising from his makeshift bed.

Before she could tell him how his tidiness and organization pleased her, he was there. Between sweet kisses, he helped her remove her scarf, gloves, and coat. Then he gathered her in his arms and gave her a proper kiss, one she returned with all the love she felt for him.

Love. Oh yes, she loved him. Mind, body, and even soul deep. Such a foolish thing to do, but she couldn't stop herself from loving him, from needing him.

His fingers fumbled with the buttons of her bodice as hers struggled to get his coat open. When she realized how funny the predicament was, she let out a laugh, one mimicked by Drake. She took a step back and began to remove her clothes, keeping an eye on him as he did the same. They quickly found themselves staring at each other—and shivering—in their undergarments.

Drake lifted one of the quilts from his pallet and draped it around Kayla's shoulders. Taking her hand, he led her to his mattress. Then he sat, pulling her down to sit on his lap.

She pushed his shoulders down and straddled his hips as he awkwardly tried to cover them with the quilt. "We're gonna freeze."

"Maybe so," she admitted. "But we shall die happy, happy people."

Unbuttoning his long johns, she separated the sides and slid her hand down his furry chest. "You are so masculine," she murmured before leaning down to flick her tongue against one puckered nipple.

Now, entirely buried by the thick quilt, Kayla helped him shrug out of the top of his undergarment and then pushed it past his hips as he raised his pelvis off the mattress. Having very little light was erotic, and feeling her way around his body excited her.

Her fingertips brushed his abdomen, finding firm muscle that quivered at her touch. A line of soft hair led her to the prize that she sought. She wrapped her fingers around his thick cock, loving how firm and hot it was.

"Kayla, darlin'," he whispered as she used her hand to glide up and down his length. "I want you. Bad."

"I want you too," she admitted. Yet when he put his hands on her hips and tried to guide her to lie down, she resisted.

"Kayla?"

"Let me be in charge. This time, I want to please you."

Drake uttered what probably would've been a protest, but what he might've said ended on a hiss of inhaled air when her lips touched the tip of his erection.

Emboldened, Kayla licked his length and then used the tip of her tongue to tease the crown. The salty taste of his skin pleased her, as did the way he grew even harder.

He laced his fingers through her hair, giving light tugs every time she put her tongue or lips against his cock. When she finally granted him quarter and took him inside her mouth, he let out another hiss and rocked his hips up.

The power she felt at being in charge of their intimacy was intoxicating. She felt her core growing wet and hot. He hadn't even put his hands on her yet, and she was nearly frantic to have him inside her.

Drake was on fire. Kayla had always been a great lover, and he'd enjoyed teaching her not only what pleased him but what pleased her. Having her take the lead had sent heat through every part of him, and he knew she had no idea of how excited she was making him.

Each time they made love, he seemed to discover something new that she liked. This time, though, she was the one on the quest of discovery, and each action, each confident movement, made him want her more.

"Kayla…" He gently pulled on her hair. "I can't take much more."

"No?" Her warm tongue caressed the head of his cock. "Grit your teeth, love, and hold on tight." She took his entire length inside her mouth.

He almost came right then and there. "Sweet lord."

Kayla gave him a wanton chuckle before rising over him and kissing him long and deep.

Drake wrapped his arms around her, and he quickly realized he was guiding her hips to a place where he could take advantage of the slit in her pantaloons to thrust himself inside her. "I want you. Now."

After another long kiss, she shifted from his lips to the side of his neck. Stinging nips were followed by soothing licks. No doubt she would be leaving love bites on his skin, but he cared little if the others saw proof of her being his lover. They had to know anyway. Each look she gave him and each longing glance he returned had to scream the knowledge to the world.

If only he were the kind of man who could take her to wife… He wasn't, but the mere thought of another man holding her, loving her, made his need to be inside her greater than he could bear.

She was his. Now and forever.

"Now, Kayla. Please."

Granting him mercy, she straddled him, guiding him past the soft material of her undergarment, through the opening, and to her entrance. Pushing down with her hips, she took him deep into her warmth.

There was no finesse to their coupling, no more sweetness and teasing. She rode him hard and he answered with deep thrusts in their race to reach fulfillment.

Drake came first, spilling himself with a near shout. Not wanting to leave her behind, he kept pushing himself into Kayla as she leaned forward to grind her hips against him. Her back suddenly arched, and then her body tightened around his cock. The quilt had fallen back with her, and she looked so beautiful to him. Her eyes were closed, and her head had dropped back. There was a knowing smile on her face, and she was the sexiest thing he'd ever seen in her lacy camisole, riding him as though he were a bucking bronco.

The cold chilled his damp skin, so he eased out of her and helped her roll to his side. After he wiggled his long johns back on, he lay down, tucked her up under his arm, and jerked the quilt back over them.

"I wish we could sleep in a proper bed," he whispered before kissing the top of her head. "You shouldn't sleep on the floor of a barn loft."

"I am quite comfortable, thank you. And after such a grand experience, I believe I could sleep outside in the snow and it wouldn't bother me a whit." Her knee rose to drape over his thighs. "We could be quite bold and tell Drew and Gideon that we wish to share my room from now on."

Drake let out a derisive snort. "I'm sure they'd *love* that idea." He kissed her head again. Although that was what he would love most, sharing a room with her and everyone knowing she belonged to him, he wouldn't ruin her like that. "Besides, you're so loud when I love you that—"

She playfully swatted his chest. "I am not loud."

"You spooked the horses."

Another swat. "For shame, Drake. Besides…you probably woke both

Drew and Gideon with *your* shout. I fear Brigit may suddenly come up the ladder to check on us."

He laughed at that image. Using his best Irish brogue, he said, "Dear Jaysus, I heard such a ruckus that I come runnin' to check on ye! Are ye wee ones well?"

This time, she just laughed at his teasing. "Get some sleep, love. I shall slip back inside before dawn. Never fear! I will protect your reputation at all costs."

Drake fell asleep with a smile on his lips.

Chapter Twenty-Five

Two Months Later—April 1887

Kayla could almost smell spring in the air. While there still might be snow covering the ground, she caught a faint whiff of hope and renewal and wondered how long it would be before she could rejoice at seeing the budding of her early crocuses breaking through their snowy blanket to announce the changing of seasons.

The town was awash in dirty snow and mud, and traveling had been slow. Brigit drove the wagon as though born to the task, managing to avoid getting them stuck into any of the deep ruts along the road to town. Since the men had chores and hadn't accompanied them, the women would've been hard pressed getting the wagon out of the mud. If supplies hadn't dwindled so low, Kayla would have been tempted to wait another week to head to White Pines.

"I shall check on the mail," she said to Brigit. "Why don't you go ahead to the store to look for that fabric we wanted for the curtains in your room?"

"I wish Master Drew…er…Drew wouldnae spend the money on me," Brigit replied. It had taken her weeks before she stopped calling the men "master," but each time she used their simple names, she seemed to settle in a little more to her new place in their "family."

Family. Together with Drew, Gideon, Brigit, and Drake—especially Drake—Kayla felt as though they formed a tribe that not only complemented each other but shared genuine affection. No doubt the townsfolks would think them an odd group, and there was surely mountain of gossip about three men being alone with two women. Kayla couldn't have cared less what the people of White Pines thought. Let the old biddies talk behind their hands and swish their skirts when she walked by. They could never know how long she'd waited for a place to belong.

For a home. A real home.

The only hurt in her heart was knowing that when her house was done, Drake would leave. Her mind knew it; her heart couldn't understand. Why couldn't he be happy staying on the farm—with her?

Yet she knew that when she watched him ride away, her new "family" would help her through. She would survive. But for now, she would keep finding ways to go to him in the night, make love with him, and then sleep in his embrace. There would be many cherished memories she could cling to on the cold, lonely nights to come.

Kayla was humming to herself as she headed toward the marshal's office. A small addition had been erected the previous August, and it now served as the town's post office. The bell above the door rang as she let herself in. Stepping up to the counter, she called out a greeting. "Good morning, Mrs. Pike."

The fifty-something woman who was sorting through a burlap bag of mail glanced over her shoulder. "If'n you say it is. Got me four bags of letters on this morning's stage after pert near two weeks of nothin'. I swear I'll be workin' on this all day."

Since the woman was known to be a bit of a grumbler, Kayla tossed her an understanding nod. "I am sorry to take you away from your important work, but I would like to know if there are any messages for Mr. Pearson, Mr. Young, or Mr. Myers." She quickly added, "Or Brigit. Miss Brigit Ryan. She might have received more messages from her brothers."

Straightening, Mrs. Pike put her hands against the small of her back and groaned. "I'll have to check. My memory ain't what it used to be." With another groan, she ambled over to the wall of wooden cubbies that held the sorted mail. After looking all around as though she couldn't remember which niche belonged to which family, she finally stood on tiptoes to reach for a small pile of letters. Then she returned to the counter and handed them to Kayla. "Here you go, Miss Backer."

"Thank you." Kayla flipped through the letters. There was a thick envelope for Drew from his mother, and there were two missives for Brigit, which would make her very happy. Gideon had a message from his lawyer in Chicago and another from the man who managed a one of the buildings he owned in Billings. "I shall be sure these find the proper recipients." She turned to leave and had her hand on the doorknob when Mrs. Pike's voice stopped her.

"Did that man find you yet?"

Whirling back to face Mrs. Pike, Kayla frowned. Surely, she'd heard her wrong. "I beg your pardon?"

"That man. The one from New York City. Was here lookin' for you. Had your pitcher with him." She let out a barking laugh. "Not too bright that one, though. Didn't even know your name. Called you Carolyn...something... Oh wait. Gimme a minute. Like I said, my memory ain't what it used to be."

"Carolyn Burton," Kayla whispered.

Mrs. Pike snapped her fingers. "That's it. That's the one. You'll be glad to know that I set him straight. Told him it was Kayla Backer and that you be livin' out at Mr. Young's farm. Figured he'd found you by now. Saw him over two weeks ago. Said he needed to tell someone 'bout where you were. Maybe that person'll find you."

Chantal Carrington has found me.

Nearly blind with panic, Kayla ran out of the post office, not even apologizing to the man she bumped into in her haste. All she could process was fear that Chantal was sending someone for her and that if she didn't leave, she would die. Just like her father.

Drake. Dear God, Drake was sure to be killed if Chantal put that brute of a man-servant on Kayla's trail.

And what about Drew, Gideon, and Brigit? Otto would never leave witnesses so that he could never be connected to the dirty deeds he committed for Chantal Carrington. If he came to the farm—a guarantee now that her location had been discovered—the people she loved were in danger.

There was only one choice.

To save her family, Kayla would have to run.

* * *

Drake knew something was wrong the moment he saw Kayla. He'd been working on her house, enjoying the warmth of the sun against his cheeks as he pounded a few more boards into place, when he saw the wagon moving down the road toward the farm. It never ceased to amaze him at how just knowing that she was near could make him smile.

But seeing how upset she was, he wasn't smiling now. Brigit was animatedly talking to her, but all Kayla did in response was frown fiercely and keep shaking her head. He slung the hammer through the loop on the burlap tool apron Kayla had crafted for him and hurried over to help the women out of the wagon.

Kayla had climbed to the ground before he could get to her. When she started to hurry away, he followed her and grabbed her hand. "Whoa there, darlin'. What's wrong?"

Brigit was the one to answer him as she threw the brake on the wagon. "She's planning on leaving, *that's* what."

He frowned at Kayla as he turned her to face him. Hands on her shoulders, he asked again, "What's wrong?"

Kayla tried to pull away. "I have to go. I have to."

"Go where?" Keeping her anchored, he shook his head. "You ain't going anywhere, 'specially not until you tell me what in the devil happened in town to have you so scared."

"I have to go."

He was surprised at how hard she was struggling to get away from him. "Kayla. Stop." He let out a frustrated sigh. "Talk to me, love. Tell me where you have to go, and I'll take you."

When Kayla shook her head, he shifted his gaze to Brigit. "What's going on?"

"Some man was looking for her," Brigit replied. "A man with her picture, and that gossip Mrs. Pike told him that she be out here with Drew and Gideon."

"What man?" Then it dawned on him. "Carrington."

Kayla tried to pull away. "I have to go. Don't you see? I have to leave. Now."

"Stop, Kayla. Just stop." Drake tried to embrace her but she quickly ducked under his arm and hurried toward the house. He caught her at the porch at the same time the door opened.

Drew stepped over the threshold, and after a quick look at everyone, he frowned. "What's wrong?"

Hurrying from where she'd crawled down from the wagon, Brigit got to them. A bit out of breath, she said, "There was a man lookin' for Kayla. Had a picture of her. Mrs. Pike told him where she be."

"Carrington," Drew said to Drake. Then he looked at Kayla. "What do you want to do, Kayla?"

"I want to leave." Her eyes were full of fear when she let them capture Drake's. "I *have* to leave. Don't you see? Chantal Carrington has found me. If her man comes here, you'll all be in danger."

How like her to think of everyone else at the farm instead of herself. He wasn't about to let her go. "You have to stay here, Kayla."

Her eyes were filled with panic. "Have you lost your wits? Chantal will send her man. I cannot allow that." Her gaze shifted from Drake to Drew and then to Brigit. "I cannot lose you. *Any* of you."

Drew beckoned to Gideon, who had begun to unhitch the horses from the wagon. With a nod, Gideon jogged over to stand with them on the porch. A quick glance at the scene made him scowl. "What's wrong? Y'all look like your dog just died."

"I am done speaking of this," Kayla insisted. "My only choice is to leave."

"Leave?" Gideon's scowl deepened. "What in the hell's going on here?"

"Might I suggest," Drew said in that "let's be reasonable" voice he liked to use, "that we adjourn to the house, where we can all sit down and discuss this rationally." He took her hand but she pulled it away.

Kayla shook her head. "You simply don't understand. I have made up my mind, therefore we have nothing to discuss."

As usual, Drew got his way. Too many times, Drake had seen that all the man had to do was take her hand again and keep staring into her eyes.

She finally huffed a frustrated sigh and let him lead her inside.

Relieved that they might be able to talk some sense into her, Drake followed.

* * *

None of them understood. Worse, no matter how hard Kayla tried to explain, not a one would agree with her plan to flee.

"Your stubbornness is going to get you hurt." She folded her arms under her breasts, leaned back in her chair, and glared at them. While they had all touched her heart by insisting that she stay, she would never allow the Carrington evil to touch a single one of them.

Drake rose from the sofa to crouch in front of her. Then he placed his hands on her knees. "Kayla, look at me."

Although she didn't want to peer into those handsome eyes, she did as he asked. The affection she saw there was almost her undoing, but she refused to cry at everything she would lose.

Knowing she had to stand her ground, she put her hands over his. "Drake, I…I love you. I do. But I cannot stay." There, she'd said it. In front of everyone. Maybe now he would understand that he meant too much to her to allow him to be in danger.

His gaze was filled with a tenderness that said very clearly how much he enjoyed her declaration. "Well, I ain't gonna let you go."

Her temper ignited. She pushed his hands away and stood. Wringing her own hands, she began to pace. "You don't understand what she's capable of. None of you have seen what I've seen."

"I damn well do understand," he countered. "You told me she had your pa killed."

Gideon jumped to his feet. "What did you say?"

"Dear lord," Drew said. "Kayla, is this true?"

Giving Drake a frown for spilling her secret, she said, "I fear it is. I did not wish to burden you and Gideon with my…problems."

"Problems?" Drew swiped his hand over his face and then put his fists on his hips. "Your father was murdered, and you didn't say a word?"

"You shoulda told us," Gideon insisted.

Brigit stepped into the fray. "Perhaps I should get us all a cuppa tea so we can sit and have Kayla tell us the whole story."

Kayla threw up her hands, wondering why she was so tempted to give each of them a smack upside the head in hopes of getting them to come to their senses. "Why does it even matter? There is still only one thing I can do. I must leave as soon as I can pack a few things."

Drake took her hands and held them tightly in his. "It matters, because I ain't lettin' you go." Leaning in closer, he whispered in her ear. "I can't lose you."

Tears stung her eyes. "Drake…"

He shook his obstinate head.

"I have to go."

"No."

Shifting her gaze to Drew, she pleaded with him. "Please understand."

His answer was the same, a shake of his head. Then he stepped closer and said, "We won't let you go."

"It's time," Drake said.

"Time?" She knit her brows.

Gideon joined them, standing at Drew's side. "You ain't leavin', Kayla."

Then Brigit was there, putting her hand on Kayla's arm. "Stay. Please stay."

"Time?" Kayla asked again. "What time, Drake?"

"Time to stop running, *Cara*," he replied.

Chapter Twenty-Six

Two weeks had never passed so slowly, and Kayla had worried herself into nervous exhaustion. Her head hurt, and her stomach had little tolerance for food. But she pressed on. She still woke each day to complete her chores, work on her home, and read.

Drew and Gideon had taken the news that her real name was Cara Burton in stride. They also agreed that even though her whereabouts might be known to whomever was seeking her, there was no reason for her to use her real name around town. Drew had claimed it would be akin to waving a red flag at a bull. Since everyone in White Pines knew her as Kayla, then Kayla she would stay. For now.

She worried incessantly about Otto coming to find her, and nightmares of him hurting Drake or the others plagued her. Her temper was short, and she wondered now if they all wished she had simply gone ahead and left. It wasn't as though she was good company for any of them.

Drake hadn't acknowledged the declaration of love she'd made in front of everyone, and for that, she was grateful. Perhaps he thought that she'd simply said the words in reaction to her overly emotional state that day. Or he might even have hoped he'd misheard her. Since he didn't seem at all concerned that she'd told him of her love right there in front of Drew, Gideon, and Brigit, she would pretend that the words had never passed her lips. Make believe could be easier than dealing with an issue as tricky as love.

Snow had begun to fall in earnest by noon, and by the time they'd finished washing supper dishes, she was convinced they were going to be snowed in for several days. Sweet heavens, she was sick of it. Would spring never arrive?

"Kayla, come and sit by me." Brigit patted the empty chair beside her.

Realizing she'd lost herself in her thoughts as she gazed out the window, Kayla let the curtain drop back into place and turned back toward the people in the room. She slapped a smile on her face. "Of course. I dare say that we shall once again render the men a sound defeat." She took the empty chair to Brigit's right.

"We'll kick their arses," Brigit added with a grin. *"Again."*

Drew had taught them all the most amazing parlor games, and tonight, he'd chosen the favorite for all five of them to play. He pulled his chair over to the circle that was rapidly forming, and as always, Gideon sat at his side. Drake completed the group and closed the circle when he sat next to Kayla.

"Drew, you must begin now!" She smiled from where he sat across from her.

He favored her with a charming grin. "'Love is patient, love is—'"

"'…kind,'" Kayla interrupted. "First Corinthians, verse four. Now start the game, you rascal!"

His exaggerated sigh was so dramatic, as was his fashion, that he made her chuckle. "Very well. I shall obey your command." He slapped his palms against his knees and then clapped his hands, starting the rhythm of the game. "The minister's cat is an amiable cat."

Gideon was next. "The minister's cat is a boring cat."

"The minister's cat is a cautious cat," Brigit said.

"The minister's cat is a dandy cat," Kayla said and then glanced to Drake.

Clapping along, Drake said, "The minister's cat is an eccentric cat." His smile told her that he was pleased at how his vocabulary had increased.

So many nights, he'd lain his head on her lap and listened as she read to him. They shared a bond, a love for stories that allowed them to explore the world without ever leaving the coziness of the barn's loft. After a hard day's work, he often fell asleep before she finished the chapter, so she'd continue reading it silently to herself, allowing her to be familiar with what she would read to him the next night.

Drew chimed in for his turn. "The minister's cat is a fortuitous cat."

Kayla let out a laugh as she tried to keep the pace of the clapping. How like Drew to toss in a word that might confound them all.

It was Brigit who ended the rhythm by stomping her foot on the floor. "I call foul. Exactly *how* can a cat be fortuitous?"

"My dear Brigit," Drew replied, "we have a barn cat who is quite fortuitous. Why, just this morning, I saw her relaxing on some hay when a mouse happened to wriggle up from that very same bale. I thought to myself, what a fortuitous feline to have her breakfast delivered right to her."

As everyone chuckled, Gideon started the game again by clapping, and everyone followed his lead. He said, "The minister's cat is a grey cat."

"The minster's cat is a happy cat," Brigit said, clapping along.

Kayla had to think quickly. "The minister's cat is an imaginary cat." She laughed at her own silliness.

Drake didn't even miss a beat. "The minister's cat is a jumpy cat."

"The minster's cat is a...is a... Damnation," Drew said as everyone broke into laughter. So seldom did he lose a game, his frustration was palpable. Hand to his chest, he bowed his head. "'There's an old saying that applies to me: you can't lose a game if you don't play the game.'"

"*Romeo and Juliet!*" both Kayla and Drake called out together, forcing more chuckles from everyone. She'd never been prouder of him. Of course, *Romeo and Juliet* had been his favorite of Shakespeare's works, and she'd read it to him many times. So it was an easy quote for him to remember.

"Shall we continue?" Drew asked. "I believe I have the perfect *k* word now." He slapped his knees and clapped. "The minister's cat is a keen—"

There was suddenly a loud pounding on the door.

Gideon was the first to react, jumping from his chair and hurrying to the door. Drake was right on his heels, grabbing his gun from where it rested in the holster that hung from the pegs that held their coats.

Gideon picked up the double-barrel Remington shotgun that was always at ready, thumbed back the right hammer, and aimed it at the door. "Who's there?"

Any reply was lost in the wind, so Kayla hurried to the window to try and see what kind of dimwit had come all the way out to the farm in the middle of a snowstorm. A lone figure was bundled up against the cold, but she couldn't tell who it was. A man, judging from the fact the person wore pants instead of a skirt. "I believe it's a man. Is it the marshal? Or perhaps Ty?"

Drake frowned and flipped his hand at her. "Get away from that window. Ty wouldn't knock. He'd get his ass in outta the cold."

"Might I suggest that we at least let the man in?" she replied. "What if he's a friend who needs our help? If we don't let him in, he'll end up a frozen corpse on our front porch. I would hate to explain that to the marshal—or the man's wife."

"She is correct," Drew added. "It would be inhospitable to allow anyone to become an icicle simply because we are too cautious."

"Fine," Drake said. "Gideon, you cover me. I'm gonna open the door."

Although he grumbled about them being foolish, Gideon stepped back to stand a few feet in front of the door. If anyone charged in, there would be a hole blown right through him.

Drake opened the door, and the man rushed inside, bringing along a harsh wind and quite a bit of snow. He was shorter than Drake and wrapped in layer upon layer of scarves.

Shouldering the door closed again, Drake held up a hand when Kayla and Brigit moved toward the man. "Who in the devil are you?" he asked.

"How on earth do you expect him to answer?" Kayla said, stepping forward again. This time she ignored Drake's signal to stop. She took the end of one scarf and began to unwind it around the visitor's head. "Drake, will you please get a broom and sweep up the snow before it melts?"

"Not before I see who he is," Drake replied, earning him a frown since she doubted anyone who was freezing to death was much of a threat.

Brigit joined her in getting the man unbundled, and in a few moments, his face was revealed.

Blinking, Kayla couldn't help but think that what she was seeing was nothing but a figment of her imagination. The image refused to change.

"Sir, what be yer name?" Brigit asked.

Kayla was the one to answer. "His name is Gregory Carrington."

* * *

The moment the name registered on Drake's mind, he wanted to put a bullet in the man's head. His hand was clearly smarter than his brain, because he released the cock on his revolver and lowered it.

Gideon, however, kept his weapon pointed right at Gregory despite the fact that Brigit was moving around him, sweeping up the snow and dumping it in the sink. "Why are you here?"

Gregory looked to Kayla, and Drake saw the pleading in his eyes. He also saw how violently the man was shivering. Before he could suggest that they get him warm, Kayla went to work stripping the gloves and coat from him.

"Drake," Kayla said in a voice that brooked no refusal, "build up the fire. Drew…"

Drew gave her a snappy salute. "Yes, ma'am. What are my marching orders, ma'am?"

She rolled her eyes. "Go fetch a quilt from the linen chest."

"I'll get towels," Brigit offered. Then she set the broom aside and hurried after Drew, who'd headed toward the bedroom where they kept the extra linens in a cedar-lined chest.

Kayla took Gregory's hand and tried to lead him toward the fire, but he shook his head. "I d–didn't b–b–believe," he said as his jaw quivered. His whole body trembled.

Kayla shook her head. "We shall talk later. You must get warm, Gregory." She tugged at him again.

This time he obeyed, following her toward the hearth, where Drake had knelt and was tossing pieces of wood on the pyre. In his peripheral vision, he saw Gideon leaning the shotgun against the wall.

Drew returned with the quilt, and Kayla had him set it on the sofa while she continued to remove clothing from their visitor. Brigit came jogging down the hall, her arms full of towels. As soon as she left her burden on top of the quilt, she joined Kayla in getting Gregory stripped down to his underwear.

The moron hadn't even put on proper long johns. Under his clearly expensive and now quite wet clothing, he had on short pants and a sleeveless shirt. Drake snorted and shook his head.

Kayla rubbed Gregory's arms with a towel. "We're going to get you warmed. I promise."

The man nodded rather than replied, probably because his teeth were chattering incessantly.

She kept barking out polite orders. "Drew, please get a kettle on so that we can make some hot tea." When Drew started to salute her again, she added, "And please spare me the sarcasm this time."

With a chuckle, Brigit crouched to dry Gregory's legs.

Feeling as though his whole world had suddenly tilted on its axis, Drake tried to think of the ramifications of Gregory's arrival. Kayla had been expecting Chantal Carrington's servant to come to hunt her down. Instead, she found herself tending to her fiancé.

Former fiancé, Drake reminded himself. Or was that wishful thinking? They'd discussed everything that had happened between her and the Carringtons, with one big exception. She'd never told him whether she'd been in love with Gregory. The relationship had ended because of Chantal's disapproval, not because Gregory or Kayla had fallen out of love.

What if she still had feelings for the man?

But she'd told Drake that she loved him—right out loud and in front of witnesses. She had blurted it right out without any prodding, so he tried to put stock in that declaration. He'd never heard her mention that she loved Gregory. At least he didn't remember having heard it.

Why was Gregory here?

The only reason Drake could think of was that Gregory was still in love with Kayla. What other reason would find a man going across the entire country and riding all the way to this isolated farm in the middle of blizzard?

Had he ridden or walked from White Pines?

As if he'd picked up on Drake's thoughts, Gideon reached for his coat. "I'm gonna go take care of this fool's horse."

"How do you know he had a horse?" Brigit asked, standing to face Gregory. "Yer gonna have to take this off." She tugged on his damp undershirt, trying to peel it from his arms.

Gideon buttoned his coat. "'Cause he would've died coming out here from town without a damned horse."

Drew plucked a hat and scarf from the pegs and helped get Gideon ready to go out. "Would you like my help?"

"That would be most welcome."

As Drew bundled himself against the cold, he said, "I am quite sure we would both appreciate some hot tea when we return, so if it isn't an inconvenience…"

"We'll make sure you get some, too," Kayla said.

As Drew and Gideon headed out the door, Drake looked over the man who had caused Kayla so much misery. It wasn't as though Gregory was an intimidating specimen. He was shorter than the other three men in the house. Hell, Brigit was only a couple of inches shorter than this man. His hair was dark, his frame lean. There just seemed to be nothing special about the man.

Except his fortune.

"Drake," Kayla said, "please go get a pair of your long johns for Gregory."

As if he wanted to share his clothing… But Drake obeyed. In his room, he fumbled through his three extra pairs of underwear to find the one that still had holes that Kayla hadn't mended yet. Then he brought that pair back to Kayla.

She frowned at him, no doubt knowing why he'd chosen that one. "I need you to help Gregory get out of his undergarments and into these."

"Thought you'd take care of that." Heaven knew she'd done the same for him more than a few times this winter after he'd braved the elements to get to the barn and tend to the animals.

Her cheeks flushed red. "I cannot see him…*naked.*" The last word was more mouthed than spoken, and for some reason it pleased Drake more than he could say that she was hesitant to do that chore.

"Go on, then." He shooed the women away with the back of his hand. "I'll get him dressed."

Having never dressed a grown man before, especially a grown man who seemed as helpless as an infant, Drake quickly learned how difficult a task it could be. Although he was a smaller man, Gregory was dead weight, and moving his limbs to help get him in the long johns quickly left Drake out of breath. The whole time, Gregory watched him closely but said nothing. Probably because the poor man's teeth were still chattering. After Drake got him dressed, seated on the couch, and wrapped in a quilt, he stared down at the man and shook his head. "You done a fool thing riding out here in this snow."

"Had to s–s–see C–C–Cara."

"She's been living here a year or more," Drake replied.

"C–couldn't f–find her."

"What do you want?"

"That," Kayla said as she came into the room and glared at Drake, "is none of your business."

Brigit gave him the same kind of glare, so he simply threw up his hands in defeat and went to get the teakettle, which had begun to whistle. But Brigit hurried over and beat him to it. "G'on now. Go help Miss Kayla." Her voice dropped to a whisper, and she added, "I donnae trust that man. Ye need to protect yer woman."

My woman. If only Kayla were his woman. Now that Gregory had come all the across the country to find her, everything she had shared with him might be ending.

And in that moment, Drake realized exactly how much he loved her and exactly how much it would hurt if Gregory was here to win her back.

Chapter Twenty-Seven

"Thank you," Kayla said as she took the cup of tea from Brigit. Then she sat down next to Gregory. "You need to drink this. It will help you warm up."

"Th–thank you." His hands were steadier now that he was dry and bundled up in front of the fire. Funny, but she'd never noticed how smooth his hands were before. So unlike Drake's, which had rough skin and calluses from hard work. Gregory's appeared as soft and pale as the hands of a pampered woman.

He sipped at the tea and sighed. "I'm f–feeling m–much better."

Knowing that Brigit and Drake were watching them, Kayla was close to biting her tongue to keep from asking Gregory why he was there. In all of her worries about being discovered, she'd never once thought about him being the one who sought her. The Gregory she'd known would never have gone against his mother's wishes. Never. Besides, Chantal had clearly let them both know that she would never approve of them marrying.

When Otto had killed her father, Kayla had immediately run away, so she'd never had a chance to tell Gregory the truth of what happened. God only knew what he thought about her now, although traveling all the way to Montana told her he might still have feelings for her. His cryptic greeting had left her curious and wanting to hear what had made him decide to find her.

She had so many questions about what had happened after she fled, but most of all, she was heartsick to find out if her father had received a proper burial. Tears of regret blurred her eyes. *I'm sorry, Papa. I'm so sorry.*

Setting her jaw, she pushed the remorse aside to think through her present situation. Gregory was in Montana, and she needed to deal with that fact.

If he still harbored feelings for her, he was in for a rather rude surprise. She loved Drake. Falling in love with her own cowboy had taught her that what she'd felt for Gregory had been more admiration and respect than love. His kisses, the handful they'd shared, had never sent her reeling, yet all Drake had to do was look at her and heat filled her body.

If only she and Gregory could have some privacy to talk—an impossibility since they were now snowed in.

The door opened, bringing with it cold wind, more snow, Gideon, and Drew. Kayla used their return as a reason to leave Gregory alone on the sofa. She grabbed the damp towels and used them to get the snow swept into a pile, then she and Brigit did their best to get the stray snow to the sink before it melted and left the floor wet.

Brigit went about getting Gideon and Drew some tea, but Drake came to help Kayla with the towels. Together they took them to Brigit's room, where they often hung things to dry. She seemed to think that moisture in the air was healthy, but Kayla figured it was more likely that Brigit was accustomed to her room having multiple uses since she'd been a servant for so long. She and Drake laid the wet towels over the twine stretched from wall-to-wall near the hearth.

Since he hadn't made any comment about Gregory's arrival, she broached the subject first. "I had no idea he would come here. I truly didn't."

"You don't need to explain anything to me," Drake said.

"I feel as though I do. I could tell how…surprised you were at his arrival."

"Damned right I was surprised. We all were. Including you."

She nodded. "I always assumed Chantal was behind the men searching for me."

"You really thought she wanted you dead that badly? You weren't gonna marry her son anymore."

After Kayla hung the last towel, she turned to face Drake. He put his hands on her shoulders and gazed down into her eyes. "I saw what she'd done to my father. She had to believe I might come back to seek justice one day. I also thought perhaps she wanted to dispose of any witness to what Otto had done."

He gave her a quick kiss and then tugged her into his arms. His embrace was tight, and she loved how it felt to be enveloped by him. To feel cherished by him.

Everything would change now that Gregory had found her. That was what Kayla feared most. She'd found such happiness at this place, with these people.

With Drake.

God, how she loved him. Didn't matter that he'd never given her the words, she still knew that he cared. His every action, his tender care, declared his feelings for her. He might never love her the way she wished he would, but she was bonded to him and him to her. Always would be.

She used to dream about revenge for Papa's death, and she'd said many a prayer to beg for forgiveness for her sinful thoughts. Now, she dreamed of a life with Drake. Of him, the house he was building was for them, and perhaps, one day, a family. Fanciful though it was, she wanted it all—her own happily-ever-after.

In that moment, she decided that she would never go back to New York City. She didn't want to be a part of that world again. No matter what Gregory wanted, she was staying in Montana.

Kayla was just about to tell Drake of her decision and to ask him to stay, to share her home, when Drew called from the other room. "Kayla! Gregory would like to speak with you!"

She hesitated. "Drake, I…I want—"

He gave her a quick kiss. "We'll talk later. That man just came all the way from the other side of the country to find you. Best to go hear what he has to say."

"But I need to ask you—"

Another no-nonsense kiss. "Come to me tonight, like you always do. We'll have plenty of time to talk then."

Kayla let out an inelegant snort. "You never seem to want to *talk* at night."

His laugh always made her smile. "That's 'cause you're such a temptin' little minx." He turned her around and gave her bottom a pat. "Now go. Find out what that varmint wants."

With a sigh, she obeyed. Drake followed closely behind.

* * *

Drake took a chair and watched the drama playing out before him between Kayla and Gregory. He imagined that she wished she had some privacy with her former fiancé, but he couldn't make himself leave. The woman he loved was coming face-to-face with her past—a past that had frightened her enough to force her to flee all the way across the country. He wasn't about to leave her alone with Gregory when he was somehow involved in that past.

Brigit frowned. She stood behind the sofa upon which Kayla and Gregory sat. That frown was shot at Drake and then directed at where Drew stood in front of the fire. He was sipping tea while Gideon leaned his back against the wall, arms folded over his chest.

"We should leave them be and let them talk," she said.

Thankfully, Drew chimed in before Drake could. "My dear Brigit, it has been such a long time since I was able to see a dramatic performance on the stage. Would you deny me the pleasure of witnessing a perfectly wonderful chance at entertainment that is here, right before my eyes?"

A small smile on Kayla's face was there and quickly gone. Drake doubted anyone else even noticed it. In the time Drew had been back home, Drake had noticed their special connection, one that saw them doing their best to make the other laugh or smile. Just like Drake, Drew clearly knew Kayla was uncomfortable and was trying to ease her distress.

Brigit, on the other hand, wasn't amused. She rolled her eyes and drummed her fingers on the back of the sofa. "They should be alone."

"Nonsense," Drew said as he placed the teacup on the mantel and gave a flourish of his hand. "We are all family here. Right, Kayla?"

Her eyes grazed Brigit, Drew, and Gideon before settling on Drake. "You're right, Drew. We *are* family. So speak freely, Gregory. Please tell me why you've come so far to find me."

Gregory drew his lips into a grim line. "I had hoped to speak to you alone. Dirty laundry and all, my dear. Don't you wish to speak in private, Cara?"

"I mean what I say," Kayla replied. "These people are my family now. You can hang up all my dirty laundry, and I will not hide it from them. And I prefer Kayla now."

He set his teacup on the table that sat beside the sofa. "As you wish... I came west to find you because I simply couldn't believe what was being said about you. I loved you and knew you would never have done something so...so...heinous." He wiped his hand over his face. "Tell me the truth, Cara...er...Kayla. Please."

"I'm confused." She glanced at Drake and then returned her gaze to Gregory. "What do you think I did?"

The tremble in her voice was unmistakable, causing Drake's thoughts to focus. There was only one thing that Gregory could possibly accuse Kayla of doing, and that horrible conclusion came spilling out of Gregory's mouth. "Tell me you didn't kill your own father."

Drake jumped to his feet, glad to see the same reaction from Drew and Gideon. "Have you lost your fuckin' mind?" he asked, fisting his hands.

Gideon chimed in. "Kayla wouldn't hurt a fly, let alone her pa."

For the first time in Drake's memory, Drew was at a loss for words. His reactions this time were pure body language as he set his hands on his hips and glared down at Gregory with narrowed eyes and a clenched jaw.

Sitting still as a statue, Kayla blinked a few times as if trying to process

Gregory's accusation. "You think that I… That I… Dear God. How could you possibly believe—?"

"But I *didn't* believe," Gregory said. "I couldn't accept that the woman I loved, the woman whom I wanted to marry, could do something like that."

"Is that what everyone believes?" Kayla asked, her eyes wide. "That I killed Papa?"

Gregory frowned. "I fear that they do. Although there is no formal charge pending against you, Mother said that your running away proved that—"

Kayla let out an indignant gasp. "Whatever your mother says is nothing but…but…pure…"

"Bullshit?" Drake offered.

She nodded vigorously. "Yes, it is *bullshit*." Her angry stare could've scorched Gregory's skin. "Your mother is the one who killed my father, not I!"

This time, it was Gregory who rose. "I beg your pardon? Did you just accuse my mother?"

"Damn right, she did," Drake replied. It was time the whole story was out in the open. "Your bitch of a mother had Kayla's pa murdered."

"You've all clearly lost your minds," Gregory insisted. "My mother is the gentlest woman in the world. How could she possibly have anything to do with such a…a…monstrosity as murder?"

"I was there," Kayla said. "I witnessed what happened."

"You saw my mother kill your father?"

She began to wring her hands. "Well, no. I didn't *see*. But—"

"Ha! I knew it," Gregory said. "My mother could never—"

"You refuse to see your mother's true self," Kayla said. "She is a dictator. Pure and simple. She wouldn't allow you to settle for someone as lowly as me for a wife. She told my father so that day. Then she left to send in Otto, and he killed my father."

"So now it's Otto's fault? Have you no shame that you will cast blame on others simply to keep it from yourself?" Gregory's tone was taunting. Then he folded his arms over his chest. "Perhaps I misjudged you, Cara. You are throwing out unfounded accusations against people I care for."

Three stomps put Drake in front of Gregory. He fisted his hands in Gregory's shirt and lifted him off the ground, bringing their eyes level. "How dare you! Do you know how much your people have put her through?"

Gregory's words came out in frightened squeaks. "What are you talking about?"

"Your mother threatened Kayla's pa, then her man murdered him. Kayla thought she would be murdered, too. Sent her running across the whole damned country like some fugitive, then started tracking her like an animal. Spent all this time lookin' over her shoulder, expecting someone to kill her, too."

Gregory pushed against Drake. "Turn me loose, sir."

Drake narrowed his eyes. "What I oughta do is punch your lights out."

"Unhand me," Gregory said, his voice gaining some strength.

Kayla put a gentle hand on Drake's arm. "Please let him go."

Although he obeyed, Drake gave Gregory a rough push back.

Straightening his shirt, Gregory turned to Kayla. "I…apologize. This has been a long ordeal. Finding you, I mean. I had Pinkertons spread all over searching for you. Once you were found, I hurried here to find out the truth."

"They scared the devil out of her," Drake said. "Made her think your
mother was wanting to hunt her down and kill her."

"My mother didn't kill anyone!" Gregory shouted.

Drew finally found his voice. "Maybe not by her own hand. But this Otto
person was clearly acting on her orders."

"I do not believe it," Gregory insisted. "Any more than I believed Cara to
be capable of such a crime. But the evidence shows—"

"What evidence?" Gideon asked at the same time the same words fell out
of Brigit's mouth.

"The fire," Gregory replied.

Kayla frowned. "Fire?"

"After your father was…gone, a fire consumed your home. The police
believed it was set deliberately and theorized it was to try to cover the crime."

She let out a little cry of distress. "The house is gone?"

"I'm afraid so," Gregory said. "And then there was the missing money.
Your father was known to keep a large amount of cash in the home. After the
fire, the police found an open safe, and it was empty. There was no money in
the house."

"Might've burned up," Gideon commented.

"Or was taken by the person who killed him," Brigit added. "That's what
they thought, aye?"

Gregory nodded. "The police think that Cara—"

"Kayla," Drake insisted.

"Fine. *Kayla* wanted the money and that her father had refused her. So she
simply killed him, took the money, and fled." He looked to Kayla. "I couldn't
believe it, though. Did you even know about the money?"

"I did. He kept quite a bit of what he called 'reserve' in the safe," Kayla
confirmed. "He didn't trust banks. But how would anyone else know that? He
would never have revealed that secret."

"My mother knew," Gregory replied. "And she shared that information
with the police."

"How could she possibly know anything about my father?"

"Because he asked her about investing the money in our bank, in Mid-
Atlantic."

Drake threw his hands up. "See? That proves that your mother killed him."

"Yep," Gideon added. "Didn't want you marryin' our Kayla, and she
wanted that man's money."

Gregory wagged his finger at Gideon. "My mother is quite wealthy, thank
you. She would never resort to something so heinous for mere cash. Why, she
probably has more in her handbag than Cara…er…Kayla's father kept in that
damnable safe."

"Kayla ain't got a dollar to her name," Drake added. "Had to come out
here to get a husband to keep from starving."

Whirling to face Kayla, Gregory demanded, "You are *married?*"

Kayla shook her head.

"Then what exactly is he talking about?"

"I didn't have to marry because I have money," she replied. "I took some from the safe to ease my escape. Papa would've insisted. I took some gold coins and a banded stack of bills. I wasn't even sure what I was grabbing. I was in such a hurry."

The confused looks on both Gideon and Drew's faces told Drake that was a fact they were not privy to. Considering they were paying for her house, they had to feel confused…and perhaps a bit betrayed at knowing she had access to money.

Raking his fingers through his hair, Drake couldn't get his own wayward thoughts to settle. He'd believed Kayla's tale. Every word of it. But then she confessed to having money. Perhaps she'd only picked up small bills and a handful of coins?

"Where's the money now, Kayla?" Gideon's voice was whisper quiet.

"My aunt helped me sew it into the lining of my carpetbag."

"So you still have it?" Gideon asked.

She bowed her head. "I do."

"But you told us you were flat broke." His jaw tightened.

Kayla's eyes rose to capture Gideon's harsh stare. "I had planned to give you the money when the house was completed. It was to be a surprise."

"Surprise?" Gideon snorted. "You let us believe… And you let us build… I don't know, Kayla. I just don't know."

"I was afraid, Gideon," she said. "I didn't know who I could trust. And then I came to you and Drew, and I found people who truly cared about me. I was going to tell you. I was!"

Gideon just shook his head.

"Might I suggest," Drew said, "that we all sit down and try to figure out exactly what happened."

"I'll tell you what happened," Gideon said. "She lied to us."

"Not about everything," Drake insisted. His own emotions were roiling. He loved her, and he wanted to trust her. He *did* trust her.

Don't I?

He thought he knew her, what motivated her, what she wanted. But then Gregory showed up, tossing around accusations, some of which made sense.

"Well, she didn't kill her pa," he finally said. "She didn't lie about *that*."

Drew chimed in again. "Let's all calm down, have a brandy, and straighten this out. We clearly have much to discuss."

Chapter Twenty-Eight

Kayla took another sip of her tea, which had no taste at all in her dry mouth. Her head was still spinning at everything Gregory had told her. That, and at the idea he'd actually traveled across the continent to find her and ask her whether she'd killed her own father because he didn't believe the accusations.

Did that arduous trek mean he loved her?

How could it when he could even entertain the notion that she was capable of such a sin?

Drake would never think that about her.

Would he?

She'd once read about earthquakes, and the author had described them as having the ground under a person's feet constantly shifting and moving. Funny, but that was an accurate depiction of her world right now. Everything was happening so quickly that she couldn't keep her balance.

She set the cup on the table instead of throwing it at Gregory's head as she dearly wished to do. Whether he loved her or not seemed irrelevant. By coming here, he'd turned her new world—a world she loved—upside down.

Their little melodrama hadn't ended and wasn't likely to have the curtain rung down for some time to come. No, the play had merely moved from the parlor to the dining table, and now she stared at the lot of them drinking their brandy. While she understood the men turning to strong drink, even Brigit seemed to need one.

Everyone, except Drake.

He had opted for tea along with her, and she was pleased at his choice. She wasn't, however, pleased with the scowl he kept tossing her way. Ever since Gregory had given her the news of how everyone in New York City believed she'd despicably killed her own father, Drake had looked as though he wasn't sure what to think. How could he possibly believe that she would be capable of hurting anyone, let alone her beloved Papa?

Did any of these people know her—the *real* her—at all?

Perhaps not, for she'd never shown them who she truly was, had she? She'd taken a new name, lied about the money she'd stashed away, and come to this town to hide, not to take a husband as she'd claimed. Kayla Backer was nothing but a mask. A fabrication.

A lie.

"Kayla…" Drew's hand covered hers. "Please don't think that any of us believe that you harmed your father."

"I loved Papa," she whispered. "I couldn't ever hurt him."

"We know that," Brigit said. But it was hard to take solace from the words of someone she'd only met a handful of weeks ago.

Kayla shifted her gaze back to Drake, the person whose opinion mattered the most, waiting to hear his affirmation of her innocence.

It never came.

Instead, Gregory pushed his chair back and stood. "I think it prudent to clarify a few things."

Although she wanted nothing more than to find some privacy with Drake, to find out exactly what he was thinking, she nodded curtly at Gregory as everyone turned their attention his way.

He put his glass down. As Drew withdrew his hand from Kayla's, Gregory picked it up. "I want you"—his eyes fell on each face at the table before returning to Kayla—"*all* of you to know that I simply cannot believe Cara harmed her father. I would never have come all this way merely to toss an accusation at her feet. I came because I wanted her to know that I still love her and want to help her through this ordeal."

"Help her?" Gideon asked, leaning back and glaring at Gregory. "How can you *help* her? People are sayin' she killed her pa."

"I want you to know that I have already put detectives and lawyers to work on the problem," Gregory replied. "They are going to do whatever needs done to clear her name."

Kayla cocked her head. "You have?"

Gregory squeezed her hand. "Of course, my dear. I want your name scrubbed clean. That way, when we marry, there will be no black cloud hanging over our heads."

"*Marry?*" As he shouted the word, Gideon pushed his chair back and jumped to his feet. He narrowed his eyes at Kayla. "You're gonna marry him? After what his mother did to you and your pa?"

His anger was a surprise, and the vehemence of it hit her like the lash of a whip. She had to fight hard not to flinch. "I never said that."

"Gideon, please," Drew coaxed. "You have heard everything that the two of them have said from the moment Gregory arrived. Nothing of the sort has been proposed, if you'll pardon the pun. Calm yourself."

Although Gideon sat back down, he breathed hard enough that a small whistle came from his nostrils. She couldn't recall a time she'd seen him so angry, and she couldn't help but wonder if that rage was directed at Gregory or her. Since she'd brought this whole mess to his doorstep, she was pretty sure she was the target. The guilt weighed heavily.

Drake sat quietly, arms folded across his broad chest as he kept an intense stare fixed on Gregory. She wanted so very much to be alone with him and learn what he was thinking. Was he as angry as Gideon? If so, at whom?

"I believe," Drew said, "that we should look at this…puzzle with less passion." When Gideon sputtered, Drew held up his hands. "Please hear me out." Since Gideon quickly settled down, Drew continued. "Gregory has given us quite a shock, and we have many things to consider where Kayla is concerned. There is some good news here, and that is the fact that no charges are pending back in New York."

"I agree," Brigit said. "She willnae have to be watching over her shoulder."

A relief, Kayla admitted to herself. But that didn't change the fact that people believed her capable of such an atrocity.

"There is nae reason for her to go back," Brigit added.

Gregory shook his head. "She cannot restore her reputation from this…wasteland. And if she is to be my wife, then she must know that she will be living where I live. My life is in New York."

"Where your mother is," Drew said with a frown. "How can you expect her to be your bride when your mother and her man killed her father?"

Hands fisted, Gregory shot back, "I have told you before that you are all mistaken. My mother would never—"

Drake stood so quickly, his chair hit the floor, cutting off Gregory's word. "How about we all stop talking about her like she ain't sitting in that chair right there?" His anger didn't seem to abate when he spoke to her. "Kayla, what do *you* want to do?"

I want to rewind this wretched day. "Right now," she replied, her throat constricted from her need to scream in frustration, "I want to go to bed and think about all of this. It is simply…too much." Standing, she bowed her head, hoping everyone at the table would allow her to leave without a quarrel. She walked toward the hallway, stopping to turn back and look at Drake. He was still unreadable, and after months of feeling a connection to him, she suddenly felt horribly alone.

Tears blurring her vision, she retreated to her bedroom.

* * *

Drake paced the length of the loft and back again so many times that he lost track and flippantly wondered if he was wearing a path in the wood beneath his feet. His mind was at war, and he was pretty damn sure a ceasefire wouldn't be called for a good long time.

He should be asleep. Morning would be greeting him soon and there would be chores to do and decisions to be made. Important decisions. About Kayla's future, which meant about *his* future—which he'd hoped would be tied to hers.

But that hope might have ended with the arrival of Gregory.

Thoughts twisting and turning like tumbleweeds on the prairie, Drake agonized over everything that had been said—everything that Kayla had told him about her father's death by Otto's hand and the new things that Gregory had shared that made Kayla seem responsible.

So what was the true story?

She lied to me.

That hurt. While she'd claimed that the lie had only been about money she'd spirited away when she ran, it was, nonetheless, a lie. That money pushed the scale harder to the side of her guilt. After all, that was what the law in New York City believed, that Kayla had argued with her father over money, and that she'd simply taken what she wanted, killed the man, and run. Then she'd invented the story of Chantal Carrington and Otto Schneider so she could cast blame elsewhere.

Wouldn't any other criminal do the same?

Hell, that was what Sara had done to him! Drake had been minding his own business, just scratching an itch that every man had, and what had happened? She'd stolen his money and run to White Pines, where she told everyone she was nothing but a typical mail-order bride. Take the money and run, except Kayla killed the person with the money instead of simply waiting for him to pass out drunk.

Dear God, he was putting Kayla in the same class of female with Sara, a woman he had hated with every fiber of his being. Sure, he might've found it in himself to forgive Sara for destroying the life he'd known, mostly because he'd come to see how pathetic her world had been and how much she'd needed to escape. But he would probably never forget what she'd done to him.

Is Kayla exactly like Sara?

Maybe he didn't even know her at all.

Drake hated himself for the doubt. He loved Kayla—*Cara*. She'd lied about her name, too. She might've confessed that, but it was another lie to all the other people in town. Could she really be trusted?

Shit, he wasn't sure he still trusted her, and that seemed…wrong. Didn't love mean you trusted another person with no reservations?

Since he'd never been in love before, he had no clue what it entailed.

Damn, but he wanted a drink. Badly.

He knelt before the potbellied stove and opened the door, cursing when he realized he'd forgotten to pick up a rag to protect his hands from the hot metal. After he tossed in some more pieces of wood, he slammed the door. All it did was bounce back open. With a weary sigh, he grabbed the rag, shut the door, and turned the handle to keep it closed.

"Drake?"

Her voice jerked him out of his reverie. "Kayla?"

She was at the top of the ladder, staring at him as though waiting for an invitation. That was new. Normally, she'd simply come into the loft, taken his hand and led him to his pallet, where they would make love. Then they would talk or read. Now, she hesitated, her gaze wary as she nibbled on her bottom lip.

Drake strode over and offered her a hand. She grasped it and allowed him to help her up onto the loft's surface. "You shouldn't be out here."

"Because?"

That one word held a lot of questions. Was she asking whether she shouldn't be with him because Gregory might find out? Was she questioning whether Drake wouldn't want her to be with him even though she stayed with him most nights? Or was she worrying about where Drake's thoughts traveled, especially his thoughts about her, after all the revelations back at the house?

"Because it's too damn cold for you to be traipsing out to this barn," he finally replied.

Now that Kayla was here, he had a million things he wanted to ask her, to say to her. They all seemed to crowd together and prevent a single thing from falling out of his mouth. Instead, he merely stared at her until her gaze made him uncomfortable and he glanced away.

A first. Normally, he loved to look deeply into her eyes—those beautiful, intelligent, chocolate eyes. Sometimes he felt as though he could drown in them.

Tonight, he felt ashamed at his own doubts.

"We should discuss…things," she said, her voice soft and tremulous.

"Things?"

She began to wring her gloved hands and bowed her head. "Ever since Gregory arrived, you have said very little."

He shrugged. "Ain't got much to say, I guess."

Her head snapped up. "But you *should*. Have something to say, that is."
Kayla paced a few steps away, turned on her heel and walked the other
direction, taking the same pacing path he'd followed only minutes before.
"Gregory told you that there are people back home..." She shook her head.
"Back in *New York* who believe I–I...murdered my father." Her pacing became
more urgent. "How anyone could possibly... Why would they... I couldn't
ever..." Half statements kept spilling out until she finally threw her hands up.
"I didn't kill Papa!"

His first instinct was to hurry to her and gather her into his arms.

He didn't, because that doubt still hovered over him like a raincloud.

"I loved him, Drake," Kayla insisted. She rushed over to stand in front of
him. "I loved him so much. How could anyone think I would hurt him?"

"Gregory says he believes you." Damn if that didn't bear the tint of
accusation.

She looked up at him, blinking a few times before she knit her brows.
"Are you saying that you *don't* believe me?"

"Kayla..." What was he supposed to say? That he was having doubts?
That somewhere deep inside, he wasn't sure he could trust her?

Her eyes flew wide. "Dear God... You think... Drake, you actually think I
killed my father?"

"I didn't say that," he said, giving his head a quick shake.

Kayla fisted her hands at her sides. "You didn't have to. All you needed to
do was look at me the way you're looking at me right now."

"I ain't lookin' at you any way," Drake insisted. "Look, I don't think you
did it. Not really. It's just... Gregory knew about the money, and you didn't tell
us you took it."

The woman's temper was clearly aflame. Her eyes had darkened, and
there was a flush on her cheeks. "Are you telling me that you believe me
capable of cold-blooded murder simply because I lied about bringing money
with me?" She was practically shouting at him now.

Not that he could blame her. When she put things that way, he felt lower
than a snake's belly.

"I thought we were in lo—" She sucked in a deep breath and blew it out.
"I was clearly quite wrong about...us." She bowed her head again. "I fear I
have misjudged this situation, whatever it is that is between us."

He didn't like the solemn finality in that statement. "What's that supposed
to mean?"

"That means that I shall not bother you any longer, *Mr. Myers*." Marching
to the ladder, Kayla hiked up her skirts to climb down.

Drake hurried over to help her. "Here. Let me—"

She slapped his hand away. "No, thank you, sir."

"Kayla..."

Now on the ladder, Kayla looked up at him. "I'm sorry."

The woman always had a way of confusing him. "Sorry? Why in the devil
are you sorry?"

"I'm sorry that I ever got my life mixed up with yours. I promise to keep
my distance from this moment on. Good evening, sir."

Despite having so much more to say to her, Drake let her leave. He hadn't craved a drink so desperately since, well since ever. While there was plenty of alcohol—good stuff instead of his typical rotgut—back at the house, he pushed the craving aside.

Getting drunk wasn't going to solve his problems.

Kayla didn't kill her father.

That thought suddenly settled on Drake, giving him absolute confidence that he was correct. The woman he loved wasn't capable of hurting someone, especially someone she loved.

He remembered the tender way she'd cared for him as she helped him see what alcohol had been doing to him, to his life. He thought about how carefully she tended the animals, talking to each animal, offering affectionate pats, and gently nursing any of their wounds. And he thought about the way her voice had trembled and tears had filled her eyes when she'd told him the story of her father's murder.

The Kayla he knew could never cause harm to anyone or anything, let alone commit murder.

He practically threw himself down the ladder and sprinted out of the barn. There was a deep path in the snow where Kayla had trudged back to the house. He caught her at the porch. Grabbing her arm, he tried to turn her around.

Kayla resisted. "Unhand me!"

"I need to talk to you," he insisted. "I'm sorry, sweetheart. I'm so—"

"Sorry?" She let out a rueful laugh that bordered on hysteria. "*Sorry?* For what? For thinking I'm a murderess?"

"Yes. No. Kayla, we need to talk."

"I have no wish to talk to you. Now or ever."

"I don't think you killed you pa."

Her eyes narrowed and her breath came hard and fast. "I. Do. Not. Care."

"Sure, you do. You said you loved me, remember?"

"I was mistaken." She tried to jerk her arm away. "Let go of me. Now." Drake shook his head.

"Listen to me, and listen to me good, Mr. Myers. I do *not* love you. I do not, at this moment, even *like* you. From this point forward, I prefer that anything you have to say to me concern my home and nothing more. Do you understand?"

The door opened, and Gregory stood there for a moment before he frowned. "Cara, are you well?"

Her gaze was on the hand that restrained her. "I will be when this man releases me."

"Kayla," Drake pleaded. "Please. Let's talk."

"Sir," Gregory said, "if you do not unhand her…"

"You'll what?" Drake said, his own voice rising in anger and frustration. "You'll let me pound you into the mud?"

Gideon elbowed his way past Gregory. "Let her go, Drake."

Great. Another champion to her cause. Drake dropped her arm. "Gideon, I need to talk to her."

Kayla hurried to the door, brushed past the men, and disappeared inside.

"Let her be for now," Gideon said. "She clearly don't wanna talk to you. So just let her be."

While Drake wanted to argue with the men, he realized his cause was lost. At least for tonight. Kayla needed time to calm down, and for now, he would give her some room to breathe.

His heart heavy, Drake gave Gideon a curt nod and headed back to his cold, lonely bed.

Chapter Twenty-Nine

Kayla was grateful to finally be alone. Gregory, Gideon, and Drew had all tried to get her to sit down and talk with them about why she and Drake had been quarreling, but she had no desire to share anything about tonight's humiliation. After excusing herself, she went to her room, shut the door, and just stood there, hugging herself. In a house stuffed with people, she felt utterly alone. There was only one thing on her mind.

Drake.

The dichotomy of the man was sure to drive her to the madhouse. She loved him more than she'd even imagined was possible; she loathed him for not believing in her innocence. He made her want to weep; he made her want to find something heavy to throw at his hard head. Part of her wanted to run back to him and demand he listen to her and trust her; the other half wanted to slap his face and tell him she never wanted to see him again.

Letting out a snort, she began preparing for bed. Sleep wasn't likely to find her until the wee, small hours, but she found the ritual of changing into her flannel nightgown and braiding her hair comforting.

What was she supposed to do now? Everything had seemed settled. Planned. Kayla was going to live in her beautiful new home, spend time with her friends, and simply…live. There had been dreams about Drake at her side, and while she admitted to herself that she still loved him, it was quite clear that he didn't return her feelings. On that, she'd been mistaken. There was no love there on his part, and she sniffed back threatening tears.

It wasn't as though she hadn't known this was how their love affair would end, with her alone. She'd just assumed it would happen after her home was completed. He had left her a few months early. So what?

Why did she have to fall in love with an obstinate, mistrustful, frustrating cowboy?

There was a knock at her door. "Go away," she said.

"Cara?"

Gregory. Great.

She ignored all the politeness that had been drilled into her. "What do you want?"

"May I speak to you? Please?"

"It's late."

Another soft rap. "Please, Cara. It will only take a moment."

With a sigh, Kayla grabbed the afghan she'd crocheted from the foot of her bed and wrapped it around her shoulders. Gregory was almost as stubborn as Drake, and if she didn't talk to him now, he'd probably stand by her door the whole night. That, and she really didn't need Drew, Gideon, and Brigit listening in. They were already too privy to the tragedy that was now her life.

She opened the door enough for them to talk. "What do you want, Gregory?"

He glanced over his shoulder as though concerned about someone being in her bedroom. "May I come in?"

Her first inclination was to deny him. But in hopes of this conversation ending swiftly, she sighed and opened the door a little wider. After he stepped inside, she left the door ajar so no one would think anything illicit was happening.

Old habits die hard.

Gregory strode to the fireplace and held his hands out toward the heat. "This place is so very cold. I feel as though I shall never be warm again."

"New York is cold, too."

"I suppose it is, but out here in this wilderness, it just seems...extreme. I keep scurrying from fireplace to fireplace like some house mouse." He smiled at her.

That smile had been charming, still was. Yet she felt no pull to him, not like she felt with Drake.

She pulled the edges of the afghan closer, weary and heartsick at everything she'd lost this evening. "What do you want, Gregory?"

Turning to face her, he cocked his head. "Why are you so hostile to me? We were engaged to be married. I was to be your husband, Cara."

"*Kayla,*" she corrected. "I'm not Cara anymore. Cara Burton is...gone."

"You'll have to forgive me if I have difficulty making the change. *Kayla*...I would like to know why you are being so cold to me, especially after I have come all this way to find you."

Kayla let out another sigh. "You're right. I'm sorry. Your arrival was just such a...shock. And then when you told me that you believe I killed Papa... How did you expect me to greet you after hearing that?"

He put a hand on her shoulder.

She shrugged it away. "Don't."

"Don't what? Touch you?" His brows gathered. "I thought we loved each other."

"We never loved each other, Gregory. We were marrying, but...love?" She shook her head. After all she'd shared with Drake, she couldn't listen to this man refer to what they'd shared as love. "We honestly didn't even know each other. I'd assumed we'd learn to love each other after we were husband and wife."

A fierce frown filled his face. "I love you, Cara. I wouldn't have agreed to marry you if my heart hadn't been involved."

Kayla let out a weary sigh and walked to the window. The drapes were only half-drawn, and she opened them a little wider so she could see outside. The beauty of this land always amazed her, and the farm looked like a wonderland. Moonlight flooded the yard, and the snow glistened and winked as though crystals were hidden on its surface.

Her sadness made the beauty fade.

Gregory came to stand at her side. "I'm very disappointed to hear that you don't feel the same about me as I do about you."

"What does it matter anyway?"

"Because I still want to marry you. I told you that. I have people working to clear your name. When we return to New York—"

"I will *not* return to New York City," she insisted as she turned to face him.

He turned as well, staring down at her. "We *will* return to New York, because it's home."

"I have nothing there." She bowed her head, wondering if she would ever have the comfort of a true home again. She'd thought she'd found it here, with Drake and her friends.

She'd been wrong.

His crooked finger went under her chin, and he lifted gently until she was looking into his eyes again. "You have *me*. You may not love me, but I love you. I want to be there for you through this…ordeal."

"Gregory…"

"Just listen to me for a moment. Please." When she nodded, his hand dropped away. "As I told you and your friends, I would never have come all this way if I hadn't believed you were wrongfully accused. I want to clear your name, and I want to marry you. You are smart and kind and I want no other woman for my wife. You will learn to love me. I know you will. Marry me, Cara. Marry me and come back home."

She didn't even try to correct him, because it was quite clear that he was never going to call her anything but Cara. "Not only would your mother never approve," she couldn't help but point out, "but I have no desire to be anywhere near that woman." Not that Kayla was considering his offer, but he seemed to be entirely ignoring the fact that his mother had been the catalyst of her father's murder.

His offer seemed utterly ridiculous.

Or did it?

Right now, people believed her to be a murderess. If she never faced those people and proclaimed her innocence, they would always think she was guilty. Lord knew that she had no means to hire people to help prove her innocence. Gregory did, and he'd already put lawyers and detectives to the task.

"I can't marry you," she blurted out.

"Why not?"

Why not, indeed? She doubted he wanted to hear the myriad reasons. She started with, "Your mother—"

"Stop," Gregory snapped. "My mother has nothing to do with us. We will not have to see her often, and I'm sure time will help mend any rift between you."

"Rift? She had that buffoon of hers kill my father! I will never be able to forgive her for that, and simply being near her would be agony." When Gregory started to protest, Kayla shook her head. "Enough. Please. I need to get some rest."

As he followed her to the door, he asked, "Will you at least think about my offer?"

Kayla nodded, knowing full well that she would be declining it again and again before Gregory would finally accept her answer. When he leaned in as though to kiss her, she turned her head so he was only able to give her a peck on the cheek. "Good night, Gregory."

"Good night, my love."

Rude though it was, she rolled her eyes after he turned and headed back toward the sitting room. No doubt a night on the sofa would be a rude awakening for a man so accustomed to luxury.

After she closed the door, she strode to the window to shut the curtains.

Hands on the material, she stopped when her gaze settled on the barn. Was Drake still awake? Was he thinking about her? Or had he dismissed her from his mind the same way that he'd forgot about other women he'd taken to his bed?

That thought felt like a knife to the heart, and her stomach began to churn. How could she still love someone so much when he had no faith in her?

Angry, she jerked the curtains shut. To hell with him then! She was strong. She would survive this the same way she'd survived losing her father.

Alone.

* * *

How am I going to fix this?

Drake resumed his pacing, unable to even consider trying to get some sleep. He'd made a mistake, a horrible mistake, and he had no clue how to repair the damage.

How could he ever have believed that Kayla was capable of hurting anyone? What a fool he'd been. He'd seen into the woman's very soul, and what he'd seen there had been pure and loving and trusting. Yet when she'd asked for his trust, Drake had hesitated.

Why? Because a woman in his past had betrayed his trust.

What did it truly matter that Kayla had some money with her? The poor woman had just witnessed her father's murder and had been running in fear for her life. She fumbled around, grabbing whatever she thought she needed. Of course, she'd taken some money. And why would she bother telling anyone that she had it? She had come here, to a town full of strangers, to marry a man she didn't know. Instead, she'd become a housekeeper to two men she'd just met. Why should she brag that she had some gold and a stack of bills?

Kayla said she trusted Drew and Gideon now, and she'd claimed she was going to surprise them with a payment for the home they were having built for her. There was no reason not to believe her—other than Drake's own stubborn stupidity in thinking she was like the other women he'd known.

Kayla was unique, and he loved her. Deeply.

His thoughts, like his unending pacing, always brought him back to the same place.

How am I going to fix this?

Constantly measuring the length of the loft with his feet wasn't going to mend this situation. Drake stamped his foot hard. "Damnation." It was time for action.

He snatched up his coat and managed to get it on before he climbed down the ladder. A miracle that, considering he was moving as fast as he could possibly move. It wasn't until he had thrown the barn door open and stepped outside that he realized he hadn't buttoned up against the cold or grabbed his hat, gloves, and scarf.

To hell with it. If he froze, he froze. What did it matter if Kayla wasn't in his life anymore?

Figuring the best thing to do to save them both some embarrassment was to knock softly on her window and hope she'd let him inside. He could crawl through and then they would be alone to talk all this nonsense out and figure out where they would go from here.

Drake skidded to a stop when he caught sight of the figures in the window. Nothing but silhouettes backlit by the hearth, a man and woman stood facing each other. His hand went to her shoulder as they spoke, and Drake wished he were a fly on the wall so he could hear what they were saying. He realized it was Kayla and Gregory. In her room. Alone.

What were they talking about? And why would Gregory possibly need to speak to her in her bedroom at this hour? Drake had to remind himself he'd been hoping to do the same thing, but he was her lover. Gregory might've been her fiancé, but he had never laid claim to her body—the thought of him even touching her make Drake's blood boil,

The cold was numbing him in too many places to count, so he waited only a moment more, long enough to see the silhouettes step away from the window. He turned and marched back to the barn, shivering all the way.

Drake managed to get back up to his loft despite his nearly frozen fingers and feet. The first thing he did was pile some more wood in the stove and stoke the fire. Then he dragged a blanket closer and sat on it, staring into the flames since he'd left the stove door open. They spiraled and turned as the wood popped and crackled. Slowly, warmth returned to him, making his hands and feet sting.

He'd been stupid to stand outside, barely covered, in the cold. The moon had been out, making the night eerily beautiful as it shone on the snow. But the beauty had been lost in wake of the anger over Kayla being alone with Gregory. Drake's jealousy was running hot, and he tried to tamp it down.

He was failing.

Had Gregory been discussing marriage with her again? Had she been willing to entertain his proposal? Not only did that anger Drake because he couldn't swallow the notion of Kayla ever being with another man, it also meant that she'd be leaving Montana, heading back to New York City to be with her husband. That meant danger.

Chantal Carrington had instigated the murder of Kayla's father—had made sure her man Otto had killed him simply to keep Kayla from marrying her son. How would she react when Gregory dragged Kayla back east with him? The moment Chantal realized that Gregory still intended to marry Kayla, Kayla's days would be numbered. Surely, there'd be some "accident" when she went riding. Or a runaway carriage would hit her. Or…

Drake had to rein in his overactive imagination. Another impossible task. The more he thought about the threats Kayla faced if she agreed to go with Gregory, the more Drake realized one very important thing.

He could never allow her to go. Not if he had any say in the matter. He'd nag, he'd beg, he'd demand—whatever he had to do to keep her safe. Drew and Gideon were sure to lend their voices to the argument, and their sway might help.

Besides, she said she loved me.

She won't marry him. She won't.

She'd been extremely upset that people believed her capable of killing her own father. Perhaps she wanted to head back to clear her name. Drake understood that. Oh yes, he did. Hell, he'd chased Sara all the way to Montana to get back the money she stole, return it to the cattle company, and scrub his own name clean.

His trip to Montana hadn't put him in danger the same way Kayla would be in danger. There'd been no Chantal and Otto waiting to kill him.

But what if after Drake did his best to try to convince Kayla that she shouldn't go, that she belonged here with him, she was going to head east anyway?

Well, if she was still determined to go to New York City, there was no other choice.

If Kayla decided to go, Drake would go with her. He might not have Gregory's money, but he would do everything in his power to not only protect her, but to try and help her clear her name.

Maybe then, she'd think he was worthy of her.

Chapter Thirty

Kayla had put up with about as much of Gregory's fuss and bother as she could handle. The man had followed her around like a puppy for four straight days. When she was cooking, he was looking over her shoulder. If she went out to the barn, he followed. Every time she turned around, she bumped into him.

It wasn't as though he had anything better to do since he seemed to think whatever she was doing was "women's work" and never once offered to help. Heaven forbid that he get his clean, soft hands into dishwater, and no one should expect him to do something as mundane as laundry.

Whenever she suggested Gregory might want to help Gideon with the animals or Drake with the construction of her home, he acted as though she'd asked him to commit a mortal sin. Manual labor was something the man simply wasn't accustomed to.

This morning, his persistence at tailing her was making her stomach knot, and working on scrambling the eggs for breakfast wasn't help her queasiness. For some reason, the look of the runny whites made the bile rise in her throat, and added to Gregory's cologne, the combination almost made her gag. When he stood by her side, scrutinizing the lard melting in the skillet as though it were the most fascinating thing he'd ever seen, she had to resist the urge to stomp on his foot to get him to move.

"Perhaps you'd like to find a nice book?" she suggested.

Gregory snorted. "Your...*library* leaves much to be desired."

Had he always been so pretentious?

Probably, although she most likely hadn't noticed because she'd been spending her time amongst people of his ilk, trying to help her father establish himself in society. Gregory wasn't a bad man; he was just a rich one.

The wealthy like him had no idea what life was like for other people. They had everything done for them, so they never learned how much effort went into making a life. What did he know about keeping a typical family fed and clothed? Household tasks were unknown to him, and he didn't seem to have any interest in learning them, other than keeping a close eye on everything she was doing. And that wasn't to acquire new skills. He trailed her around to keep trying to convince her that she needed to go back to New York City—something she had absolutely no intention of doing.

"If our books aren't sufficient for your needs, I'm quite sure your library back in New York is anxiously awaiting your return," Kayla said, not even trying to disguise her irritation. The heat of the kitchen was beginning to wear on her already frayed nerves. She wiped some sweat from her brow with the back of her sleeve.

Gregory didn't seem to notice her distress. "As I told you," he said, "I will not be returning to my home until you are traveling at my side." The same thing he'd said—ad nauseum—since that first night he'd arrived, and his constant following her seemed to reveal his fear that she would run again if given the opportunity.

Kayla wasn't running. Never again. "How many times do I have to tell you that I'm staying here?"

He shook his head. "You'll change your mind. I know you will."

When hell freezes over.

Thankfully, Drew interrupted the fruitless argument when he came in from his trip to the barn and hung his coat on a peg. "Good morning, Kayla." He didn't even politely nod at Gregory, showing his irritation with the man by simply ignoring him as much as possible.

Kayla wished she could follow suit. Alas, she seemed stuck with Gregory for a while.

She glanced over her shoulder as she continued to turn the eggs cooking in the hot skillet. "Good morning to you as well, Drew. Is the weather clearing up?"

"'I'll say she looks as clear as morning roses newly washed with dew,'" he replied, with a lopsided smile.

"*The Taming of the Shrew*, and I'm glad we aren't facing more snow," she said, returning the smile. "Are Drake and Gideon about ready to eat?"

"I believe Drake's comment was that he was hungry enough to eat the south end of a northbound steer."

As she chuckled, Gregory's eyes widened. "How...uncouth," he drawled.

"Oh, Gregory." Kayla shook his head. "You are truly not meant for Montana."

"Does that mean we can leave soon?" he asked, his voice rising in what she assumed was feigned hope.

She just shook her head again and began to scoop the eggs onto the platter.

"Is Brigit supposed to return today?" Drew asked as he strode closer to sniff at the eggs. "Smells heavenly, Kayla."

To her, it smelled like a breakfast she was considering skipping. She wasn't sure her stomach could keep the eggs down, so she decided all she would eat was a piece or two of the toasted bread. "I'm not sure if she'll be back today or tomorrow. Depends on now Mrs. Gaines is doing with the new baby."

Drew nodded. "Thankfully, you're here to cook for us while she is away."

Gregory turned his attention to Drew. "I have been meaning to ask you, sir, whether it might be possible to afford me the use of a bedchamber. While I do not wish to question your hospitality, especially since I came to your home uninvited, I must say that your sofa leaves much to be desired in the way of comfort."

"Where, pray tell, do you expect me to find another bedroom?" Drew asked, his tone snide—a rarity from a man with impeccable manners. She couldn't blame him. Gregory had come unannounced, unwelcomed, and had done nothing but pressure Kayla to leave from the moment he'd arrived.

"I was thinking that with Brigit being away, I could use her room," Gregory replied.

"She might be back today," Drew said.

"If she does return, then perhaps she could sleep in Cara's room. There's a large bed, and it shouldn't be difficult for the two women to share."

Drew gaped at him. "Surely, you jest."

"Not at all," Gregory insisted, adjusting his cravat. It was wrinkled and for some reason, that fact pleased Kayla. She wasn't about to offer to press it, and if Brigit got wind of his plan to displace her from her bedroom, she'd probably chase the man around the house with a broom.

With one of his wicked grins, the type he always got when he was getting ready to rile Gideon with some kind of outrageous idea, Drew snapped his fingers. "I believe I have a solution!"

Gregory smiled back at him, no doubt misunderstanding that he was about to receive some sort of verbal smack upside the head. "Do tell!"

"You and Drake should share the loft in the barn!" Drew announced.

With eyes wide and mouth open, Gregory gaped at Drew. "Surely, *you* jest."

"Not at all, my good follow. I think it might be a bit…enlightening to see how Drake handles his chores, and what better way to do that than to spend your days—and nights—together."

Kayla let out a laugh, unable to control herself any longer. "Drew… Your humor is as warped as a board left out in the rain."

He held out his hands as though innocent. "But I'm not trying to be funny, Kayla. Don't you think it would be good for Gregory to see how it is for people who must work for a living?"

Now, Gregory was sputtering in anger. "I assure you, sir, that I work. Why, I spend hours at the bank almost every day, dealing with loans and managing investments."

"I'm quite sure it is very difficult *work*," Drew said. "Very well then. I shall tell Drake that he avoided a bullet." He headed down the hall, ignoring Gregory and his clearly ruffled feathers.

"That man is… is…"

Kayla let out another laugh. "I believe the word you're looking for is *correct*, Gregory."

"I beg your pardon?"

"Have you ever shod a horse?" she asked. "Or mucked out a stall?"

He grabbed his lapels and gave his jacket a shake. Even here on the farm, the man dressed as though he were ready to go to some society function. "I have people whom I pay to handle things like that for me."

She gave a snort. "How about changed and washed your own linens? Or emptied your own chamber pot?"

"Again, I have staff for those matters."

"Exactly!" she exclaimed. "Haven't you ever thought about how difficult the lives are for the people who work for you?"

"Cara—"

She slammed down the spatula. "That is exactly what I'm talking about! I have asked you to call me Kayla, yet you do exactly as you please."

"But you are Cara. Cara Burton. My fiancée," Gregory insisted.

Grabbing a towel to hold onto the hot handle of the cast iron skillet, Kayla moved it aside. This conversation was getting nowhere, and it merely reinforced her idea that, exactly as Drew had said about Drake, she had dodged a bullet. "As I have told you repeatedly these last four days, I am *not* your fiancée any longer."

The door flew opened, and Drake hurried into the house. "Ty was just here. There's a fire at the Beck's barn. We need to get out there to help."

Drew grabbed his coat. As he was shoving his arms into the sleeves, he looked to Kayla. "I fear breakfast will have to wait." Then his gaze shifted to Gregory. "Grab your coat."

"Why on earth would I do that?" Gregory asked, making Kayla strongly consider hitting him with her skillet.

"Because," Kayla replied, "there are people who need our help—*your* help."

Drake strode over to where she stood. "Damn. Those eggs smell delicious."

She grabbed a plate and scooped some eggs from the platter. Then she handed the plate to Drake. While she gave him a fork, she said, "Eat. You'll need your strength. Drew, would you like some, too?"

As Drake became to shovel the scrambled eggs into his mouth, Drew came over to take another plate she'd readied. "Thank you, Kara."

"I'll get a plate for Gideon so he can eat before you ride." She didn't bother to offer one to Gregory since he was surely going to stay home where it was safe and warm.

He surprised her by going to the table, picking up a piece of toasted bread, and piling it with eggs. "I shall accompany the other men," he proclaimed before hastily eating his impromptu breakfast sandwich.

There was no way she'd heard him correctly. "I beg your pardon?"

"I am going with the men to help fight the barn fire," he said around chewing. If his prissy mother could see him talking with a mouthful of food, she'd no doubt have an apoplectic fit.

"Why?" she couldn't help but ask.

"Because you seem to think I don't have any useful...skills. Perhaps if I show you that I am not immune to hard work, you will stop fighting the idea of returning to New York with me."

The scowl Drake leveled at Gregory could've set a forest ablaze, yet he said nothing. Instead, he scooped the last of his eggs into his mouth, muttered something that sounded a bit like, "Thank you," as he handed her the empty plate, and then left. He slammed the door behind him.

Things had been tense between them, and Kayla hadn't found an opportunity to clear the air with him since their last conversation. Her heart hurt knowing that he had believed her capable of murder, especially of her own father, and he'd done nothing to show her that he'd changed his mind. Since the last time they were alone, he'd barely spoken ten words to her, and she felt abandoned.

So why did she still love him so much? She really did, and she cursed herself for her own stupidity.

Drew gave her his empty plate as she passed him one that she'd prepared for Gideon. "I hate that we will be leaving you alone."

While she wanted to blurt out that alone was exactly what she wanted to be simply to get Gregory out of her hair, instead she said, "The Becks need all the help they can get. I shall be fine."

He kissed her forehead. "'She is clothed in strength and dignity...'"

Her cheeks flushed hot at the wonderful compliment. "Proverbs chapter thirty-one, verse—"

"Twenty-five," Gregory interjected with a crooked smile that revealed the dimple in his left cheek.

There was the appeal that had drawn her to him back in a world long gone. While he was a bit too privileged, she had to admit, Gregory wasn't a bad person. He could be charming when he chose to be, and his looks were pleasing with his wavy, dark hair and green eyes. One day, he would make some woman very happy.

But I'm not that woman.

The door shut behind the men, and Kayla went to grab a piece of toasted bread. She had only taken her second bite when her stomach went into full rebellion. Thankfully, she made it to the sink before what little that was in that stomach came right back out. As she leaned over the sink, eyes watering, the epiphany came. Her missed monthly. Her queasiness. Her fatigue.

There couldn't possibly be a worse time for her to be with child, except perhaps if she was actually wanted for her father's murder and potentially faced time in prison.

A few long minutes passed before her body settled and her heart stopped pounding. She made her way to the table, pulled out a chair, and just sat there, contemplating her next move as though life were a game of chess. Was the fact she was going to have a baby going to equal checkmate?

Stop being fanciful, Kayla.

Kayla. She'd begun to think of herself as exactly that. Kayla Backer, not Cara Burton. That woman was gone, hopefully never to return. Montana had changed her in positive ways—ways that would help her survive this tough world.

Her hand dropped to her abdomen, and she stroked gently as though caressing her unborn child. *Drake's child.*

If her cowboy knew he was going to be a father, he'd probably help the Becks put out their barn fire and then keep riding any direction except back to her. The man was never meant to be tied down, and there was no way he'd welcome the news of her pregnancy.

What do I do now?

After some quick math, Kayla realized the baby would come in the autumn—probably late October or early November. By then, her home would be completed, and Drake would be long gone. If the weather kept up its steady march toward spring, he might have the house done by June or July. Which meant she might be able to keep her situation hidden from him until he left. He would never have to know that they shared a child.

That thought made her so sad, her eyes suddenly brimmed with tears. Just as quickly, she pushed the melancholy away. He was the one who had ended their relationship because he didn't trust her. He didn't deserve to share her life or this child's life.

But he *did* deserve that. He was the baby's father, and she wasn't sure she could keep herself from telling him the truth. Had circumstances been different, she'd be shouting the wonderful news to the whole world.

Her thoughts were tumbling and turning, and she needed something to do to help crowd her worries out of her mind. She began to gather the breakfast dishes to clear away the table. How much time had she spent sitting there, worrying about something over which she had no control?

Too long.

The knock at the door startled her, making her squeal and drop the plate she was taking to the sink. The china shattered, sending shards flying across the wooden floor. "Damnation." Stepping around the ruins, she headed toward the door. When she saw that she hadn't thrown the bolt to lock it after the men left, her heart began to beat frantically. "Who is it?"

There was no answer.

Kayla picked up the shotgun. "Who's there?" Keeping the weapon pointing at the door, she eased to the window, pulled the curtain aside, and glanced at the porch. Her mouth dropped open.

Chantal Carrington had arrived.

Chapter Thirty-One

"No," Kayla whispered to the empty room. Standing on the front porch were the two people she feared most in the world—Chantal Carrington and Otto Schneider.

"Carolyn, open the door," Chantal demanded. "I've come a long way to speak to you."

Kayla's first inclination was to run, to head out the back of the house, jump on a horse, and flee. The mere sight of Otto was enough to make her stomach heave. Thankfully, nothing was left to expel, but she had to set the shotgun aside and steady herself against the wall until the dry heaves stopped.

The knocking continued. "I demand you let me in, Cara!"

"Go away."

This time, the knock was a heavy pounding—no doubt Otto's fist was being applied to the door. Chantal would never put her dainty hands through so much abuse.

"Open the door," Otto ordered, "or I'll kick it in!"

Kayla was in a panic and snatched up the weapon again. There was no way to keep the shotgun pointed at the door and open it, so she chose holding on to the gun. "It's unlocked."

The door swung open, and before she could even gasp, Otto hurried through, grabbed the shotgun, and jerked it right out of her hands. Then he tossed it out the door into a snow bank.

Chantal followed him through the door. She was impeccably dressed in a thick coat trimmed with fox, and she wore a hat of the same red fur. "Where is Gregory?"

Although still reeling from the way Otto had so swiftly disarmed her, Kayla tried her best to put up a brave façade. "What makes you think Gregory is here? There is no reason whatsoever for him to travel to Montana."

Otto let out a scoff and shook his head. Although he wore a full-length beaver coat, his bald head was bare, making Kayla wonder if the man even felt the cold.

One finger at a time, Chantal removed her expensive kid gloves and then slapped them against her palm. She hadn't changed a bit. Her dark hair still had a faint fan of gray against the temples, but her face appeared young enough that people might question whether she was old enough to be Gregory's mother—until someone saw that her eyes were the same shade of emerald as her son's. "Don't play coy with me, my dear. He sent a telegram that told me he was here and that he'd finally located you. I have come all this way to try to talk him out of his ridiculous plan to go ahead and marry you."

Kayla's first instinct was to blurt out that she was never going to marry Gregory, but until she could be sure she wasn't in danger, she felt it best to play her cards close to her chest and say nothing. Instead, she folded her arms under her breasts and glared at them both.

"I will never understand his fascination with you," Chantal continued. "There are so many women of much better breeding and fortune. He could have his pick."

"She's a witch," Otto commented. "Must've cast some kind of spell over him."

"Hardly," Chantal countered. "More likely, she simply used her feminine...*favors* to convince him that they should marry."

Kayla let out a derisive snort that made Chantal's eyes narrow.

Chantal slapped the gloves against her palm again. "Pray tell, Carolyn, why do you believe my Gregory is so enamored of you that he'd pay great expense to have detectives chasing you all across the continent?"

"What do you want?" Kayla finally asked.

"I want you out of my son's life," Chantal replied.

"I left New York. I didn't ask him to come here," Kayla insisted before she fixed a hard glare at Otto. "You made it quite plain that you wanted me gone when you killed my father."

Chantal let out a gasp. "How dare you! You killed your father when you stole his money, and yet you make baseless accusations against my fiancé!"

Jaw dropping, Kayla couldn't believe what she'd heard. "You're going to marry him?"

"Although it is truly none of your business, yes, I am," Chantal replied.

"How can you even consider being his wife?" Kayla asked. "He's a murderer!"

Otto took another step closer. "Shut your mouth!"

"I will *not*," Kayla replied. "I was there. I saw what you did." She shook a finger at Chantal. "I saw what *both* of you did. You were the one who told Otto to kill him."

"How dare you!" Chantal stomped her booted foot. "How dare you cast aspersions at your betters. You killed your own father, stole his money, and burned the house down behind you to hide your crimes. Yet you stand there, bolding accusing two innocent people."

"I was in the attic, and I could hear everything you said to him," Kayla said. "Papa knew you were the one ruining us in society. Then you told him you burned the betrothal papers and that you'd do *anything* to make sure Gregory and I didn't marry."

"Which is clearly what made you desperate," Chantal explained as though speaking to a small child. "You weren't going to be able to take my son's fortune, so you stole your father's."

Kayla shook her head, her anger growing, making her heart pound and her stomach lurch. "No! *You* were the one who killed him. *You* told Papa that you would protect Gregory at all costs. Then *you* left Otto to attack my father."

"Such nonsense," Chantal said with a frown. "You simply wish to avoid the gallows."

"I have proof," Kayla insisted.

"Proof?" Chantal shook her head. "You are a liar."

Righteous anger in full flight, Kayla fisted her hands. "Otto beat my father before he shot him. Papa was able to grab one of his cufflinks. He gave it to me before he died."

"A cufflink? That's your proof?" Otto snorted and shook his head.

Chantal stared at Kayla for a few moments before she finally spoke. "What does the cufflink look like?"

"Chantal, don't be ridiculous," Otto scolded. "The girl has nothing but a wild story that she's trying to use to save herself."

"Hush, Otto," Chantal said, her gaze still on Kayla. "I asked you to tell me what that cufflink looks like, Carolyn. Now."

At least the woman was listening. "It's silver."

Otto let out a scoff. "That proves nothing!"

"Be silent!" Chantal snapped.

"It has a brown stone," Kayla continued. "A very odd brown stone."

Otto butted in again. "Chantal… This is ridic—"

Chantal interrupted him. "Does the stone look a bit like an eye looking at you?"

"You know it does," Kayla replied. "You were with Otto when he threatened Papa. You had to have seen it."

"I want to see it, Carolyn. Now."

"No."

"Please."

There was a thread of worry in Chantal's plea, and doubt bloomed for the first time in Kayla's heart. While she might remember what Chantal said that night, Kayla's memory of was filled with gaps about what exactly Chantal had *done*. The woman had left before Otto went after her father, and now Kayla searched her memory for Chantal's exact words.

"This ends our association, Jamison. So I shall bid you a fare-thee-well."

Then Chantal had left. The angry words—the shouts and the threats—had all come after and from Otto. Chantal had merely informed Papa that she'd burned the betrothal papers and that she wouldn't allow Gregory to marry his daughter.

"May I please see it?" Chantal asked again.

Kayla nodded. "Come with me. I'll show you."

"Chantal, don't so this," Otto said in an angry voice.

"Stay here, Otto," Chantal ordered. "I will be back in a moment."

"Chantal…"

"I said *stay here*."

Kayla led Chantal to her bedroom. What she sought was in her bureau, so she jerked the door open, tossed aside some clothing, and pulled out a small wooden box. Her hands were trembling so much, she could barely open the lid. She tried to pick up the precious piece of jewelry, but her fingers wouldn't cooperate. Finally, she plucked it from its home. "Here." She held out her hand to reveal the silver cufflink she'd protected since the night her father had died. When she'd knelt at his side, Papa had been clutching it in his hand, and he gave it to her right before his last breath.

After staring at it for a few long moments, Chantal looked as though someone had struck her. Hard. "Dear God…"

Otto came stomping into the room, making Kayla close her fist around the precious cufflink. "Get out of my room! Now!"

For a big man, he was swift, crossing the room in a mere moment as he snatched for the cufflink. "Gimme that!"

Kayla turned aside, protecting the jewelry against her chest. "I will not! You killed my father, and this will prove it!"

When Otto reached for Kayla again, Chantal pushed his arm away. "Leave her alone!"

A storm brewed in his eyes, and his brows gathered in anger. "Chantal…"

Chantal turned her back to Otto and held her hand out to Kayla. "Carolyn, please. Hand it to me."

"No," Kayla replied. "You'll just give it to him."

"Please hand it to me. I will protect it…and you. I swear to you on my son's life."

The pleading and sincerity in her voice cut through Kayla's resistance. Reluctantly, she held the cufflink out to Chantal.

Chantal held it between her finger and thumb, bringing it close to her face as her mouth bowed in a deep frown. "Otto, this is yours."

"Don't be ridiculous," he said with the flip of his wrist. "It's just a silver cufflink."

"It's *yours*," Chantal insisted.

"It's *not* mine," he said, his voice growing gruff.

Chantal kept staring at the cufflink she held. "You forget, Otto, that I gave you this cufflink—and its twin—two years ago. It was a gift for you to wear when we went to the governor's ball."

He shook his head. "I still have those. They're both back in New York."

"Then why haven't you worn them since Jamison Burton died?"

"You're mistaken. I've worn them. I've worn them several times," he insisted.

Chantal shook her head and her gaze shifted to Kayla. "I got him these…*this* cufflink, you see. They were specially made. See the cat's eye stone in the center? I chose two of them the exact color…" She swallowed hard. "They are the exact color of Otto's eyes." She turned it to look at the back. "I commissioned them from Black, Starr, and Frost on Fifth Avenue. Here is their mark."

"Stop this foolishness, Chantal." Otto tried to take the cufflink, but in a move that mimicked Kayla's earlier actions, Chantal balled her hand around the piece of jewelry and pulled it to her chest.

"He killed my father," Kayla said again. "Was it on your command?"

"No!" Chantal shouted. "I would *never*… I didn't ask him to do anything to Jamison except put some fear into him. To threaten him. If I wanted to hurt your father, I would've simply seen to it that my bank put a financial squeeze on him. I wouldn't… I couldn't…" She shook her head, and her eyes shimmered with tears. "I would never commit such a sin as condoning murder. I swear *on Gregory's life* that I didn't tell Otto to kill your father."

Kayla believed her. Chantal had done exactly what she said. She'd threatened. Which meant it was Otto who had made the choice to kill Kayla's father.

Chantal turned on him, her face filled with anger and disgust. "What did you do?"

A calm seemed to settle on Otto, which made him appear even more dangerous. "I did what needed to be done. The family needed to be protected from her. She's nothing but a poor harlot who wanted our money."

"Dear God…" Chantal shook her head.

"You're a murderer," Kayla said to him. "And I will be sure everyone knows about what you did."

Chantal was still shaking her head, appearing hurt and confused. "You're…a monster." She stared at the cufflink she still held. "And to think…I was going to marry you."

With a weary sigh, Otto reached into his pocket and pulled out a gun. He pointed it at Kayla. "Look what you've done, you stupid bitch."

Knowing there was no escape, Kayla faced him bravely, swiping away angry tears with the back of her hand. The child she'd only just learned about would never draw his first breath. "May you rot in hell."

Chantal surprised Kayla when she suddenly rushed in front of her, blocking Otto from shooting. "I will not let you harm anyone else. You're going to prison, Otto. For a long, long time."

He let out a chuckle that sent shivers racing the length of Kayla's spine.

"You're *laughing*?" Chantal held up the closed fist that still held the cufflink. "I assure you, sir, you won't be for long."

"Such a shame," he said. "If you hadn't listened to this little bitch, we could've taken Gregory home. But now?"

Chantal narrowed her eyes. "Now, what?"

"Now, I have to kill you both."

* * *

Drake could've sworn he heard Kayla calling him. The sensation was so vivid that he dragged Rusty to a stop. The horse flicked its tail in agitation, probably at how hard Drake had pulled on the bit. Drew and Gideon kept galloping up the road, not even glancing back as they hurried to help the Becks with the fire in their barn.

Gregory, who'd been trailing a bit behind, slowed his horse and then stopped at Drake's side. "How much farther to the farm?"

Instead of answering, Drake strained to listen. Was that Kayla calling again? He shifted in his saddle to check behind them, almost expecting to find her riding hard to catch them.

Turning to glance the same direction, Gregory frowned. "What's wrong?"

"Did you hear Kayla?"

"Kayla?" Gregory turned to stare. "Do you think she followed us?"

"I don't know. I just… I coulda sworn I heard her shouting at me." Drake was tense, his muscles tightening as his stomach knotted. Why couldn't he figure out what was wrong? She wasn't there. She wasn't calling out to him. So why was it impossible to make himself get Rusty back in motion and catch up with Drew and Gideon?

"She's not there," Gregory said, shifting in his saddle. "I have excellent vision, especially at a distance. There is no one following us."

All Drake did was frown. Everything inside him was screaming for him to hurry back home—back to Kayla. But the Beck family was losing their barn. Every passing minute could see the fire spread to their home.

His heart implored him to turn back, and the message was simply too strong to ignore.

Jerking the reins, he turned Rusty. "I'm going back."

"Why?"

Instead of replying, Drake gave Rusty a kick, sending the gelding leaping into motion. A few moments later, he heard the sound of hoofbeats behind him. A quick glance over his shoulder found Gregory on his tail.

When he pulled close enough to be heard, Gregory shouted, "I don't understand why you're going back."

"Kayla needs me," Drake shouted back.

With a curt nod, Gregory kept his horse in pace with Rusty.

They rode in silence back to the farm.

Chapter Thirty-Two

Kayla couldn't believe that Chantal had positioned herself as a shield. The woman now stood between Kayla and Otto, and every time Otto shifted to his left or right, Chantal would adjust.

"Chantal," Otto said in a scolding tone, "don't make me do this."

"Do what, Otto?" Chantal asked. "Murder another person? I cannot believe you killed Jamison!"

"I *had* to," he insisted. "It was the only way to protect the family." His gaze shifted to Kayla, and the hatred blazed in his eyes. "She was supposed to die, too. Then their greed wouldn't taint my— *Your* fortune."

Kayla was trembling in fear—as much for her unborn child as herself—but she took strength from Chantal's stalwart stance. Chantal faced Otto with apparently no fear, folding her arms in front of her and drumming her fingers on her arm. "Exactly how were you protecting *your* fortune, Otto?"

"We are engaged, my love. What's yours is mine. Had I allowed Gregory to make such a foolish choice for wife, I have no doubt this whore would've bled him dry. Then she'd start draining away our money."

With a shake of her head, Chantal said, "There is no 'our.' Not any longer." She handed the cufflink to Kayla and then jerked a ring from the third finger on her left hand before hurling it at him. It bounced off his chest and hit the floor. "I will not be wife to a…a…common criminal."

"Of course, there's an 'our,'" Otto countered. "You forget, we have already signed all the betrothal contracts, and those have that delightful contingency that should something happen to either of us before we exchange vows, we inherit the other's money." He let out a grating chuckle. "It would seem that when our Cara kills you—and I will be sure everyone believes that is exactly what happened—I shall become a very wealthy man." He cocked the gun. "I suppose you might want to know that you were never returning from this trip," he said, an arrogant lilt to his voice. "I had always planned for you to have a convenient *accident*, but this? This is even better! I can rid myself of both of you bitches at the same time. Goodbye, Chantal." He raised the gun.

"You're wrong about the money, Otto," Chantal said with an edge of steel in her voice. "Dead wrong."

"Wrong?" Another irritating laugh as he let the gun drop a little. The man was clearly enjoying toying with them and had no intention of ending it quickly, as though the need to brag about his plan couldn't be stopped. "No,

I'm not. You're just stalling. Remember that *I* was the one who insisted on that clause. I knew exactly what I was doing. I've waited a long time for the Carrington fortune to be mine."

This time, Chantal laughed. "You're a fool. An utter fool."

Kayla had been praying for deliverance, and she was beginning to believe the woman she'd hated and blamed for her father's death might be that deliverance. She'd never seen someone so brave in the face of danger. Had she not fisted one of her hands in the back of Chantal's coat, she would never have realized that Chantal was trembling.

"I am done talking to you." He aimed the gun again.

"I'm not speaking of the clause, you ignoramus," Chantal said in a snide tone. "You're wrong that the papers have been signed. I was in such a hurry to find Gregory that I never found the time to sign them. If anything happens to me, you inherit nothing. Not a damn penny."

"You're lying!" he said with a scoff.

"I suppose," Chantal drawled, "that you'll just have to find out the hard way. A pity to lose all that money simply because you forgot to check if I'd followed through."

Taking courage from Chantal, Kayla moved to the woman's side and held out her hand. Chantal took it in hers, and the women faced Otto as a united front.

"So, here we are, Otto," Kayla said. "Two women who know exactly what you did. But if you kill us, you'll walk away a pauper."

His face flushed red, and sweat was beginning to bead his forehead. "You're lying, Chantal. I know you. I've seen you bluff men in business deals for years, and you're bluffing now. If I kill you and this interfering little bitch, I will inherit the Carrington fortune."

"What about Gregory?" Kayla asked. "Surely you know that he'd inherit, not you."

"Half," Otto said. "Only half." Then he chuckled. "I suppose he shall have to meet with an accident as well."

Movement in the hallway caught Kayla's eye, and she tried not to react to alert Otto that someone else was in the house.

* * *

The moment he saw the carriage, Drake thanked God that he strapped on his gun every day. While that habit went back to his cattle drive days, it wasn't one he'd tried to break. Today, that custom might just save Kayla's life.

He'd ridden hard until he got to the barn door, then he jumped out of the saddle, slapped Rusty on the rump to get this horse heading into the barn, and grabbed the reins of Gregory's horse. "Get off."

Gregory obeyed, and Drake sent his horse into the barn as well.

"Who's here?" Gregory asked.

"Not sure," Drake replied. "But Kayla was alone, and I want to be sure she's safe."

Gregory took a few steps toward the porch. "By all means then we'll go see—"

Snaking a hand around Gregory's upper arm, Drake dragged him to a stop. "We're not charging in there. Not until we get the lay of the land."

"Pardon?"

"The lay of the land. We need to know what's going on in there first."

"We can figure that out quite nicely by going inside," Gregory said, his tone condescending.

Drake swiped his hand over his face, trying to keep his patience. This man had no idea of the kinds of dangers in this part of the country. While the carriage boded well, meaning someone had wanted to travel in comfort, he couldn't help but feel as though something here was very wrong. "What if there's someone in there threatening her?"

"Why on earth would anyone threaten Cara?" Then Gregory's eyes widened. "You think Otto has come here, don't you?"

"I do," Drake replied. "Judging from the carriage, I'd say your mother is with him."

"Well, then, shouldn't we go greet them? My mother is no threat to Cara."

Drake let out a derisive snort. "My guess is she's the *biggest* danger Kayla faces. You might not believe her about your ma, but I do."

It was easy to see that Gregory was still convinced his mother was innocent, but he finally nodded. "What do you want to do?"

Drawing his gun, Drake scrambled for a plan that would be safest for Kayla. "We need to go around the house and peek in the windows. Find out what room they're in. Then we'll regroup here and figure out what to do next." He gestured with his gun to the right. "You go that way. Stay low. Don't be seen."

Gregory nodded, went to the right side of the porch, and crouched to look into the closest window.

Assured that Gregory was going to be careful, Drake headed to the other side of the house. Three windows later—the window into Kayla's bedroom— and he saw them. His heart took a leap when he saw the gun that Otto was pointing at the women. They stood side-by-side, facing him with expressions of sheer challenge on their faces.

Something had obviously changed in Kayla's view of Chantal Carrington, which made Drake focus on Otto.

He was a big man, tall and heavy. But he'd chosen a poor weapon. A .22. *A woman's gun.* But it would kill, and Drake needed to disarm Otto as quickly as possible. He'd just decided to take his best shot through the window, hoping the distortions in the glass wouldn't hurt his aim, when Gregory came bursting into the bedroom. He held a large vase above his head, and he rushed at Otto.

Everything happened so quickly, Drake couldn't think, only react. Otto whirled and fired his gun at Gregory, and Drake took quick aim and pulled the trigger, shattering the glass. Ears ringing, he used the back of his heavy sleeve to brush aside the shards in the window. Then he looked into the room, saw Otto on the floor, and hurried to crawl inside.

Kayla was there, grabbing his arms to help him. When she tried to embrace him, he pushed her behind his back in case Otto wasn't incapacitated.

He'd hit Otto right between the shoulder blades, leaving the man sprawled on his stomach. The gun had slid across the floor and was laying near the door.

Relieved Otto was no longer a threat, Drake shifted his gaze to Gregory, who was on his knees, his right hand pressed against his upper left arm. "Did he shoot you?"

Gregory nodded, then he pulled his shaking hand away, revealing a torn jacket but no blood. "I–I think he m–missed."

"Gregory!" Chantal, who had appeared to be a trance, rushed to her son and fell to her knees. "You're injured!"

His hand still shaking, he put it on his mother's shoulders. "I am f–fine, M–mother."

"My darling boy!" She pulled his head to her chest, nearly making them both topple over. "You were so brave!"

"I was supposed to wait," he said, his voice still a bit shaky, "but I saw you were in danger, Mother. I had to do something."

With a snort and a shake of his head, Drake turned to gather Kayla into his arms, wondering if he'd ever be able to let her go. She laid her cheek against his shoulder and took a few deep breaths. Slowly, her trembling began to subside. He doubted, however, that his would abate for a good, long while.

He rubbed her back. "Are you okay, love?"

"I am now." She let out a sweet sigh. "How did you know to come back?"

How could he tell her that his intuition had been screaming at him until he'd turned Rusty around and rode for home as though Satan himself was on his tail? All he did was shrug.

Pushing her arms around his neck, she rose on tiptoes to brush a kiss over his lips. "Thank you."

He grunted a response, feeling a bit flustered at her gratitude. He'd only done what was necessary to protect her, and he didn't think it deserved praise.

"You saved my life."

"A man protects his woman," Drake replied.

Kayla pulled back and stared up into his eyes. "Is that what I am, Drake? Your woman?"

He grabbed her around the waist, jerked her against him hard enough that she gasped, and covered her mouth with his. Then he kissed her with all the love he had for her deep inside himself. The kiss was consuming, and all he wanted to do was toss her on the bed and show her exactly how much he wanted her—needed her.

Loved her.

When he eased back, her cheeks were flushed and her lips wet. Feeling a bit smug at seeing her so flustered by his kiss, Drake smiled. "Of course, you're my woman. And I don't care if I'm not worthy, you're gonna marry me anyway."

She smiled in return. "You think I'll marry you?"

"Damn right." He nodded to show how serious he was. "Soon."

"For the love of Saint Peter," Chantal said. "You two may stop this little…display before I lose my breakfast." Then she got to her feet, put her hand down for her son to grasp, and helped him rise. "It would appear, my dear son, that you will not be taking Cara as your bride after all."

Gregory just sighed.

* * *

Kayla didn't mind Drake following her around the same way Gregory had. It seemed as though he wouldn't let her stray more than a few feet away since they'd left her bedroom. He'd even followed her to the outhouse, which made her feel awkward as she'd conducted her business.

Drew and Gideon had returned about an hour after Otto's death, saying the Beck's barn had only sustained a small amount of damage. They were very surprised to hear about the showdown at their home. Gideon had ridden for the town to fetch Marshal Riley while Drew and Drake had covered Otto's body with a blanket and made some temporary repairs to Kayla's window. When the marshal arrived, he'd needed little time assuring himself that the story Kayla, Drake, Chantal, and Gregory had told him was exactly how events occurred. The men had loaded Otto's body onto a wagon that Gideon had hitched up for the marshal to take back to White Pines.

"I think that wraps everything up," Marshal Riley said, indicating the wagon by jerking a thumb over his shoulder. "I'll get him to the undertaker." His gaze shifted to Chantal. "Unless you're wantin' to take him back to New York City. We can arrange rail transport and—"

Chantal waved away the thought with a flip of her wrist. "Burn him. Bury him. Throw him over a cliff. It matters none to me."

"Well then…" The marshal tipped his hat to Chantal and then to Kayla. "I'll be headin' back to town." He went to the wagon, crawled up onto the bench, and took the reins in his hands. Soon, he was traveling down the tree-lined road, on his way back to White Pines.

Drake didn't seem inclined to let go of Kayla's hand, and she had no intention of asking him to do so. She was his woman—he'd said so. When they were finally able to be alone, she would tell him her secret, and she hoped with all her heart that he would be happy that they were going to have a baby.

"Kayla's gonna marry me," Drake blurted out in a matter-of-fact tone.

"Is that so?" Drew stroked his chin with his thumb and fingers.

Drake nodded. "Soon. As soon as we can arrange it."

Drew kept stroking his chin, looking smug. "'Remember that 'whoever hastens to be rich will not go unpunished…'"

Gideon rolled his eyes. "Give it a rest, will ya, Drew? They *gotta* get married, the sooner the better."

"Is that a fact?" Drew asked. "And why exactly do you think that?"

"'Cause she's in the family way."

Kayla gasped, her hand dropping to her stomach.

"She's *what*?" Drake's question ended on a squeak.

"You're gonna be a pa," Gideon replied. He considered Kayla for a moment then said, "I'd say by autumn. Prob'ly late autumn."

"How could you possibly know that?" Kayla asked. Her face felt as though it had burst into flames, and there was no doubt that her embarrassed reaction screamed to everyone that Gideon was correct.

Gideon shrugged.

Drew, who had begun laughing the moment Gideon had said she was pregnant, got a grip on himself. "Didn't you know, my dear, that my Gideon has always had a sort of…instinct about such things?"

"I beg your pardon?" Chantal asked.

"He always seems to know when any of our livestock have conceived." A mischievous grin and a twinkle in his eye made Kayla brace for his next comment. "He has a special knack for knowing when the cows are expecting."

While everyone else was chuckling, Kayla released Drake's hand and crossed her arms under her breasts. She leveled a hard glare at Drew. "Did you just call me a cow?"

Feigning innocence with a hand on his chest, Drew shook his head. "How you impugn me, Kayla. I said no such thing."

She suddenly found her upper arms seized in a tight grip as Drake whirled her to face him. "Is it true? Are you gonna have a baby?"

"We," she replied, keeping her voice calm when what she really wanted to do was shout her happiness. "*We* are going to have a baby."

"Hot damn!" He swept her into his arms and spun her in a circle. "I'm gonna be a father!"

Epilogue

Kayla took a step back and held her palm out to her dance partner. "I fear I have had far too much dancing. I need a moment to rest. I'm sorry." She had to nearly shout to be heard above the enthusiastic fiddler.

The cowboy—she'd already forgotten his name—frowned and dropped his chin, looking a bit like a sad puppy. He walked away, shoulders sagging and feet dragging. While his reaction might have been flattering, she realized he wasn't regretting leaving her in particular. He was regretting that there simply weren't a lot of women to dance with. There were many lonely men in Montana.

Even before she could turn around and exit the dance floor, Drake was immediately at her side. "Are you okay, love? You're lookin' a bit pale."

"I am quite well," she replied. Her hand dropped to cover her stomach. "*We* are quite well. I am simply tired of having my toes repeatedly trod upon." Then she admitted, "I suppose am a bit overheated. Perhaps we could get some refreshments and sit for a spell?"

He wrapped his arm around her waist and led her to the benches along the far wall. While she sat down and fanned herself with her hand, Drake headed toward the long table that was filled with cakes, snacks, and a large punchbowl.

Brigit sat at her side. "Sweet Jesus, it's hot in here."

As she continued to fan herself, Kayla nodded. There were so many people dancing that they were constantly bumping into each other. The sight made her smile.

It had been quite a wedding reception.

"Looks like near to the whole town came out," Brigit said.

"I suppose Chantal Carrington meant what she said when she claimed Drake and I would have a big wedding," Kayla said. "I dare say she invited everyone within riding distance."

"Ye told me she'd insisted on helping."

Kayla let out a snort. "Helping?" She shook her head. "The woman handled *everything*. Not that I'm complaining. Drake and I have been so busy trying to get the house completed, I had no time to spare."

"'Twas kind of her," Brigit said.

"I agree, and I have thanked her many times." Kayla let her gaze wander the church, which Chantal had hired people to rearrange and decorate to become a reception hall immediately after the wedding. She and Drake had no sooner exchanged vows in front of the guests when Chantal's workers had descended like locusts on a field of fresh grain. Benches were moved, festive bunting was draped, and food was brought in. Musicians set up and began to play, and everyone dove into celebrating. "I will continue to thank her in the future. I could never have arranged all of this."

Brigit touched the lace border of Kayla's veil. "Yer a beautiful bride."

"That's because Chantal has impeccable taste. She designed the dress and veil," Kayla replied. "The lace was shipped all the way from New York City."

Drake handed cups of punch to both Kayla and Brigit. "The dress isn't why Kayla is a beautiful bride."

Offering her new husband a smile, Kayla asked, "Then why, pray tell?"

His handsome grin always made a warm ripple race through her, and she hoped she always felt that way. "You're just beautiful, sweetheart. In or out of a dress." He winked.

Brigit laughed loud enough to set a few heads turning their direction. "Yer a wicked man, Drake."

"That's why I love him," Kayla said.

Gregory came over. He was holding a silver flask instead of a cup of punch.

Kayla frowned. He hadn't handled things well since the day of Otto's death. While Chantal had wanted to help with the wedding, claiming she owed Kayla for not believing her, Kayla knew Chantal also wanted her son to remain single. What better way to ensure that than marrying off the woman her son wanted?

Gregory had tried to talk Kayla out of marrying Drake several times. It wasn't until he finally realized that she truly loved Drake that he finally gave up. Since then, he'd been in an extended pout.

"And how are the newlyweds?" Gregory asked with a bit of slur in his voice.

"We're doin' dandy!" Drake slapped Gregory on the back, probably a little harder than necessary, sending Gregory stumbling a few steps forward. "Sorry 'bout that, Gregory."

"When are you returning to New York?" Kayla asked.

"Didn't I tell you?" Gregory replied. "I've decided to stay in White Pines. I'm going to start my own business, and your husband is going to be my first customer."

Kayla blinked a couple of times. "I beg your pardon?"

With a faux contrite look, Gregory said, "I didn't mean to let the cat out of the proverbial bag. I simply assumed he'd told you."

"Drake? What is he talking about?"

Drake shook his head. "We'll talk later. Okay?"

She nodded, although worry bloomed. Then she realized that Drake always had her best interests—and their child's best interests—at heart. He would explain, and after, she'd scold him for not confiding in her first.

Husbands, evidently, required a bit of training.

Gregory went on. "He wants to build homes for people around here, and I am starting a new building and loan company to help fund the venture. I can also help his buyers with mortgages."

"You're stayin' here? How does your mum feel 'bout that?" Brigit asked.

Gregory's gaze dropped to the floor as if something very interesting suddenly appeared there. "Actually, I haven't told her about it. Not yet."

Kayla and Brigit exchanged knowing looks of concern. "I don't envy you that task," Kayla said.

As though she knew she was the topic of conversation, Chantal came striding across the church. She clapped her hands when she reached the small group. "There you are! Everyone up and at 'em! It's time for the happy couple to depart! You need to toss your bouquet, Kayla!"

After a resigned sigh, Kayla stood up and followed Chantal to the next thing the woman had planned for the wedding. Thankfully, it would be one of the last.

* * *

The wagon ride to the house was quiet. Spring had arrived, but the nights still held a chill. Kayla squeezed herself up against Drake and leaned her head on his shoulder. Even though Chantal had been bossy, Kayla had to admit the woman had given them a wonderful affair. And letting Chantal do all the planning had allowed Kayla to give the house some finishing touches. Now, she was heading there to start her new life with her husband.

Husband. The word made her smile. Never would she have believed that Drake Myers would be a man to take a wife, nor would she have thought that she would be the one he chose. But she was his wife now. They'd said their vows before God and most of White Pines, and she felt a contentment she hadn't known possible.

"Why didn't you tell me about working with Gregory?" she asked. "I would have been supportive. I know how much you love building things."

"I knew you would," Drake replied. "I just wanted to be sure it would all work out first. The money, I mean. I knew I could do the work, but it takes capital. That's what Gregory calls it. He thinks we can make some money with all the new people comin' out here to settle."

"Our house is amazing. If anyone sees it, he will want one exactly like it."

"Won't make another one *exactly* like it," he said. "This is a one-of-a-kind, and I intend it to stay that way."

"And it's ours."

"Damn right." The wagon passed Drew and Gideon's house as the newlyweds headed toward their new home. "You know, I think I always kinda knew it would be mine. When I was buildin' it, I made it as perfect as possible."

"I think you're right," Kayla said. "After all, you made that model for it. Remember? The one Drew said looked like my drawings."

"I remember. I remember *everything* about you, Kayla. Every last detail." She sat up, surprised at the emotion behind his statement. "You do?"

"Of course, I do. I love you."

Tears sprang into her eyes, blurring her vision. "You love me?"

Drake pulled on the reins, bringing the team to a halt. Then he turned to look into her eyes. "I know I ain't said it before, and I should've. I guess I was a bit of a coward. But I do love you, Kayla." He pointed to the lush full moon that was lighting their way home. "I love you all the way to that moon and back again."

"Oh, Drake…" She threw her arms around his neck and kissed him. "I love you too."

"Let's go home, Mrs. Myers. We got a honeymoon to start." He gave her another quick kiss and then got the horses back in motion. "We've had a helluva interesting journey getting here, haven't we?"

Kayla smiled and leaned her head against his shoulder again. "We have. And you know what?"

"No. What?" he teased.

"I dare say we shall have a helluva interesting journey ahead of us as well—one that I will be happy to share with you."

The End

And now a preview of Safe Havens Book 5, False Pretenses…

Chapter One

New York City—April 1888

I'm in hell.

No, not hell. New York City—a place that Willie might've named if someone had asked her where she'd least like to spend eternity.

Finding the building had been a trial. The streets were crowded with people, trolleys, and carriages, and it seemed as though myriad wires ran from large poles to almost every single building. Telephones, no doubt. She sure didn't see many of those in the northern Dakotas. Didn't see this many people, either. In fact, she could go weeks without coming across another soul unless she ventured from her homestead to go to town—to *Nuni Oyate*.

A young man in a well-tailored black suit came out through one of the ornate double doors Willie had been staring at for close to an hour. He came to stand directly in front of her. "Miss Marchand?"

"That's me."

"Mrs. Carrington is ready to see you now." He swept his arm toward the door that he'd left open. "If you'd please…?"

After such a lengthy wait, Willie was sorely tempted to give him one of her typical sarcastic replies. This meeting was too important to risk offending a man who was barely old enough to shave, especially when he likely had Chantal Carrington's ear. "Thank you."

He followed her through the doors and nearly ran into her back when she planted her feet to gape at the sight before her. The cavernous room was like nothing she'd seen before. The walls had to be twenty-feet tall, drawing her eyes up until she gasped at the mural on the arched ceiling. She'd heard of such art before, even reading that there was a famous one in Rome that people believed was divinely inspired. This mural wasn't of God or Bible stories. It was a tribute to American history.

Willie recognized images of George Washington, Thomas Jefferson, and Benjamin Franklin. There were scenes from the Revolution that shifted into pictures of Civil War battles where Yankee soldiers stood victorious over their fallen Confederate foes. Abraham Lincoln was at the center, being portrayed as an angel—halo and all.

The young man cleared his throat loudly. "If you wouldn't mind…" He gestured toward the enormous desk at the front of the room.

Room? Hardly. She'd explored caves that were smaller than this…this…cathedral. The intimidation factor was obvious, so Willie gently lifted her skirts, gave herself a mental bracing, and strode confidently to the desk.

Chantal Carrington sat in a highbacked leather chair with brass tacks as edging. She was holding a piece of paper, scanning it with her eyes over a pair of spectacles sitting on the end of her nose. When she glanced up, she didn't lift her head. Instead, she considered Willie over the wire frames.

She was dressed in what Willie thought of as a lady's suit—a long-sleeved, snugly fitted jacket of green velvet with shiny satin lapels. Her white blouse sported a cravat, making her appear much like any normal businessman. She'd pulled her dark hair into a tight bun, and several strands of gray fanned from her temples. Although she wore no rings, large emerald and silver earrings dangled from each ear.

Willie gave her a polite nod. "Mrs. Carrington. I'm Wilma—"

"Wilma Marchant. Wilma Shappa Marchant." Chantal let the paper fall to her desktop. It flitted down slowly, like a lazy bird preparing to land. "Quite an unusual name. Indeed, *quite* unusual."

Not one to put all her cards on the table, Willie simply nodded.

"I'll admit curiosity about the Shappa. Care to enlighten me."

Even knowing her ethnic heritage was often looked down upon by a lot of people, Willie didn't hesitate to reply. One of the reasons she'd chosen Chantal Carrington was because she flaunted her femininity in a world full of men. She knew how it felt to be the underdog. "It's a Sioux word that means red thunder."

"Interesting… Perhaps one day you shall tell me why that particular name was chosen for you." Chantal swept her hand toward one of the two chairs that rested in front of her desk. "Have a seat, Miss Marchant."

"Thank you." Setting her portfolio beside the chair, Willie sat down, keeping her spine straight and her chin high just as her grandmother—her *Unci*—had taught her.

Never show fear. One of Unci*'s best lessons.*

But Willie was afraid. This proposal was her best chance to achieve not only her wildest dreams but to help her town. "I truly appreciate your time, Mrs. Carrington. I know how busy you are. I want to tell you a little about myself and why—"

With a snort, Chantal interrupted. "I know everything there is to know about you, Willie. There's only one thing I don't know."

"And what exactly is that, Chantal?"

The left corner of Chantal's mouth rose, just enough to make Willie believe she was amused by her brash reply. "Bravo, my dear."

"Pardon?"

Leaning back in her chair, Chantal took off her glasses and set them down. "You are a woman who is trying to create a business. You will need to keep that cheeky attitude if you have any chance to succeed."

"I never realized that I was *cheeky*, as you say."

"Don't lie to me. You are quite aware of your ability to get what you want, and you are quite brazen in doing so. Please don't mistake my choice of term as insult. Quite the opposite. I applaud you. But if we're to work together, I demand that you never lie to me."

Chantal had been correct. Willie had been called everything from cheeky to sassy to bold to being a bitch, she couldn't help but smile. "Touché."

"You want me to invest in your venture. What exactly makes you believe it would be profitable for me to do so?"

Willie moved to the edge of her seat, so excited that she had the ear of the most powerful woman in the country. "I know there's gold on my land. I *know* it. What I need is—"

"Money. Capital."

"I might be able to raise that," Willie said. Not a lie, but perhaps an exaggeration. To try to get enough funds to mine her land could take a year. Or years. One thing she lacked was patience, and her town couldn't afford to wait that long. "But in addition to the capital to start a mine, I could use a name…one that people recognize and respect."

"Like Carrington."

Willie nodded.

Chantal stood and walked to one of the large windows behind her desk, staring out as though she had nothing better to do.

Feeling bold, Willie got up and strode to Chantal's side, where she followed her gaze to see what was so enthralling. The view of the Manhattan skyline was breathtaking, and normally she would gawk for a long time trying to take it all in. But not today. "I will make money for you, Chantal."

Arms crossed over her breasts, Chantal looked up at Willie. My, she was a short woman. Willie had always felt awkward being so tall, and she often wore less-than-fashionable shoes that had flat soles instead of heels so that she didn't tower over everyone. Today, in the name of etiquette, she wore shoes that took her nearly forever to button. Her hands had shown a slight tremble that made it difficult to use a buttonhook on such tight leather. At that moment, she wished she would have gone with shoes that didn't make her feel as though she were a giant.

Drumming her fingers along her forearm, Chantal asked, "You could have gone to any number of 'names' to try to finance your venture. What exactly brought you to Mid-Atlantic Bank?"

"You."

"Pardon?"

"*You* brought me here," Willie said. "The desire to work with a woman who has been successful in what we both know is a man's world."

"Interesting…" The word Chantal spoke was a long, drawn-out affair, and for a moment, Willie wondered if she'd overstepped. A woman like Chantal Carrington probably didn't want to be reminded of how difficult her job—her life—was among the barons of industry. Then a slow smile filled Chantal's face. "Have a seat, my dear. We have much to discuss."

"You'll finance the mine?"

"I might. But there will be a quid pro quo," Chantal replied. "It involves my son."

* * *

Gregory Carrington locked the front door after his last client exited his business, Western Building and Loan. Things were going swimmingly, and he couldn't help but smile when he thought about the fact that he'd helped a lot of people with the loan he'd just closed. The man and his family would be able to build their home, and Drake Myers and the men he employed would be paid well to build it. Everyone won.

Gregory flipped the sign to CLOSED, and waved at Marshal Matthew Riley as he walked down the wooden boardwalk toward the shops along Main Street that were still open. Most would roll up their sidewalks soon, although a few—like the Four Aces Saloon—catered to the evening crowd. More businesses were popping up every day, and White Pines was poised on the verge of a population boom. Word from out east was that Montana was going to be named a state soon, and the benefits of the promotion from a territory would help influence more families to settle here.

As he prepared to mount the steps to his upstairs household, he cast a glance back to his desk and frowned. There were two new telegrams from his mother this week lying next to his telephone, and he wondered if she'd ever stop pestering him to return to New York City. She simply didn't understand why he wanted to stay in the small town he now called home. When would she realize that he was thriving here and had no intention of ever going back to the Carrington mansion?

White Pines hadn't been a deliberate choice. He'd come here in pursuit of his fiancée—a woman he loved who was now another man's wife. He'd known her as Cara Burton, but she'd taken a new name when she fled to Montana. *Kayla Backer.* Now, she was Kayla Myers. And why had she run away from him?

Because of his mother.

Chantal had never approved of Kayla. When Gregory fell in love with Kayla, Chantal tried to force Kayla and her father out of New York society. Then her man-servant—her lover—had taken matters into his own hands, killing Kayla's father and sending Kayla fleeing in fear for her own life. She'd landed in White Pines, and Gregory had spent more than a year hunting her down.

But he'd been too late. She'd fallen in love with Drake Myers, eventually marrying him. Gregory held them no animosity, and his working relationship with Drake was helping both of them prosper. Yet the torch for Kayla still burned brightly.

He picked up the latest message.

Please come home. I need your help at the bank. You owe the family and me your support.

He ripped the telegram into pieces, tossing them at the small wastebasket next to his desk. The motherly guilt she was showering over him wasn't going to work this time. Not now, not ever again. He loved her, but it wasn't until he'd started to make his own way in the world that he'd realized exactly how much power she'd exerted over his life. Her interference with his *fiancée* was only a symptom of that excessive control. On the day he'd lost Kayla, he'd decided that the time had come for him to be his own man, and it felt wonderful.

He was never going back.

There was a knock at the back door, making Gregory smile. His poker friends had arrived for their weekly game. He went to the door and prepared to greet some of the men who'd become his friends in White Pines.

Opening the door, he gaped when he found the woman he'd just been thinking about standing there. "To what do I owe this pleasure?"

Kayla quickly bowed her head, a remainder of the New York City manners that weren't routinely practiced in Montana. "Drake and I came into White Pines for supplies. I thought I'd stop by for a friendly visit."

Since the two of them were seldom seen in the town without their son, Jamie, Gregory had to ask, "Where are your husband and son this fine evening?"

"They are at the general store visiting with Grace and Adam Morgan." She nodded at the wicker basket she was carrying. "I thought you might want some of the cornbread I baked the morning. I know it's one of your favorites."

"I would, indeed," he replied. "My own cooking leaves much to be desired."

"You should hire someone to cook for you, Gregory." Kayla pulled a plate from the basket that held a towel-wrapped brick of what he assumed was the promised cornbread. "Surely, there are women around here who could use the work."

Gregory couldn't help but chuckle. "My dear, Kayla, there are no women around here who are unmarried and willing to take on cooking for a bachelor."

"You could hire a married woman," she countered. "I'm quite sure some of them are excellent cooks and could use the income."

"I will consider that." He took the plate when she offered it. "Thank you for this."

Instead of bowing her head again to take her leave, she nibbled on her bottom lip.

He recognized the nervous action. "What's wrong?"

"I wasn't sure whether I should tell you, but Drake insisted."

"Tell me what?"

Kayla let out a weary sigh. "I am still receiving telegrams from your mother."

He closed his eyes for a moment in a silent prayer of patience, something he was sorely lacking where his mother was concerned. "I'm so sorry. I have asked her repeatedly to stop bothering you. What did she want this time?"

"She was inquiring on how well your business was doing and whether I knew if you had plans to return to New York."

"She wants you to spy on me," Gregory said, shaking his head. "I shall send her yet another message to ask her to leave you in peace."

She frowned. "There was a bit more..."

Gregory rolled his eyes. "Let me guess...this time, she was offering you money to convince me to go back."

"She did. A rather large sum. I have already sent her a telegram telling her I don't see you often and that I am the wrong person to be asking these questions. I wanted to tell you, because you and I both know she will keep trying to get her way. I suppose I wanted to put you on notice."

"That's very kind of you," he said. "But I am always on notice where my mother is concerned. *Always.*"

With a quick bow of her head, Kayla smiled and turned to go.

Gregory stopped her with a question. "How are you doing?"

She whirled to face him. "Oh, Drake and I are quite happy."

"I meant *you*, Cara." He winced when he realized he'd let her old name slip out, the name of the woman he loved who didn't truly exist any longer.

"Me?" Her hand flew to her chest as though she were surprised at the question. "I am quite well, thank you. Jamie keeps me busy, and I'm still adding some touches to the house. But I assure you, Gregory, that I am content. I… Well, I hope you feel the same." She hurried back to him, rose on tip toes, and brushed a kiss to his cheek.

Then she was gone.

Gregory shut the door and then leaned back against it, holding the plate of cornbread she'd been kind enough to bring. He should be over her by now. It had been almost two years since they'd been engaged. She was a married woman with a husband who clearly adored her and a son.

So why couldn't he get her out of his mind?

Could his mother possibly realize he still carried a torch for Kayla?

Mother. Dear lord, the woman was going to make him daft. Tomorrow, he'd send her yet another message that he hoped might finally convince her to stop meddling in his life.

Another knock heightened Gregory's morose mood. His friends were here, and it was time to take as much of their money as he could manage.

Money, after all, was what he did best.

ABOUT THE AUTHOR

Sandy lives in a quiet suburb of Indianapolis, where she teaches psychology. Published through Grand Central Forever Yours, Carina Press, and indie-published, she has been an Amazon #1 Bestseller multiple times and has won numerous awards including two HOLT Medallions. Please visit her website at sandyjames.com for more information or find her on Twitter and Facebook. Represented by Danielle Egan-Miller of Browne & Miller Literary.

Other Books by Sandy James:

Damaged Heroes Series
Murphy's Law (Book 1)
Free Falling (Book 2)
All the Right Reasons (Book 3)
Faith of the Heart (Book 4)
Twist of Fate (Book 5)

Safe Havens Series
Saving Grace (Book 1)
Runaway (Book 2)
Redeemed (Book 3)
Hideaway (Book 4)
False Pretenses (book 5 ~ Coming soon!)

Ladies Who Lunch Series
The Bottom Line (Book 1)
Signed, Sealed, Delivered (Book 2)
Sealing the Deal (Book 3)
Fringe Benefits (Book 4)

Alliance of the Amazons
The Reluctant Amazon (Book 1)
The Impetuous Amazon (Book 2)
The Brazen Amazon (Book 3)
The Volatile Amazon (Book 4)

Single Titles
Turning Thirty-Twelve
Rules of the Game
The Seeker

Nashville Dreams Series
Can't Walk Away (Book 1)
Can't Let Her Go (Book 2)
Can't Fight the Feeling (Book 3)

www.ingramcontent.com/pod-product-compliance
Lightning Source LLC
Chambersburg PA
CBHW070850120626
46556CB00002B/942